BROKEN REIGN

By the Author

Rocks and Stars

The Odium Trilogy

Daughter of No One

Broken Reign

Visit us at www.boldstrokesbooks.com

BROKEN REIGN

by

Sam Ledel

2020

BROKEN REIGN

ISBN 13: 978-1-63555-739-8

This Trade Paperback Original Is Published By
Bold Strokes Books, Inc.
P.O. Box 249
Valley Falls, NY 12185

First Edition: September 2020

Credits
Editor: Barbara Ann Wright
Production Design: Stacia Seaman
Cover Design by Tammy Seidick

Acknowledgments

Thank you to Bold Strokes Books. A big thank you to my amazing editor, Barbara Ann Wright. She is a masterful wordsmith and makes this story sound like I knew what I was doing the first time. Also, thank you to Alyssa for your love and support, and for always pointing out when I use the same adjective five times on one page. The earlier drafts wouldn't improve half as much without you.

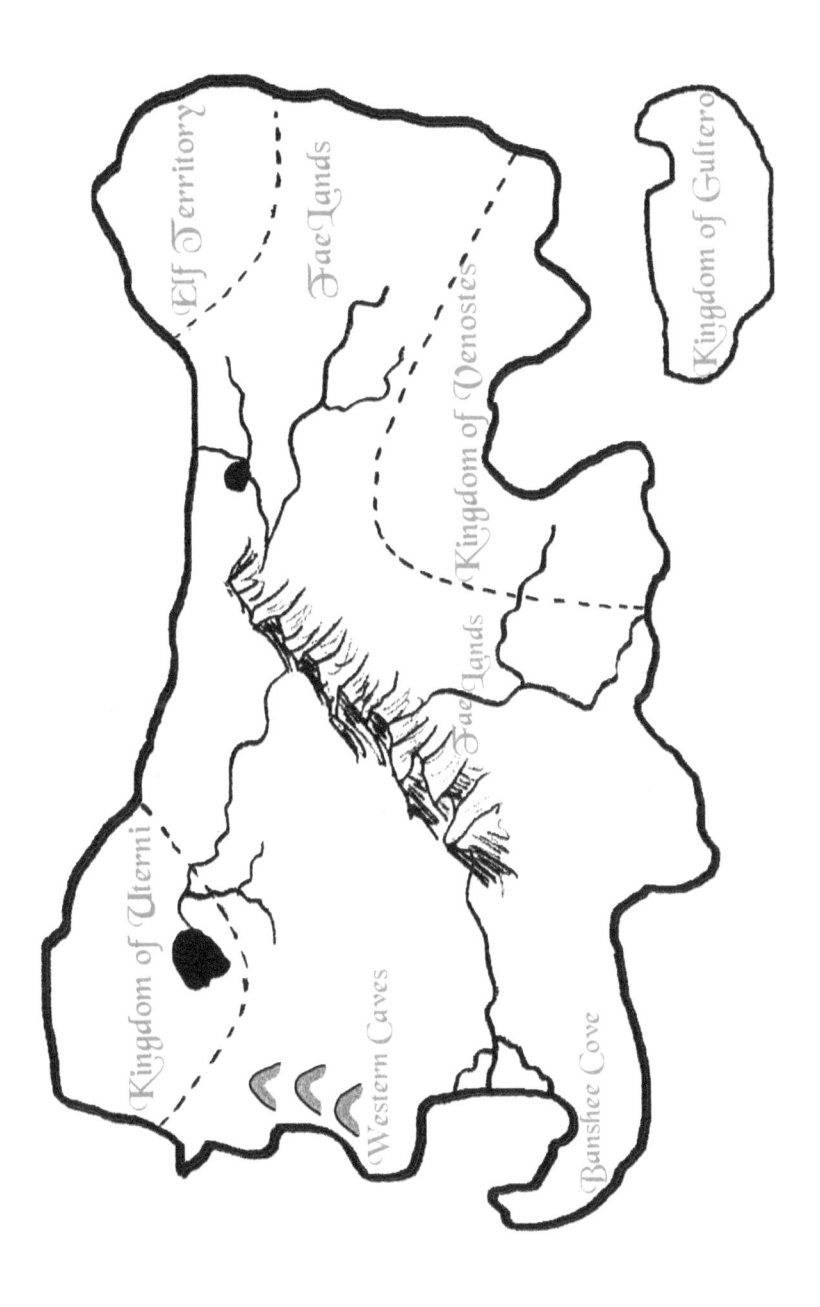

Chapter One

How could you?"

Jastyn didn't respond. She couldn't. The way Princess Aurelia Diarmaid was looking at her now swept away every word she'd ever learned and stole the air from her chest.

"After everything we've been through…after everything I gave up for you." Aurelia's typically fair cheeks were now a bright pink. Tears brimmed in her clear blue eyes, reminding Jastyn of the river where, not two weeks before, they'd spent a happy day fishing. The water had been nearly translucent as it rushed over smooth rocks on its way to the sea. Those moments had been blissful.

Jastyn desperately wished she was back there now.

Like her words, the memory was washed away. Jastyn scolded herself. She knew good moments never lasted. She'd known that her entire life.

A different memory blazed like fire in her mind: an arrow streaming from the trees as she ran toward Aurelia. She imagined another arrow now, willing the pointed tip to plunge deep into her shoulder like it had a month before. Perhaps then Aurelia would see the pain Jastyn felt at being the cause of her hurt.

"I left everything behind. I left it behind for you."

Finally, Jastyn's words returned. "I understand. I know what you gave up."

"Do you?" Aurelia's gaze turned hard. "Do you realize what I risked coming with you? What I laid in your hands?"

"Aurelia, I—"

"I trusted you, Jastyn. I gave you everything I had. Yet you still saw fit to betray me?"

Now Jastyn felt like she was in that clear river, floundering beneath the rapids. Tears stung her eyes. "I was going to tell you."

The princess swiped at her nose, her cheeks tearstained. "When? After you had gotten what you needed from the caves? Once I'd been sacrificed to gods know what, left alone? Or dead."

"Let me explain." Jastyn stepped forward. "The Red One told me what I need to do in the caves." Months ago, the leprechaun had traded Jastyn banshee blood to quell her sister Alanna's suffering, but the remedy was temporary. The blood's vial was to be taken to the western caves. There, a noble sacrifice needed to be given in exchange for the true cure.

Aurelia glared. "You let a fae send you on a chase across the realm knowing I was only a token to be bartered?"

"No. I only—"

"What?"

"I had plans to tell you what the Red One said." Jastyn ran a hand down her braid, her breath uneven. Her vision grew hazy as she struggled to speak. "I was going to tell you."

Crossing her arms, Aurelia muttered, "Your argument is chasing its own tail."

Jastyn's jaw tightened. Her chest felt like that arrow in her shoulder was now splitting its way through her ribs. Meanwhile, her mind drowned in the water. How did this happen? She never meant for Aurelia to find out about the sacrifice like this.

When she met Aurelia's gaze, she saw in it what she had feared most since beginning this journey: disappointment.

Aurelia spoke just above a whisper. "My mother was right. I regret ever having set foot beside you."

Nausea and dizziness overwhelmed Jastyn, and she felt as if she was spinning endlessly against the raging river swells.

Fighting the urge to be sick, Jastyn barely registered the sight of Aurelia packing her satchel. Her voice was devoid of emotion when she said, "I can't stay here."

Reeling, Jastyn couldn't stop a laugh, though it was hollow. "What are you talking about?"

Aurelia ignored her, throwing the satchel over her shoulder as she started for the line of trees opposite their camp.

"Stop, Aurelia, wait." She reached out, but her feet didn't move. Looking down, she found nothing holding her in place. Calling out again, Jastyn didn't recognize the desperation in her own voice. "You don't know the way. Aurelia. Wait!"

Her words fell on deaf ears, and Jastyn watched helplessly as the princess walked away from her without looking back.

"Wake up, Jas."

Something cold and wet hit her face. For a moment, Jastyn feared she was still adrift in the river, watching Aurelia retreat into the Wood. Blinking, she wiped her face. Her best friend Coran sat beside her in his navy tunic and black pants, a topless flask in his freckled hand.

"What'd you do that for?" Jastyn scowled at him while she brushed strands of strawberry-blond hair away from her face before resetting her long braid. Sunlight peeked over the eastern treetops, and the morning air was already heavy and humid.

Coran eyed her as he recapped the flask. "There's only two reasons I'd wake you. Either we're being ambushed by a nymph eager to get her hands on you, or…" He dipped his chin as his voice trailed off.

Jastyn glanced around, and upon finding no wood or lake nymphs nearby, she sighed. "It seems all is quiet."

"All save for you." Coran stood, running a hand through his wild shock of red-orange hair, which had grown taller in the last three weeks.

Guilty, Jastyn rubbed her eyes, forcing the lingering image of Aurelia disappearing from her mind.

"Was it him again?" Coran held her gaze, his hazel eyes filled with concern. Jastyn quickly and happily reported that the Dark Fae had not seen fit to visit her last night. In fact, the ghastly fae had come only twice since their journey began.

"It was something else," she added, allowing her gaze to drift to the figure sleeping on the other side of Coran. They both watched Aurelia's chest rise and fall slowly.

"I see." He opened his mouth as if to speak, then seemed to think better of it.

Jastyn lingered on Aurelia. Relief washed through her. Their argument had only been a terrible dream, and Aurelia was still there. *Here with me.* Aurelia's dark blue tunic ran past her waist and fell over the worn pair of pants that had belonged to her brother. Long dark brown hair framed her delicate face, which was the picture of peace while she slept with one slender arm wrapped around the end of a blanket.

Another splash of cold hit Jastyn's cheek.

"Coran!"

He snickered and put out the flames of their campfire. "Don't you think it's time?"

Jastyn hesitated. Was he referring to her plan to get to the caves? She'd told him pieces but not the part she dreaded most, the part that required a noble sacrifice in order to obtain the medicine her sister Alanna needed.

Deciding to feign ignorance, she asked casually, "What do you mean?"

His look was incredulous. "You and our fair princess." At the same time, Aurelia stirred and inhaled sharply as she woke.

"I'm sure I don't know what you mean," Jastyn said, pitching her voice to do her best Aurelia impression before Aurelia yawned and sat up. Another day in the wild stretch of fae lands and Jastyn was still in awe at how beautiful she was.

Aurelia smiled and stretched. "What a lovely day. Good morning, Coran."

"Good morning, Your Highness."

"Coran, I've told you to please call me Aurelia," she said, a slight pout to her bottom lip.

He blushed, then returned to extinguishing the embers of their fire.

When she met Jastyn's gaze, her smile returned. "Good morning."

Jastyn stood and wiped off her pants. She moved closer, reaching down. "Good morning, Princess," she added with what she hoped was a charming grin.

Aurelia reached up, an amused twinkle in her blue eyes that made Jastyn's heart beat faster than she would like to admit.

"Whatever am I going to do with you two?" She placed her hand in Jastyn's before being helped to stand. Aurelia's hand lingered a moment longer than it needed to before she brushed the leaves and grass from her legs. Jastyn was grateful for the stark contrast this moment held in comparison to her dream and relished the fact that this Aurelia was still here, standing happily before her.

The feeling of frivolity made Jastyn's head light. She let the feeling fill her up, then transform into words that spilled out before she could stop them. "Oh, I imagine you can think of something."

Coran coughed, and Jastyn stepped back, grinning at the blush in Aurelia's cheeks as she quickly turned her attention to the blanket and began folding. A moment later, Jastyn could feel Aurelia's gaze on her but pretended not to notice.

Eventually, their things were packed. Jastyn announced, "Rigo is a good mile ahead of us. We need to follow his trail and reunite with him at midday." Their elf companion had left at dawn to scout the trail ahead.

Aurelia's voice was light when she asked, "A new adventure?"

Coran and Jastyn exchanged glances. She couldn't help but smile at Aurelia, whose eyes were filled with hope and anticipation, reminding her that her fears and dreams were only that, intangible visions meant to scare her. Jastyn never wanted to see anything but that bright spark in those blue eyes. She would need that spark to carry her forward on the journey ahead.

A journey that she had expected to take in solitude. Instead, she was surprised by her best friend's company and stunned when Aurelia decided to forsake her family and join in the search for Alanna's cure. While she was certain the royal family would not let Aurelia go easily, Jastyn would not deny her this chance at freedom. Part of her recognized that Aurelia was choosing a reality that couldn't last. A reality where an Odium and a Diarmaid walked together was unimaginable, a fleeting fantasy that would eventually end. But who was Jastyn to deny her this small chance to see the world? As long as Aurelia wanted to, Jastyn would fight with everything she had to keep that spark in Aurelia's eyes.

That same spark, while breathtaking, frightened her. That spark would go out when they reached the western caves unless Jastyn could think of a way around the Red One's words. A noble sacrifice was required in exchange for the cure, and it didn't escape Jastyn that a woman of noble blood had fallen into her world at that same time. She had intended to trick Aurelia upon their encounter in the Wood a month ago, but now...that spark made Jastyn want to be better. It made her want to find an alternative to what she feared would be needed.

It was a long trek to the western shores. She would have time to figure things out.

Jastyn shook her head. Journeying alongside a Diarmaid. What could possibly go wrong?

Chapter Two

Rigo believes we're only another week from the Mountains of Ionad?" Aurelia focused on her feet as she spoke, careful to match her steps to Jastyn's on the forest floor. Thus far, she had found it difficult to believe simply walking could be so, well, difficult. So problematic, in fact, she thought it a bit ridiculous. She often found herself caught up in the magnificent scenery surrounding them... literally. Accustomed to only witnessing such wonders in the pages of her books, she was pleasantly overwhelmed with the Wood she had once longed to explore.

As far as she could see stretched endless, tightly packed birch trees, all hosting patches of shamrock-colored moss up and down their thin trunks. Boulders the size of melons, tree roots that crept from the ground like serpents, and conspicuously hidden gnome hills, while lovely, added another set of obstacles for her poorly prepared feet. Then there was the flora, a stunning array of purples, yellows, and fiery reds erupting from the never-ending wall of green. How could she not want to take it all in?

Alas, this morning she had already tripped three times. Her boots—formerly a polished tawny, now a dull and dirt-covered walnut—clipped the edges of needled shrubs the rest of her party had no trouble avoiding. She envied the way Coran and Jastyn were at ease while they hiked two paces ahead, their heads high as they scanned the path. It was impossible to compare herself to Rigo, as the tall slender elf possessed feet that seemed to float above the forest floor.

A tree-dweller scurried past. Aurelia yelped, prompting a glance from Jastyn while Coran, who led their group, called out an answer to her earlier question.

"It'll be five days at best before we get there. If we keep our pace, we should have the peaks in sight in two days' time."

"Splendid." Aurelia's gaze fell on a bright siskin as it landed in its nest to her right. She stepped carefully over a trickling creek as the yellow bird greeted a trio of offspring squawking hungrily from their perch.

"Isn't summer lovely?" Aurelia breathed deeply as a wave of happiness overcame her. "Everything is so alive. The entire realm trills with vigor, wouldn't you agree?"

Coran turned, no doubt to share a look with Jastyn. Aurelia sighed. She had been trying not to let her naivety show the last three weeks since their adventure began. She didn't have the same knowledge of the Wood as Jastyn and Coran. Her time outside of the Kingdom of Venostes, even her time outside of the castle, was extremely limited. Still, she imagined her friends understood.

It was difficult to believe almost an entire moon had passed since that night in the Wood. Stumbling on a rock, she recalled the intense night when she had helped destroy her brother's best friend before he could hurt her or anyone else the way he had Brennus. It was the same night she'd left the safety of the life she'd known for twenty years, a life of comfort and familiarity confined within the high stone walls of the Diarmaid castle. It was a life that no longer included her dear brother but still hosted her parents, who no doubt continued to mourn Brennus's passing into the Otherworld.

As quickly as her mind retraced its steps, the pain of grief overwhelmed her. The tightness of her chest bound her breath, and she paused, leaning one arm against a tree. She focused on her breathing, then on the sound of Jastyn's voice. She let it pull her back to the present, and the pain slowly subsided.

"Summer is always nice. Your kingdom hosts many foreign visitors, each prime for pilfering. Coran, remember that sultan from the East? His pockets were so filled they clanged like cymbals each step he took."

"We collected so many coins that day, I bought my mum a new cauldron."

Aurelia—grateful her companions hadn't noticed her momentary lapse—rejoined the trek, one hand raised to shield her eyes from the midmorning sun shooting through a break in the branches overhead. "I'll pretend I didn't hear that," she said, inhaling deeply to catch her breath. After so much time spent traipsing through the Wood, she could feel her body handling the physicality better, though her lungs still had to catch up. She felt less disappointed in herself when Jastyn had mentioned the week before that they had climbed to a higher elevation. This provided a good enough excuse for occasional wheezing.

She paused again to catch her breath when Coran asked, "Your summers are spent riding mostly, aren't they, Princess?"

Deciding to ignore his insisted use of her title, she replied, "Yes. Nearly every day I'd take Tully out for a ride. She and I would fly together over the hills." Briefly, she lost herself in the memory of sitting astride her best mare. She could feel the horse's strong body beneath her while they galloped along the Wood's edge on a crisp, clear day.

Too quickly, the memory shifted, and she was atop her other horse, Keller, sitting behind Drest. His broad shoulders bounced as he took her farther from her brother. When his elbow swung in her mind, her shoulder smacked into a low-hanging fairy nest.

"Oh!"

The high buzz that erupted snapped Aurelia back to reality. She stepped backward as a dozen fairies, each no bigger than her hand, swarmed angrily around her.

"I'm sorry. I didn't mean to disturb you." Her frantic gaze landed on a particularly perturbed-looking fairy wearing a tiny crown of young birch leaves. He said something in a language she didn't recognize before making a beeline for her face.

A blue saol flame flew toward her, halting the angry fairy in midair, inches from her nose. Aurelia peeked from behind her raised hands to see Jastyn retracing her steps, one hand out to control the movement of her companion flame.

Jastyn placed her free hand on her hip, eyeing the frozen fairy. "Was that necessary? It was an accident this human stumbled so rudely into your nest."

Aurelia's first reaction was to argue this choice of words, but catching the hint of a smile on Jastyn's face, she went along, nodding sympathetically.

"Please forgive her," Jastyn said. Then she leaned forward to whisper. "Between you and me, this isn't the first time she's wandered somewhere she shouldn't." She rolled her eyes. "And it probably won't be her last."

Aurelia frowned, glancing sideways and ready to protest this degrading of her character. But she saw the playful light in Jastyn's hazel eyes and lost herself in the handsomeness of Jastyn's broad face. Then the blue flame vanished, releasing its captor, who led his subjects back into their nest, which glowed hotly until Jastyn and Aurelia were several paces away.

Coran stood with his hands on his hips. "Is everything all right?"

Jastyn pushed aside a low-lying limb, holding it until Aurelia passed beneath. "Our princess seems to be a beacon for trouble."

Aurelia turned to object, but her words faltered when Jastyn smirked. She swallowed. Her feelings for Jastyn were climbing to new heights. She had been instantly taken by the village woman when they first met three months ago. The initial mystery encompassing Jastyn's identity had pulled Aurelia in like a ship to a siren. Her intrigue had developed into attraction, which had paired with admiration once she and Jastyn were thrust together during the frantic circumstances following Brennus's death. Now Aurelia's feelings for Jastyn dazed her at times, but in the happiest of ways.

These happy feelings helped squash any qualms she had about her family naming Jastyn an Odium Child, a fatherless individual meant to be extinguished for fear of the Odium Uprising that had occurred a half century before the great famine. According to legend, a pair of illegitimate children had attempted to claim the throne of the first Diarmaid king. They'd gained such support that the citizens of the kingdom had joined the children, fighting alongside them against the royal army. Their revolt had nearly been successful, almost killing and overthrowing the king and queen to take what the Odium Children had believed was their rightful place.

Aurelia couldn't believe the woman standing before her was such a person. Odium Children were a legend, a cautionary tale, not unlike those Aurelia had read about in texts from faraway kingdoms. The Odium Children who had attempted to usurp the Diarmaids had been executed for treason. The royal family had been so afraid of unrest in their kingdom afterward that all Odiums from then on were questioned and typically found guilty of plotting against the Diarmaids, even though most had been innocent. Those who hadn't been killed had fled. Ever since, the women of the kingdom were careful to never bear such a child.

Jastyn Cipher might have been born from a woman without a husband, but why should that demote her to society's lowest rung?

She was a young woman who carried herself with more pride than anyone Aurelia had ever met. Sometimes too much pride, if she was being honest. She adored the way Jastyn stood strong as she moved through each day, her face filled with determination in life's current venture. Her unending quest to help her sister was more than commendable; it was one of the most selfless acts Aurelia had ever known someone to commit.

Aurelia was falling fast for her, Odium Child or not.

Despite Jastyn's obvious appreciation for her, too, she had thus far been unable to decipher how Jastyn truly felt about her. Or rather, if she felt anything for her at all. She had been making her desires obvious, but Jastyn was difficult to read.

Smiling, Aurelia figured it couldn't hurt to keep making her intentions known. Moving out from under the branches, she squeezed Jastyn's left shoulder before running her fingers the length of Jastyn's arm. Aurelia clung to her forearm when she said, "We had better continue on, don't you think?"

Jastyn swallowed, her gaze flickering to Aurelia's lips.

Flashing another smile, Aurelia moved past. She pulled her shoulders back, regaining her composure. *I may not be able to handle my two feet, but gods know I can navigate my own heart.*

That night, Aurelia dreamt of her brother. The two of them sat at a sturdy oak table in the castle's west wing study. She smelled the musty pages of old volumes, their ink faded from the steady march of time. It had been a few days since her first meeting with Jastyn in the stables, and her mind was filled with thoughts of the mysterious village woman and not focused on the Asian tonic recipes laid out on endless rolls of parchment.

"Something the matter?"

She glanced up. Brennus sat catty-corner to her, his blue tunic complementing his fair complexion, the same as hers. His hands, only mildly rough from hunting on castle grounds, worked diligently to carve something into the edge of the table. His hazel eyes narrowed on his handiwork, and a piece of auburn hair fell over his brow as he concentrated the point of his blade into the wood.

Aurelia watched him work. "I was only daydreaming."

A fire roared in a nearby hearth, filling the room with warm light. From the opposite corner near the door, Roisin snickered.

Brennus glanced up, his gaze flickering between the two. "Oh?"

Aurelia shot her maiden a look, but Roisin's gaze was locked on the needle she threaded through an old cloak. "M'lady is rather fond of a member of the village."

Aurelia sat up. "Roisin!"

"Come now, m'lady. Your brother already suspected."

Huffing, Aurelia crossed her arms.

Brennus finished the final cut and blew away flecks of curled wood. "I'm afraid she's right. You were not terribly subtle at dinner the other night. Not to mention you spent more time in the stables yesterday than you have all month."

Aurelia blushed. "You two are completely intolerable." He laughed as Roisin smiled and continued her patchwork. Eager to change the subject, Aurelia leaned around the corner of the table. "What have you been doing, anyway? Clearly not studying."

He pushed a large, unopened, leather-bound book farther away. He leaned back in his chair so Aurelia could better see the carving he had made.

The image was simple, the outline of a great ship. Its mast stood tall, and a triangular sail waved in a permanent wind. When she looked at him, she caught a glint of sadness in his face.

"What's the matter?"

He replaced the knife at his hip. "I was only thinking how wonderful it will be to leave this place."

Roisin slowed, and Aurelia knew she was listening. "Soon, brother." She reached out. He smiled. When his fingers gripped hers, his touch was cold as ice.

"Brennus?"

His gaze lost its light, as did the fire nearby. The room fell into darkness until he and Aurelia sat alone. His skin turned an eerie ash, his lips a shade of purple. His voice was a frightened whisper when he spoke. "Aurelia, he's not done."

Before she could respond, he fell backward, slipping away into the dark abyss.

"Brennus!"

"Aurelia."

In a jolt, she woke to darkness. But this darkness was warm and held figures that were fast growing familiar. The tall, lean outline of Rigo stood watch twenty yards away, one arm propped on his bow. His square jaw sat firm below his hooked nose, and his keen gray eyes peered into the distance. Coran slept to her left behind a lulling yellow fire, snoring softly. Blinking, Aurelia found Jastyn leaning over her, her hazel eyes dark with concern.

"I'm sorry," Aurelia said. "I was dreaming." She accepted the water flask.

Jastyn sat back, eyes curious. "Your brother?"

"Yes." She took another drink, the cool liquid quenching her dry throat. The air was heavy, and she pushed back her long hair to allow the faintest wind to reach her neck. She glanced at the gathering clouds blocking the moon.

Jastyn recapped the flask. She seemed to lose herself in thought before glancing back at Aurelia. "What was he like?"

Aurelia released a long breath. "My brother was kind and generous. He loved to hunt and adored outings with my father into the Wood to catch game."

"Sounds like we would have gotten along."

"You would have."

Jastyn smiled. "Maybe I could have even taught him a thing or two about hunting."

"Perhaps," Aurelia said, her mood lifting. The night air was humid, and she let the heaviness envelop her like a comforting blanket. She rearranged herself so that she sat cross-legged, facing Jastyn on their makeshift bedding. "He loved going into the market to mingle with the villagers on solstice days." She laughed, recalling a memory. "Three years ago, some local fisherman talked him into an archery contest to see who could shoot an apple hanging from a branch. My idiot brother decided to make it more challenging and placed the apple on his own head for the villagers to take aim at."

Jastyn's eyebrows arched. "You're not serious?"

"I am." She smiled. "Fortunately, right before the first arrow, our mother caught sight of this latest folly from a nearby hill. She shouted so loudly, the entire kingdom turned to watch her march down to scold him."

Jastyn's eyes were bright. "I bet she wasn't too happy."

"Not at all. She grabbed the apple and hurled it into the trees. She was furious. Of course, the villagers got a good laugh at Brennus's expense." Aurelia pictured him, embarrassed but soaking up the crowd's laughter, happy to have provided a moment's good humor. "He was quite the character, my brother." Her thoughts drifted, and they both sat quietly by the fire.

After a moment, Jastyn said, "I'm sorry to have missed that. I never went to many kingdom events." She seemed to study the flames.

Aurelia could guess why she hadn't attended. It was the same reason Aurelia hadn't seen her prior to their first meeting in the stables. As an Odium Child, it would have been easier for her to hide.

Unsure how to broach that particular topic, Aurelia said, "I wonder if the gods knew what they were doing, making sure we met when we did." As she spoke, she conjured and sent a small red flame from her fingertips into their campfire, adding to the warm glow. A quick *snap* from the charred logs broke the quiet.

Jastyn's snort surprised her. Seeming to realize who she was with, Jastyn glanced sheepishly sideways. "I'm sorry, but I'm not one to put faith in the gods. They haven't done much for me in this lifetime. Or for anyone I care about."

Aurelia nodded. She had learned bits and pieces about Jastyn's life since their adventure began. She knew Jastyn's sister was nine years younger and an avid reader as well as a lover of numbers. She had also overheard Coran ask about Elisedd, Jastyn's stepfather. From Jastyn's curt replies, it was evident their relationship was uneasy. She seemed to tolerate Elisedd's presence while her love for her sister was clear. It was also obvious how much she cared for Coran and vice versa. Aurelia often caught the two of them throwing fruit at one another or attempting to shove each other into a brook. What Aurelia found most curious was the lack of discussion about Jastyn's mother.

Shaking out the saol from her fingers, Aurelia sighed. It wasn't the gods.who had been unkind to Jastyn and her mother. It was the Diarmaid family—Aurelia's family—who had created the laws stating that women like Jastyn's mother were fit for punishment due to bearing a child out of wedlock. It was an archaic rule, but a rule she'd only learned as theory...until she'd met Jastyn.

Touching Jastyn's knee, Aurelia said, "If I had known what your family had gone through..." Her voice drifted off. What could she have done? She was royalty, yes, but it was her mother and father who implemented the laws set in place by their ancestors. Rules established to keep the kingdom of Venostes safe and its people in order.

Seeming to sense Aurelia's uncertainty, Jastyn placed her hand atop Aurelia's. "It's all right. It's not your fault my childhood didn't have the comforts of others."

"But I—"

Jastyn cut her off, her voice heated. "The Diarmaid legacy runs deep. History put my mother in the dungeon and forced us to live like dogs." Coran moaned and rolled over. She took a breath, lowering her voice. "You had nothing to do with it."

They held one another's gaze. "Nevertheless," Aurelia replied, "I am a part of it. I promise, I will work to right our wrongs when all of this is done."

She gently squeezed Aurelia's hand. Her eyes gleamed, and she smiled. Aurelia once again lost herself in those eyes, wondering at the glimmer of vulnerability in them. She savored the feel of her hand in Jastyn's and longed for this moment to never end. Her heart beat faster, and she was overtaken by an even greater longing, this one physical. She imagined herself leaning close, shrinking the distance between them. She had thought about kissing Jastyn since they'd survived the skirmish with Drest, each of them coming out battered and bruised but alive.

As they sat together now, Aurelia bit her lip to quell her urges. Was Jastyn's pulse quickening, too? Before she could discover, the look in Jastyn's eyes changed. She cleared her throat and, to Aurelia's dismay, pulled back her hand.

"Your sense of duty is admirable, Princess." Aurelia's brow furrowed as Jastyn lay next to the fire, one hand behind her head. "I appreciate your words. But it's late, and we should rest for tomorrow's walk. We have a lot of ground to cover."

Aurelia swallowed. Each time she felt Jastyn opening up, this happened. She seemed to realize what she'd said and quickly slammed the door before Aurelia could venture too far inside.

If only she knew how I long to know her. "I suppose you are right," she said softly. "Good night, Jastyn."

Jastyn had rolled onto her side, her back to Aurelia. Her voice was filled with something Aurelia couldn't pinpoint when she whispered, "Good night, Princess."

CHAPTER THREE

The next morning brought a short summer shower, forcing everyone to work quickly to pack up their belongings and start on the day's hike. Jastyn handed out handfuls of boysenberries and the last chewy strips of tree-dweller Coran had roasted the night before.

Rigo sipped thistle milk as he eyed their scraps. "In another day's time, I will hunt something larger than rabbit for us to eat. You humans have the most peculiar tastes," he said as he treaded lightly beside Aurelia through the Wood, which was beginning to grow sparse as they neared the rugged terrain separating the Wood from the Mountains of Ionad. His knee-length green tunic shimmered as he strode effortlessly in ankle-high tan boots over collapsed tree trunks with his large bow resting over his chest.

"Don't know what ya mean," Coran said between chews. "I thought the stew I made was rather tasty."

Jastyn grinned. "Not quite your mum's, but it was digestible."

"I don't see you roasting much, Jas," he replied, swiping crumbs from his speckled face. His hair had grown even more unmanageable and was in desperate need of a wash, as was his round, ruddy face. Jastyn was sure a dip in a cool lake would do them all good, including the impeccable Rigo, who never seemed to appear the worse for wear.

"I'm sure Jastyn is a fine cook." Aurelia spoke cheerily as she stepped over a fallen cluster of tree limbs with moss damp from the recent rain. She glanced at Jastyn, who smiled. They were only two hours into their walk with the sun at their back, and Aurelia had already found three different instances to compliment her. Coran shot her a knowing look, which she ignored. Aurelia was not holding back when it came to flirting. And Jastyn had to admit, she rather enjoyed it. She had been attracted to Aurelia immediately, and against all of her efforts, she liked Aurelia's company more than she expected to. This, of course, only deepened her growing feelings. Conversation with her was effortless, though Jastyn was careful to only share information she was ready for her to know.

Aurelia's medicinal knowledge was also quite welcome. Jastyn hated to admit it, but she had been weary following their fight with Drest. The arrow she'd taken in the shoulder had been one of the most painful things she'd ever experienced. She'd been grateful that the queen healed her that night, but her right shoulder now boasted a coin-sized patch of healing skin on either side of her shoulder blade where the arrow had entered and been extracted. She still felt the lingering effects on her muscles when she extended her arm.

While the queen's proximity that night had made Jastyn's skin prick with fear, Aurelia had a way of putting her at ease. She was quite the caretaker and was efficient in reminding Jastyn to clean and care for her recovering wound. Jastyn would roll her eyes but always looked forward to after dinner each evening, when Aurelia fussed about, making sure everybody was clean and tending their cuts and bruises as she pulled an endless supply of herbs and crushed tonics from Coran's bag, which had transformed into a makeshift apothecary's kit. It also didn't escape Jastyn that once everybody else had been tended to, Aurelia carefully applied calendula to her own knee, which seemed to be healing well. Jastyn hardly noticed a limp in Aurelia's stride anymore.

As the sky cleared, Jastyn breathed in the cool breeze that drifted between the trees. They were leaving the densest part of the Wood, reaching the point where the land turned bare and rocky near the base of the mountains. Jastyn had never been this far west but knew what lay ahead thanks to Eegit's diligent teaching. The hedgewitch had instructed Jastyn on the realm's geography at a young age, something Jastyn had soaked up eagerly, already longing to know faraway places. Places that, according to her mother's stories, might be host to her wandering father.

As they walked, Coran listened to Aurelia explain why she'd plucked five fistfuls of lavender. The steady hum of conversation lulled Jastyn's mind, and the scent of lavender led her to the last conversation she'd had with her mother, Branna. She had revealed that Jastyn's father had not only left before Jastyn was born—the reason for her mother's banishment to the outskirts of the kingdom with no money and no shelter—but also that he was a fae. The news had seemed unreal at first. Outside their humble home, Jastyn had felt suffocated by the information. She'd spent her whole life dreaming up visions of who her father might be. Perhaps a sailor, according to the fantasies her mother had helped weave, exploring far corners of the realm. Jastyn had envied him, even looked up to his freedom. She hadn't considered that he had left her and her mother willingly, let alone that he was a magical being.

She had spent little time ruminating on the fact that she was half-fae on top of being an Odium Child. As the weeks passed since she'd hotly left her grief-stricken mother outside their home, Jastyn had inklings of guilt. As quickly as the guilt came, though, she reminded herself that her mother had twenty-two years to tell her the truth. Yet she decided that the night before Jastyn was to leave was the best time to reveal everything. Frustration overran her guilt, and she once again fumed with renewed anger.

Despite all of that, she missed her family. Even Elisedd's looming presence elicited a sense of longing to return to her beloved sister. Jastyn spent nights looking at the stars twinkling behind a screen of gray and willed her sister to hold on. She knew the banshee blood she'd gotten from the Red One was effective, but it had an expiration date that fast approached. She wasn't sure where in the western caves to find the cure. The Red One had been cryptic in her details, and Jastyn had gone over and over what she could have meant. More than anything, she hoped the noble sacrifice the Red One had spoken of wasn't what she feared: something to do with the blood of Aurelia.

Another day of walking came and went, followed by a night sleeping under thick branches of ash trees to shield them from another storm. Jastyn and Coran pulled their hoods up while setting a saol shield. The invisible dome acted as a small-roofed hut, albeit one with leaks. But a few sprinkles of moisture were better than the onslaught outside of their modest, one-room-sized protection spell. Rigo seemed unfazed by nature unleashing her waters and watched them curiously from beneath a towering pine.

"It is only water. We will dry," he said, humor lining his words.

Jastyn added some damp twigs to their fire. She swiped her hands clean and placed one on her hip. "Since you're not eager to join us, how about you take watch again?"

Coran muttered, "He had last night's shift."

Jastyn frowned but stood her ground to the elf looming two heads taller than her. Though they had traveled together for nearly a month, she was not completely comfortable with him. After all, he had been one of the people who'd helped kidnap Aurelia following her brother's Remembrance. Aurelia was convinced of Rigo's allegiance; Jastyn remained skeptical.

She and Rigo stared at one another, and Jastyn was glad to see Aurelia preoccupied with shaking out their blankets. She didn't always understand Jastyn's distrust. Perhaps, Jastyn reluctantly decided, she needed to learn more about him.

Eventually, Rigo relented. "I would be happy to keep watch again. Sleep deeply, friends." He bowed, then wandered to his post.

After a rain-soaked night with little sleep, Jastyn approached Rigo as their group passed through a boulder-filled stretch of woodland teeming with gnome hills.

"Are you still planning to hunt?" she asked.

He glanced sideways. "Yes. At twilight."

She cleared her throat, keeping her chin high. "May I join you?" She watched Aurelia, who walked ahead with Coran and spoke animatedly while pointing to a pine tree several yards ahead.

"Certainly," Rigo replied. "Once we set up camp for the night, we can begin."

"Wonderful."

That evening, they picked a camping spot in a meadow. The wind was harsh, the formerly thick layers of trees giving way to puny shrubs and haggard weeds unable to block the blaring gusts. Coran sharpened a walking stick into a point for skewering. Aurelia sat next to him on a log, her tongue sticking slightly between her teeth in concentration as she analyzed the day's herbal collection.

"Shall we?" Rigo asked Jastyn, who added a few leaves to their fire before standing. She wiped her hands and nodded.

Aurelia looked up, surprised. "Are you going somewhere?"

Jastyn briefly lost herself in the brightness of her eyes. "I'm joining Rigo in a hunt. He seems to have tired of our meager human offerings and craves something more substantial." She grinned. "We won't be gone long."

Aurelia stood. "Oh. Well, do hurry back. I was just examining our medicine supply and determined we need more calendula. An onion wouldn't be bad either. I can grind the two into a paste that will expedite healing your shoulder." She fingered the torn material of Jastyn's navy tunic. Her fingertips grazed the fresh skin.

Jastyn's entire body warmed. She wrapped her fingers around Aurelia's before bringing them back down. "If I see an onion lying around, I'll be sure to grab it." Their hands fell to their respective sides. Tension filled the air between them, and Jastyn noticed Coran watching them, amused. To break the silence, Jastyn added, "I'm sure Rigo can smell an onion from a mile away."

He raised an eyebrow but didn't say anything as Jastyn punched his arm. "Well, what are we waiting for?"

Aurelia checked both their flasks and handed the fuller one to Jastyn. "Do be careful." She leaned closer but shifted back awkwardly. She smiled sheepishly, then returned to her seat next to Coran.

"Keep an eye on things, yeah?" Jastyn asked him, gesturing to Aurelia.

He waved her off. "Just go catch somethin', will ya? I'm starved." They exchanged grins before Jastyn and Rigo set off.

They didn't speak for several minutes, only gesturing as Rigo pointed in the best direction. Eventually, Jastyn said, "I wanted to apologize for yesterday. It was rude of me to expect you to take two nights' watch in a row. The rain had me in a foul mood."

Rigo stepped nimbly half a pace ahead. He could have easily been five yards ahead with his long stride. "I am not accustomed to human ways," he said, his voice lilting and rising like a song. Jastyn wondered how, even if he was upset, his voice sounded like a melody. She hadn't known any elves before and wondered if they all sounded as elegant as him when they spoke. "However, your animosity toward me seems to stem less from your dislike of elves and more from your desire to protect the princess."

Jastyn felt her face flush. Deciding to make light, she said, "Can you blame me? She's fallen into two riverbeds and disturbed seven fairy nests since we began."

Rigo smiled. "While that may be true, it seems to me that your feelings for her have built a wall between us."

Taken aback, Jastyn's words stumbled. "I don't...my feelings are..." Rigo gave her a pointed look. "What I feel for Aurelia is complicated."

Shaking his head, he replied, "Human mating rituals are foreign to me, but from what I've seen, they appear entirely too complex. It seems things would be much easier if you all simply conversed with one another about the matter."

Laughing, Jastyn said, "Human mating rituals? Now I must know, how do elves decide their partners?"

He looked into the distance, his thin lips curving into a smile. "At our fiftieth birthday, we are able to leave our clan and live amongst the other elven people. That is often when we find our mates. Once there is a mutual agreement from both parties, we spend the next ten years courting. At our joining ceremony, a lock of hair is exchanged, binding the two together for eternity."

He reached into a pocket at his left hip and pulled out a shining silver locket. On its cover, it sported intricate letters, though Jastyn couldn't read them. "The name of your clan?" she asked.

"Yes, and the word my mate and I chose to represent our love." Jastyn waited. With a smile, Rigo added, "*Muinin*. It translates, roughly, to confidence. Confidence in one another. Confidence in ourselves to be enough. And confidence in this world that brought us together."

Impressed, Jastyn's thoughts went to Aurelia. She was surprised to picture herself standing before her, their hands clasped, and Aurelia looking at her with adulation. Shaking herself from the thought, she said, "What is your mate's name?"

Smiling wider, he said, "His name is Daylor. I miss him."

"Does he know of this journey?"

He shook his head. "He knows I left on a mission from our queen. However, this part of my journey was unexpected. Yet I know he can sense my longing and knows I am thinking of him. We will be reunited one day."

After a moment, she asked, "The mission for your queen, it was to kill Aurelia, wasn't it?"

His face fell. "Yes."

She nodded. It made sense. The prince had already been disposed of when the elves attacked during his Remembrance ceremony. If they could eliminate the only remaining heir, the throne would be vulnerable.

"My queen had aligned herself with that man." His face scrunched. She felt bitterness on her tongue when she said, "Drest."

"He promised that if my queen could ensure the end of the Diarmaid reign, it would mean everlasting security for the elves."

"But how?"

Rigo watched the ground as they walked. "He claimed to have the power to take out the Diarmaids and bring about 'the old ways.'" He shook his head. "That part never made sense to me. The realm used to function harmoniously. Once humans invaded, borders were drawn and unrest began."

Pondering this, Jastyn said, "He sounded like a madman bent on control. Perhaps he saw the Diarmaids as a threat to something."

"I do not know. I sent word that he had been imprisoned. My queen will hopefully see reason, but I fear she may be too far gone."

Jastyn asked the question that had been bothering her for weeks. "Why change sides?" She met his gaze. "Why help us escape that leprechaun lodging? Why help me, when the Dark Fae was at my back?"

Rigo held her gaze, then turned to scan the surrounding trees. "My clan has a saying. 'When every eye is turned to the sky, question what is on the ground.' I saw the thirst my people had for isolation, for a life of superiority over the rest of the realm. They became so fixated on pulling apart from everyone else, there had to be a larger plan at work. A reason for this desire. So when the queen asked for volunteers to find Aurelia, I saw it as an opportunity to learn more about what was really going on."

"You got close to Drest."

"Each night that we had Aurelia in the Wood, he would go off somewhere. I never learned where, but he would come back…changed."

Jastyn furrowed her brow. "Changed?"

"Reinvigorated may be the better word. Like a new darkness had taken root, enlivening him to march another day." He tilted his head as if remembering. "He offered a vial of something to us each night. I don't know if it was the same thing he was using to continue. My companion and I never took what was inside." He pulled a small vial from his tunic. The liquid was a dark blue, nearly black.

Jastyn's mind flashed to the Dark Fae. Was he a part of all of this? But why would the Dark Fae care for the workings of the kingdom?

"Maybe Aurelia will know what it is."

"Perhaps." He pocketed the vial again. Eventually, he said, "The princess proved a worthy captive. She even managed to knock me and my companion out with a sleeping draught one night." He chuckled at the memory, and Jastyn snorted.

"Sounds like her."

Rigo smiled. "That only solidified my belief that she was innocent of any dark doings. The princess only wanted to be free. So I decided that even if my queen couldn't see reason, I could at least try to help in any way I could."

Understanding the allure of Aurelia, Jastyn said, "Thank you for telling me all of that."

He nodded. After a while, he broke the silence. "There is a buck within a mile. Keep your eyes sharp."

She nodded, though her eyesight wasn't nearly as keen as his. Nevertheless, she grew excited to show off a bit and hoped they could bring back something worthy of Aurelia.

Rigo raised his arm, and they halted. He squinted into the distance, then asked quietly, "What do you know of the Mountains of Ionad?"

Following his gaze, she said, "Only that they are the dividing line between the Kingdom of Venostes and the western realm. I've heard stories of people crossing them, though most choose to venture north and travel around the farthest peaks in order to pass through places like Uterni."

"You have no knowledge of the fae that dwell within the range?"

Jastyn's pride stung, though the question wasn't phrased rudely. Eegit had taught her a lot but often got distracted by mineral elements contained within the mountains. She hadn't told Jastyn much about who or what resided in Ionad. "I would imagine there are dwarves." The mineral-loving fae typically dug mines filled with gold and diamonds, riches being their main desire in life.

"There are some, yes. Though many have moved north to live nearer to Uterni. There is a colony of elves who reside in the mountains, those who refused to leave after the war that claimed the land for Venostes."

Jastyn listened carefully. As they tiptoed between trees, a faint rustle sounded ahead in the brush.

"That is the extent of my knowledge," Rigo said. "However, I imagine there is a plethora of unknown fae who call the mountains home."

Jastyn's body hummed with anticipation as her senses heightened. She could feel the buck's presence as they moved. "I have a feeling you may be right."

The sun was at its lowest point above the horizon, and Jastyn felt the Wood shift from day to night. Smaller creatures scurried into their burrows at the base of the trees. Leaves rustled as songbirds perched in their nests, while the hoot of an owl broke the air. Insects chirped their nightly greetings, and a distant howl signaled the wolves waking.

Together, she and Rigo stepped toward the unsuspecting buck. She decided to follow his lead and had to admit his ability to sneak up on an animal was unprecedented. She had always been proud of her stealth, in part thanks to her petite stature and years of tracking creatures in the Wood. Elves, on the other hand, had a natural advantage in their grace and precision and their ability to see and hear better than any human. Together, they were a pretty good team.

Pausing next to a sturdy ash, Jastyn saw the buck. He was nearly as tall as Rigo, his massive antlers stretching skyward atop his wide head. His fur bristled, his body alert as he grazed. Jastyn inched closer to Rigo. She steadied her breathing. They were only thirty yards away, and the anticipation of conquering such an animal sent a wave of elation through her. It had been some time since she'd hunted something other than rabbit and tree-dweller.

Slowly, she reached for the blade that rested on the outside of her boot. Her eyes stayed on the buck while her fingers traced the outside of her right leg. As soon as she felt the empty loop that typically held her hunting blade, she grimaced.

"Gods be damned. I forgot I've lost my knife." Two days after they'd started this journey, she had discovered her blade missing and figured she must have lost it in the battle with Drest.

The buck paused, his powerful neck rising to scan his surroundings.

Rigo nodded. Silently, he plucked an arrow from the quiver. He nocked it in his bow. For a moment, the entire Wood stood still. This was the part Jastyn loved. The moment right before. She watched the buck and silently paid her respects to the animal. Then Rigo let the arrow fly.

❖

"Gods, where did ya find such a catch?" Coran gawked as Jastyn and Rigo entered their camp, the limp buck resting on their shoulders as they walked one in front of the other.

"He's already cleaned out. We've just got to skin him before we cook."

They carefully placed the buck on the ground. Coran ran over, rubbing his hands as he examined their menu for the next few days. "Mighty fine, he is. Well done."

Jastyn placed her hands on her hips, standing proudly as she scanned their camp. The sun had set, but the fire burned brightly. A few fairy nests shined in the branches around them, providing a soft glow of light. Three logs had been arranged around the fire, a setup Jastyn recognized as Aurelia's signature addition. She sat on one now, wearing a look of shock, her eyes wide as she stared at their catch.

"Aurelia?" Jastyn tilted her head. When she didn't answer, Jastyn moved closer, stepping around the fire. Aurelia continued to stare at the fallen buck even as Coran and Rigo began to scrape off the fur. Her face paled. "Aurelia, are you all right?" She sat next to her and nudged her knee.

Finally, the spell broke, and Aurelia turned, though she still wore a look of surprise. "Forgive me. I…" She glanced at the buck. "We eat venison quite regularly in the castle. However, I fear…I fear that despite the many occasions I've enjoyed such a meal, I have never actually *seen* the preparation process."

Jastyn followed her gaze and laughed. "Oh, Princess."

Aurelia blushed. "You should know by now there are many things I'm not privy to." She looked back at Jastyn, who was still chuckling. She took a deep breath, eyeing their food warily. "Perhaps…perhaps I could learn?"

Jastyn admired her gusto. Aurelia's face was a light shade of green, and as fun as it would be to watch her attempt to skin their food, Jastyn thought of something else. She placed a hand on Aurelia's knee where her pants were torn and a wide scar peeked through. "I have a better idea. Why don't you help me apply some of your magical herbs to my shoulder? It's itching more than I'd like it to."

Her eyes filled with gratitude, and she smiled widely. "I can help with that. Did you happen to find any more calendula?"

"I'm afraid not, but we can look tomorrow."

"Very well." She reached for Coran's satchel and dug through it eagerly. "I'd like to find that onion, if possible. I've noticed a few along our trek but forgot to pluck them." She inhaled sharply, her nose crinkling. "If I don't get a proper bath soon, I may simply turn into one. That would make things easier, wouldn't it?"

Jastyn laughed. "You don't smell anything like an onion." She leaned close and gave an exaggerated sniff. "Well, not completely."

Aurelia's mouth fell open. "You!" She shoved Jastyn's knee, making her laugh harder. In reality, all she could smell when Aurelia was near was orchids and the warm musty scent of the earth, a smell Jastyn was fast growing fond of. Before she could stop herself, she placed a strand of hair behind Aurelia's ear, running her fingers the length of the smooth tresses as she gazed at the soft curve of Aurelia's jaw before wandering to the fullness of her lips.

"I think you are the most beautiful woman I've ever known."

The words surprised Jastyn as much as they seemed to surprise Aurelia. Both sat silent, stunned by the confession. Aurelia's eyes softened, and she dipped her chin. "Shall we proceed with your shoulder?"

Jastyn swallowed, running a hand down her messy braid and wishing she could drench her face in water to calm herself. Why did she say that? She wasn't supposed to feel this way about Aurelia. Moments like this, when she was completely at ease, made Jastyn want to tell her everything. Tell her about the noble sacrifice in the caves. She wanted to tell Aurelia that it might be her blood that was needed to claim the cure. Moments like this made her head swim.

Unable to manage the torrent in her mind, Jastyn stood. "I'll just grab my flask." Quickly, she fetched it from Coran, who was already carving the meat free thanks to Rigo's quick work.

When she leaned down, he muttered, "Any day now, Jas," and threw her a grin.

"Hush," she replied, splashing him before returning to Aurelia's side.

Fortunately, the rest of the night was filled with less tension as Coran and Rigo skewered and cooked a surplus of venison. Once everything was done, Aurelia admitted to feeling useless and volunteered to wrap the leftovers in linden leaves to better store them.

The next morning, before midday, they cleared the final line of trees. Before them lay acres of barren gray rock that unfurled like jagged parchment. The healthy trunks of birch gave way to shrunken, twisted junipers. At their end, the towering black peaks stood like giants against the bright cerulean sky.

"Nearly there," Coran said, awe in his voice.

Aurelia stepped out from the trees and let out a gasp as she fell in line beside Jastyn, who couldn't help but smile at the look of wonder.

Proudly, Jastyn said, "Princess, welcome to the Mountains of Ionad."

Chapter Four

B y the gods, it's amazing."

Aurelia shielded her eyes from the bright sun. She had read dozens of books on the lands that lay west of her kingdom and had spent countless days poring over renderings of the vast, open lands beyond the Wood. She had admired detailed charcoal sketches of the mountains that hung on the castle walls. None of those compared to the stunning, rugged beauty of the dark cragged peaks and astoundingly wide, tree-littered bases of the great Mountains of Ionad. Her own imaginings had paled in comparison, unable to conjure the appropriate grandeur to encapsulate the wild, windswept terrain filled with endless treasures waiting to be discovered.

"It's breathtaking."

Her voice was captured by the ceaseless wind and was carried away across the open stretches of land. The ground was harsh, the lush green of the Wood fading to patches of sickly yellow sticking up from the black earth, itself an endless sheet of rock. The occasional tree sprang from the ground, but they were few and scattered haphazardly, their scrawny, twisted trunks tangled in the brutal winds. What few leaves clung to their branches were small and gripped their thin twigs with desperation. Aurelia shuddered at the stark contrast to Venostes, and she felt a pang of something unfamiliar. She was happy to be out of the castle, far from her kingdom, staring at a chance to explore a new land all on her own. Yet this opportunity was laced with melancholy.

I wish Brennus could see this.

Her brother would have loved to be here. For a moment, she imagined him standing beside her, one hand resting on the hilt of his sword, the other raised to shield his eyes. His blue tunic blew around him in the wind. She turned, and he grinned, ecstatic and eager to explore.

"Can't wait to tell Roisin about this." Coran swiped a hand through his hair, his eyes wide with wonder. Aurelia blinked, and the image of her brother disappeared. To her left, Jastyn stood between her and Rigo. He peered toward the peaks, no doubt analyzing the massive cracks in the mountains' intimidating faces. Jastyn seemed impressed, and Aurelia was glad that, even if her brother couldn't be here, she was experiencing this with people she cared about.

The sky to the south hosted a gloomy stretch of gray, but ahead and to the north were clear skies, save for the occasional tuft of cumulus. To Aurelia, the fluffy mounds resembled sheep's wool drifting lazily through the sky.

She glanced at Jastyn, who explained, "The southern shores lie near. Clouds always coat the edge of land next to the sea."

Aurelia nodded. "Does that mean we're close to the caves?"

Jastyn shook her head and pulled a red apple from her satchel. "I'm afraid not. We could follow the shoreline, but it's extremely treacherous. The cliffsides often tumble into the sea due to constant battering from the ocean waves. It will take longer, but the safest way will be to find a passage through the mountains."

"Any idea what we'll see in there?" asked Coran.

Aurelia's mind raced back to her mother's texts. She pointed right. "That's the native chaparral plant and appears to be of the scrub oak genus. They can live in poor soil such as this and hardly require any water. I see a smattering of foxtail over there," she added, gesturing ahead. She scanned the area closer to them, then drifted back out. "There's a few splashes of color. Do you see? That light blue over there?" She smiled. "Even wild lilac can thrive in such conditions. It's quite stubborn. I imagine we'll see some thistle and ragged robin once we get closer to the mountains, too."

When she glanced around, Jastyn's lips were pursed as if holding back a laugh. Coran nodded politely but looked overwhelmed. Confused, she turned to Rigo.

"Your Highness, I believe he was inquiring about the fae who reside in the mountains. Not this region's collection of flora."

"Oh." She blushed. Jastyn grinned after another bite into her apple. Aurelia shrugged, regaining her composure, which in itself was becoming more difficult to do the longer she was around Jastyn. Particularly since Jastyn's confession of attraction. Initially, Aurelia had been overjoyed. Her suspicions and hopes were confirmed, and she was happy to know that she wasn't completely mad, pining after a woman who maybe didn't feel the same way. But now, there was a spark between them, and the attraction was mutual.

"Rigo says there may be elves who reside in certain parts of the mountains, those who never left once your family claimed the land." Jastyn said the last part softly, and Aurelia appreciated her attempt to lessen the sting of history.

"Of course. And dwarves?"

Jastyn nodded. "They'll be deep within the mountains, so I don't imagine we'll run into many."

"Mighty good scavengers, dwarves," Coran said. "Wouldn't mind picking their brains on swiping tactics, gold sifting tips, and the like."

Aurelia eyed him, and his face reddened.

"Not that I'd use those techniques in the village, o'course. Only for my own curiousness." He looked pleadingly to Jastyn, who smiled and started forward, tossing her apple core into the trees behind them.

"I do hope there are no more snares," Aurelia said with an exasperated sigh. She had run into three snares already, two hidden near rivers and one in a leaf-covered meadow. Fortunately, all three had been meager, and Aurelia had been able to free herself using a quick counter spell. Her parents had laid the snares. There was no mistaking them. She supposed they had been more reluctant than she'd initially thought to let her go. Back in the castle, her mother had set many snares, typically to catch a nimble-fingered maiden or a slippery guard who had their eyes on her parents' possessions. The unsuspecting thief would quickly find themselves caught in a saol snare, trapping them in place until they could be interrogated. They could be cast from anywhere.

Jastyn hesitated before saying, "You're the heir now, Aurelia. Your mother is only trying to keep you safe."

"Jastyn."

Jastyn held up a hand, squaring up to face her. "Please." Her face was conflicted, and Aurelia wished she didn't feel the need to go through this. Didn't she know by now this was where Aurelia wanted to be?

Ignoring the eyes on her, Aurelia focused on a spot below her feet. "I am well aware of my status."

"It will be dangerous."

"I understand." Aurelia gestured to the Wood behind them. "We've made it this far with little incident."

"Your Highness," Coran interjected, "if somethin' *did* happen to you…the queen and king…"

"My mother and father will be fine," she said, her voice sharper than she'd intended. "They need to understand I am no longer a child." She glanced around sheepishly at admitting something she'd felt for years but had never known with whom to share it. "Brennus and I are"—she swallowed, the familiar pain rising up in her chest—"they have kept us in the dark for far too long." Taking a shaky breath, she lowered her voice. "The least they can do is let me have this time. And if they won't, I'll take it for myself." She blinked back tears. Her mother and father couldn't understand; she was finally free. Of course, she knew her eventual destiny, but that required accepting the fact that her brother was truly gone. It meant returning to a place vacant of his presence, a place where she would be completely alone.

For that, she was not yet ready.

She turned to Jastyn, her voice soft. "I know what you're going to ask. I know you think this is your mission alone." Jastyn squinted, her mouth open to say something, but Aurelia continued. "But I meant what I said in the Wood." Looking from Jastyn to Coran, Aurelia placed her hands on her hips. "I want to be here. I'm staying."

Smiling, Jastyn said, "If Her Highness insists."

Coran clapped his hands. "We'll keep an eye out for those snares."

"And anything else my mother decides to send our way."

"There's only one way to find out what we'll run into." Jastyn turned back, reaching out a hand. A rush of heat swam in Aurelia's chest, and she happily let Jastyn lead her on the first steps of their journey through the great Mountains of Ionad.

The first half of the day passed pleasantly enough. Aurelia munched on raspberries she'd plucked in the first hour, knowing the chance that they'd find much in the way of fruit slimmed the closer to the mountains they got. The strong sun forced all of them to roll up their tunic sleeves, and they passed their flasks around generously in the glaring heat.

They decided to continue directly west. According to Rigo, there were several wide passages between the second and third peaks, something his excellent vision had determined after a quick trip up a sickly looking pine.

They'd found a thin river lined with sparse pines, with a few fish swimming lazily through its waters. Aurelia tried to contain her enthusiasm as they followed it. She attempted to take in everything at once, much as she had during her time in the Wood. Unlike the kingdom's dense, moss-covered forests, this land was open, like an ink-filled page in a book. Despite its openness, it was dark and hostile to much of the plant and animal life she was accustomed to seeing. She relied on the memory of her familiar texts to give her a sense of comfort as she moved further from the life she'd known.

Coran walked beside her. "What do ya wager Roisin would say if she was here?" They were nearly the same height, with his tangle of red-orange hair standing tall and giving him a couple of inches more.

Aurelia breathed in the fresh air that carried the scent of pine as it blew uninterrupted around them. "Honestly, I'm not certain she would care for this region. It's not the most welcoming, is it?" He shook his head. "Besides, I'm afraid my maiden's adventurous spirit has been diminished by the comforts of castle life."

Smiling, he said, "She much prefers a light stroll through the Wood than a trip to the shores. I do believe you've spoiled her." She raised her brows, and he paled. "I forgot who I was talkin' to. Forgive me, Your Highness."

Laughing, Aurelia said, "It's fine, Coran. You may speak plainly to me. And please, call me Aurelia."

Blush fading from behind his smattering of freckles, he nodded.

A gust of wind blew over them, the sound like a horde of arrows whipping through the sky. Aurelia saw Jastyn falter, her slight frame little match for the blistering gusts. She regained her step quickly and fell easily again into what looked like a serious conversation with Rigo.

Aurelia wondered what they could be discussing. Their route, she supposed. Her eyes fell to Jastyn's back, landing on the rip in her tunic over her right shoulder blade. She made a mental note to patch it once they found a public house or any settlement. The road thus far had supplied little in the way of company, but Aurelia had chalked that up to the Fae Lands hosting creatures who probably weren't fond of humans and preferred to keep to themselves. She pictured herself sitting before a warm fire, a goblet of spiced wine before her. She could mend Jastyn's tunic, humming happily while Jastyn and Coran swapped coins in the corner. She couldn't help but miss the idea of a warm bed covered in layers of pelts. While she quite enjoyed the outdoors, she had to admit her back was growing quite sore from sleeping on the hard ground each night.

She sighed, chagrined that part of her still missed aspects of her old life, though she'd never say so. She missed Roisin. She missed their conversations in the dining hall. She hoped her maiden was faring well and that her parents had informed her that she and Coran were all right.

It seemed Roisin was on Coran's mind too, as he recounted a particularly humorous story about trying to teach Roisin to ride. Aurelia enjoyed hearing it from a paramour's perspective. The two were obviously smitten.

While she listened, Aurelia took another opportunity to watch Jastyn. She loved the confidence in Jastyn's stride and the way her head was always high, even if she was uncertain about which direction to go. Over the last month, Aurelia had noticed other things as well: how Jastyn clenched her jaw when she was frustrated, like on the rare occasion she came back empty-handed from a hunt. There was the way Jastyn's eyes lit up when she spoke of Alanna, then darkened when the conversation turned to her stepfather or mother. And Jastyn's shoulders relaxed only when she thought nobody was looking.

Now Aurelia tracked the gentle sway of Jastyn's braid, her right hand as it traced the top of the woven strawberry-blond strands before running down the length of the thinner tail. This was another common gesture, usually signifying she had a lot on her mind.

"Those two seem to be getting along better." Coran's voice pulled her from the trance. She blinked, realizing her gaze had fallen lower than she'd intended. Thankfully, Coran hadn't noticed.

"Yes," she replied, adjusting her flask over her shoulder. Jastyn had been suspicious of Rigo's intentions since the night Drest had been taken into her parents' custody. At first, Aurelia had been flattered, assuming Jastyn's animosity was a sign of her protective nature. As the days passed and Jastyn was no kinder to him, Aurelia realized that Eegit and Coran were right. Jastyn simply didn't trust easily. Even after Rigo had spent the first two nights reiterating his story, how he did not agree with his queen's alliance with Drest and believed there was more to her sudden blind trust in humans, Jastyn had seemed to scrutinize his every move or critique his suggestions. As Aurelia began to understand more about Jastyn's upbringing, she didn't blame her for the distrust. Jastyn had lived a life of unjust cruelty and unforgiving circumstances. It only made sense that she'd be wary of strangers.

"Perhaps," Aurelia mused, "their hunt proved beneficial for their relationship. There seems to be a bridge of understanding between them now."

"You might be right," Coran said, his gaze thoughtful.

After another two days, the river diverted south, and they said good-bye to their steady supply of water. The skies had been kind, with no storms, though this also meant no more water.

One particularly blustery night, they camped below an overhang of black rock. Around the campfire, Aurelia listened while Jastyn, Rigo, and Coran discussed their plans for when they reached the base of the mountains.

"The northwest passage is the one I favor most," Rigo said. "While it features the steepest elevation gain, it also contains the most welcoming footholds. It will take us five, maybe six days, to cross the peaks entirely."

"From there, how long until we reach the caves?" Coran bit off a piece of venison they'd cooked over a red-flamed fire. The wind proved unfriendly to keeping the flames lit, forcing Coran and Aurelia to repeatedly add their saols to the embers.

Jastyn and Rigo exchanged glances. He nodded to Jastyn, who said, "Once we reach the other side of the mountains, it will be a two-week journey to the shoreline."

"And the home of Alanna's cure." The group turned to Aurelia. Coran nodded while Rigo watched the fire, his face a blanket of concentration against the eerie silence of the rock walls surrounding them. Aurelia met Jastyn's gaze, and she smiled at the anticipation.

Jastyn's smile faltered, and Aurelia wondered what she was thinking as her gaze went to the skewer she rubbed between her hands.

"The western caves lie near the banshee's cove, do they not?" Rigo asked from his spot across the fire.

Nodding, Jastyn said, "Eegit ventured to the cove once. She doesn't recommend it." They all chuckled.

Aurelia, asked, "Have you any word from Eegit?"

Coran said, "I swore I saw her about four days ago when we were in the Wood. There were two giant eyes peering at me through a layer of branches, and they were framed by a wide, sunken face. I thought I even heard her cackle."

Jastyn laughed, placing a hunk of venison on the end of her skewer and hanging it over the fire.

"Turned out to be an owl. But I wouldn't be surprised to turn around one day and see the old loon marching along behind us." He took another bite as a rustle sounded behind him. They all paused, and Coran's eyes widened, but there was nothing.

Eventually, Jastyn said, "I'm sure she's in her meadow, mixing spells and working on her potions."

"What was she working on?" Aurelia asked, picturing the old hedgewitch who had seemed quite kind, if a little unsettling in her demeanor.

"She's been trying to bottle luck for years."

Aurelia's brows rose. "Has she? They say it's against the elements to try to bottle luck."

Jastyn's grin spread wider. "I told her the same thing." Their eyes met, and a flutter stirred in Aurelia's chest. "Eegit's never cared much for rules."

Aurelia nodded, noting this as one of the reasons Jastyn probably took to Eegit.

Coran tossed a burned scrap of meat into the fire. "Well, without her steady supplier of stones and minerals, it may be a while before she succeeds."

Jastyn dipped her chin, glancing at Aurelia, who asked in mock disappointment, "How many items *have* you stolen from the royal market?"

Jastyn and Coran exchanged glances, the latter returning his focus to the meat he tore apart. Jastyn laughed. "Enough to fill ten apothecary stands, I'd imagine."

Rigo snorted, and Aurelia gaped.

Jastyn pulled her dinner out of the fire, and the smell of the cooked meat wafted over them on the wind. Jastyn's shoulders rose and fell as she took in their surroundings, the jagged wall of the overhang sitting haphazardly over their heads, the unforgiving earth beneath them, and the scrawny logs they sat upon. Aurelia's gaze went to Jastyn's fingers as they traced the empty place on the outside of her boot where her dagger had been as if missing it.

"Anyway," Jastyn said, "I haven't heard a single thing from Eegit. But if I do see her, I'll tell her we could all use a bit of luck in the coming days." Looking warily at the fire, she added, "I have a feeling we're going to need it."

CHAPTER FIVE

The first day of their ascent went by with little incident. However, as time passed, Jastyn grew anxious. She could deal with the uncertainty of the journey. After all, she'd had a lifetime of not knowing what the next day would bring. It was the endgame of this that drove her mad as she dwelled on what they might encounter in the western caves. Each night, she tossed and turned, dark visions filling her mind. When sleep proved futile, she would volunteer to stand guard, letting her mind wander in the solitude of a cool night. She contemplated the future, considering every possible way she could talk about the truth of the noble sacrifice.

Each morning, she was left feeling the way she always did: as if she was being pulled in opposing directions. With each sunrise, she could feel the closeness of Alanna's cure. She longed to hold the answer, and at times, she felt light-headed with the prospect of finally giving Alanna the life she deserved.

On the other hand, each sunset signified another day she'd kept her secret from Aurelia. Jastyn had yet to decipher the Red One's true meaning regarding the noble sacrifice required in exchange for the cure. She'd considered many variations, but each one featured something from Aurelia: the shedding of noble blood, her forced captivity at the mercy of some horrible creature, or what Jastyn loathed most, a bargain for Aurelia's life. The idea made her sick. The thought that the only way to obtain the cure meant endangering Aurelia's life was unbearable. Aurelia, whose eyes held a zest for life that both frightened and invigorated Jastyn. It was a joy Jastyn had felt fading inside herself for years, but it had been bolstered since their meeting.

How am I going to do this? How do I tell Aurelia the truth of the Red One's words?

She had played out the conversation in her mind, and each time, it ended in disaster, with Aurelia staring at her in shame and disbelief before turning her back on Jastyn forever.

Thus, the cycle continued. Every day, Jastyn woke with renewed hope that today would be the day. Alas, more than a month had passed since their journey had begun, and Jastyn had failed to be brave. The longer she waited, the stronger her feelings grew, and the more difficult it became to tell her the truth.

When the whirlwind of her mind proved too much—and it inevitably did—Jastyn focused on the hike. The first day's climb between the second and third peaks was uneventful. The barren, rocky earth was not easy to traverse, but they managed well enough. Rigo, not surprisingly, fared best. He walked ahead, leaping nimbly from rock face to rock face, hanging easily from precarious cliffsides and large boulders that looked ready to tumble into the passage. Coran appeared rather nervous at their ascent, which Jastyn was more than happy to tease him about.

She also chuckled at Aurelia's insistence on collecting each tiny sprig, root, and herb she laid eyes on, though not before making sure whatever she touched held no secret snare waiting to grab her. She kept pace as they climbed, though her breath grew laborious around midday. By the end of the first day, Jastyn, Coran, and Aurelia were so tired, they all fell asleep within minutes of setting up camp on the interior of a wide crevice wedged between two cliff faces, twenty yards off the main path.

On the second day, Jastyn woke to the distant caw of a raven. She jerked awake, reaching for the blade in her boot. Remembering it wasn't there, she conjured her saol as she shoved off her blanket and stood.

Rigo's voice came from behind her. "Take comfort. It is only ravens overhead."

Jastyn stepped onto the path and looked up. She craned her neck, her sleepy gaze skyward. A trio of large black ravens circled to the north.

She grimaced, then turned to Rigo. Standing at the entrance of their rocky inlet, he leaned against his bow. Her saol, its blue light vibrant against the dark morning, hovered over her open palm a moment more. Finally, she exhaled, closing her palm as the saol vanished.

"I thought for a second it was…" She'd dreamt of the Dark Fae. However, unlike her dreams over the last twelve years, where his menacing presence was contained to the Wood, he now followed her into the village. In the dream, she'd been running from the cloaked rider, passing shadows of homes that led to her family's dwelling at the outskirts of the kingdom. He'd never been that close to her family in her dreams. She feared it might be an omen, that maybe the Dark Fae was closer to finding her in this world.

"The dark force has penetrated many facets of this realm." Rigo seemed to read her thoughts, speaking softly as Coran stirred. "His shadows have already begun to stretch over my homeland. They have breached your Wood as well."

Jastyn walked back into their campsite and shook out her blanket. "I prefer not to think about him."

For a moment, it seemed as if Rigo wanted to say something, but before he could, Aurelia yawned and stretched, an adorable look of sleep still on her face.

"Good morning," she said cheerily.

Jastyn rolled her blanket and stuffed it into her satchel. "Good morning, Princess." She shot Rigo a look, signaling she was done with their conversation. "Ready for another day?"

Aurelia's smile widened. "Always."

On their hike, Jastyn's stomach growled. They'd eaten the last of their venison for breakfast. She was grateful when Aurelia hadn't seemed to notice that Jastyn had given her the last good piece of meat, while she split an apple with Coran. They'd shared a handful of gooseberries that were now more sour than sweet, and the flask that bounced gently on Jastyn's hip was nearly empty. She hoped that wherever they found shelter tonight would have something to offer in the way of food and drink, though that prospect wasn't promising. This didn't faze Jastyn. She'd grown accustomed to hunger pangs, having spent the first half of her life as a scavenger skirting the edge of starvation. In the village, she'd learned to pick up after families who threw out scraps, scrawny bites of chicken clinging to gnawed bones. Making do with the little she could find had been normal, with puny tree-dwellers and spoiled fruit a staple in her diet.

Aurelia was not accustomed to meager meals at odd hours. Her face had lost some of its roundness, though her legs had gained lean muscle, according to the new tightness of her leather pants, something Jastyn couldn't help but notice. Aurelia, continuing to surprise her, never complained when food was scarce.

Coran, on the other hand, was quite vocal about the food situation and didn't hesitate to share the sting of their low rations. "Gods, I could eat a whole cauldron of my mum's stew."

He gripped his stomach as it growled noisily. The four of them climbed slowly upward on a sloped path littered with piles of broken black rock that had accumulated over decades of uninterrupted solitude. The weeks were beginning to wear on everyone, and Jastyn knew their pace had slowed since reaching the mountains. The wind wasn't helpful either, its gusts berating them with fervor as they blew by the peaks. The steep mountain walls stretched skyward around them, often blocking the sunlight. Their formerly sundrenched days on the moors were gone. Now they were left in an unnerving, perpetual feeling of twilight.

More rumblings came from their stomachs. Aurelia stepped carefully over a pile of rocks, one hand landing gingerly to balance her steps. "I must admit, a plate of roasted lamb sounds quite appetizing at the moment."

Without thinking, Jastyn replied, "Never tried it."

Aurelia paused, turning to face her with a look of surprise. "You never…Oh, it's a delectable dinner. Our cook prepares the most scrumptious leg of lamb with a gravy that warms the very core of you. He garnishes it with radishes and parsley. Paired with a mulled cider, it's absolutely delightful."

Jastyn pursed her lips in mock envy. "Well, I'll be sure to order some next time I venture onto royal grounds." She grinned, relishing the hint of pink that swam to Aurelia's cheeks.

"I didn't mean for that to sound as pompous as I fear it did."

Coran chimed in behind Jastyn. "Mostly sounded tasty to me."

Aurelia's eyes, swimming with embarrassment, moved from Coran to Jastyn. She reached out, gathering one of Jastyn's hands. "I'm sorry. That was thoughtless of me."

Jastyn hardly heard. She was caught in Aurelia's eyes, admiring how the color was even more vibrant in these dark mountains, a bright anchor to cling to in this foreboding and frightening land. Jastyn loved Aurelia's eyes, not only for their beauty, but because in them, she saw the unwavering conviction about what they were doing. In her eyes, she saw what this meant not only for herself and Alanna but what this newfound freedom meant for Aurelia, too.

Overwhelmed, Jastyn dropped her gaze to Aurelia's hands. She traced the pink scars running like thin reeds around Aurelia's wrists. Her heart ached when she recalled the kidnapping. It seemed like another lifetime when they'd fought against Drest as he sought to bring about the downfall of the royal family. They'd come a long way since then.

"Think nothing of it," she said, her voice quivering at the surge of emotion. She placed her free hand on top of Aurelia's. "Maybe you can introduce me to the fine dining of Diarmaid castle one day."

Jastyn couldn't believe those words had left her mouth. Had she just willingly proposed a visit to the royal castle? Gods, what was Aurelia doing to her?

Light welled like sparks in Aurelia's eyes. Jastyn's chest filled with something she was beginning to understand but was not yet ready to name.

"Oy, you two! You're gonna want to look at this."

As Aurelia turned, Jastyn let her hand linger in Aurelia's, and they moved forward together. Coran and Rigo had continued ahead and were now standing thirty yards up the increasingly narrow path that cut through the mountainside. Jastyn stepped ahead, holding on to Aurelia's hand and helping guide her through the unstable and shifting rocks. Once they'd caught up to the others, Jastyn pulled Aurelia up carefully beside her.

She was surprised to find a stretch of flat, even ground ahead. The space was larger than Eegit's meadow, and on the opposite end, the wide mouth of a cave opened to their right, and the most wonderful smells drifted from inside. Jastyn caught whiffs of heady flowers, not unlike the ones on the nymph she'd encountered some months before deep in the Wood. A thin line of smoke wafted out, carrying a hint of spices and fruit.

She thought she might be imagining things, but Coran said, "Can you believe it? Looks like we've been given a bit of luck after all."

Jastyn released Aurelia and stepped forward. The clearing was a nice reprieve from the suffocating closeness of the peaks, and Jastyn enjoyed being able to see the evening sky, currently a deep pink as the sun set ahead. She took a deep breath, filling her lungs with fresh air that wasn't bursting with dust. The clearing was home to a couple of scraggly bushes and clusters of thin, wheat colored reeds that whistled when the wind blew through them. Otherwise, it seemed deserted.

Aurelia moved forward, but Jastyn held up a cautious arm.

"Do you think someone lives there?" Coran asked, taking a sip from his flask before replacing it on his hip.

Jastyn frowned, taking a good look at her crew for the first time in days. Coran's arms and face were covered in a layer of dirt, and his tunic, formerly a bright navy, was now nearly black. Aurelia, though still radiant, had smudges on her hands from bracing against the rock, and her long hair had collected bits of stray scrub. Jastyn looked at her own pants and tunic, appalled at the filth.

"It is definitely occupied," Rigo said, his own appearance relatively unscathed save for faint dark circles beneath his eyes.

Aurelia's expression shifted from curiosity to determination. "We should introduce ourselves."

Jastyn exchanged glances with Rigo. Coran licked his lips. "They're probably makin' dinner. We could offer, um, something." He rummaged through his satchel, pulling out a half-eaten apple and three blueberries.

Jastyn turned to Rigo. "What do you think?"

He looked thoughtfully into the cave. He placed his bow in front of him, its base landing with a thud onto the ground. He resembled a statue, his arm stretched before him, and peered into the dark opening. "I sense no immediate threat."

He had barely finished speaking when Coran said, "Good enough for me."

Coran went first, followed by Jastyn, who was trailed by Aurelia. Rigo followed. Upon entering the cave, they became enveloped in darkness. Her eyes adjusting, Jastyn reached out to feel that Coran was still in front of her as she heard Aurelia's light tread at her back.

"Should we conjure our saols?" Coran's voice was a whisper.

Jastyn thought for a moment. They'd walked roughly fifteen yards down a stretch of the cave that was wide enough for them to walk two by two. The smells grew stronger, and the floor of the cave seemed damper.

"I don't see why not. Whoever's in here can probably hear us coming. If they were going to do anything, they'd have done it by now." She conjured her blue companion flame, and Coran did the same, his orange saol bouncing in greeting. Their lights fell into step at their sides.

"Is that water?" Aurelia grabbed Jastyn's arm, prompting her to listen. She paused and heard the unmistakable fall of a steady stream.

"Keep moving."

Together, they shuffled along. The ceiling of the cave lowered the farther they walked. The path twisted to the left, then took a sharp right around a corner. They grabbed at the walls, following the grimy rock.

A voice penetrated the darkness.

Jastyn and Coran held an arm over Aurelia. Jastyn raised a finger to her lips. Aurelia nodded and stepped back toward Rigo. Jastyn and Coran walked around the corner, their saols ready in their hands.

The light of a new chamber made Jastyn stumble, and she raised her hand to shield her eyes. A man of average height with black hair wound into braids that zigzagged down the back of his head to his shoulders stood casually over a boiling cauldron. An array of coins emitted a soft jingle from the ends of his braids. His ebony skin appeared smooth, and his full pink lips puckered as he whistled a tune Jastyn recognized as the song of a bluebird. His lanky frame bore a ragged tunic full of patches with a few holes yet to be mended. The sleeves were gone, and the deep V-neck exposed his chest. His pants had been cut off at the knee, with threads hanging over his shins. His bare feet stepped lightly along the small pools of water on the floor.

Jastyn glanced around the large cavern. The space could hold at least four village homes and had a domed ceiling where dozens of thin stalactites hung, their tips dripping moisture.

A similar passageway opened up on the opposite side and allowed a constant flow of air from one end to the other. That entrance was taller than the one they stood in, and to the right, a screen of smoke rose from the ground. Squinting, Jastyn realized it wasn't smoke like the thin plume crawling out of the cauldron but steam.

The whistling stopped. "Well, are you going to come in or not? One foot in the river never got anybody clean, I can tell you that."

The rich baritone carried no malice, and Jastyn raised a brow to Coran, who shrugged. They vanquished their saols as Coran waved for Aurelia and Rigo to follow.

"You've come at a good time. I'm nearly finished with another batch of fine wine." The man leaned over the cauldron. His face, featuring a wide, square jaw outlined in a fine goatee, looked peaceful as he inhaled deeply. Jastyn and the others crept closer, stepping carefully around puddles. Some bore floating water lilies, while others, somehow, held an assortment of small fruit trees. Confused, Jastyn directed her gaze back to the man, who flourished his right hand. A small green sprig appeared between his long thin fingers.

Aurelia squeaked out a noise that Jastyn knew was an attempt to keep quiet. This proved futile as she said, "Is that mint?"

For the first time, the man turned to face them. His features were plain, and large ears framed a face that seemed chiseled from stone, with hard lines and a sharp nose. Rich brown eyes looked softly at them, then lingered on Aurelia.

"It is, indeed. I find it adds a kick to the wine."

"I completely agree," she replied, moving past Jastyn.

"Wait," Jastyn muttered, but she was already standing in front of the cauldron, one arm out in greeting.

"Hello. I'm Aurelia. It's lovely to meet you."

Much to Jastyn's surprise, he took Aurelia's outstretched arm after dropping the mint into the bubbling liquid. "I am Vreis."

"Vreis. That is a wonderful name." Her eyes lit up. "It means 'strong arms,' does it not?"

They released each other, and Vreis threw up his arms, his fingers splayed. "You are a clever one. That is its meaning." Then he flexed, showing off meager biceps. "Bit ironic, wouldn't you say?"

Aurelia giggled, and Jastyn motioned for Coran and Rigo. They gathered around. Within moments, Aurelia had introduced them, holding Jastyn's hand as she spoke. She accurately guessed that Vreis was brewing blackberry wine. To his credit, he seemed perfectly content to divulge that this was his three hundred and forty-seventh batch in twenty-five years' time.

"You've been here that long?" Coran asked, admiring a collection of handmade bowls and spoons, all appearing to have been made from rock.

Vreis nodded, his almond-shaped eyes sweeping the cavern. "Twenty-six this winter. There were more of us in this peak before the big snowfall two years ago. Only little old me now, as far as I know."

Jastyn nodded politely, but questions brewed in her mind. For as long as he claimed to have lived there, he still looked fairly young. He was probably ten years older than her mother, but his face betrayed little sign of the years.

Aurelia seemed completely enraptured by him. Along with Coran, she asked question after question about the various concoctions held in dozens of cauldrons and gourds scattered in the cavern. Candles emitted a soft yellow light from every available surface. A circle of standing wax-dripped branches surrounded the cauldron, their flickering tips providing ample light. The farthest recesses of Vreis's cave were less well-lit, with a handful of large sticks popping out from crevices, their charred tips lit with red flames and throwing shadows onto the walls.

Rigo nudged her elbow, motioning for her to follow him.

"I think it wise we exercise caution and don't overstay our welcome." His eyes were a darker gray, and his pale, nearly iridescent face pinched in concern.

"Of course. Though he seems harmless." She tilted her head. "Do you not agree?"

He looked past her. His nostrils flared. "Perhaps. But I cannot deny what my senses tell me." He paused, and Jastyn's heart sank. "I'm afraid our new friend is not what he seems."

CHAPTER SIX

Aurelia was elated. She wasn't sure how she knew, but she was certain she had made a new friend in Vreis. There was something about him. Perhaps it was his candidness or the gentle way his hands moved when he spoke. His voice, smooth as silk, reminded her of the lowest notes of a kithara, and his words filled her with a feeling of comfort. Perhaps the fact that they'd finally found another living soul on this arduous journey was what drove her to throw herself wholeheartedly into meeting somebody new.

There was no denying her relief at stumbling upon his home, which they were given a tour of after he'd divulged his blackberry wine recipe. Aurelia listened happily while Coran stood beside her, studying the food supply Vreis kept on the flat surface of a large, square-shaped boulder. As he explained the various fruits growing from his trees— which included a type of nectarine she'd never heard of before—Jastyn and Rigo stood off to the side. They conversed quietly, watching Vreis.

What now?

"Do you mind if we ask some questions?" Jastyn and Rigo stepped closer to join them. He made his way to the cauldron, staring intently into the magenta liquid that smelled quite delicious.

"Jastyn." Aurelia sighed. They'd only just met this man. She was not ready to start an argument. She craved nothing more than a seat on the warm cavern floor and a respite from their hike through these taxing mountains. Jastyn threw her a reassuring smile.

Vreis blinked, seemingly lost in his concoction that bubbled over the small fire. "Be my guest. Would you all like to sit? Please, let me pour us a drink. I'm eager to try this."

"That sounds lovely, thank you." Aurelia smiled and happily plunked down on a smooth rock beneath the leaves of a miniature apple tree. She patted the spot next to her, looking at Jastyn, who sighed and joined her.

Rigo continued to stand as Vreis gathered four wooden cups and one empty gourd. "I haven't had guests in a while." He moved to the cauldron. When Rigo didn't budge, Vreis smiled. He was half a foot shorter than Rigo but didn't appear intimidated by his presence or the way he gripped his tall bow. "You're skeptical. The best elves always are." Vreis dipped one of the cups into the cauldron. Aurelia licked her lips, suddenly aware of how thirsty she was.

Vreis offered a drink to Rigo. "Try it. I promise, the only thing it will do is enliven your senses. And maybe help you relax." His smile stretched wide, small lines framing it in waning crescents. Aurelia noticed a couple of gaps in his lower teeth. Rigo took the cup, his sloped nose hovering over the rim. Slowly, he brought it to his lips.

Aurelia could feel the tenseness of Jastyn's body beside her. She rested a hand on Jastyn's thigh. "It's okay." Jastyn grimaced.

Rigo licked his lips. Holding Vreis's gaze, he nodded. "It is fine wine."

Clapping his hands, Vreis laughed. "You elves never fail. Eternally cynical, the lot of you." In a flurry, he handed out the other cups after filling each with blackberry wine.

Aurelia clinked hers with Coran and Jastyn, then gulped the first taste of mulled fruit she'd had in months. "By the gods, that's good."

Vreis took a spot on the floor, his long legs crossing easily and his back straight as he took a long drink. "One of my better ones, I must say."

"The mint was a wonderful idea," Aurelia said, her lips tingling. On her empty stomach, the wine went directly to her core. It washed through her like a pleasant wave, and she felt relaxed for the first time in days.

After another sip, Vreis sighed. "Very well. You may proceed with the questions. What would you like to know?"

"What brought you to the Mountains of Ionad?"

Vreis turned to Rigo. "Jumping right in, I see." He took another drink, and Aurelia leaned forward to listen.

"I'm afraid it's not a happy tale. And one that began decades ago."

He reached behind him and pulled out a pouch. He poured out a handful of seeds, tossing a few into his mouth. "I find it best to recount stories of woe with something else to focus on." He paused, then glanced around their group. "I hail from the southeastern shores of Venostes. That is where I was born, some fifty-odd years ago." Aurelia coughed on her wine. Jastyn threw her a look as Vreis continued. "You all are too young to know, but back then, the kingdom was in an uproar. The royal family had recently written the laws as you know them now, one of which states that there was to be absolutely no fraternizing between humans and fae." Jastyn stiffened. "The Diarmaids were determined to rid the land of mixed couples. One of those couples was my parents."

Aurelia glanced from Coran to Jastyn. She had an inkling as to where Vries's story was going.

"You see," he continued, "my mother was a member of the kingdom. She'd sailed from the East to the island of Gultero as a child and migrated north to Venostes to sell her skills as a weaver. She'd done well for herself. When she was twenty-three, she did even better and found love."

Vreis's face shifted, revealing the smallest hint of emotion. "My mother fell in love with a water nymph, my father. It's not an uncommon pairing but typically only leads to a brief spree and not the meeting of two soulmates. It also does not typically result in offspring." At this, he raised his hands, pointing both index fingers at himself.

Rigo spoke after a moment. "Your parents fled persecution."

Vreis took another drink. "That is correct, my wise friend. There were two options for my parents: leave the kingdom they'd called home for years or face the wrath of the Diarmaids. So after I was born, they journeyed north. For a while, they took refuge in Uterni, known for its more accepting laws. Venostes sent search parties, though, and my parents and I were forced to flee again."

For a moment, he grew quiet. "For a while, these mountains kept us safe. We'd managed to go twenty-one years without a run-in with the hunting parties. That's what they really were," he added, the first hint of malice lacing his voice. "Then one day, my father went to a nearby spring where water nymphs were known to gather. He might have been on the run, but a nymph cannot truly live without a social hour now and then." He smiled wryly, then looked at the ceiling. Aurelia's heart hurt at the tears welling in his eyes.

"A hunting party was waiting there. When my father arrived, they ambushed him." He paused. "Do you know what they do to water nymphs as punishment?"

Coran shook his head, as did Aurelia. It was Jastyn who answered. "They're forced to keep their water form eternally. Trapped inside what should be their freest state, unable to change back."

Vreis nodded. "When my mother and I went to find him, the other nymphs led us to where he'd been taken. His human form was lost. Where he'd stood, the most stunning lake had appeared near the top of this peak," he said, gesturing overhead. "I remember looking into the clear waters and my father's eyes looking sadly back. Each winter, his waters would freeze, his spirit forced to hibernate." His smile was small. "But the gods are merciful. Each spring, the sun emerges new, and his waters thaw. The snowmelt carries traces of his lake water down the edges of the peak, landing in scattered fragments along the mountainsides. I like to think that he visits me each spring, pieces of him reminding me to carry on."

Aurelia wiped at her tears. "I'm so sorry."

He shrugged. "My mother fell ill five years later. I buried her at the base of the mountain and have been here ever since."

A hush fell over the cavern, the only sound the distant, lonely drip of water.

Jastyn's voice broke the quiet. "You're a child of broken laws."

Vreis looked at her, seeming to see a part of Jastyn he hadn't noticed before. "Your tone implies you know the path someone like me is forced to walk."

They held one another's gaze as she replied, "That's why this cave pulled us in. It's why all of this can flourish in a place made to harbor only darkness."

"Your nymph magic makes these plants take root." Coran's mouth was open, his face slack in awe.

Vreis held out his arms in a showy gesture. "The rules were against me from the beginning. I figure I can break a few while I'm here, wouldn't you agree?"

Aurelia reeled. Vreis's story hit her like a stable door. She'd overheard conversations between her parents in her youth, plans for scouting parties to go out and "ensure the laws of Venostes were upheld, even in the farthest reaches of the kingdom." She'd thought these outings noble, necessary even, to the safety of the kingdom's people. She hadn't realized those individuals were the only ones being protected. The laws gave little protection to fae and, as she knew, none who possessed the blood of both.

Aurelia tried to imagine what Vreis had been through. She pictured his mother, alone and isolated after being forced to leave the only home she'd ever known, all to protect her child from a life full of fear and dread that had been forced upon her by Aurelia's family. She shook her head, unable to comprehend her family's fear of fae. Human and fae had been separated for more than a century, after the fae were blamed for the famine in Gultero. She knew the legends, but she couldn't understand.

What were they really afraid of?

A thought hit her then: Was that what her parents were grooming Brennus for? Preparing him with that scouting party so that, when his reign came, he'd be able to continue the extinguishing of half-fae like Vreis? Or of Odiums like Jastyn?

Though it had seemed the laws had softened, perhaps the passage of time only moved her family's dark doings into the shadows.

She gripped the edge of the rock. She felt weak, and her stomach turned in on itself. When she glanced at Jastyn, she expected to find anger in her eyes not unlike the anger currently raging in her own veins. Instead, she saw sympathy and admiration as Jastyn launched into a series of questions.

For the next several minutes, Vreis divulged more of his youth. Jastyn seemed to listen eagerly, resembling a hungry stray lapping up his stories like scraps of meat. Her eyes lit up with each tasty morsel he shared. After recounting how he came to find this cavern—a rather entertaining story involving a rabid mountain goat—he stood.

"Well, this has been fun, but it's obvious from your haggard appearances that you all have come far."

Coran snorted.

"Was that rude?" He frowned sympathetically. "I apologize. It's been some time since I've had guests. May I offer you some food? I've a bit of goat's cheese and plenty of fruit to go around. More wine?"

He refilled their cups, the steaming drink cupped between their grateful hands as plates appeared filled with stacks of white cheese and an assortment of berries. Jastyn reached for a shining red apple, biting into it with gusto before Aurelia and Coran followed suit, diving into the bountiful offerings.

Relishing the taste of fresh food, Aurelia closed her eyes. She forced the dark thoughts of her family's hatred to the back of her mind. There would be time to unravel the tangled tapestry of her family's history later. She leaned back, her full stomach gurgling happily.

Through a mouthful, Coran said, "It's no royal treatment, but it'll do, wouldn't you say, Princess?"

Aurelia's eyes flew open. The warmth of the wine turned scalding hot as her face flushed. She felt Jastyn inch closer, her fist tightening.

"Princess?" Vreis stood between two of his apple trees. Perhaps it was only her imagination, but Aurelia thought she saw the tips of the leaves begin to blacken.

Jastyn stood. "As you no doubt guessed, we are fellow travelers from Venostes."

Aurelia hurried to stand beside her. She was not about to let Jastyn put herself in the line of fire again so soon.

Vreis only stared. "You're a Diarmaid?"

Aurelia's entire body buzzed, and she felt miniscule, like the beetles her brother had kept in jars to study when they were young. Coran gulped, and Rigo clenched his bow.

Finally, she found her voice. "It is true. My name is Aurelia Diarmaid, daughter of Queen Dechtire and King Grannus Diarmaid."

Vreis blinked, tilting his head. "Grannus married?"

The question surprised her. "Y...yes?"

"The young Prince Grannus...married?"

They all exchanged glances.

"Forgive me," Vreis said between fits of laughter. "Prince Grannus was one of the unruliest souls the kingdom had ever produced. Quite the opposite of his straight as a line mother and father. Word was that no one would ever be able, or willing, to put up with his wild ways."

Aurelia sat back down, searching for the rock to steady herself, unsettled by Vreis's reaction. She had never heard somebody speak of her family in this way. Of course, she'd never given much thought to her parents as, well, people. They'd led lives before she and Brennus, of course, but it wasn't something she'd truly ever thought about before. And frankly, it was something she found difficult to imagine.

Rattled by Vreis's words, she said, "My mother is of the village.

She's a healer." Aurelia felt compelled to share her life. She'd expected a negative reaction upon his learning who she was. As evident by his bemused laughter, he only seemed intrigued.

"I know not of her. She must be beautiful. She gave you her eyes, no doubt." Aurelia couldn't look anywhere but at him. "Nobody in Venostes has eyes like yours."

Aurelia felt as if she was being pulled into his brown gaze. Flecks of gold swam around his irises, mesmerizing her. Her head felt light.

"Vreis." Jastyn's voice cut through his trance. Aurelia blinked.

Across from her, Vreis popped a raspberry into his mouth. "Forgive me. Comes with the territory."

Rigo spoke for the first time in a while. "Explain something. How is it you mean no harm to Aurelia, knowing she is a Diarmaid? Every fae we've encountered either runs in fear or seeks to hurt her."

Vreis stoked the embers below his cauldron, staring into the red-orange glow. "Insightful elf, aren't you? I like you." He grinned. "I harbor no resentment toward the family Diarmaid. Not anymore."

"How?"

The desperation in Jastyn's question made Aurelia shiver despite the warmth of the cave. Thousands of emotions raced over Jastyn's face, and Aurelia ached at the turmoil Jastyn had experienced at the hands of her family.

"Time is a wonderous healer." Vreis's soft gaze shifted from Jastyn to the others. "I watched hatred, resentment, and distrust destroy my mother. After my father was condemned, she was never the same. When she fell ill, it was like she took that as a reason to give up. Her will to live diminished with her health, and she withered away. She let the disease ravage her body and with it, her resolve. All because of her hatred for your family."

Tears fell onto Aurelia's cheeks. Jastyn was quiet, but her eyes were glazed as if lost in thought. Or perhaps memories.

"Once she died, I admit it was tempting to let myself give up alongside her. Oh, was it tempting. That was when the first snowfall began to melt." He smiled. "The waters from my father's lake made their way down the mountain, and the smallest trickles found their way to the clearing outside. I collected a small pool and brought it here." He reached for one of his apple trees, whose roots were gnarled and twisted with age. "That was when I wove my first magic and made this.

I realized that even though their lives had been lost to prejudice, I could use their memories and the love they shared to make something new. After that, I never stopped."

The cavern was quiet again. Vreis breathed deeply, his fruit trees and berry shrubs seeming to shudder with him. Moments later, brightness returned to his face.

"My, you are a solemn bunch." He gestured around the circle. "I know not what your journey entails, but I can see it has worn hard on you. Well, most of you." He raised a brow at Rigo. "You are welcome to stay as long as you need. It's not every day you get a member of the royal family knocking on your door."

He collected their plates. When he took Aurelia's, he added, "I mean no offense when I say this, but you look like you could do with a solid scrub. There's a hot pool just beyond those rocks." He nodded to the far corner. "You may air out your clothes in the passage. I have a few spare tunics you may wear in the meantime."

"Thank you." Aurelia felt more tears surfacing. She reached out to him. "I cannot change what my family did, though I wish I could. And I'm afraid I don't understand why they did such horrible things. I thought things were changing. I thought I understood, but…" She cleared her throat. "But I am eternally grateful to you for your hospitality. I fear it is undeserved."

Faint crows' feet gathered at the corners of Vreis's eyes when he smiled. "Your Highness may be a Diarmaid, but in only our brief meeting, it is clear to me that you are far from the ones I once knew." He threw a glance to Jastyn, who was busy talking to Coran. "You travel with an Odium, something my mother and father could never have anticipated a member of Diarmaid family ever doing. It is an honor to know you."

Chapter Seven

Jastyn had lingered near the cauldron after dinner, wrestling with the knowledge that she had met somebody else like her: half-fae, half-human. She could only imagine the fear he'd grown up with. At least now they only persecuted Odium mothers, forcing them into prison for a time, then relegating them to fight for survival at the kingdom's edges. Jastyn had heard of the awful extent to which the previous monarchs had gone; now she had met living proof.

She was surprised to find that she had so many questions. Her life of solitude and wondering had, unbeknownst to her, lent itself to a lifetime's supply of inquiries. On top of that, she enjoyed Vreis's company, and together they talked about their lives, each shaped by the laws of Aurelia's family.

Now she stepped quietly into an alcove on the right side of the cavern. A semicircle of waist-high stalagmites created a barrier between this part of the cavern and the rest. This area they'd designated as their camp. Coran, freshly bathed, slept soundly on a bed of blankets. Jastyn couldn't help but smile at his ruddy face and the formerly dirt-covered freckles she hadn't seen in weeks scattered on his forearms and cheeks.

Stepping over him, she grabbed his satchel and pulled out the poultice of lavender and calendula. Aurelia had taken it upon herself to prepare several before they'd begun the climb into the mountains. Jastyn wondered at her preparedness, another quality she hadn't expected her to possess when they'd first met.

"Would you like some help?"

Jastyn spun around. Her throat went dry at the sight of Aurelia. Her dark brown hair, now wet and nearly to her waist, hung over exposed shoulders. The tunic she'd borrowed was far too big, its wide neck clinging to her upper arms. She'd tied it so that it pinched at her waist, but in doing so, it pulled the neckline lower. Her fair skin shined anew.

Unable to find words, Jastyn handed the poultice to her. She smiled and motioned for them both to sit. Two blankets had already been laid out, and Jastyn sat carefully, one leg in front of her while she held the other to her chest. She was painfully aware of how filthy her boots were and again missed seeing the silver of her hunting blade tucked against her right leg.

"You could take those off, you know." Aurelia gestured to her boots. "Allow yourself a moment of comfort."

Jastyn considered it. "The smell might make Vreis's flowers wilt."

They both laughed. "Later, then." Aurelia sat in front of her in a crouch. "Let's see."

Jastyn sat still as Aurelia pulled back the torn fabric from her shoulder, revealing her wound. "Wonderful. The poultice continues to work. The new skin is beginning to grow."

"Great." Jastyn feigned disinterest but actually focused on the rapid beating of her heart. She wasn't sure if it was the atmosphere of Vreis's cavern—full of aromatic flowers and warm air—or the blissfully intoxicating scent of Aurelia, but she found it nearly impossible to think about anything other than Aurelia.

Taking a slow, deep breath, her gaze fell to Aurelia's lips as her typically steady hands trembled slightly as they worked.

"How are you feeling?" Jastyn managed to ask, hoping her heartbeat couldn't be heard over her voice, which she tried to keep low so as not to wake Coran.

Aurelia's lips pursed in concentration as she focused on Jastyn's shoulder. "Refreshed. I was growing rather faint during our trek this morning."

"You were?"

She nodded. "I'm glad to know it wasn't obvious. I felt foolish, knowing how common it is for people to endure journeys much more difficult than ours." Jastyn raised a brow but didn't say anything. "Vreis is lovely."

"He is kind. We're lucky to have found him."

Aurelia pressed the edges of the new poultice against Jastyn's wound, assuring it stayed. Seemingly satisfied, she lowered her hands. "All done."

Jastyn's heart thumped like the legs of a jackrabbit. As she licked her lips, she regretted their chapped feeling. Aurelia's lips, also worn from the harsh winds, glistened from her bath. Glancing up, Jastyn found Aurelia's gaze unfocused, possessing a look she hadn't seen before.

"I should probably clean myself up now." Jastyn's voice was hoarse. But she didn't move, save for reaching out, her fingers seeming to move of their own accord, dancing over Aurelia's right hand resting on the ground. Her skin was warm, and Jastyn relished the smoothness.

Aurelia leaned closer.

Swallowing, Jastyn whispered, "The others…"

"They're not listening." She pressed her forehead to Jastyn's, and they leaned into one another. Jastyn's mind raced. She recalled their first meeting in the royal stables and how Aurelia had commanded attention despite the overbearing presence of Drest. She thought about the prince's Remembrance Day and how she'd felt after seeing Aurelia again. She recalled the fierceness of her posture, how she exuded a quiet power that was more impressive than the king and queen combined.

Gazing up through her lashes, Jastyn looked at the beautiful woman before her and tried to tell herself to pull back, to not give in.

Then, only for a moment, she imagined what it would be like to let go.

"Jastyn."

She pressed forward, her lips meeting Aurelia's. A feeling like wildfire raced over her skin, and that was all it took for her to come unraveled. She kissed Aurelia deeply, cupping her face. Aurelia returned the kiss with just as much passion, if not more. Her lips parted with the tilt of her head, and her breath caught, and Jastyn knew her heart was beating as wildly as Jastyn's.

Aurelia leaned forward, and Jastyn pushed softly back. Aurelia grabbed her waist, and she relished the firm grip that pulled her closer. She let herself relax, her tense limbs opening to Aurelia. Jastyn kissed her harder, savoring the softness of her lips, the warmth of her mouth, the feeling of her body as it pressed into Jastyn's.

Then Jastyn remembered why they were here. She remembered

the western caves. She remembered the sacrifice and what she would need to do to get the cure for her sister. She remembered that it was impossible to believe she and Aurelia could ever be together.

Gasping, Jastyn pulled back, breaking their kiss. Aurelia shook, her cheeks pink. Jastyn couldn't stand the smile she wore, knowing she was about to be the cause of its end.

"I'm sorry," she said, unable to look. "I shouldn't have."

Aurelia grabbed her chin, tugging it so Jastyn's eyes met hers. "Do not apologize for that. I wanted it as much as you did." She paused, taking a shuddering breath. "I have wanted that for some time, if I'm being honest."

The words shook her. *Honest.* All at once, the truth rushed to her tongue, the words gathering in line, ready to spill out and tell the truth of what the Red One had told her. But how could she after a kiss like that? How could she look Aurelia in the eye and tell her the truth about what would need to be sacrificed?

Jastyn shook her head, her thoughts a deafening stampede while her body ached with need.

"Jastyn?"

"We can't do this."

Aurelia frowned. "There are no rules against a royal and a villager."

Jastyn breathed a laugh. "Are you choosing to overlook the obvious?"

She was quiet a moment. "Maybe I am." She palmed Jastyn's cheek. "Jastyn, I don't care if your mother raised you alone. I don't care that you're an Odium."

Jastyn could only shake her head. Aurelia didn't understand what she was saying. Perhaps she could live with Jastyn, knowing she was an Odium, but what of the other half of Jastyn's truth? What would Aurelia say knowing she was also half-fae?

Her throat dry as tree bark, Jastyn fought tears. "Aurelia…it's not that simple." She winced at her use of her mother's words and regretted them immediately. To ease her own pain, she placed her hand over Aurelia's and repeated, "We can't do this."

"I don't accept that."

Jastyn couldn't bite her tongue. The entitled words fueled her retort. "Aurelia, this is not your castle. I may be your subject, but you cannot simply dismiss something because you don't accept it. The world doesn't work that way."

Aurelia's hand fell, taking Jastyn's with it. She leaned back, her gaze hard as she stared. "I would hope by now you know I'm more than my title."

"Of course I do. But you can't deny that the entire realm runs on the basis of our living separate lives. It lives on ravaged fae land and thrives on the fear of Odiums like me. All of that says that what we have…" Her voice faltered. "Whatever this is between us, we cannot pursue it."

Each word was like a dagger to her heart, and Jastyn forced her voice to remain neutral as she spoke.

Aurelia didn't seem to care. She grabbed Jastyn's hand, kissing it hard. "The world changes, Jastyn. It's already changed leaps and bounds," she said, gesturing behind them toward Vreis. Then she paused, steadying her breathing. "I cannot deny what I feel for you. I refuse to."

"Aurelia."

"Perhaps you are right. Perhaps I prefer to sweep things under the bearskin when I don't like what I hear." She stood and transformed from Aurelia into the princess Diarmaid. "We will table this conversation until further notice."

Confused, Jastyn also stood. "Aurelia, you can't—"

"I can and I just did." Her voice softened. "Jastyn, please." She stepped closer. "Let us have that kiss. Let us have it, if only for one night."

When Jastyn started to protest, Aurelia cut her off. "I won't hear it. Now, it's your turn for a bath. I will see you after."

With that, Aurelia wandered to the center of the cavern, adjusting her tunic and braiding her hair as she moved to where Vreis and Rigo conversed by the cauldron.

Jastyn could only watch. A kindling of hope lit itself deep in her heart. Had Aurelia meant what she'd said? Had she been willing to accept Jastyn as an Odium? It seemed impossible. Maybe she was in a dream, one brought on by the nymph magic thick in Vreis's cavern. Or perhaps she'd fallen into a world where she could be loved for every part of who she was: Odium, fae, and human. She had spent her life believing herself undeserving of such affection. Yet here was Aurelia, telling Jastyn she was worth more.

Running a hand down her dirty braid, Jastyn wanted to believe. She recalled the horror on Aurelia's face when the queen and king had begged her to come home, their hands shaking in regret after touching Jastyn. She remembered Aurelia's defiance and tried to hold on to her words of devotion.

Jastyn took a breath, drinking in her reality again. How could she hold on? How could she hope for a chance with Aurelia when life had given her nothing up until now? How could Aurelia ever be with someone like her? It was impossible.

Heading to the back of the cave, Jastyn tried once again to vanquish her feelings. She turned to gaze to the hot pool. Perhaps the scalding waters could scrub away the feeling growing inside her. She threw a glance back to the middle of the cave.

Why, of all people, does she have to be a Diarmaid?

Chapter Eight

The next morning, Jastyn woke from pleasant dreams. She had tried to suppress the memory of the kiss, but it was useless. She relived it in the quiet moments following her bath as she donned one of Vreis's spare tunics, laying hers to air alongside Aurelia and Coran's. She thought only of the kiss the following day over her plate of cheese and fruit while Aurelia slept in.

Coran and Rigo sat around the cauldron with her in the morning, discussing the day's plans, and she tried to quiet the memory of the night before. They decided to stay one more day but would scout the land in order to determine the best route. Vreis, meanwhile, had gone to fetch more water for their flasks.

"I'm gonna miss this place," Coran said with a wistful look between bites of an apple.

"Is it the place you're going to miss or the food?" Jastyn smirked, and Coran chucked a blueberry in her direction.

Rigo caught it midair before tossing it into his mouth. "Can we return to the plan for today?"

Laughing, Jastyn said, "We should head out once Aurelia wakes. I'll let her know our plan. Vreis can watch over her while we're out."

Coran asked, "You trust him?"

Jastyn considered for a moment. "I do." She felt a connection to Vreis. He was like her, in a way. And he emitted only kindness. There was nothing that gave Jastyn the impression he meant any harm to any of them.

Rigo stretched his long legs. "I will take the northern path, which ascends most steeply. The two of you can walk west, no more than two miles. That will be sufficient to get an idea as to what lies ahead."

"Then we meet back here at midday," Coran said, finishing his breakfast before standing. "I'll get my satchel."

Vreis wandered back in through the western passage. The bucket that swung heavily in his right hand sloshed water onto the floor.

Coran called, "Successful trip?"

Vreis didn't answer. He stared at the floor. When he finally looked up, he muttered, "Oh, yes. Quite."

Jastyn and the others exchanged looks. "Are you all right?" she asked.

He appeared preoccupied with a cluster of cauldrons and vials sitting among his possessions. He grabbed each one, inspected it, then replaced it before moving on to the next.

Rigo's soothing voice was calm as he asked, "Did something happen outside?"

"If by something, you mean I found a lovely new stream cutting through the southern face, then yes." He turned. His eyes had regained their usual gentle shine. "Aren't you all heading out today?"

"We are, as soon as—"

From off to the right, Aurelia yawned.

"As soon as Aurelia is up. Which appears to be now." Jastyn stood.

Coran returned with his satchel, tossing her a knowing grin. "You go on, we'll meet you outside."

Jastyn nudged him playfully. After crossing the cave, she knelt beside Aurelia, who rubbed sleep from her eyes before propping herself up on her elbows.

"Are you heading out?" She stretched, lazily peering up.

"Yes. Rigo, Coran, and I will scout the trail in order to leave at first light tomorrow. We'll be back by midday."

Aurelia sat up. "You'll be careful."

Jastyn smiled. For a brief moment, she heard the echo of a similar sentiment prior to beginning this journey. "Of course. Vreis will stay with you." She glanced toward the center of the cave. "I fear he may be a bit lost in his own mind this morning."

"No matter. I'm eager to ask him more about his gooseberry cider. It will be a lovely morning."

Chuckling, Jastyn replied, "Good. We won't be long. Try not to get into any trouble."

They shared a smile, and Jastyn felt an urge to hug her good-bye. To fight it, she moved to stand and forced her gaze to the cave floor. But Aurelia stopped her, placing a hand on her knee. When she leaned in, Jastyn pulled back.

"Aurelia, please don't make this harder than it is."

Aurelia watched her a moment. "I'm not sure *I'm* the one guilty of making this difficult."

Jastyn met her gaze. "Just…stay safe."

After a dissatisfied huff, Aurelia snuck a kiss to Jastyn's cheek. "Hurry back."

"Is everything okay?" Coran spoke between bites into his apple.

Jastyn stepped onto the mountain's ledge, a rocky precipice providing only enough room for one person to stand and featuring a breathtaking view of the land below. She peered over the western side of the mountain's rocky base. From there, the barren land stretched toward the dry scrub grass that turned a deeper green once it reached the marshlands, which then gave way to sand dunes visible below a thin marine layer. Beyond that were the western caves and Alanna's cure next to the sea.

"What do you mean?"

"You're quiet."

"I'm always quiet."

"Sure." He gnawed around the apple's exposed core. "But something's different."

Jastyn sighed. "Aurelia and I kissed."

When there was no immediate response, Jastyn turned. Coran gawked, a smile stretching between his speckled cheeks. Jastyn jumped from the ledge, moving back to the main path where he stood. When it finally looked as if he found his words, Jastyn held up a hand. "I don't want to hear anything about it."

Tossing the remains of his apple off the side of the mountain, Coran let out a low whistle. "That good, huh?" She shoved him, and he laughed. "Jas, come on. That's amazing." Then he added, "Can't say I haven't seen that coming."

She picked up a smooth pebble and ran her thumb along its edge. "Yeah, well, it's something I was trying to avoid."

His brow furrowed. She threw the rock off the side, then motioned for him to follow. "Come on. There's something I should tell you, and we might as well finish the last leg of this passage while I do."

For the next mile, Jastyn explained what the Red One had told her that night when she'd gone to bargain for a cure. She told him that the banshee blood she'd procured was only a temporary fix, and that without the true cure, Alanna would die within six months. And through a shuddering breath, she revealed the final piece of the puzzle: the noble sacrifice.

When she finished, they stood on a narrow part of the path, the earth beneath their feet dry and empty save for the scattered rocks that had been shed like skin from the peaks above.

Coran slowed. "I'm sorry, Jas, but I don't see what this has to do with Aurelia."

"Isn't it obvious? 'A noble sacrifice' will get me the true cure." She looked at him expectantly.

Slowly, his eyes widened. "You don't think…"

She only stared.

Vehemently, he shook his head. "No. Jas, there's gotta be another explanation." He began to pace. "It could be anything. Noble's got a dozen meanings. Doesn't mean the princess is the one meant for the sacrifice."

Jastyn spoke softly. "Doesn't it?"

Coran squared up with her. "Don't do that. Not this time."

"Don't do what?"

He crossed his arms. "This. This spiral you start when all you can see is red. Red and black, nothing but the worst. Like when Elisedd banned you from the Wood for a month when we were late getting back from the market. Or when the nightmares got really bad. Not this time. I won't let you."

She bit the inside of her cheek. "The Red One told me what I need to do. I don't know how, but whatever waits for us in the caves needs something from Aurelia. I know it does." She took a breath. "And I have to be the one to get it."

"You can't take anything the Red One says at face value. You know that. Eegit herself told ya—"

"Eegit!" Jastyn threw up her hands. "She's twice the loon the Red One is."

He frowned. "I know ya don't mean that."

She only sighed.

"If Eegit didn't mention her in any of the Red One's musings, what makes you so certain about Aurelia's nobility being the missing factor in this sacrifice?"

"I just know." She started her own pacing, trying to fit the pieces together. "Think about everything's that's happened. Alanna fell ill. Who's the best healer in the land?"

He eyed her. "The queen."

"Yes, the queen. But who did we meet in the stables that day?"

"Aurelia."

She moved closer. "Not the queen. Aurelia. It was she who gave me the bracelet to trade with the Red One. It was she who was kidnapped, and it was the search for her which led us into the Wood. It's *Aurelia* who's with us now." Jastyn didn't realize her breathing had quickened, and she took a deep breath to slow her racing heart. "That's why I couldn't get too close to her." She looked down. "It's why I can't. Coran, I can't bear the thought of having to ask her to do this for me. I couldn't bear it if anything happened to her."

Coran searched her eyes, and she knew he was trying to think of an alternative. He'd be trying to think a way to comfort her, to tell her this was not the only way things had to be. But like she knew he would, he came up empty-handed.

"What about the two of you?" he asked.

Jastyn clenched her fist, staring at the sky. "There is no me and her. There can't be."

"I know it seems like a stretch, but—"

"But nothing, Coran. It's impossible." She met his gaze, daring him to speak. She saw the words forming in his eyes, but that was as far as they went. They walked back toward the cave in silence. When the sun was directly overhead, a faint thud sounded behind them. They turned to find Rigo.

Grateful for a break in the quiet, Jastyn asked, "How was it?"

Rigo leaned his forearm on his bow. "The northern path is quite steep. I handled it fine, and I imagine you two could do so as well. But Her Highness might have a difficult time navigating the terrain."

Jastyn nodded. "Then we'll take the western route. I saw no indication that we couldn't handle the path. It will take another day's time, but that's fine." She thought of Alanna but forced her worry aside. Coran stood silently.

Rigo glanced between them. "Is everything all right?"

Before Jastyn could answer, Coran tilted his head. "Did you hear that?"

They listened. Rigo squinted against the sun shining down through the clouds. Then Jastyn heard it: a groan came from off to their left where a cluster of tall, fallen boulders huddled together. Their lumpy forms reminded Jastyn of an old man she'd often seen in the market who sat hunched over his goods. Quietly, she stepped closer, kicking up swirls of black earth. There was no denying the distinctive moan, the sound of somebody in pain.

Rigo drew an arrow from his quiver and nocked it. Jastyn and Coran readied their saols. Together, they crept toward the source of the noise.

When they peered over the top of the rocks, Rigo sheathed his arrow.

Coran squeaked. "Vreis?"

Rigo leapt between the rocks, kneeling over the body. His large hands pressed against a massive gash in Vreis's right temple where blood trickled onto his ear. His eyes flickered. Rigo ran his hands over his body, checking for more injuries.

"What happened?" Jastyn asked.

"He's been stunned. The attacker attempted to take him out with a blow to his head, and when that didn't work…"

"They knocked him out with a spell," Jastyn finished.

"Yes."

Vreis moaned, then muttered something. "Don't try to speak, my friend." Rigo ran a hand down his face. "We will take you back to the cave."

Jastyn glanced at Coran, who read her mind. "Wait," he said, his voice shaking, "if Vreis is here, then who's in the cavern?"

She paled. "Oh no. Aurelia."

Chapter Nine

A fter you've let the rosemary sit in for half a day, what do you do?" Vreis appeared thoughtful, his face scrunched as if he was truly struggling to remember. He'd been like that all morning, quieter, almost bothered by her questions. She'd chalked it up to a late night and early morning, but she sensed something wasn't right.

"I let it simmer for a day," he replied, pacing around the cauldron and throwing looks to the cavern's western entrance.

"I see. Do you add anything else?"

"No. Nothing else."

Watching him, Aurelia stepped backward but continued with her questions. "It only simmers for a day? Silly me, I thought at least three days was typical."

He was definitely antsy about something. He rubbed his hands together when he said, "Three. Oh, yes, of course. That's what I meant."

Now she was certain something was not right. But what was it?

A sudden flurry of quick steps, like someone running, sounded in the depths of the western passageway. Aurelia glanced over Vreis's shoulder, and he too turned to look as Jastyn sprinted into the cavern, her face washed in dread.

"Finally," he muttered, facing Aurelia once again. Confused, she only watched as Jastyn conjured her saol and called out.

"Aurelia, get behind me, now!" She rushed around the cauldron where Vreis stood, then positioned herself between him and Aurelia, one arm out protectively.

"Jastyn, what are you doing?"

"He's not who he seems."

"What do you mean?"

"Remember when he went out to fetch water this morning?"

Aurelia's pulse quickened as what Jastyn was saying became clear. "Yes."

"Something happened then. This isn't Vreis."

Aurelia kept her breathing calm. "I knew something wasn't right." She kept her eyes on him or, rather, the imposter who had taken his form.

Smiling, he finally spoke. "I've been waiting for you." He spoke to Jastyn, who held her blue saol steady above her right palm, her left holding Aurelia's waist.

"I take it you're not one of the Red One's minions?"

He cackled, his typically handsome features appearing disjointed. "The Red One has no part in this."

Aurelia racked her mind as she tried to understand his meaning when Jastyn said, "Reveal yourself."

His body shifted. His strong, rounded shoulders grew narrow, the bones jutting upward and stretching his flesh. His square jaw pulled itself downward as an extra set of pointed teeth sprouted behind the originals. His legs seemed to tear themselves apart as they grew to twice their length, twisting up and in awkwardly until he was double his original height.

"Get back," Jastyn muttered, and Aurelia shuffled with her toward the eastern entrance. The figure before them continued to lose its mask of humanity. For a moment, Aurelia feared they were witnessing a werewolf transformation as jet-black fur sprang up on every part of his body. Gods, she had no idea how to handle a werewolf. Then she remembered it was a quarter moon, and therefore impossible. Still, the creature possessed a bizarre, wolfish figure, if a wolf stood on two unsteady legs, but she'd never seen one with a triangular face. Its long snout gnashed at the air as it continued to change, large padded feet struggling to gain balance on the cave floor.

"What is that?" Aurelia stood behind Jastyn as they made their way to the other side of the cave, keeping the transforming creature in their sights.

"I'm not sure."

They stopped to stare as the creature let out a piercing screech, and its large eyes opened, bright yellow surrounding small irises enclosed by a blood-red ring. The creature snarled, saliva dripping from its lips while its clawed hands scratched at its own back in apparent agony. When it doubled over, Aurelia saw two protrusions sprouting between its shoulder blades.

"Are those…wings?"

Thin, bat-like wings erupted from its back, and the creature emitted a final, piercing howl.

Jastyn turned with fear in her eyes. "We need to go. Now."

Together, they sprinted into the eastern passage. Engulfed once again in darkness, Aurelia stumbled, but Jastyn pulled her up. Another screech sounded behind them.

Aurelia didn't dare glance over her shoulder. "What do we do?" It was so dark she could hardly make out anything and hoped to the gods Jastyn knew her way out to the mountain.

"Just keep running."

Distant steps started behind them. Aurelia's heart pounded, but she quickened her pace as much as she could.

"This way," Jastyn called, and they took a sharp right.

A burst of wind, like from the wings of a bird taking flight, flew at their backs. At the same time, a cramp started below Aurelia's ribs. "Jastyn."

"We're almost out."

Wincing, she forced herself to keep pace with Jastyn, the pounding of their boots in near synchronicity. She imagined the creature's breath at her neck. When they took another turn, the entrance appeared.

"Nearly there," Aurelia said between pained breaths.

The beating of wings was on top of them now, but Aurelia didn't stop. She extended her stride, wincing at the pressure on her knee, but she didn't stop. She couldn't.

"Keep going," Jastyn shouted, falling a step behind.

Once Aurelia cleared the entrance, she threw up her hands to block the sudden light. Jastyn was almost clear of the entrance, but the menacing yellow eyes were right behind her.

"Go!" Jastyn yelled as a claw ensnared her left shoulder, pulling her back into the darkness.

"Jastyn!"

Aurelia fell back, conjuring her saol as Jastyn tumbled to the ground, the creature rolling with her in a tangled heap out of the cave. Aurelia let her spell-fire go, and it hit the creature's thin right arm. Jastyn rolled out of its grip and forward, narrowly dodging another attack.

Readying another saol, Aurelia ran to help. Jastyn had barely stood when the creature flew ten feet above and swooped down, talons first. Aurelia fired her saol but missed, and they were forced apart, rolling opposite ways to avoid the creature. It circled back, its wings sending waves of choking dirt into the air. Covering her face in her elbow, Aurelia knelt, Jastyn following suit a few yards away. Aurelia conjured another saol, which flickered uncertainly when Jastyn held up an empty hand.

"We don't want to fight," she called to the creature, whose snout was froth-ridden and whose eyes were bloodshot. "Please, what do you want?"

The creature screeched again. Aurelia scampered over to her. "What are you doing?"

Jastyn kept her focus on the creature. "I think we're dealing with a pooka."

"A pooka?" Aurelia looked at the huge, rabid, winged creature high in the air. "But they're small, impish creatures who only come out during the autumnal equinox." She threw up a hand. "They're harmless bedtime stories."

Jastyn looked at her incredulously. "I'm afraid not. Pookas are underlings."

Another screech made Aurelia jump. "You mean, it answers to somebody?"

"Or something."

The sky darkened, and the sun retreated behind a pile of bleak cumulus clouds. A thunderous boom shook the ground, and Aurelia was reminded of her brother's Remembrance. She half expected an eclipse of arrows to come plunging down. A shiver ran up her back, and she leaned into Jastyn. The pooka cackled as if invigorated by the change in the air, its wings beating joyously.

"I have a feeling we're about to meet its master."

They crouched behind an outcropping as the sky continued to shake, turning sickly green as the clouds split open. Above the pooka, a funnel formed at the clouds' base, then stretched and spun its way to earth. Aurelia had never seen anything like it. The wind picked up, and she shielded her face from the debris of rocks and sticks scattered by the raging winds.

A final, gleeful howl from the pooka announced the arrival of a dark horse that galloped from the twisted tunnel of wind. Aurelia had never seen its like; its massive hooves clapped against the tumultuous air, emitting more thunder that Aurelia felt in her very core. Beneath her feet, the earth quaked.

"Gods," she whispered. "Who is that?"

The cloaked rider wore a hood that covered his face. Aurelia didn't recognize the dark colors, faded blue with pale stitching of yellow on the edges of gloves that gripped his horse's reins. As the hooves took to the earth, Aurelia felt washed in dread, as if every ounce of happiness had been stripped from her mind until only the most horrifying of memories remained. "Jastyn," she said, "what are we going to do?"

When she finally tore her gaze from the rider, Aurelia's courage shrank. Jastyn's face was utter terror, and Aurelia wasn't prepared for the fear that filled her eyes.

"Jastyn?"

Only her mouth moved when she replied, "No."

Aurelia took her arms, shaking her gently. "Jastyn?"

"No. It can't be. He couldn't have found me."

"Who?" When she got no response, she asked again, "Jastyn, who is that?"

The horse and rider stood below the pooka. The clouds descended with them, shrouded the clearing in a heavy mist.

"It's the Dark Fae."

Aurelia felt faint but didn't let go. Looking over her shoulder, she took in the rider's ominous figure. Beneath his hood, in the space where his face should be, was only darkness.

Then she remembered. The clearing in the Wood that night with Drest. She remembered Jastyn's screams and how she'd run with Rigo and Coran, and she remembered the black clouds and the dark figure that sat before them.

The rider spoke, his voice hollow. "Odium Child."

The hand Aurelia held balled into a fist, and Jastyn's face shifted from terror to fury. When she stepped forward, Aurelia pulled her back.

"What are you doing?"

When Jastyn's gaze met hers, it was dark. "He's here for me."

"And you're going to, what, go out and greet him?" Fear coursed through her, fear of the unknown, fear of what the Dark Fae could do, and most of all, fear of losing Jastyn.

"I have to face him."

"Says who?" She tightened her grip.

The figure and his horse seemed to float around the clearing, watching. The pooka flew down, and the rider spoke to it in a low voice.

"Aurelia, please. This is my fight."

Aurelia was speechless. She didn't understand. She stared at Jastyn—handsome, proud Jastyn—and knew there was no way she was letting her go. "We're in this together. I don't care who that is or what he's capable of." She searched Jastyn's gaze, which softened for a moment.

"That is the Dark Fae from my dreams. The one who's haunted me for years."

"Why?"

Jastyn shook her head.

"Because you're an Odium?"

"I don't know. Maybe."

"If he's a fae, he may be powerful, but he's got to have a weakness." She recalled her brother's teachings, then her mind returned to the last encounter they'd had with this Dark Fae that night in the Wood. "Where's Rigo? His arrows seemed to ward him off last time."

"I don't know. I'd hoped he and Coran weren't far behind me. But they were tending to Vreis. Perhaps his wounds were worse than I'd thought."

"We'll think of something," Aurelia said but looked at the Dark Fae as he said something to the pooka that prompted another screech.

"Aurelia, let me go." Jastyn gathered her hands. Tears stung her eyes, then fell to her cheeks when she kissed Aurelia's knuckles. "Please."

Taking a breath, Aurelia summoned her resolve. "You'll have to get through me first."

Jastyn opened her mouth as if to respond but stopped. Her brows knit together, and Aurelia noticed the thunder had halted. "Is it quiet to you?"

Before she could look behind her, two massive claws wrapped themselves around her shoulders, clenching beneath her arms.

"Aurelia!"

Thrashing, Aurelia kicked the air. Jastyn held tight to her hands as she was lifted from the ground. Her arms stretched as she flew higher, and her fingers slipped from Jastyn's. She reached up to scratch at the pooka's feet, but its claws only gripped harder, their sharp edges scraping through her tunic, cutting her flesh. She tried to conjure her saol, but she was in too much pain to summon anything more than a flicker. Below, Jastyn sent a blue flame at the pooka. It dodged, hissing and flying higher until Aurelia hung nearly twenty feet off the ground.

"Odium Child."

The rider had dismounted. Jastyn, another saol ready, turned to face the Fae. "Leave her alone," she shouted. "It's me you want. Let her go!" She hurled her saol at the fae. He laughed, deep and mocking, and deflected her flame easily. Jastyn threw another, then another, but it didn't stop him as he marched closer.

Aurelia continued to scratch at the pooka's legs, thrashing in the hope of releasing herself. "Let me go," she shouted, managing a light flame that she threw into his face. To her dismay, the pooka opened its wide jaws and he consumed her saol, a thin, black tongue licking his lips as if satisfied.

It felt as if her arms were being ripped from her body. Panic rising, Aurelia looked on helplessly as the Dark Fae closed on Jastyn. His cloak billowed, almost regal as it framed his proud stride.

"Please, Jastyn," Aurelia shouted. "Run!"

But Jastyn couldn't or wouldn't hear her. She sidestepped, pressing two flames she'd conjured into one. She shoved it at the Fae, but he walked right through it.

"Luck does not walk with you this night."

"I hate you!" Jastyn conjured another flame, but it was smaller. Aurelia's stomach churned, knowing this was a sign of diminishing strength.

Three more saols flew at the Dark Fae as he closed in. His horse, standing nearby, whinnied. "Come now, Odium Child."

Aurelia screamed as sharp, spindled fingers sprang out from beneath his cloak and wrapped around Jastyn's throat.

"Jastyn!" The pooka howled as Aurelia cried out. "No, Jastyn!"

The Dark Fae lifted her off the ground, her throat wrapped in his grip. She tried to pry herself free, but it was to no avail. Squirming, Aurelia felt sick at the gurgling sound that came from Jastyn's throat, and she watched helplessly as the Dark Fae opened his mouth and slowly began to drain Jastyn of her life.

Chapter Ten

Jastyn couldn't breathe. Her throat was on fire. She wasn't sure if it was the Dark Fae's grip or the heat seeping from his fingers that made her feel like she was caught in a blazing ring of scalding flames. She was light-headed and closed her eyes so as not to stare into the horrid, serrated mouth opening in front of her.

Overhead, Aurelia's desperate cries cut through the air. Jastyn wanted to shout, wanted to tell her she was sorry. She wanted Aurelia to know the truth about everything. But it was too late.

Each breath grew labored. She peeked. The rancid blackness of the Dark Fae's mouth opened wider. It smelled rotten, like decayed flesh and spoiled earth. A white mist formed inside its depths. Her strength waned, and dread weighed heavy over her body. Then she realized the white mist wasn't coming from the Fae; it was her own life force being stolen.

Aurelia's screams continued. Jastyn tried to hold on to her voice. She tried to be strong. She could hear the awful choking noises from her own throat, and she kicked at the air in an attempt to make contact with something, anything.

Lights filled her vision, and she began to float. She looked down at herself. How small she seemed, caught in the grasp of the Dark Fae who was gradually pulling the life from her body.

"Jastyn."

Alanna. Her sister stood beside the Dark Fae, arms crossed and a sullen look on her pale face. She spoke to the Jastyn trapped on the ground. "You told me you would stay safe."

The pain in her throat began to wane. In its place, emotions swelled. "I tried, Alanna. I tried to get the cure."

Her lips in a pout, Alanna looked every bit the angry teenager. "You have to stay safe. You told me you would."

"Alanna, it's not—"

"That simple?"

Jastyn balked when her sister's gaze turned upward, locking on where she floated high above the ground. "I never wanted to fail you."

"Then don't."

Jastyn's lightness dissipated, her feet heavy.

"I need you, Jastyn. We all need you."

Up in the air, Jastyn was now eye level with Aurelia, who continued to struggle against the airborne pooka. Every ounce of her fought to survive, fought for Jastyn.

Alanna spoke again. "Do you remember the promise you made to yourself when this journey began?"

Jastyn glanced down. "I promised to never stop fighting." She looked from Aurelia to her sister. "I promised I'd never stop fighting until this journey was done."

Alanna smiled. "Keep going, Jastyn."

The heaviness in her feet tugged her downward as searing pain tightened around her throat. She returned to her body, caught by the Dark Fae. Burning fire scorched her lungs, and she battled the overwhelming desire to give in.

She reached one shaking hand up and held on to the slimy, rotted wrist of the Dark Fae. With her other, she willed her saol to appear. Feeling the smallest of flames, she thrust her fingers into the pit where the Fae's face should have been.

A deep laugh rumbled from the Dark Fae. Jastyn forced her saol deeper, working to loosen his grip with her other hand. But he only clutched harder, and she gasped for breath as more of the white mist drifted from her mouth into his.

She looked to the side. Alanna was gone. Aurelia shouted overhead. Jastyn closed her eyes and pictured her sister. She pictured herself standing before her with the cure. Holding on to that image, she conjured one final push of strength and kicked. A bright purple light zoomed past her right ear and landed in the center of the Dark Fae's face.

A four-foot spear now protruded from beneath the Dark Fae's hood. A low, guttural moan erupted from the black emptiness. Through her bleary vision, she saw the white mist stop flowing. His grip loosened, and Jastyn freed herself, falling hard onto the ground.

"Jastyn!"

She looked up as two golden lights sped by. One landed in the pooka's gut while the other lodged in its left knee. The pooka howled, releasing Aurelia. She screamed as she fell.

"Aurelia!"

Jastyn sprinted to catch her, knowing she'd be too late. She tried to run faster, but her lungs were filled with fire, and she could hardly breathe. Somebody ran past, and Jastyn stopped as a well-built, toned woman with short, curly hair opened her arms and caught Aurelia seconds before she hit the ground.

Stunned, Jastyn struggled to stand. The woman set Aurelia down quickly and asked, "Are you all right?"

Aurelia, seemingly as shocked as Jastyn, stuttered, "I'm…I'm okay."

The woman, slightly taller than Aurelia but with a boyish figure, nodded and leapt toward the pooka. Jastyn's legs gave out, and she fell as the woman easily grabbed hold of not golden rods of light, but two sai, and dislodged them from the pooka, but not before twisting them in the creature's flesh for good measure.

Aurelia ran to Jastyn.

"Gods, are you all right?" She ran her hands over Jastyn's body, one sweeping over her hair and face. Aurelia kissed her forehead and pulled her into a hug. Leaning back, she rested a few fingers on Jastyn's neck. "I thought I was going to lose you."

Jastyn coughed but felt the prick of grateful tears. Her throat burned when she spoke. "I'm still here."

She nodded to the other side of the clearing where the pooka had fallen, and the woman kicked his leg. Her bright, nearly magenta hair stood out in the gloom, one side cropped short as it ran around her ear where a three-inch sword-shaped earring dangled from the lobe. She grinned as she conjured a purple saol, lighting her pixie-like face mischievously. She chucked the saol at the pooka, who screamed as the flame engulfed him.

Still reeling, Jastyn realized the woman was not alone. An equally fit man appeared to wrestle the spear from the Dark Fae's face. He struggled as the Dark Fae gripped his shoulders, a sickly inhale searching for a new life to take. As he fought, Jastyn noticed the man looked uncannily like the woman, his face hosting the same pointed chin, small sharp nose, and arching eyebrows. Except while her hair was short and bright, his straw-colored locks were tied back in a long, thick ponytail, with two thin braids running from his temples past his ears and a third down the center of the tail.

"Who are they?" Aurelia asked, crouching beside Jastyn, one arm around her shoulders.

The man managed to shake the spear loose, but he stumbled, tripping on a rock. As he fell, Jastyn moved to stand. "He needs help."

The Dark Fae cackled and towered over the man, who readied the spear and showed no flicker of fear. The woman shouted something and fired a purple saol that temporarily halted the Dark Fae. This gave the man enough time to conjure his own golden flame. Together, their saols wrapped around the Dark Fae like vines.

"You stay here," Aurelia said. Jastyn tried to stop her, but she was too weak to do anything more than raise a worried hand. Aurelia rushed toward the others and conjured her red saol. The others nodded, and the three let their saols fly. A blazing wall of light lit up the mountainside. The dark horse bayed at the air before galloping to its rider. After another screech, the Dark Fae leapt atop his horse, retreating into the clouds. The piles of gloom lifted with the Fae until he ascended higher and, with a clap of lightning, vanished.

Jastyn, her legs shaking, stood and walked unsteadily to Aurelia. The man and woman shared an exuberant hug.

"I saw that extra twist you gave the pooka," the man said, dimples appearing in his light-skinned cheeks as he smiled. "I thought you were gonna go easy on him."

The woman brushed off her forest green tunic, the same color as her eyes, and dusted her fitted brown pants that came to the ankle where polished tan boots covered her feet. At the same time, she tossed the man the two sai while he lobbed the spear to her. She examined it as she replied, "I said no such thing. I should've picked your guy. He looked like more of a challenge." Her voice was feminine but held a cadence that implied confidence, as if she was accustomed to speaking and having people listen. "That was a nice throw. We should switch things up more often."

The man, a few inches taller than her and wearing the inverse of her outfit—a brown tunic that fell over forest green pants and tan boots—ran a large hand down his ponytail and then flicked a stray piece of brush that had attached itself to the end of one of his sai. "We should. It was fun." His voice was only a little deeper but held the same intonations of somebody who liked to hear himself speak. In a showy routine of spins and flips, he sheathed the sai into leather sheaths on his hips.

Aurelia stepped closer to Jastyn. They exchanged glances, and Jastyn cleared her throat, which currently felt as if it was being squeezed and torn apart at the same time. The two strangers paused, looking surprised to see Aurelia and Jastyn staring.

"Oh," the woman said, a frown falling to her bow-shaped lips. "Have we not introduced ourselves? Forgive us." In unison, they both turned and straightened. "I'm Keeva." She held out a toned right arm, which, like her left, was lined with tens of leather bracelets. Jastyn and Aurelia greeted her as the man followed suit.

"And as my sister so rudely forgot to mention, I'm Donovan."

Jastyn embraced his arm. "You're twins," she said, wincing at the pain in her throat.

"Twins," Aurelia said. "I've never met twins."

Keeva pouted. "I was hoping people would notice less with my hair like this."

Donovan rolled his eyes. "I suppose today's your lucky day." He sighed dramatically. "Sadly, we've been stuck together our entire lives. Twenty-seven years with this one. I should be rewarded for my good behavior."

Keeva shoved him, hardly making her well-muscled brother budge an inch.

Aurelia gawked while Jastyn, exhausted from the ordeal with the Dark Fae, leaned into her. Aurelia wrapped her right arm snugly around Jastyn's waist, and she couldn't help but relish the feel of being in Aurelia's arms.

Keeva's eyes lit up. She bit her lip excitedly. "You two are adorable."

Jastyn straightened, willing her legs to hold her up without the support of Aurelia, who frowned disapprovingly. "That is very kind of—" Aurelia started.

"We're not together," Jastyn finished, her voice scratchy as she rubbed her neck.

Aurelia crossed her arms. "We're also not, *not* together."

"It's complicated."

"And whose fault is that?"

"Not now, Aurelia."

"Aurelia?" Keeva's voice intruded on their conversation.

"Forgive my manners." Aurelia dipped her chin and gave a small bow. "My name is Aurelia Diarmaid, daughter of Queen Dechtire and King Grannus Diarmaid."

Donovan whistled low, his face impressed. "Hear that, sis? We're in the presence of royalty."

"Venostes's very own," Keeva added, sizing Aurelia up from head to toe.

Jastyn didn't like the look in her eyes and once again stepped closer. "We are grateful for your help," she said, hoping to turn their attention away from Aurelia. "But we should be getting back."

"To your friends?" Keeva asked. "The lovely elf and the extremely freckled young man?"

"You saw them?" Jastyn asked, her throat scratchy.

Donovan waved nonchalantly. "About, oh, what would you say, two hundred yards back on the path?" Keeva nodded. "They were helping a poor fellow back to his cave."

"That's Vreis," Aurelia said. "Is he okay?"

Keeva casually turned her spear in her grip as she spoke, and Jastyn noticed the shining onyx tip. The strong-looking shaft held grooves from years of use. "He looked like he'd been through a rough ordeal, but he was walking with little assistance."

Jastyn sighed, and Aurelia's body relaxed beside her. "That is happy news."

"The Mountains of Ionad usually don't host such an offering of activity," Donovan added.

"We've been out here dozens of times and rarely see anyone or anything else."

"Dozens of times."

"We usually only encounter one…maybe two—"

"That one time we had four."

"That's right. That was a blood moon."

"Was it?"

"It was."

"Oh, yes. The imp and the tree nymph?"

"That's the one."

Jastyn's head hurt. These two were odd ones, all right. They seemed caught up in their own world. Jastyn felt bewildered in their presence, though her recent near-death experience wasn't helping her ability to understand. She pinched the bridge of her nose. Her entire body throbbed, and she ached for a drink to quench the searing dryness of her throat. "Please, Keeva, Donovan. As Aurelia said, we are extremely thankful for your help. But…exactly what are you doing out here in the first place?"

The twins, who had been exchanging a whispered banter that ended in Keeva slapping the back of Donovan's head, refocused. "Well," he started, rubbing his neck, "the Mountains of Ionad are a sort of training ground."

Jastyn glanced between them. "Training ground?"

"Yes." Donovan shot Keeva a pleading look. "A training ground for…"

"Guard exercises."

"That's right. Royal guard exercises," he added enthusiastically, though Keeva slapped him on the head again.

Bewildered, Jastyn was struggling to follow. Thankfully, Aurelia jumped in. "Are you both members of a royal guard?"

Their faces lit up. "Yes," they cried in unison.

"That's exactly it." Keeva positioned her free hand on her hip. "Donovan and I are members of the royal guard from the Kingdom of Uterni."

"Uterni?" It was Jastyn and Aurelia's turn to speak in unison.

"That's correct, Your Highness," Donovan said, his arms crossed. "We are sent often to these mountains, thanks to their close proximity to our kingdom which, as you no doubt know, lies to the north along the cold, rain-covered shores of this realm. The, um, royal family sends their soldiers here for training purposes. If we come back alive, we've made the cut."

Aurelia blinked. "That's…quite the training program."

Donovan elbowed Keeva, who quickly added, "Well, it's under revision."

Jastyn shot Aurelia a look. She appeared to be just as confused. "I see. Well, we're lucky you were here."

"Yes," Aurelia added. "Is there any way we can repay you?"

"Well," Keeva started, but Donovan cut her off.

"No need," he said, lifting his chin. "We are grateful to have been of service. That rider was one nasty fae. If I hadn't known better, I'd say he was just like the stories of the dark force we've been hearing about, the one that's making its way across the realm."

Jastyn felt light-headed again. Her vision swam out of focus. When her knees buckled, Aurelia helped to steady her, then said, "That *was* the dark force."

For once, the twins were silent. A breeze blew over the sun-drenched clearing. "You mean to say, it has reached this far west?" Donovan's voice filled with concern.

Jastyn tried to speak, but she was exhausted. Thankfully, Aurelia carried the conversation. "I'm afraid so. My kingdom has fallen into darkness the last few months. The elf queen has succumbed to his temptations and sent her kind to attack Venostes. There is tumult within my kingdom, and it is spreading fast."

The twins listened intently. "What has befallen your kingdom? Have the elves conquered it for themselves?" Keeva's eyes widened. "Is that why you flee?"

"No," Aurelia started to reply, but she faltered.

Forcing herself to speak through the pain, Jastyn said, "Prince Brennus Diarmaid has passed into the Otherworld at the hands of the dark force."

The twins turned their incredulous gazes from Jastyn to Aurelia. Keeva spoke softly. "We are sorry to hear such news."

Aurelia nodded. Jastyn asked, "His passing has not reached your kingdom?"

This time, they looked guilty. "We are extremely isolated in Uterni. News takes time to travel to us."

Nodding, Jastyn winced and leaned more into Aurelia. Her legs trembled, and she felt the little strength she had left fading. "We should probably get back," she said, looking at Aurelia, who seemed to catch her pleading gaze.

"Yes, our friends will be worried. And I should attend to Vreis's wounds as soon as possible. As well as yours," she added softly, leaning her forehead into Jastyn's.

"We'll walk you back," Keeva said.

"Yes," Donovan added before nimbly leaping to Jastyn's side and pulling one of her arms around his shoulders to support her. "It's the least we can do before we have to get back for our—" Keeva cleared her throat, and he stammered. "Our, um, our next training session."

Jastyn was too tired to care about how strangely these two were acting. She let herself be guided by Donovan and relished the feel of Aurelia's hand, which didn't leave her own as they trudged back toward the safety of the cavern. Jastyn tried not to focus on the fact that the Dark Fae had gotten closer to her than ever before.

CHAPTER ELEVEN

Upon arriving back at the eastern entrance of Vreis's cave, Donovan gingerly handed Jastyn to Aurelia, who used her height to keep Jastyn propped against her. Aurelia ached at the state Jastyn was in; she had drifted in and out of consciousness the entire length of their walk, her legs dragging along the dirt path, with Vreis's borrowed tunic stretched and torn at her neck. Aurelia had already made a mental list of antidotes, teas, and various herbs to prepare in order to bring Jastyn's spirits back to their original state. It wasn't until the Dark Fae had disappeared, taking the body of the pooka with it, that Aurelia had noticed the pain in her shoulders. She stopped the bleeding that had been inflicted by its claws with her saol. But now, each rotation of her arms shot pain through her chest down to her fingertips. Still, she'd have time to mend herself later. She had important people to attend.

"Well," Donovan said, standing next to his sister as they scanned the cave's entrance. "This must be it."

Aurelia grasped each of their forearms with her free hand. "Thank you again. I hope one day I can repay you for saving us. I have no doubt that you have made your royal family proud." Then a flash of memory returned, an old conversation with her mother. "Your queen, she's not well."

Both pairs of eyes grew dark. Keeva replied, "That is correct. Queen Asta fell ill three summers ago. She's fought bravely, but I fear she may not recover."

Aurelia thought their intense concern for their monarch curious. They were only guards, after all. Then again, she hoped that the men and women who helped protect the Diarmaid castle might feel the same should a similar fate greet her parents. "I am sorry to hear that."

Keeva started to say something, but Donovan held up a hand, smiling kindly. "That is nice of you to say. I am sure we can get the message to her and the king upon our return." A deep sadness flashed in his green eyes before he added, "Perhaps one day, we shall meet again. I hope wherever you are going, you find safe passage. We had best return north to share the news of what we've learned with our…with the royal family." He bent at the waist and kissed the top of Aurelia's hand.

"Take care of one another," Keeva added, then mimicked the kiss, placing her lips atop Aurelia's knuckles. Jastyn groaned and muttered, and Aurelia couldn't help but chuckle when Keeva quickly pulled back.

"Safe journey to Uterni." Aurelia bid farewell to the twins and began the dark trek through the cave.

When she finally pulled Jastyn through the cavern doorway, Aurelia was elated at the familiar warmth, the fragrant flowers, and the welcoming sight of the smattering of fruit trees filling the candlelit space. But her joy was short-lived when she saw Vreis lying motionless on the floor near his cauldron. Rigo was bent over him, muttering something.

Coran noticed them first. "M'lady!" He rushed over, helping to prop Jastyn between himself and Aurelia. "I'm so glad to see ya. Vreis is heavier than he looks, and we struggled bringing him here. I wanted to go out and look for ya, but Rigo said something out there wasn't right." He dipped his chin. "I shoulda gone to find ya."

"It's all right," Aurelia said. "We had some unexpected help."

"Oh?"

Shaking her head, she asked, "How's Vreis? He doesn't look well."

Coran took the change of subject in stride. "Whatever spell was used was a tough one. But Rigo thinks he can get him back."

Aurelia watched Rigo as his hands drifted over Vreis's body, then she helped Coran lead Jastyn to the cluster of boulders where their blankets were still laid out from this morning. "I do hope he will be all right," she said as they placed Jastyn carefully onto a makeshift bed.

Coran bundled another blanket up to slide beneath Jastyn's head. He sat back on his heels. "What happened to her?"

Aurelia straightened Jastyn's legs. She groaned, her face contorted in pain. "The dark force…the Fae and his beast, they found her."

Coran's eyes widened. "The same one from her nightmares?"

"I believe so."

"How?"

Aurelia shook her head, taking his flask and lifting its uncapped top to Jastyn's chapped lips. "I'm not sure."

She took a drink but coughed and leaned back tiredly. Aurelia had never seen her looking so exhausted.

Coran frowned. "He hasn't been that close to her since she was a child. Something must have changed."

Aurelia looked up. "Something about Jastyn?"

He shrugged. "Maybe. But he hasn't gotten this near to her in years." He teared up as he took in the red and blue bruises around her throat. "Can you help her?"

Aurelia took a shaky breath. "Gods know I am going to try."

Jastyn awoke to the low murmur of conversation. Her eyes felt sewed shut, and she slowly worked one heavy eyelid open, then the other, and glanced around. Her entire face hurt, and when she turned her neck, a massive twinge, like a wire pinching her throat, pierced her senses. She tried to swallow, but that hurt even more. Her tongue felt swollen and intrusive. The pain ran all the way to her chest, and her lungs filled painfully when she breathed.

"You're awake."

Jastyn blinked, her vision adjusting to find Rigo standing near the steam pool, opposite the disarray of blankets she lay on. His eyes looked tired.

"Don't try to speak," he said.

Her body turned hot with panic. She reached to her neck. With blistered, sore fingers she felt along inch-wide imprints that ran like thick stems where the Dark Fae had held her. She found four distinct indentions but could hardly run a finger on one spot before her own touch was too much to bear. If the bruising looked as bad as it felt, it must be horrible.

"It looks worse than it is." Rigo held one hand atop his bow as he gazed solemnly at her. "Aurelia told me your voice was intact immediately after. A product of shock, I imagine, as I'm afraid your throat has suffered significant damage. I was able to repair most of it with a healing spell. You should regain the ability to speak within a couple of days. I plan to heal the scars once you're more rested. The bruises will take time, but they will heal on their own."

Jastyn propped herself on her elbows, grabbing her throat and wincing. "The pain," Rigo said. "Well, I'm not sure how long that will last. Aurelia is working diligently on something for you now."

Forcing herself to sit up, Jastyn looked toward the center of the cavern. Aurelia puttered busily between four different cauldrons. She spoke to herself in hurried whispers, her delicate hands gesticulating with each new ingredient she added to a steaming concoction inside each black pot. Jastyn smiled, but even that hurt. She rubbed her jaw when she spotted Coran collecting an assortment of berries from the bushes near the back of Vreis's cave. For a meal? She'd lost all sense of time. How long had she been in here? How did she get back?

She glanced at Rigo, who seemed to read her mind. "Aurelia and those twins brought you back. That was before sunset. I imagine it's a few hours before dawn now." She raised an eyebrow. "No," he said, "I did not have the good fortune of meeting the twins. From what Her Highness told me, they sound…interesting."

A small laugh escaped her throat, making her wince. Then she remembered Vreis and shifted to look into the main chamber. He sat on the cavern floor, his back resting against a waist-high boulder. He looked tired but was happily examining the latest berry batch from Coran. The large gash on his head had been covered with a worn piece of cloth running from his hairline down to his earlobe.

"Aurelia's doing," Rigo said, again following Jastyn's train of thought. "He is much better. In a bit of shock, but that's to be expected."

Sighing, she closed her eyes. When she did, she was once again face-to-face with the Dark Fae.

Odium Child.

She squeezed her eyes shut, forcing away the horrible image. Her throat burned, and she opened her eyes in search of water.

In a moment, Rigo knelt beside her, a full flask ready. She took it gratefully and drank as if she'd been without water for weeks. The liquid tore through her throat like broken glass, but she drank anyway.

She wiped at her lips with the back of her hand, which was dirt-covered with tiny cuts. Taking a deep breath, her mind once again filled with Aurelia's cries, and she was caught in the Fae's grasp. She shook her head, hating that he had gotten so close. His evil, hollow voice echoed.

Luck does not walk with you this night.

Her head ached, and she handed the flask back to Rigo. She tried to tell him thank you, but when she opened her mouth, only faint gasps of air came out. She reached up to her neck, surprised.

His eyes were the saddest she'd seen since they met. "You are strong, Jastyn. I know it is difficult. But time will heal this."

Her eyes burned with tears. She nodded when he stood. There were footsteps, followed by the appearance of Aurelia, who ran around Rigo and crouched in front of Jastyn, her eyes wide.

"You're awake. How do you feel?"

Again, Jastyn tried to respond, but this time, only a small croak escaped her ravaged throat. Aurelia palmed Jastyn's cheek. Her eyes filled with tears, and one of Jastyn's escaped and fell onto her fingers.

Eventually, Aurelia whispered, "I'm so sorry, Jastyn."

Rigo excused himself. Jastyn noticed a wooden cup in Aurelia's left hand. It smelled peculiar, and steam furled from its top. She nodded toward it.

Aurelia glanced down. "Oh yes. I prepared this. Well, I prepared several things. But the licorice root is still steeping and won't be ready for a few hours. Vreis says there's a hive nearby for honey, but I will collect that when its light. This"—she held up the cup, and Jastyn sniffed, then cringed—"is one of my mother's specialties." When she looked into Jastyn's face, she frowned and said, "It may not smell like a rose, but it will help your throat."

Jastyn grimaced.

"It's a combination of marshmallow root and water. I started it as soon as we were back and Vreis was up and talking. He told me it grows near his father's lake and had a collection of it on hand." She lifted the cup. "That was a bit of luck, wouldn't you say?"

Luck. She recalled the Dark Fae's words. *Luck does not walk with you this night.* That wasn't the first time she'd heard him say something like that. The first time they'd met, out in the Wood when she was ten, he'd said something similar. Except then, he'd told her luck *was* walking with her.

"Jastyn?"

She started to explain, but the pain in her throat proved too much. Aurelia lowered her hand, resting it on Jastyn's knee. "It hurts, I know. This will help." She passed Jastyn the cup. "The root has properties that aid in reducing pain. My mother often used it when my father had gone off on a hunt and came back with a terrible cough."

Jastyn shifted to sit cross-legged, delicately holding the cup. She found she hardly had the strength to do so. Fortunately, Aurelia appeared caught in a memory as Jastyn struggled to lift the cup. The smell was quite unpleasant, like spoiled dirt and rotten flowers.

"It doesn't taste as bad as it smells," Aurelia finally said.

Smiling, Jastyn took a drink, coughing in disgust.

Aurelia huffed. "I said it didn't taste *as* bad. I never said it tasted good."

Grimacing, Jastyn forced herself to take another drink. At first, the liquid scalded her throat. Like the water earlier, it seemed to tear through her like a knife. Swallowing felt as if she was choking down a rock.

Aurelia placed her hands on Jastyn's knees. "That's good."

Jastyn took another drink. This time, there was less pain. She glanced hopefully over the top of the cup.

"See? It helps." Aurelia smiled. "Try to finish it. A batch of chamomile is next to help you sleep. Then I'll have more prepared in the morning."

Jastyn paused. She'd forgotten another day had passed. Another day in the mountains meant they'd lost more time. They and Alanna. They'd also lost another day to unravel the riddle awaiting them in the caves.

"What's wrong?" Aurelia asked, her eyes searching Jastyn's face. "Is it something about the Dark Fae?"

Jastyn opened her mouth to speak, then remembered she couldn't. She looked pleadingly to Aurelia, who said, "All right. Give me a moment. Does it have to do with one of us?" When Jastyn only stared, Aurelia frowned. "Your family?" Jastyn grimaced, and Aurelia sighed. "Your sister."

Unable to meet her gaze, Jastyn moved aside part of the blanket. In the dirt, she drew a circle, then a crescent.

"The sun and the moon?"

Then Jastyn drew a line that cut through each.

Aurelia placed her hand atop Jastyn's. "You feel as if we're running out of time." Jastyn met her gaze. "I understand." She licked her lips, hesitating. "But I'm afraid you're not in any condition to travel."

Jastyn set the cup down, taking Aurelia's hands. She hoped Aurelia could see her desperation, could see how much she wasn't going to let what had happened slow them down.

Apparently, Aurelia did pick up on this and looked at her sympathetically. "Jastyn, I know. I know you want to go. And we will. As soon as you've rested."

Jastyn dropped their hands into her lap.

Aurelia straightened. "I was going to suggest three days' rest."

Jastyn squeezed her hand.

"One day? Valiant effort." She smiled, and Jastyn couldn't help but return it. "Fine. Two days. We will take two days of rest and then continue on."

Reluctantly, Jastyn gave a small, painful nod.

"Good," Aurelia said before handing the cup back. "Finish this and I'll bring you a batch of the chamomile." Then she helped Jastyn sit back, bundling the blanket so Jastyn could lie propped up. "Try to rest. Are you hungry?"

Jastyn shook her head.

"All right, tomorrow morning, then." She leaned down and kissed Jastyn's forehead, her lips lingering when she whispered, "I'm so happy you're all right."

When she pulled back, Jastyn felt that same feeling from the other night, and her gaze flickered to Aurelia's lips as the energy vibrated between them. She wanted to reach out, despite her pain and tiredness.

Aurelia inhaled sharply, and Jastyn was sure she was trying to shake the same feeling. "Rest well."

She turned to go, and Jastyn lay back, taking slow sips of the marshmallow root. Two days. She could wait two more days. Two days and she'd return to her quest to save Alanna. Maybe by then, she'd think of a way to tell Aurelia the truth.

Maybe.

CHAPTER TWELVE

Over the next two days, Aurelia kept them all on a strict schedule of herbal remedies, light food, and bedrest. Their quartet, she decided, looked like something the horse had dragged in and was in desperate need of care. She included herself. Aurelia had never been so tired in her life, and that included the weeklong solstice and equinox festivities that had often kept her up with the moon for days at a time. While lengthy kingdom frivolity had prepared her for mingling with foreign guests, it had not prepared her for anything resembling what they'd gone through in the last few days.

It seemed another lifetime when she had longed for adventure outside of the castle. Of course, after everything, it was difficult to keep the sturdy stone towers and torchlit halls in her happy memories. Each corner of the castle she'd known was now cast in shadow, a bleakness so thick it seemed impenetrable. Perhaps that was how it was supposed to be, a dreary homage to the death of her brother. It helped assure her that her place was here and not in a kingdom dressed forever in black.

She had to laugh at the gods' interpretation of her wish to leave. Still, she could not complain. The journey was arduous, yes, but she had seen spectacular places, made new friends, and even found a woman she yearned to build a future with.

The night after the attack, Aurelia had brought Jastyn some chamomile to wash down the marshmallow root. She'd found her sound asleep, face slack with much needed rest. Aurelia had watched for a moment, wanting to heal the horrible bruising around Jastyn's delicate throat. Alas, she set the drink nearby and let Jastyn sleep in peace.

Coran and Vreis drifted off shortly after, and only Rigo sat awake as Aurelia crushed more marshmallow root next to the dormant cauldron. She let the methodical turning of the pestle take over, quieting her mind while she worked.

"How are you?"

Aurelia looked up, surprised to find Rigo sitting cross-legged across from her, his lithe limbs folded neatly beneath him.

"I'm fine." She worked the pestle harder into the bottom of Vreis's stone bowl. Rigo touched her shoulder where the pooka had held her.

She winced, pulling away.

"You are not fine."

She waved a hand. "It's a flesh wound." Her gaze flickered to Rigo's incredulous face. "Very well. It's two flesh wounds." She paused to shake out her shoulders, staring at the crushed bits of root smeared inside the bowl. Reluctantly, she carefully lifted her arm and pulled back the torn material of her tunic, a slit that ran the length of her underarm. Trying not to think about the pain she was in, she examined the bruise and fresh scratches beneath, which she'd covered in a thick layer of calendula to prevent infection. When Rigo continued to watch, she added, "I will be fine. It's Jastyn I'm concerned about."

Looking thoughtful, Rigo said, "She is incredibly strong."

Defensively, she replied, "She is. Unlike me, one of the weak members of man." His eyes widened in surprise. She smiled wryly.

"You remember my saying that?"

She stared into the bowl. "I remember everything from those days."

After a moment he said, "Well, I was wrong." Sighing, he glanced over his shoulder toward Jastyn. "I find it impressive she has fought off the dark force's presence for as long as she has."

Surprised, Aurelia said, "She's talked to you about him?"

A small smile graced his lips. "Fret not, Your Highness. Jastyn did not confide in me. She mentioned him offhandedly on one of our hunts when I asked her how her shoulder was healing. The rest, I was able to put together. 'Comes with the territory,' as our friend Vreis would say."

Aurelia laughed. "I see." She set her work aside. "Rigo, is it safe to say that the Dark Fae from Jastyn's nightmares, the one we met last night, is the same dark force sweeping over the land?"

"Yes. I believe they are the same."

Considering this, Aurelia asked, "The Dark Fae is the one your queen fears?"

He tapped his knees lightly. "You find it difficult to believe my queen would fear him."

"I mean no disrespect, but—"

"But if the Dark Fae is no more than a vision in the night or a hooded rider who can be chased away when he is outnumbered, why fear him? Aurelia, his presence has frightened many. It's made them lose sight of reality and brought fear and mistrust to much of the realm."

"I still don't understand all of this."

His slim shoulders rose and fell, and Aurelia was irked by the fact that she was likely testing his patience or perhaps his own lack of understanding. Either way, she was glad when his next question came out softly. "What do you know of him?"

"Me?" She straightened. "I've never heard of such a horrible monster." She thought for a moment. "Well, there are stories, of course. There always are. I have heard old tales of a hooded rider, tales said to have begun in the time of the first kings. King Bradan of Venostes and King Andrus of Uterni. Gultero was ruled by King Taranis." She began to recall a rather chilling story her father had told her and Brennus when they were young, on a late summer night next to a fire that threw shadows across the walls. The story of an old withered man who'd wandered from Gultero to Venostes, a hooded man with a dark horse said to have sprung from the Otherworld. His blood had been drawn from the molten earth and his bones collected from the ashes of the dead.

"His soul was born rotten, black and full of hate. So King Bradan banished him to the Wildlands. Out there, the man found a new target for his hatred, the fae. Particularly those who lived their lives with humans." She paused. "It was said that when a child was born of an illegitimate union, the man would lurk in the corners of their home, determined to collect each Odium child until there were none."

Her hand flew to her mouth. "How did I not remember that before?"

"It was an old memory. An unpleasant one, at that. Your mind most likely locked it deep away."

Aurelia tried to put all of this together. "But he's a story. He was nothing but a cautionary tale. A warning to young people to tell us how hatred leads to a life of loneliness and solitude."

"Even stories begin with a drop of reality."

Her body buzzed. "Wait. This madman, this withered being who roamed the land, he was said to be of the time of the first Diarmaid king."

"Correct."

"The first Diarmaid king is the one who banished him to the Wildlands." The buzzing roared louder, and she struggled to maintain her train of thought. "The laws written by the earlier kings that my ancestors adopted…they sound as if they came from the mouth of that madman." She rubbed her temples with her forefingers, muttering, "I don't understand. Who was that man?" She looked up. "Did he have some sort of influence over the ones who wrote the laws?"

"Perhaps."

She shook her head. "He must have. His awful words and beliefs, they must have infiltrated the king's mind. King Bradan must have been under some sort of spell or ancient magic. That must be it."

Aurelia was shaking now, but Rigo remained still. "Your Highness?"

"That has to be it. The laws of Venostes…those terrible, archaic laws my mother and father cling to are the workings of a spiteful lunatic, not the Diarmaids."

"Aurelia, are you saying the line of Diarmaids who have upheld the laws are not responsible for their actions?"

She sat back, the buzz beginning to die down. "Gods, no, of course not. But don't you see? The root of all this is an outside force. He came from Gultero. Why didn't King Taranis do anything? Why did King Bradan have to banish that monster?" She took a shaky breath. "Maybe his influence is what prompted the laws to be written. What if he had worked some sort of spell over the Diarmaid king?" Most of all, why didn't King Bradan repeal the laws once the wandering man was banished? With him gone, wouldn't the influence he held lessen?

Rigo spoke slowly, as if choosing his words carefully. "I know not the history of your people but am aware of the brutality of your laws."

Aurelia opened her mouth, but realizing the truth of his words, she said nothing.

"There are endless possibilities, but I suppose it could have been that an outside force, like the Dark Fae, manipulated his way into the inner workings of the Diarmaid family."

They sat in silence for a time. What if she'd discovered the truth? Rigo was right; all stories began from somewhere. What if the Dark Fae and the wandering man were one and the same? What if he found a way to force his ideas on King Bradan, turning the Diarmaids into a lineage blindly upholding his bigoted laws for the rest of time? She shuddered at the thought. Did her mother and father know about this? Specifically, her father, the blood of the Diarmaids? King Bradan was his great-grandfather three times over. Maybe there was something in the castle, some shred of evidence she could find to explain all of this. Proof to help overturn the laws. But how? And more importantly, when?

Rigo pulled her from her thoughts. "Whoever he is, we must not underestimate him. The Dark Fae has survived through five Diarmaid kings, feeding on the lingering fear of change and prejudice. He despises Odiums like Jastyn and has woven that hatred into the fabric of your society. He thrives on the fear of a new way of things and taps into that same fear in others."

"But nobody thinks that way today," Aurelia said, though she instantly conjured her parents and their reactions to who Jastyn was. "Well, they shouldn't think that way. The Odium curse is ancient history, if it even is that." She scoffed. "I have a feeling it may well be another fabrication, written to ensure 'peace over the kingdom.'" She sneered at those last words, mimicking her parents. Then, feeling inspired, she said, "Rigo, we can turn all of this around. We can convince the realm to come together to fight against him, fight with us"

Rigo's face was solemn. "That may prove difficult. My queen is a confident leader, but she has maintained the elves' success by being cautious. This means putting her own kind first. Due to this, she has fallen prey to those dark ideals."

Aurelia's shoulders fell. "She believes she can keep her clans safe by keeping them pure and isolated from the rest of the realm."

He nodded.

"That's why she sent her soldiers to do Drest's bidding. He convinced her that if he was given the throne, he could keep the humans and fae apart from one another, keep them 'pure.'" She sneered as she used Drest's word. It remained difficult to fathom he'd harbored such a hatred for Odiums and fae all his life. How could she not have known?

Still, something remained unclear. "Why now?" she asked. "I've read stories of the hooded rider, but he was relegated to the moors near these mountains. Obviously, he is more than story, but why has he infiltrated Jastyn's mind? How is he now able to fulfill his dark agenda and hunt down Odiums across the realm?"

"I do not know the answer to those questions."

She sighed. "How did he get so close to her this time?" She glanced toward where Jastyn slept.

"I don't know. But something must have changed."

"Coran said the same thing."

Rigo smiled. "He is a smart young man. I can only hope the truth will be revealed to us in time."

Aurelia nodded, but she was beginning to think they might have to start making the truth come to them. Since her brother's death, she had questioned the gods and the plans they had for her. Perhaps it was her turn to make the plans. After all, she was in a hurry.

Realizing she'd lost herself in thought, she cleared her throat. "Well, I could go the rest of this journey without another Dark Fae encounter. I don't know about you."

"Indeed. Still, it would do well to take caution over the next weeks as we venture to the caves. Something tells me an unexpected meeting awaits us upon our arrival."

The day they were to leave, Jastyn woke before any of the others. She packed her satchel with a blanket and wandered to the center of the cavern where she was surprised to find Vreis standing over his cauldron.

"Good morning," he said. "You look rested."

She smiled, feeling infinitely better than the night of the attack. Sleeping on a cave floor didn't hold a candle to a night in an open meadow, but it did provide a nice, cool place to recover. She adjusted the flask over her shoulder.

"Ah, yes, you'll be needing water on your journey." He found a gourd nearby and poured its contents into the flask. "There we are." He recapped it, handing it back. Jastyn tucked it inside her satchel.

"I was hoping to finish this batch before you left, but that little incident the other day put a damper on my plans." While stirring the bubbling liquid, he reached up to dab at the injury on his head. Jastyn followed his long fingers as they traced the jagged dark line of red beneath the white cloth. It was significantly less swollen, and she was glad to see it healing.

"Your princess is quite the curator of cures," he said, smiling at his own words. "I'm glad to know her."

She smiled. "So am I." Her voice was just above a whisper, but it seemed to surprise them both.

Jastyn reached up to the markings on her neck, now almost gone thanks to Rigo's magic. She said, "My voice." It had only been a couple of days, but the hoarse whisper sounded oddly foreign.

"Quite the healer indeed." He grinned, then added, "Welcome back to the land of the living."

Still smiling, she stepped closer, adjusting the satchel. "Vreis, I..." Now that her voice was back, she found it difficult to explain what she was feeling, how she was thrilled to have met someone like her, somebody who understood the lonely life she'd led. She wanted to tell him what it meant for her to know he existed, and how his ability to not just survive but thrive in a world made to bring him down was an inspiration to her.

"Thank you," was all she said, holding out an arm, which he took and gripped.

"It's been lovely getting to know you all these past few days. Well, aside from that pooka you brought along," he added behind a wry smile. His brown eyes shone, and he busied himself with his fruit trees. "Go on and get yourself changed. Your pants and tunic are aired out in the back passage near the steam pool. Your boots, too. I hope you don't mind. I couldn't stand the state of them. The others will be up soon, and I'd better get breakfast ready before you go."

Jastyn wandered to the back of the cavern, passing Rigo, who leaned against his bow. His eyes were closed in a rare moment of rest. Coran's snores came in steady bursts from the other side of the boulders as Jastyn found her wonderfully clean clothes. She slipped out of Vreis's tunic and happily donned her pants and worn navy tunic before wrapping her pleated belt around her waist, the tail resting against her thigh like an old friend. As she tugged on her boots, she heard a splash. Aurelia sat on the opposite side of the steam pool, washing her face with the warm water. The blush in her cheeks told Jastyn the water wasn't the only thing she'd had her eyes on.

"Oh," Aurelia said. "Good morning."

Jastyn adjusted her boot and stood, feeling like herself for the first time in days. "Good morning."

Aurelia stopped. Her hands parted, water dripping from her wrists and fingers. She stared. "Did you just…did you…"

"Talk?" Jastyn asked, clearing her throat to combat the annoying catch her voice kept doing. "What do you know? Guess I did."

Jastyn grinned as Aurelia hopped up and scurried around the pool. "Jastyn, that's amazing. How does it feel? Does it still hurt?"

"Not as much as before," she replied, listening to the gravelly whisper. "Your remedies helped."

Aurelia's eyes lit up, and she bounced on her toes. "That's wonderful. I'm so glad."

Jastyn caught several droplets of water trickling from Aurelia's chin. She grinned when Jastyn asked, "And you?" She gestured to the torn parts of Vreis's tunic.

"Oh, I'm all right. Like I'd let a pooka get the better of me."

"Uh-huh." Jastyn noted the smell of calendula on Aurelia's wounds. She had known that this journey wouldn't be easy, but she had not imagined the peril she'd be putting her friends in. Or Aurelia. She wondered if Aurelia was beginning to regret her decision to stay.

"I'm all right, really," she told her as if reading her thoughts. "We're all okay."

They shared a smile, then without thinking, Jastyn pulled her into a hug, careful not to hold her too tight. Memories flooded her mind, and she heard the echoes of Aurelia's screams while fighting the pooka as Jastyn struggled to fight the Dark Fae.

"I'm sorry," Jastyn mumbled into her neck.

Aurelia hugged her tighter before stepping back, holding her at arm's length, her own eyes glistening. "Nonsense. What happened was the Dark Fae's fault, not yours." When Jastyn tried to protest, Aurelia said, "I signed on for this adventure, remember? And I'm here for every part of it with you."

"Aurelia, I…" She paused, licking her lips. She was inundated with the desire to tell Aurelia everything. She needed to. They would reach the caves within two weeks' time. She was running out of chances. Taking a deep breath, she said "There's something I need to tell you."

Her heart beat wildly as Aurelia's brow knit adorably, and she wiped more of the water from her chin and cheeks. Jastyn was overwhelmed. She never expected Aurelia to be like this, to be so absolutely wonderful about everything. She had expected a lazy, complaining, ill-prepared woman who had no idea what she was getting into when she'd agreed to come to the west. Granted, that last part might have been true, but Aurelia had never faltered. Swallowing, Jastyn really looked at her. She couldn't believe the incredibly strong, intelligent, brave woman Aurelia Diarmaid had turned out to be. Jastyn had spent the first weeks of their journey reconciling the fact that the heir to the Diarmaid throne was everything her royal lineage was not.

While her feelings had grown, Jastyn still struggled to fathom a future with Aurelia, or a long-term one, anyway. How could she have one? She was looking at the woman who would one day be Queen of Venostes. Jastyn, meanwhile, was nobody, an Odium with no money, a hunger-lean frame, and a penchant for getting into trouble. In what realm could she and Aurelia be together?

Still, maybe it would be enough to know that, if only for a short time, they could share whatever this was between them. Jastyn could hold this time they had together in that special corner of her mind where her precious memories resided. On this journey, they could simply be. When it ended, so would they. That was the way it had to be.

"Jastyn?"

Summoning her courage, Jastyn swallowed. "I have something to tell you about the caves."

"Yes?" Aurelia studied her as she began to braid her long hair, pulling it back from her face. For a moment, Jastyn lost herself in the deft work of Aurelia's fingers as they nimbly twisted the strands into a well-worked pattern.

Jastyn bit her lip. Why was this so difficult? She knew she had to tell. She couldn't keep her in the dark anymore. But what would Aurelia say? How would she react, knowing a noble sacrifice would be required in exchange for Alanna's cure? Jastyn imagined herself saying the words. She imagined Aurelia's face, lit with curiosity, fall to darkness. She could almost hear the yelling, Aurelia asking why she had kept this from her. Then she'd walk away without ever looking back.

"Oy, you two, breakfast is ready."

They both turned. Coran was standing next to Vreis in the center of the cavern. Jastyn hadn't even realized he'd woken up. Her courage failing, she turned back to Aurelia. She wore an expectant smile, her hair now in a braid over her right shoulder.

"Coming," Aurelia called, waving. "What was it you needed to tell me?"

Jastyn stammered, "I, um, I was only going to say that...Rigo thinks we may encounter more fae in the caves." She felt like a wilting flower and dropped her gaze to the floor. "I was going to tell you that we need to be careful."

Playing with the end of her braid, Aurelia flicked it over her shoulder. "Of course." She smiled and leaned in to give Jastyn a kiss on her cheek. "Come on, let's get you some breakfast."

Jastyn couldn't look at her. "You go ahead. I'll be there in a minute."

"Suit yourself. But do hurry." She skipped off.

Her knees weak, Jastyn fell into a crouch. Pretending to wash her hands in the steam pool, she fought back tears. She felt sick at her own cowardice. She'd spent her entire life being brave in the face of danger. Why, then, could she not tell Aurelia this one thing?

Standing, she looked over at Aurelia, who laughed at something Vreis said while she prepared a plate.

Of course, Jastyn knew exactly why she was afraid to tell Aurelia about the noble sacrifice. It was the same reason she had fought to come back when the Dark Fae was drawing the life from her.

It no longer mattered that Aurelia was a Diarmaid. It no longer mattered that there was no hope for them. She had been kidding herself by thinking these feelings wouldn't last. She was experiencing something she never thought she would, especially toward a member of the royal family. She was falling in love with Aurelia Diarmaid.

CHAPTER THIRTEEN

Here, let me help you with that." Aurelia stood across the campfire in her original pants and blue tunic, wiping her hands clean of splinters before reaching for her satchel.

"I've got it."

"Jastyn, I really don't mind. It's easier to apply if—"

Jastyn pulled the calendula poultice out of reach. "Aurelia, I said I can do it myself."

The crackle from the fire was the only noise. Jastyn could feel everyone's eyes on her, but she fixed her gaze on her boots. When she finally looked up, Aurelia's eyes blazed.

When the silence dragged on, Jastyn added, "Please."

Aurelia looked as if she was about to say something, but she turned and snatched up one of their flasks. "Rigo, will you accompany me, please? I feel the sudden urge to go for a walk." She threw a glare over her shoulder as Rigo stood.

"Of course, Your Majesty."

As they disappeared around the bend of the path, Jastyn dropped the poultice.

Coran cleared his throat. "Jas, what was that? Since we left Vreis's, you've been nothin' but sour."

Jastyn picked up the poultice and pretended to spread the calendula on the cloth. Coran called her name again, and when she didn't respond, he grabbed the cloth. She started to protest but stopped when she saw the look on his face. He was looking at her in a way he hadn't since they were kids and she'd tried to take more than her fair share of the coins they'd found in the market.

"Out with it. What's got your tunic in such a nasty twist?"

"I don't want to talk about it."

The sun hadn't set yet, but the midsummer air—now flowing more freely outside of the choking mountain walls—held a crisp bite. Coran frowned, then conjured and threw an orange flame onto the fire.

Taken aback by his rare show of frustration, Jastyn gingerly applied the fresh calendula to her wound, then tossed the used cloth into the flames. She fidgeted with the empty dagger sheath on her leg as he sat next to her.

"You do know that was Aurelia you were talkin' to?" he asked. "And being mighty rude to, if I'm being honest."

After adjusting her tunic, Jastyn rested her hands on her thighs, fists clenching and unclenching. "I know."

"What is it, then? Because that kinda talk to a royal could get you locked up back in Venostes."

Jastyn replied hotly, "That's the whole point. We're not in Venostes. None of this would've happened if she'd stayed where she belonged."

"All right," he said, "that was your last one. Now come on. What's really wrong?"

Her shoulders shaking, Jastyn felt cold, though perspiration prickled her forehead. She hated feeling like this but couldn't stop the bitterness as it ran off her tongue. "I should have never gone to the prince's Remembrance that day. I should have never agreed to let her come with us."

"Jas, what are you talkin' about?"

"Coran, I can't go through with this. I can't keep this from her anymore. I feel sick."

"You mean, the caves?"

"Yes. The noble sacrifice."

"I thought you were gonna tell her."

"I tried. The last day with Vreis. I was going to tell her, but…I couldn't do it. Coran, she's gonna hate me."

"Aurelia could never."

"I can't stand the idea of hurting her. The longer I keep this a secret, the worse it's gonna be. But how do I tell her when it's gonna be the thing that ends…whatever this is between us?"

He was quiet for a moment, picking up a fallen twig, one of many that littered the ground. Jastyn leaned back on one of the logs Aurelia had arranged for them. Now that they were descending one of Ionad's peaks, the terrain was becoming more familiar. Small trees dotted the edges of their less barren path that boasted lush brown soil sprouting tufts of yellow-green grass. The sound of birds had returned, along with the occasional sighting of a tree-dweller or rabbit.

"Well, my mum always says it's better to tear an old house down if its startin' to give in. You can always rebuild, but you can't keep on livin' in a place that's crumbling."

Jastyn eyed him. Her throat itched, and she took a drink from the flask. She knew what he was trying to say but hated his ability to read her so well. "You don't have to remind me you won the contest for best mum."

He stood, his eyes wide. "Look. I know we've been through a lot. You in particular. The Dark Fae is on your heels. It's scary, and you have a right to be upset. But now you're attackin' your mom. What does she have to do with any of this?"

She laughed, throwing a leaf into the fire. "I didn't tell you, did I?"

"Tell me what?"

Taking a deep breath, she let her fears loose on him. "On top of the fact that I keep putting everyone in danger, besides my sister having only four months to live unless I find a cure, and with the only way to do so is by asking Aurelia to sacrifice herself, it must have slipped my mind that before all of that happened, my mom told me my father is a fae."

He blinked. Jastyn rubbed her hands so hard into her thighs it hurt, but she let the pain distract her from the feeling that she was losing her grip on the world.

"I thought your dad was a sailor, somebody from another land?"

"That's what I thought, too."

"But if your dad's a fae..."

"I know. My mom broke all three of the laws."

"That explains why they kept her locked up until after you were born."

Jastyn wrapped her arms around herself. "It doesn't matter."

"Doesn't matter? Jas, you're half-fae!"

"And an Odium."

"Did she tell you who he is? Which type of fae?"

She swallowed, recalling that night on the hillside with her mother. "I didn't give her much of a chance to explain."

"Oh."

She brushed back her hair. "It doesn't matter. He abandoned us. He left my mom all alone."

"But if he's a fae, maybe he's still out there. What if he's from the realm?"

"I don't care where he's from. I hope I never meet him. He's a coward." She wondered if Coran could sense the lie. Despite her anger, the curiosity she'd harbored all her life about her father wasn't gone. She was furious at the man who'd left her mother, but she couldn't help but wonder what he was like, wonder if she was like him.

When she glanced at Coran, he was frowning. "What is it?"

He side-eyed her. "No offense, Jas. But...if you're half-fae, shouldn't you have some sort of power? Somethin' special?"

She flushed and clenched her jaw. "I don't know." She snorted, then added, "With my luck, he was probably a lowly fae, somebody who couldn't even conjure a saol."

"You're right. Your dad's probably a troll."

She bit the inside of her cheek to keep from smiling. "Worse. I bet he's a grogoch."

He guffawed. "That's it. Your dad's an old hunched grogoch, the kind with hair growin' from his ears."

She laughed, punching his arm. He nearly rolled off his log in a fit of laughter. She shoved him again, and this time, he did tumble onto the ground. Of course, she recognized the tactic he often used to pull her up from the dungeons, but she didn't care. She let the laughter chase out the dark mood that had drowned her thoughts.

As their laughter ceased, Jastyn wiped her eyes. "I was awful, Coran."

He picked himself up. "Nastier than a witch's wart."

She hung her head. "I don't know how to do this. How do I get the cure without Aurelia getting hurt? There has to be a way."

After a moment, he squeezed her shoulder. "We'll find a way. We always do."

"It's all so much."

"I know. But whenever you're ready to tell Aurelia, I'll be there. You don't have to do it alone."

"Aurelia." Jastyn looked up. She and Rigo would be back soon. She tried to think of something to say when they returned. A mere apology wouldn't be enough. Then an idea hit her. "There was a beehive about seventy-five yards back up the path. Will you tell them I've gone to hunt?" She stood, a renewed sense of vigor filling her chest.

"Sure, but where are ya goin'?"

"I thought of something I can do to make things up to Aurelia. I won't be long."

"She's completely intolerable. One minute, the sun beams from her strength, and the next, a cloud obstructs her vision and she's lost in the darkness." Aurelia stomped beside Rigo, leaving a heavy trail in the dirt. "I don't know how Coran tolerates her." She tripped on a boulder, glaring at the rock as she huffed and continued, her feet pounding. "You know, I understand now why her only friend is a hedgewitch. She is so…so…intolerable!"

Rigo stepped lightly alongside. "You said that already, Your Highness."

"Because it's true." She swatted a branch. It wacked her in the back of the head. "Fine, it's not completely true, but who is she thinking she can speak to me that way? I'm Aurelia Diarmaid, Princess of Venostes."

His melodic chuckle earned a halt in Aurelia's frustrated step. Crossing her arms, she glared. "What is so funny?"

"Forgive me, Your Highness. I find it difficult to not be amused by human mating rituals. They are entirely befuddling."

"M-mating rituals?" She blushed and pushed back the hair that had fallen loose from her braid, wincing at the pain in her shoulder. "Don't be ridiculous."

"If I may say so, from what I have observed, Jastyn is generally a reserved individual. She is drawn outward in instances of hunting, exchanges of humor, and physical escapades with Coran, as well as mentions of her sister, and, finally, when she is speaking to you."

Not knowing what to say, Aurelia glanced at the trees. Rigo continued. "However, Jastyn seems to always be at a point of contradiction in your presence. When the two of you are near, her body exudes all the signs of physical attraction. At the same time, she seems to be fighting against those very primal urges, contradicting the nature of her wants and desires."

Lifting an eyebrow, Aurelia replied, "That is very...observant." Then she sighed, throwing up an exasperated arm. "But why? Every time I feel us growing closer, she pulls away." She gestured back in the direction of their camp. "She closes herself off to me again."

He thumbed the string on his bow, looking thoughtful. "She has not had an easy road in this life."

She sighed. "I know. All I want is for her to let me in."

"The doors we close to others are not easily opened."

She stood quietly. What could Jastyn be so concerned about that she would lash out like she did? There had to be something more. Of course, she was worried about her sister. Aurelia ran through conversations the four of them had shared over the last two months. "What if it's something about her mother?" Her mind picked up pieces she had overheard and tried to put them together. "She's been closed off about her mother since we left Venostes. What if that's why she's acting like this? Something happened with her mother before we left. Of course."

She started walking again, Rigo falling into step next to her as they headed to their campsite.

"I fear I do not follow, Your Highness."

She stepped lightly over a boulder. "What I mean is, I might know why Jastyn has not been herself since the Dark Fae."

"You think it has to do with her mother?"

A branch snapped, and they both turned to look. Aurelia checked her hands and feet, ensuring she hadn't stepped into another of her mother's snares. Finding no evidence of a saol set to trap her, she remained still. Rigo drew an arrow, aiming it toward a towering ash tree. He stepped in front of her, his eyes narrow slits.

"What is it?" she whispered, glancing around him.

"That tree has been following us."

She glanced incredulously between him and the tree. "Come again?"

"Look around, Your Highness. This highland is littered with only pines and rowan trees." She stepped closer, noting the lowly, twisted trunk of the pale ash. He asked, "When was the last time you saw one of these?"

She stood behind him, looking up the length of the ash into its lush leaves. He was right; this didn't belong. "Those are native to Venostes." She swallowed, her throat suddenly dry. "How has one of my kingdom's trees found its way out here?"

"That is a good question." He spoke louder as if to ensure the tree could hear him.He pulled back his arrow, the string releasing a tight sound. When it did, Aurelia nearly fell backward as the tree's branches shook, covering the ground with green leaves.

"Oh!" The trunk shrank and transformed into a broad-shouldered man with rough, bark-like skin and turquoise eyes, with a smattering of green running in patches along his wide body.

"Please," he cried, his hands in front of him. "I mean no harm. P-put the arrow away."

Rigo eyed him a moment more, then sheathed his arrow. "Explain yourself. Why have you been following us?"

Aurelia was still so shocked at seeing the transformation of the wood nymph that she only listened, mouth open, as he spoke.

"I have a message f-for the prin-princess."

She stepped forward. "A message? From whom?"

The wood nymph reached up into his hair—a wild arrangement of thick twigs, each topped with a single green leaf—and dug through it. Moments later, he withdrew a skinny blue vial and held it out. "It's a m-message from the Diarmaid castle."

Taking the vial, Aurelia examined its contents. Under the sunlight, clear liquid sloshed against its sides.

Rigo shifted next to her. "Peculiar message."

Tilting her head, Aurelia turned the vial. When the light hit the contents, she saw a face floating through the magical waters: her maiden, Roisin.

"Rigo, these are from the druid's brook, the babbling waters. My mother has a special bowl full of it. It's a clever, unassuming way to share messages. Brennus and I used to steal small portions when we were younger. You need another body of water to use it, though."

"There was a small pond close to our campsite."

"Thank you," she said to the trembling wood nymph, who ran off and disappeared into the hillside.

Stumbling over her own feet, Aurelia nearly fell into the murky pond Rigo led her to. She knelt at the water's edge and uncorked the vial. Then she poured the babbling waters into the stagnant, algae-filled pond and waited.

Bubbles emerged on the pond's surface, clearing away the floating tufts of algae until a circle the size of a small cauldron opened up before her. An image swirled and shifted until she was no longer looking at her own murky reflection but that of her beloved maiden.

"Roisin." Aurelia nearly tumbled into the pond at the sight of her dear friend. Roisin's wide, fair face looked up at her from the water, and confusion knit in the lines above her hazel eyes.

"M'lady! Gods, are you all right?"

Aurelia swelled with happiness at the sound of her voice. "What do you mean?"

"Have you been eating? You look as skinny as a broomstick."

Aurelia exhaled, smiling. "I'm eating just fine, Roisin." Looking at her maiden, she found it suddenly difficult to talk about everything that had happened over the past two months. Had it really been that long? Unsure where to start, she said, "It is good to see you."

The floating image smiled. "And you, m'lady."

"How did you get your hands on druid water?"

Even through the murky pond, Roisin's sheepish smile came through. "Glanna, the daughter of one of your mother's ladies of the court, snuck some out of the study for me. Things have been a mess here, m'lady. But I'm happy to know you are all right, and that this message finally found you." She took an excited breath. "I'd never met a nymph before. Handsome creatures, they are." Aurelia chuckled at the blush in Roisin's face. "Not as handsome as Coran, o'course. How is he, m'lady?"

"He is well. He misses you."

Beaming, Roisin replied, "That is happy news." Then her face fell. "I fear this message is quite the opposite."

Aurelia's heart skipped. "What is it?"

Her voice grew quieter, as if someone might be listening to them. "Baron Louarn has disappeared."

"Disappeared?" She hadn't thought about the baron or his wife since the elf invasion several months before. Their son had tainted all memory of them, though she knew that was unfair.

"Yes. He's vanished. Whispers around the castle claim he fled in the night. They say he was overcome with guilt."

"About what?"

"About Drest, m'lady. People are saying it was the baron who put Drest up to everything." She paused. "Everything to do with your brother."

Her stomach twisted. "Are you sure, Roisin?" She had struggled for weeks to reconcile the villainous Drest with the man she had known all her life. She had not been able to see the hatred in his heart. But his father the baron had always seemed like an honorable man and had been a trusted friend to her father. "I can't believe he would do such a thing."

"It is difficult to wrap your head around, m'lady. He was always kind."

"But if he's gone...what of the baroness?"

"Baroness Enya is the consult for His Majesty now."

Aurelia adjusted her seat along the pond's edge, pulling her leg closer. "Baroness Enya is assisting my father? But what of my mother?"

Roisin looked sad when she said, "Queen Dechtire has been occupied...looking for you."

Aurelia let her head fall into her hands. "The saol snares. She's set them everywhere."

"Her Majesty has kept herself in her chambers. When she does emerge, she wanders the castle with this strange look on her face. She's requested every map of the realm be sent to her."

"I thought she would let me go."

"M'lady, you're the only remaining heir."

"But I'm safe!" The pain in her shoulders shot down her arms. Softer, she added, "I'm fine. I'm with Jastyn." She smiled. "I'm happy. Why can't she understand that?"

"The castle's not the same without you, m'lady. You or..." She trailed off.

Aurelia swallowed the sadness threatening to turn into sobs. Now was not the time to grieve her brother.

"I can't go back," she said finally. "Not yet."

Roisin's image leaned closer. "The cooks say she is wrangling fae to go in search of you."

"What? My father, what does he say of this? Surely he disagrees."

Her gaze fell. "King Grannus has not been the same since your brother's ceremony."

Again, emotion surged, and Aurelia felt faint, overcome with grief. She'd missed her brother's funeral pyre. She hadn't been there when his body returned to the elements. Sniffling, she forced herself to focus on the target of her anger. "My mother knows I am well. Let her send her snares. I am in no hurry to return to a throne built from bigotry."

Roisin seemed confused as she asked, "What do you mean?"

"I mean I will not be a part of a dynasty that despises those who are different."

Roisin fell quiet.

Sighing, Aurelia said, "I'm sorry, Roisin. I only…" She rubbed her temples, glancing over her shoulder. Rigo paced twenty yards away. "I only wish they could understand things don't need to be the way they are."

"I know, miss." The image began to shimmer and shrink.

"Roisin, before you go, tell me, how was Brennus's funeral?"

"Lovely, m'lady. Fit for a king."

Aurelia had to cover her mouth to stifle her cries.

"M'lady?"

Aurelia wiped her eyes. "I'm sorry, Roisin."

Her image began to fade as she asked, "Will you come home soon, m'lady?"

"I can't leave Jastyn." She sniffled. "She needs my help."

"We need you, too. The people need you."

The water swirled. "Roisin, wait, please, tell my mother and father—"

But her image was gone, the algae floating over where she had been. Aurelia fell backward onto the damp bank. She stared at the water. "Tell my mother and father that I'm working to make things right."

The algae floated listlessly. Aurelia wiped her cheeks on her sleeve, then stood, the empty vial in her hand.

"Is everything all right, Your Highness?" Rigo asked.

Aurelia shook her head, which felt heavy on her shoulders. "I honestly don't know."

Chapter Fourteen

Jastyn wandered through the sparse highland, walking lightly along a pebble-laden path interspersed with fallen bark and pine needles. The night sky opened wide overhead, and she craned her neck, taking in the canvas of twinkling lights. Slowly, she was feeling like herself again, imagining that she was strolling through her Wood. The time alone had proved helpful, and she'd let the sound of her footsteps chase away the sense of foreboding that had encased her mind since the Dark Fae's encounter. His proximity had signaled a warning bell: she was running out of time to find the cure and save her sister. She'd let herself get caught up in her feelings, and they'd woven a net around her heart, distracting her from the mission.

When she stepped back into their campsite—a grassy alpine meadow at the mountain's base—she tried to ignore the giddy bubble expanding in her chest at the sight of Aurelia, who sat next to Coran on one of the logs near their nightly fire. Rigo stood thirty yards off to the right, scanning the dark veil that lay atop their sparse surroundings, which hosted a single, dim fairy's nest. Jastyn reminded herself to remain focused on the reason she was out here. Distractions had only gotten her and her group into trouble.

Then why do I still care about what Aurelia thinks of me?

Coran shot up from his seat and hurried over. She waved but faltered when Aurelia only stared into the fire.

"You're back." Coran stood close, glancing back at Aurelia.

Jastyn patted the satchel against her hip. "Took me a while to maneuver around the bees, but I got it. Is everything all right?"

He lowered his voice. "She's hardly said a word since sundown when she returned from her walk with Rigo. I had to set up the logs myself."

She raised an eyebrow. "That is serious."

"I think you better talk to her."

"I was kind of hoping to wait until things had blown over a bit more." She hadn't liked the way she'd left things with Aurelia but didn't want to rush matters. Space could do them both good. Yet she felt constantly pulled toward her, like a hummingbird craving its nectar.

Coran gave her a look, and she put her hands up. "Fine, fine. I'm going." Perhaps if they were at least civil with one another, Jastyn could worry less about Aurelia and more about what she was out here to do.

He pushed her toward the fire. Unsure how to proceed, she stood, rubbing her hands together over the flames. From the side of her eye, she watched Aurelia, who held a skewered tree-dweller over the flickering flames. Her eyes were glazed and her dinner nearly charred.

"I think your food is done."

Aurelia blinked. "Oh, so it is." She pulled the smoking meat out of the fire, stared at it a moment, then set it aside.

"Not hungry?"

"Not particularly."

Jastyn looked pleadingly at Coran, but he only motioned her forward. Grimacing, Jastyn sat next to Aurelia. Her dinner lay beside her, smoke unfurling from the blackened meat. Unfazed, Aurelia had one elbow propped upon her knee, her chin resting in her upturned palm. Her eyes bore into something Jastyn couldn't see.

"Aurelia, are you all right?" When she didn't say anything, Jastyn willed her voice to be steady. "I, um, I wanted to apologize for how I acted earlier."

Slowly, Aurelia faced her. Her gaze was still distant, but confusion settled between her brows.

"I was short with you. I shouldn't have been." Taking a deep breath, she said, "I'm sorry."

Seconds passed. Aurelia's eyes shifted between Jastyn's, searching. For what, Jastyn didn't know, but the attention made her squirm. What was going on?

"Princess?"

"My brother has been returned to the elements." Shifting

uncomfortably, Jastyn sat quietly. Aurelia, meanwhile, returned her gaze to the fire. "I missed his funeral."

Jastyn had imagined this would be the case. In fact, it was one of the reasons she had been so surprised when Aurelia announced her desire to join this journey. Her brother hadn't been dead long, and she thought it odd Aurelia seemed in no hurry to return to his side. Admittedly, Jastyn had not lost a loved one to death and knew not the intricacies of grief. Still, Aurelia hadn't shed a single tear for her brother's memory in their time together.

Aurelia looked almost angry as she said, "Roisin told me."

"You've heard from her?"

"She sent a message."

Carefully, Jastyn said, "I see. It has been several weeks—"

"Two moons and five days."

"All right. It's been two moons and five days since we left and…" She wasn't sure how to handle this but attempted to tread lightly. "They couldn't have left him the way he was."

"I know." Her voice was a whisper. "I only wish…" She reached toward the fire, the tips of her fingers glowing red. Her saol bobbed gently on its way to the flames, a short pop making them jump.

"You wish you could have been there," Jastyn finished for her.

Aurelia didn't reply. Her eyes went blank again as she seemed to lose herself in the lambent fire. Jastyn didn't know what to do. She'd never seen her like this. Thinking back on everything that had happened since Aurelia's kidnapping, Jastyn wondered if she had allowed herself any time to mourn the loss of her brother. She could only imagine the turmoil of losing a sibling, a frightening reality she walked dangerously close to the longer she went without Alanna's cure.

Jastyn was about to speak when Aurelia snapped from her trance and, grabbing her skewer, gave an odd laugh. "I do believe I've burned my dinner." Her laughter was hollow, and she was plainly fighting to cling to something, anything, other than the reality of her brother's death. For a moment, Jastyn considered telling her it was okay to let go of her pride, that she could let herself grieve. But the pain behind Aurelia's smile was too much; she wasn't ready.

"I can catch another one if you'd like."

Aurelia broke her skewer in half over her knee, then tossed the creature into the fire. "It's all right. I will wait for breakfast in the morning." Then she turned, straddling the log. "And I accept your apology. We all have our moments, don't we?"

"I guess we do." She tore herself from Aurelia's gaze, remembering the satchel draped over her chest. Pulling out a cloth, she unwrapped a dripping chunk of honeycomb, the sweet smell wafting between them. "Peace offering?"

Aurelia's smile lit up her face. "How did you get it?"

"I remembered seeing the hive on our hike today, so I doubled back." She shrugged. "Bees never bother to sting me. Somethin' about my smell, so said my mother."

Taking the honeycomb, Aurelia lifted it, breathing deep. "It's wonderful. Thank you."

Self-conscious, Jastyn dug the toe of her boot into the dirt. "I figured you could use it for another batch of herbal remedies." She reached up to her throat, lightly touching the bruises running in a line around her neck. "They really do work wonders. It hardly hurts at all now to talk."

Aurelia stood, looking happy to have something to do. "I'll start one now." After grabbing a small cauldron Vreis had gifted them, she filled it with water and placed it on the edge of the fire. Jastyn watched as she began crushing more of the chamomile, her hands working deftly.

"Aurelia, I have something to tell you."

Aurelia looked up, a thick strand of hair falling across her left eye. When she lifted her arm to swipe it aside, Jastyn didn't miss the flash of pain on her face. "Yes?"

Her fists clenched over her thighs, Jastyn took a deep breath. She looked to Coran, who had joined Rigo at his watch post. She closed her eyes, conjuring the image of her sister. Alanna sat on their bed, her curved shoulders trembling from coughs but her face stoic. Jastyn drew from her sister's seemingly endless well of strength. She had to tell Aurelia about the sacrifice. It was now or never.

"My father is a fae."

She slammed her mouth shut. What had she just said? That wasn't the plan.

The gentle thump of Aurelia's pestle halted. Reeling, Jastyn closed her eyes. She had finally summoned the courage to tell Aurelia the truth but instead revealed an entirely different secret.

When she opened her eyes, to her surprise, Aurelia was smiling.

"I…um…" Jastyn ran a hand down her braid, "I'm not sure why I said that."

Aurelia bit her lip, but her smile only widened. Knocking her bowl of crushed chamomile over, she rushed to Jastyn, once again straddling the log. "Your mother told you, didn't she?"

"Right before I left to find you." She paused. "Wait, how did you know?"

Aurelia beamed. "I had a feeling." Jastyn waved an expectant hand, prompting her to continue. "You've hardly spoken a word about your mother since we left. Which seemed odd, as I imagine your relationship has to be close due to…" She licked her lips as if searching for the right words. "Well, because of everything. Yet you seemed to do all you could to not talk about her. It only seemed logical, then, that something had happened between you."

Shaking her head, Jastyn smirked. "Here I thought I wasn't giving anything away."

Aurelia's face turned serious, her voice lowering after a glance at Coran and Rigo. "How does it feel?"

"Knowing my mother kept this from me?" Jastyn scoffed. "I don't know." She glanced at the moon's slim crescent, remembering her mother's words. "I guess she thought she was protecting me, but it felt like a betrayal. Like she didn't trust me to know the truth."

Aurelia nodded, but Jastyn saw a glint of guilt on her face. She smiled. "You were asking how it felt to be half-fae."

Dropping her chin to her chest, she muttered. "I'm terrible." She hid her face in her hands.

Jastyn laughed, pulling Aurelia's hands down. "Aurelia, it's natural to be curious."

She shook her head. "Please, forget I asked. Your mother"—she straightened, speaking seriously—"what had she told you of your father before?"

Jastyn pulled her hands back into her own lap. "She told me he was a sailor from another land. I always imagined he was from the East and had been called away, sworn to serve another kingdom." She sighed. "Maybe it was naive of me to believe her. I wanted to think he thought of us, maybe even missed us from time to time." She cleared her throat. "I knew he'd left us, and that was why my mother was imprisoned once it was discovered she was pregnant. But I guess I always hoped he'd been forced to leave. I didn't want to believe he had a choice."

Her eyes glistening, Aurelia shook her head. "How long were you in the dungeons?"

"Until I was two summers old."

"Gods. Jastyn, you were…were…"

"Born into the belly of despair while my mother wore shackles on her hands and feet?" Old resentment boiled anew, and Jastyn's face grew hot. She glanced at Aurelia. "I'm sorry."

Aurelia looked shocked. "*You're* sorry? Jastyn, it's terrible what my family did to you and your mother." She inched closer, bracing her hands on Jastyn's knees. "*You* have nothing to apologize for."

Jastyn's gaze fell, and she bit her cheek, fighting back tears. Remembering where this conversation began, she said, "I was terrible… when my mother told me about who my father is. I didn't even let her explain."

Aurelia squeezed her hands. "Do you have any idea who he is?"

She shook her head. "I didn't stick around long enough to ask. I was so angry." Meeting Aurelia's gaze, she added, "I don't think I really care."

"You don't?"

Shrugging, she replied, "Why should I? He abandoned us."

Softly, Aurelia suggested, "Maybe he had his reasons."

"It doesn't matter."

Starting to say something, Aurelia paused, tilting her head. "Did you hear that?"

Wiping her nose, Jastyn listened. "What?" She watched as Aurelia stood, her face scrunched in concentration.

"Rigo," she called, and he was at her side in moments. "Was that tree there before?"

"It was." He smiled. "M'lady, I would have noticed if we were being followed again."

"Again?" It was Jastyn's turn to stand.

Aurelia waved her off. "He means the tree nymph, the one carrying Roisin's message from the castle."

There was another flash of movement behind the trees, and Jastyn stepped closer, pulling Aurelia back from the towering pines. Coran joined them, and together they stared through the layers of tree trunks, listening.

"Maybe we should set another protection spell tonight," Coran suggested.

Jastyn nodded. They'd gotten too comfortable. She rested her hands on her hips. "Good idea. It's late, anyway. We should turn in." She tugged Aurelia's sleeve. "If you need to go anywhere, let one of us know."

"Don't I always?" Aurelia asked, her tone serious. Jastyn crossed her arms, Coran picked at his nails, and Rigo smiled. She frowned. "If I weren't so tired, I would be offended."

Laughing, Rigo returned to his post while Coran readied their blankets near the fire. Aurelia finished her chamomile batch and let the liquid simmer as she turned in.

Jastyn tucked the honeycomb inside Coran's satchel, then worked with him to set their camp's protection spell around the meadow.

"That seemed like it went well," he said when they were halfway through the incantation, standing opposite where Aurelia slept.

"I didn't tell her about the caves."

"But I thought—"

"It's funny. I was ready to tell her. But when the words came out, all I could think about was my father."

"Your father?"

"The fact that he's a fae."

They shuffled to their lefts, their steps in sync as their hands pressed against their saols, lining the perimeter of their spell. "So she knows you're half-fae?"

Jastyn nodded.

"Well, that's somethin', I suppose."

"Yeah," Jastyn said, glancing past her hands to watch Aurelia hold the blanket around her as the wind picked up. "I guess so."

"Aurelia."

Bolting upright, Aurelia reached for Jastyn. Finding her sound asleep beside her, she released a shaky breath.

Coran, too, slept soundly, sprawled on his back, one arm behind his head as he snored.

Turning, she asked, "Rigo, did you hear that?"

Rigo, standing twenty yards off, showed no signs he'd heard her. She called out again, but he kept his watchful gaze locked on the meadow's opposite edge.

"Aurelia."

Crouching, she peered between the trees. The meadow grass was as high as her knees, and it swayed lazily in the night's cool breeze. Standing, she crept around their campsite.

She pulled back a low-lying branch as layers of fallen bark crunched beneath her feet. After a momentary glance at her group, she stepped through the protection spell's barrier and into the night.

Again, she heard her name. The song-like voice, no longer muffled by the barrier, was that of a woman, and Aurelia found herself drawn to it.

"Who's there?"

An owl hooted, and she spun. When she did, a pair of large, emerald-green eyes stared down at her. Gasping, she stumbled backward, tripping on pinecones until she fell. Cringing at the searing pain in her left shoulder, she hurried to stand and face the stunning woman whose emerald eyes stared hungrily down from a heart-shaped face and whose skin resembled the porcelain Aurelia's family had been gifted from the East.

Quickly crossing her right arm across her chest to brace her shoulder, Aurelia conjured her saol at her side. "Who are you?"

Small, pointed teeth appeared behind lush pink lips that pulled up in a wicked grin. The woman's waist-length silver hair fell in waves over her shoulders, where a deep blue dress wrapped around her flat chest and board-like frame. The dress sparkled beneath the faint moonlight; the tiny shimmering stones sewn into it resembled hundreds of raindrops captured from the clouds.

"I can't believe it," the woman cooed, her voice like a song. But unlike Rigo's melodic tones, hers were captivating and beguiling, wrapping Aurelia in a wave of desire. "My sisters will be entirely envious that it was I who found you first."

"Your sisters?" Aurelia readied her saol and raised her arm, but as she did, the woman caught her fist on a rush of water from her long fingers that left Aurelia's flame nothing but hot air. Her voice shook. "You're a siren."

The woman beamed. "A river siren," she corrected. "And soon to be the first river siren welcomed by the Diarmaid family. The queen offered any river within her kingdom to the siren who could find her daughter and return her to Venostes. My sisters searched the edges of the Wood, but I knew you'd travel farther."

"My mother put you up to this?"

"The rivers will go to us, the hillsides to the gnomes, the trees to the nymphs. It's only a matter of who finds you first." She shrugged. "Looks like I win."

Aurelia felt dizzy. Would her mother truly stop at nothing to get her back? First the saol snares, now this. Not only was she wasting the kingdom's resources on this manhunt, now her mother had wrangled the fae into her game? It was too much.

"Well, I'm afraid you're out of luck," she said, attempting to regain her composure. "I have no intention of going with you or anyone else back to Venostes." When the siren only smiled, Aurelia faltered. "Didn't you hear me?"

The emerald in the siren's eyes swirled, and Aurelia registered an odd sensation beneath her boots. Looking down, she found herself ankle-deep in a puddle of water that was rising quickly.

"I will not be denied my prize." The siren then screamed, a piercing pitch. Aurelia clapped her hands over her ears as she sank another inch in the snare, her calves now submerged in the enchanted waters.

Tearing through every defensive and counter spell she knew, Aurelia tried to remember a way to stop the water from rising or at least bind the siren's magic long enough for her to make a run for it. But the siren's scream continued, and Aurelia's rattled mind was lost in the numbing cacophony. She sank deeper into the earth when the scream changed. The siren turned, and Aurelia cried out. "Jastyn!"

Her eyes were fiery when she said, "Sorry to interrupt."

A hiss prompted the water to rise higher still, and Aurelia tried to kick free as the pool pulled to her knees.

"She's mine now," the siren said.

Jastyn appeared unfazed, moving to stand beside Aurelia. "I'm afraid she's spoken for."

Boisterous laughter frightened Aurelia and made Jastyn flinch. "Is she?" The siren's movements were as languid as the water she commanded. Her limbs appeared to shift and change like the flowing river. "How can she be, when I see no commitment in the hearts before me?"

Aurelia tried not to panic as the water seeped through her pants. Jastyn tensed, and Aurelia watched helplessly as she stepped forward until she was face-to-face with the siren.

Jastyn spoke through clenched teeth. "Let her go."

Amused, the siren replied, "No."

In one rapid movement, Jastyn conjured her saol and shoved the flame into the siren's chest. Screaming, the siren doubled over, sprays of moisture spiraling from her shoulders. Jastyn's face was hard when she threw another orb, hitting the siren with such force that she was flung into the nearest tree trunk. Stalking forward, Jastyn conjured another saol.

Aurelia shouted. "Jastyn, that's enough!"

Jastyn's shoulders rose and fell. Slowly, she vanquished her blue flame, then spun after a single glare back to the siren, who struggled to stand. Jastyn turned her open palms to Aurelia's boots. "Hold still." She muttered, "*A bheith gaile.*"

The water trap began to simmer. Aurelia wondered how she didn't feel a flick of heat as the water bubbled to a boil. Within seconds, it evaporated, white hot strands of steam dissipating into the night air. When not a single drop was left, Aurelia said, "How did you do that?"

"One of Eegit's tricks."

"I'll have to remember that."

"The queen will not stop," the siren said. "I'm not the only one she sent. She won't stop until she gets what she wants."

Turning, Aurelia held on to Jastyn's forearm as the siren slithered closer. Fed up, Aurelia met her alluring gaze with a will of stone. "Tell the queen I have no interest in her games. I've escaped her snares, and I will continue to elude her until she understands that I will not return to a kingdom run by people afraid of the truth."

Another hiss prompted a rush of water to flow from the siren's shoulders. It fell like a cape around her. Then in a wave like a waterfall, it encapsulated her, and she was gone.

"Well, that was a rather rude departure." Aurelia smiled, but her face fell when she looked at Jastyn, whose arms were crossed expectantly.

Shrinking, Aurelia said, "I know, I know. 'Tell us before you wander off.'" She glanced around. "Perhaps now I understand what you all were saying earlier. In my defense, I did try to get Rigo's attention."

They turned and wandered back through the trees toward their camp. Jastyn relaxed. "I believe you," she said eventually. "A siren's call can only be heard by the one they're trying to lure."

"See? It wasn't completely my fault." Aurelia grinned, relieved at the smile on Jastyn's face. "If it makes you feel better, I tripped over a pinecone. My shoulder feels like it's been pounded with a giant's hammer." She held it gingerly, giving an exaggerated pout, hoping to keep Jastyn's mood light. It appeared to work.

"Whatever will we do with you, Princess?"

Exhaling, Aurelia stepped back through the protection spell's threshold, grabbing Jastyn's hand. "I'm hopeless at this whole adventure thing, aren't I?"

Rigo rushed over to them. "Your Highness!"

"I'm all right."

"I didn't even notice—"

"You wouldn't have," Jastyn assured him. "A siren tried to pay us a visit."

"A siren? So far out here?"

"The queen is pooling her resources to bring her daughter back." Jastyn sat down on her blanket next to the fire, avoiding Aurelia's gaze.

"I'm sorry for all of the trouble she's causing," Aurelia said. "It is not my intention to make our days so difficult."

Jastyn poked a skewer into the flames. "We know, Princess."

Aurelia frowned. "Do you?" When Jastyn didn't answer, a seed of insecurity took root in her chest. She let the sting of Jastyn's silence usher the words from her throat. "Perhaps I would have been better off staying back in the castle."

Her companions shared a look, and Aurelia sat, her legs unstable. The first buds of disbelief blossomed. She glanced between them as their silence dragged on. "Is that how you both feel? Is that how you've felt this whole time?"

Jastyn reached out. "Aurelia, we're only worried about your well-being."

"You and my mother." Her words came out sharper than she would have liked, and she regretted them as Jastyn's face turned from concerned to shocked.

"Perhaps," Rigo said, "we all should rest and discuss this in the morning."

Feeling dizzy, Aurelia shoved herself under a blanket, yanking it up to her chin. She couldn't believe what she was hearing. Had they been thinking that the entire time? Was Jastyn merely putting up with her, placating her every whim? She huffed. "That is a wonderful idea."

"Aurelia—"

She tugged the blanket closer around her. "Good night."

Jastyn clearly wanted to say something; Aurelia could practically hear the way her jaw clenched in frustration. But she didn't care. She let her mind race with thoughts, recalling all the times she'd slowed them down, all the times she'd had to be saved from some trifling problem. Even tonight she'd been nearly snatched up by a siren. Gods, was she truly such a nuisance?

Tears drifted to the corners of her eyes as Aurelia wondered for the first time if she was really welcome on this journey at all.

Chapter Fifteen

Jastyn's head hurt. She'd gone out of her way to try to make peace with Aurelia last night. She'd even gone to fetch honey, not a particularly easy feat. Not to mention the fact that she had, once again, needed to rescue Aurelia from another misstep, this time in the form of a slippery siren.

How, then, did all of that turn into Aurelia being angry at *her*? Admittedly, she hadn't denied anything when Aurelia had asked if she was a liability. To be honest, Jastyn wasn't sure. Since their travels had begun, Aurelia had developed a habit of stepping in places she shouldn't. Of course, the queen wasn't helping matters, placing saol snare after saol snare in their path. Now she was sending fae after them. That sort of constant badgering couldn't be easy for Aurelia.

"I don't get it," she muttered, sipping a cup of chamomile from the batch that had brewed overnight.

Coran gnawed on his roasted tree-dweller and didn't answer. Rigo had gone to fetch more water at a river he'd spotted on a sunrise scouting.

"I don't know what she wants from me."

He grunted, tossing her a look.

She punched him. "You know what I mean. I thought she was happy out here with us."

"She is."

Gesturing to the sleeping Aurelia, Jastyn asked, "Does that look like a woman happy with where she is?"

"Jas—"

"This is exactly what I was afraid of. I told you she would realize what was happening. She would understand she didn't belong with me...with us," she added, her cheeks hot.

Chewing thoughtfully, he stretched his legs. "You're thinking about this all wrong. Her Highness is right."

"She's what?"

Waving the uneaten half of his breakfast around, he said, "Did you hear anything she said last night? She's worried she hasn't been helpful. She thinks she's slowing us down."

Jastyn considered this. She took another drink, the cup warm between her hands as the sun rose above the trees at their backs.

"I know you're worried about her," Coran continued. "We all are. I've never seen anybody stumble into so many fairies' nests." He smiled, shaking his head. "But I think she's afraid you wish she wasn't here."

Jastyn opened her mouth, then shut it when she remembered what she'd said to Coran not a week before. *I wish she'd stayed where she belonged.*

Her aching head fell into her left palm, her elbow resting on her knee. "Gods. Why is this such a mess?"

He nudged her. "Relationships are never easy."

"You're the expert?" She scoffed.

He held his hands up, finishing the last of his food. "Oh, I didn't say that."

She sat quietly. As the soothing tea made its way down her throat, warming her chest, a thought occurred to her. Perhaps she did have a bad habit that she wasn't owning up to. Communication was not her strong point. But thinking back on everything, she was beginning to see her pattern of cutting off communication before it even started. She had done it with Elisedd since meeting him. She'd done it with her mother before all of this. And she was doing it now with Aurelia.

She sighed. On one hand, Aurelia drove her absolutely mad. On the other, she made Jastyn want to run through the Wood, leaping gleefully from tree root to tree root with outstretched arms. Aurelia made her wonder what they taught in the castle, then surprised her with an endless supply of medicinal knowledge she was eager to share. She was absolutely helpless on a hike but the best of traveling companions. She was a Diarmaid, yet she stood for everything her family did not.

Aurelia was a conundrum that Jastyn was not ready to give up on, as hard as she tried.

"I'll talk to her," she said, and Coran nodded as Rigo wandered back into their camp. Meanwhile, Aurelia stirred.

"The flasks are full," Rigo announced. "There is also a surplus of trout in the river nearby. A day of fishing might be fun." The last sentence was said with a pointed look at Jastyn, who read his message loud and clear.

Across the fire, Aurelia stretched, yawned, and sat up. Jastyn tried not to smile at the cluster of pine needles sticking up in the back of her hair. Biting her lip, she cleared her throat, looking at Coran.

"Good morning, Your Highness," he said. "You, um, have a little something." He gestured to the back of his own hair.

Aurelia frowned and reached up. "Oh," she said, combing out the needles. "Thank you."

An awkward silence fell over them. Eventually, Jastyn said, "We're going fishing today."

Aurelia's eyes lit up, her face excited. Then, seeming to remember she was angry at them, she turned up her chin as she stood to fold her blanket. "I see. How wonderful."

Rigo leaned on his bow, face amused. Coran nudged Jastyn, who shook her head vehemently, kicking his shin until he said, "Our village has some of the best fisherman. We can show you a thing or two about it. Care to join us?"

Jastyn wasn't sure if Aurelia didn't hear him or was purposefully ignoring him. She only swiped off her pant legs, looking anywhere but at Coran.

"A trout sounds mighty good, doesn't it?" Jastyn asked, raising her eyebrows to Coran, who smiled and followed along.

"At this time of year? Delicious." He made an exaggerated show of smacking his lips, rubbing his stomach. "I bet we could catch ten, even twenty of 'em by midday."

"Thirty, easy."

They both grinned when Aurelia replied. "Well," she started, her hands on her hips. "I have always wanted to try my hand at fishing."

Pursing her lips, Jastyn clapped her hands. "Perfect. After breakfast, we'll head to the river." She ignored Rigo's bemused look. Maybe this could get things back on track. They could hardly spare the time, but if it meant keeping Aurelia on their good side, she was less likely to do something rash, like leave their group—and Jastyn—behind.

❖

"I got another one!"

"Good for you," Jastyn hollered at Coran, glaring downstream where he stood proudly displaying his latest catch on the end of his makeshift spear, one of four she and Rigo had carved from the fallen limbs of a nearby cottonwood. Grinning, he waved the wriggling trout skyward. Trudging through a shallow part in the river, Coran bent to roll up his unruly left pant leg before adding the fish to his robust collection on the bank. The nearly fifteen fish flopped limply in the pile next to his discarded boots and satchel.

"I must say, Coran is quite the fisherman." Aurelia waved encouragingly at him, laughing as he struck a triumphant pose.

"Don't worry, Jas," he shouted across the thirty yards between his fishing spot and hers in the steady, churning river cutting through the grassy meadowlands. "I'm sure your luck will turn around."

The Mountains of Ionad were now at their backs to the east, and the sun was high in the sky and made the scales on the fish gleam like jewels as Jastyn eyed them enviously. She mumbled, "Not likely," as she stood on bare feet with her pant legs rolled above her knees. She scanned the blue water flowing past, tracking the shadows of trout swimming in sharp, ever-changing patterns on their way downstream.

"I'm sure it's much harder than it looks."

Choosing to ignore Aurelia's teasing, she threw a sad glance to her own pile of trout—a meager four—gathered next to Aurelia on the bank near Jastyn's boots. Inhaling the fresh, late summer air, she readjusted her stance and aimed her spear.

When the shadow darted past, she struck, the tip of her spear piercing the water and unfortunately, nothing else. The trout she'd hoped for swam easily past, unfazed by her attempt.

Trudging empty-handed back to the bank, Jastyn tried not to feel unworthy as she took a seat next to Aurelia.

"It wasn't all bad," Aurelia said. "Look at our spoils." She gestured to the four open-mouthed trout next to her.

"I guess."

"Cheer up. You may not have as many as Coran, but you have infinitely more than Rigo."

Rigo was standing in the middle of the river's current. He hadn't moved in nearly an hour. Like a statue, he stood still, his palms open at his sides, his feet planted shoulder-length apart. His long silver hair looked nearly white in the bright sun while his eyes remained closed. Jastyn envied the sense of peace surrounding him.

Aurelia eyed him quizzically. "I'm not entirely certain I know what he is doing."

Jastyn chuckled. Cupping her hands around her mouth, she shouted, "Doing all right over there?" Rigo opened one eye, turning slightly in acknowledgment. "Well, carry on, then."

Aurelia laughed, and Jastyn glanced sideways to admire the light reflecting off her hair, the way her nose crinkled when she smiled, and the openness of her face as she laughed. Jastyn held on to the moment's lightness, tucking it away.

"I believe elves pull their powers from the elements," Jastyn said, fiddling with the splinters on the end of the spear resting across her lap.

Pushing back strands of hair, Aurelia nodded, still smiling. "Oh, of course. I knew that. Mother would be ashamed, considering how many weeks she made me spend over volumes of elven culture and history. It's quite fascinating, actually."

Jastyn dropped her feet in the cool water, enjoying the way Aurelia commanded attention as she spoke.

"Their magic is rooted in the four elements, much like our own. But while humans tend to command fire and on occasion, wind, the other two elements of water and earth are more commonly utilized by fae. Legend has it the northern elves have an entire lake devoted to the regeneration of their powers."

"The Lake of Agder."

"You know it?"

"Only in stories."

They both watched Rigo standing in the river. It may have been a trick of the sunlight, but he looked taller as he absorbed the strength of the water swirling steadily around him.

A rather large splash caught their attention. "Another one?" Jastyn asked in disbelief.

"That's seventeen," Coran shouted. He waved the speared fish, nearly tripping as he hurried back to add to his growing assembly.

"All right," Aurelia said, standing and kicking off her boots. She bent, rolling up one pant leg, then the other. "I think it's time we show him how it's really done, wouldn't you say?" Aurelia picked up the spear that had gone untouched thus far at her side. She gripped it earnestly, placing her free hand on her hip. Looking up, Jastyn's heart skipped at Aurelia's beauty backed by the towering mountains.

Forcing herself to focus, Jastyn turned the spear she held. "Are you saying you want a go?"

She smirked. "How hard can it be?"

Amused, Jastyn watched as Aurelia stepped carefully over the smooth boulders at the bottom of the river. Aurelia's balance, or lack thereof, reminded Jastyn of a young fawn taking its first steps. Eventually, she found her footing a few yards out. Jastyn crossed her legs, her chin propped in her upturned palms, ready to watch what would surely be an entertaining show.

"I can feel your lack of faith from here," Aurelia called over her shoulder as she attempted to find the best grip on the spear.

"You have my complete confidence."

"I see one," Aurelia shouted before jabbing the wrong end of her spear wildly into the bottom of the river. "Oh," she cried, nearly falling headfirst.

Laughing, Jastyn decided to bite her tongue as Aurelia brushed her hair behind her shoulders, her eyes everywhere except on the bank. Another jab, this time with the correct end, again yielded no trout.

"You're rushing. Be patient."

Aurelia lifted her spear above her shoulder, the tip aimed at the flowing waters. "Patience has never been my strong suit."

Jastyn smirked. Aurelia stared into the water, the end of her tongue sticking between her teeth. It was quiet for a while until Aurelia said, "Perhaps I should have considered patience before jumping so imprudently into your journey."

Tilting her head, Jastyn's chest felt tight. "What do you mean?" she asked, though she knew where Aurelia was going with this.

"Jastyn, please." She threw a look over her shoulder, still posed to strike. "Look at me. I can't even do this right."

"Aurelia—"

"You can tell me." Jastyn heard the catch in her voice. "You can tell me that I shouldn't have come."

"But who would gather the logs for our nightly fires?"

Aurelia turned, planting her spear into the bed next to her feet, a hand sitting in judgment on her left hip. "You know what I mean."

Jastyn's gaze fell. "You are anything but useless." She glanced up. "Aurelia, this wouldn't be the same without you."

"I've only slowed you down. Your sister—"

"Is strong," Jastyn replied. "Yes, I am worried about her. But I know she is fighting to hold on until I can get the cure."

Aurelia's mouth opened for a moment, then closed, her eyes thoughtful. She tilted her face skyward, taking in the sun. Lifting the spear out of the water, she turned it over so that the point aimed downward. "Still, I feel silly sometimes. You and Coran are so good at this and I'm..." Angrily, she stabbed at the river. A look of shock graced her face.

"Aurelia?"

"Gods, I've got one." Jastyn hurried forward as Aurelia cried, "What do I do?" Her other hand flew to the spear as she struggled to keep her balance. Water kicked up around her knees as the fish she'd caught flapped to free itself.

"Hold on, keep still." Rushing across the river, Jastyn smiled as Aurelia's wide eyes flew from her to the fish.

"Oh!" She lifted the spear, but in doing so, clipped the end of Jastyn's heel. Jastyn tumbled sideways into the water, landing awkwardly on her backside.

"Jastyn!" Aurelia pulled the spear from the water, the small trout she'd caught still wriggling to be free.

Standing quickly, Jastyn assured her, "I'm all right. Just don't—"

Aurelia rushed to her, but in doing so, fell hard.

"Don't try to run," Jastyn finished.

Sitting waist-deep in the water, Aurelia coughed and sputtered, spear and trout still in hand. When Jastyn tried to stand, she slipped on the slick boulders, and they both fell into a fit of laughter, sitting contentedly in the middle of the river, completely drenched.

"Oy, what're you two doing down there?"

Aurelia called to him, "We're at one with the river!"

This prompted more laughter from Jastyn, who made her way over to Aurelia on her knees. "Are you all right?" she asked, shivering from the cold water.

"Oh, I'm fine." She beamed, showing off her catch. "I've caught my first fish."

Slowly standing, Jastyn pulled Aurelia to her feet. Together, they ventured back to the grass, collapsing in a wave of relief to be on warm, dry land. Aurelia, with a look of determination, pulled the fish off the end of her spear and added it to Jastyn's previous catches. Then she fell onto her back, her chest rising and falling, a smile stretching across her face.

"If only my mother and father could see me now: Aurelia, Princess of Venostes and Fisherwoman Extraordinaire."

Jastyn collapsed on her back next to Aurelia. Their pants and half of their tunics were nearly black, soaked through.

"Thank you," Aurelia said, her gaze on the clouds.

"For what?"

"For not saying it was beginner's luck."

Chuckling, Jastyn turned to rest her cheek on the lush blades of green. Aurelia, her face in profile, seemed lost in the skies above. Jastyn felt the urge to reach out and pull her closer. She could see the quick pulse beating in her neck and ached to feel it beneath her lips.

Closing her eyes, Jastyn inhaled deeply before reaching and finding Aurelia's hand. "I'm glad you're here."

Aurelia turned. Her eyes flashed, her lips curving into a smile. "You don't have to say that."

"I mean what I say, Aurelia."

Lost in her gaze, Jastyn once again felt that force pulling them toward one another. She tried to fight against it but was lost in the radiance of Aurelia as they lay together on the river's edge.

Another big splash sounded from downstream.

Aurelia's voice was low. "Coran must have caught another one."

Jastyn's heart pounded. But another splash, too big to be the clap of a trout's fin, made her sit up. Her stomach sank.

"Coran!"

He was on his knees, his spear already floating away downriver.

"Jas! Something's got me!" His hands shot toward his ankles, tugging against whatever held him down.

Jastyn stood.

"What is it?" Aurelia was also on her feet.

"It won't let go," Coran cried. Another wave lifted from beneath the river. Jastyn thought she saw the end of a brown tail, triple the size of any trout. When the wave subsided, Coran's terrified gaze caught hers right before he was dragged beneath the water.

"Coran!" Jastyn took off. "Rigo," she shouted over her shoulder, and he opened his eyes, returning from his trance. She pointed to where one of Coran's arms poked up from deeper water, already twenty yards downstream from where he'd stood before.

Rigo leapt to the bank.

"Jastyn," Coran shouted.

She skidded to a halt, panic rising in her as his head bobbed above the surface. He gasped for air before whatever had him yanked him back under. Aurelia, still dripping wet, already had her satchel around her shoulder and was scurrying up the bank. Jastyn glanced helplessly to Rigo.

"We'll catch up," he said, hurrying with Aurelia to gather their things. "Go."

Nodding, Jastyn sprinted after Coran, her bare feet pounding along the riverbank. She tracked the sporadic splashes in the middle of the deepening river as Coran struggled to stay above water.

"Hold on, Coran," she shouted, now only ten yards behind. But as she drew closer, the flowing waters turned tumultuous, rocks and fallen logs littering its path. Jastyn considered her saol but decided against throwing it at the raging current, fearing she might do more damage to Coran than his attacker. He surfaced again, wide-eyed with fear as he choked for air. Jastyn picked up her pace, jumping over boulders, slipping along the river's muddy edge.

To her dismay, the river curved, its mouth widening as the grassy meadows gave way to sandier earth and scrub grass. Something sharp jabbed into the bottom of her foot, but she didn't stop. There was another frantic splash as Coran surfaced.

Her legs turned to lead when she saw his eyes closed, his face slack. "No!" She stopped thinking and jumped into the river. Not the strongest swimmer, she struggled to stay afloat as the current swept her up. She kept her eyes on the matted orange of Coran's hair as he continued away.

Once again, he went under. Jastyn's throat tightened. "Coran!" She treaded the deep water, desperately searching. Then she saw it.

Coran's limp body was nudged ashore by the wide snout of a seal. Jastyn's mind felt waterlogged, submerged in a raging bed of confusion. Forcing her legs to work, she swam to shore, hurrying to where Coran lay. The seal barked once, then descended into the water, its shining, brown skin glinting before disappearing.

Jastyn knelt beside Coran. His chin sagged against his chest, and she rushed to lay him flat on his back.

"Coran, wake up." She slapped his cheek once, then twice, but his head only bobbed awkwardly on his neck. "Wake up!"

"Jastyn." Rigo was at her side, Aurelia a few paces behind him, their boots and satchels gathered in her arms.

"Please," she said to Rigo, who knelt opposite Coran's body. "Please help him." Her voice cracked with emotion, but she didn't care.

He motioned her away. "Step back."

Stumbling, she felt sick. How did this happen?

Like she'd seen him do to Vreis, Rigo held his hands inches above Coran's chest as he murmured something Jastyn couldn't hear.

Aurelia fell to her knees nearby, dropping their items, her face slack with disbelief. "Gods."

Memories flooded Jastyn's mind: summers in the Wood hunting, winters huddled by the fire, comparing market spoils, all memories she'd taken for granted with her dearest friend. What if those were all the memories she would get?

When Rigo's eyes closed, none of them breathed.

A gurgle sounded deep within Coran's throat. Then he coughed, and water spewed from his mouth.

Jastyn rushed forward, helping prop him up. Still coughing, Coran expelled more water. When the last of it left him, he fell onto his side as if exhausted.

"You're okay," Jastyn said, swiping his hair off his forehead. His shoulders shook, another line of coughs shaking his chest. She looked up at Rigo. "Thank you."

Rigo nodded. All three of them, for what seemed like the first time, breathed again.

A cold sweat lined her forehead as Jastyn's tear-filled gaze met Aurelia's. She smiled, but her face fell as her gaze shifted to something behind Jastyn's shoulder.

She had barely turned to look when the pointed end of a knife came up hard against her neck.

Wincing, she didn't move as five figures closed on their group, every one gripping a blade. They had black hair and strong arms and wide-set bodies clad in fur-trimmed clothing. Each wore an empty-eyed seal skin as a headdress, its slick body gleaming like the individuals wearing them. She turned her chin up ever so slightly and stared into the jet-black eyes of the man standing over her.

He sneered, revealing large teeth, two menacing canines extending low. "You should have let him drown." He pressed the knife harder into her neck. "Now he will have to die twice."

CHAPTER SIXTEEN

"Where are they taking us?"

Aurelia didn't like the uncertainty of Jastyn's gaze almost as much as she hated the dried line of blood running down Jastyn's neck where the brute's knife had dug into her not five minutes before.

"I'm not sure," Jastyn replied, her voice low as they continued to march. It was nearly nightfall. Aurelia's bare feet ached as they walked over uneven, gritty earth filled with what had to be the world's largest collection of pointy plants. She was certain to find thousands of tiny cuts along her heels and ankles later.

Rigo's voice came from behind them. "We've been heading directly west."

Aurelia glanced back, surprised to find a hunch in his typically strong shoulders. His hands were the only ones that had been bound and draped in some sort of plant. The dark green weed wound tightly around Rigo's wrists, ensuring him no access to the arrows at his back. She and the others, apparently, showed little threat.

Past Rigo, Coran was being pushed brusquely forward every other step by one of the females of this awful group, the same one carrying Rigo's bow. His face, looking paler than normal, wore a blanket of pure exhaustion as he trudged ten paces behind them.

"Surely we'll stop soon," Aurelia said, turning to face Jastyn walking at her side. "It's nearly nightfall."

"I wouldn't pin your hopes on that, Your Highness," Rigo said before he, too, received a callous shove by one of the males. Rigo lifted his lip in disgust, but the male only laughed, slapping one of the female's arms in amusement. Aurelia eyed them curiously. If these were the fae she thought them to be, her many teachings had been proven once again to be chock-full of false fantasies.

Aurelia scanned their other abductors in the fading sunlight. They were all of average height, and none were taller than Rigo, one of the men only coming up to his chin. Still, they each carried themselves with pride. Their incessant laughter sounded more like barks, sharp and short. They all possessed chestnut skin with a glowing sheen. Their broad shoulders were draped with the arms and legs of their seal skins, with the animal's head resting atop their own. The slender snouts dipped into a point on each of their foreheads. The rest of the skin fell against their backs, over where their black hair fell in thick layers. A few had twisted the strands into braids, while others let their locks flow freely. They were all striking, with wide, flat noses and high cheekbones, but a hard edge lined their features.

Aurelia asked a question she had been afraid to utter since midday. "We've been captured by selkies, haven't we?"

Jastyn's silence confirmed her suspicion. According to her schooling, selkies kept to themselves, only attacking sailors at sea. They typically ran from humans, afraid their precious skins would be snatched away and sold. These selkies, she thought, with a furious glance around, had ventured too far inland to match such stories.

To Aurelia's dismay, the selkies marched through the night. Their endless trek continued when the quarter moon rose, and they didn't stop as it rested in its highest perch among the stars, nor when it began its descent toward the western horizon. The wind picked up with the cool night, and Aurelia caught the scent of salt on the breeze. The selkies allowed them all a moment to relieve themselves, along with time to get a drink from their flasks. That was their only respite.

When the sun rose, Aurelia wasn't sure how she was still standing. For brief moments when her eyes fluttered shut, she saw herself in the Wood, bound and gagged as Drest forced her deeper through the trees and away from her kingdom's walls. Another flash and he was being taken by the royal guard. Jerking awake, Aurelia felt relieved that nightmare was over only to realize she was in a new, horrible waking dream. The little comfort she did take was in knowing that this time, she wasn't alone.

When the sun had fully risen and Aurelia was certain she'd faint from hunger, one of the selkie men grunted. "That one's not gonna make it."

Turning, Aurelia saw Coran stumble, tripping on his own feet. His toes were red with dried blood, his shaky legs on the brink of collapsing.

"Please," Aurelia said, casting a pleading look at the selkie who had their boots and satchels draped around his shoulders like trophies. "He needs to rest. We're starving."

"Should've thought about that before you stepped into our river," the leader said. He was the tallest male and gripped the hilt of a dagger he kept in a leather belt at his side, the dagger he'd threatened Jastyn with. His large black eyes matched his companions' in their illusiveness, the lack of white unnerving at first glance.

"Your river? But—"

"Aurelia." Jastyn elbowed her.

Frowning, she shut her mouth.

"At least let me carry him," Rigo said.

"You think you're a clever elf." The stocky woman who pushed him scowled. The head of her skin, with specks of white around its eyes, fell over a wrinkled forehead. "Like we'd untie you."

"Please. You may keep my bow. He is weak."

"Too bad," the only other male said as he lumbered at the back of the group.

The leader turned, holding up a hand. His face was smooth, no lines indicating the passage of time. Even his palm held no signature of age, his skin flawless. Their group stopped. "Gorm, the council requires all trespassers to be captured for questioning. He can't answer anything if he's dead, can he?"

"But Njal—"

"Can he?"

The other selkies grumbled, ultimately nodding. Njal motioned to Rigo. "Thyra, untie him. If he tries anything, he'll have the council to answer to."

The same female unholstered her dagger from her boot and roughly cut Rigo's bonds. He scooped Coran into his arms.

"Keep moving."

Aurelia forced herself to walk. By evening, she glimpsed the shoreline. "Gods, where are they taking us?"

Again, they walked through the night with only a momentary break. The stars shone brightly as the rich meadowlands fell farther behind them. Green, thick-leaved plants grew in dense, ankle-high patches along their path. When the moon was at its highest, Aurelia gasped as her feet hit something she'd thought a dream.

Tears brimmed in her eyes as sand sifted between her toes for the first time in nearly a decade. Had they really made it to the western shores? Though she shivered with fatigue, a small jolt reinvigorated her as the sound of distant waves caressed her ears.

Shocked, she turned to Jastyn, who had been quiet, only throwing occasional worried looks at Coran in Rigo's arms.

"Jastyn," she said, trying to keep her voice low while the selkies carried on their own, boisterous conversations, as they had the last two days. "What if they're taking us to the caves?"

Concern flashed across Jastyn's face. She looked at the stars. "I don't think so," she finally replied. "We're too far south."

The flicker of hope Aurelia had harbored all but went out. She'd been naive to think the selkie could have some connection to the caves. Gods, what if they couldn't get out of this one? What if Jastyn's chance at reaching the caves before it was too late was gone? She closed her eyes, taking a deep breath. Almost three full moons had come and gone. That left three more to find the cure and return to Venostes before Alanna's time was up.

When dawn drenched the eastern sky in a blaze of orange, the leader motioned for them to stop. Jastyn huddled next to Aurelia, Rigo standing close behind with Coran. They stood atop a sand dune with thin reeds of grass waving in a strong wind.

Weak and on the brink of fainting, Aurelia knew she had to be dreaming now. "By the gods."

Against the deep blue sky topped with cerulean stretched the open sea. The shore ran out ahead of them to meet it, gentle waves lapping upon the sand in a never-ending greeting. She closed her eyes, relishing the sound. The one time she and Brennus had gone to the beach, he'd sneaked a single shell back into the castle. For months, she'd held the folded ends of the sacred keepsake to her ear, pretending she was once again standing on the beach. The magic of the ocean had pulled her in, and her composure was quickly unraveling with the reality of where they stood.

After wiping a tear from her cheek, Jastyn wrapped one arm around Aurelia's waist. "Are you all right?" she asked, her voice revealing a similar state of weariness.

Aurelia could only nod. "It's beautiful."

"I wish this was happening under different circumstances."

"At least we're together." She was glad to see the small smile grace Jastyn's lips. The moment was interrupted when the selkies dispersed.

"Gundrun and Thyra will lead most of you home," Njal said. "Gorm," he added with a glare to the selkie standing with his arms crossed over his wide chest, "that includes you."

"But, Njal, it was I who pulled the orange-haired one into the river."

"The council will be grateful. You'll still go with the others."

Dejected, Gorm started for the water alongside his fellow selkies, save for the female who carried their human things. A long pink scar ran from her right ear all the way down to her neck, then disappeared under the seal skin and her brown tunic toward her shoulder, the old injury glaring against her dark skin. "Sif," Njal said to her, "stay with me. We'll have to take them in the boat."

"Boat?" Aurelia looked around, her knees shaking as she was pushed down the dune, closer to the water. She spotted an unassuming rowboat bobbing ten yards to their right.

Jastyn stepped forward, dark circles standing out under her eyes. "Tell us where we're going."

Njal turned. Sif watched, amused. "We are taking you to the council."

"Because we stepped into 'your river'?" Jastyn asked. Aurelia could see her fury growing, the tips of her fingers glowing a pale blue.

Njal laughed. "You humans never cease to amaze me with your stupidity."

Jastyn conjured her saol, albeit a pale, flickering one and threw it at the selkie leader. Aurelia braced herself as the flame hit his shoulder, a quick hiss piercing the crash of waves behind them as his seal skin smoked.

"Maybe the council will keep her," Sif said through a laugh. "She can perform tricks at our annual gathering."

She and Njal bellowed with laughter, which seemed to make

Jastyn angrier, her small frame shaking. When she reared her arm with another saol, Aurelia ran forward, grabbing her elbow.

"Jastyn," she said into her ear. "Now is not the time."

Aurelia could feel her shoulders trembling. Rigo stepped closer. "She's right. We'll learn more if we go." He gestured to Coran. "We can regroup once we get to where we're going."

Jastyn stared at Coran's slack face, his slow chest. Swallowing, she turned back to Aurelia. "All right."

Njal was shaking his head as Sif, still laughing, walked out to pull the boat closer. The other selkies lined up along the sand five yards to their left, standing an arm's length apart and knee-deep in the sea's swirling waters. Holding on to Jastyn, Aurelia watched, mesmerized, as they raised their arms. The seal skins extended, wrapping their gleaming limbs around their human counterparts. Their figures shifted, growing shorter and sleeker. Hands and feet transformed into fins until four regal seals sat with their snouts proudly lifted to the rising sun.

"Have you ever seen anything like it?" Aurelia asked.

Only awed silence answered her.

Njal waved as his comrades each gave a satisfied bark, then dove under the waves and out of sight. "Come," he said, turning his attention back to their group.

Jastyn's grip returned to Aurelia's waist.

"If you want your things," Sif called, already in the boat, "I suggest you hop in."

"Come on," Rigo said, stepping past them.

When Jastyn didn't move, Aurelia squared to face her. "We'd better go." Her eyes filled with something Aurelia couldn't pinpoint. She stared at where the selkies had transformed moments before. "Jastyn?"

She swallowed. "We'll be okay," she said, her gaze unfocused. "We have to be okay."

Aurelia hoped her odd comments a result of hunger and dehydration and willed herself to believe what Jastyn said. A terrible feeling wrapped inside her chest, though, as the four of them crushed together in the boat and watched as the land they'd wandered for months slowly disappeared behind them.

CHAPTER SEVENTEEN

Sleep once again threatened to draw its dark blanket over Jastyn's mind, but she willed herself to stay awake. Her stomach was so empty it felt shriveled like a leaf in winter, and her throat was so dry it hurt to swallow. Fortunately, the selkies didn't seem interested in talking as they rowed their boat farther from shore. They'd gone west for a few hours, rowing farther than Jastyn had ever gone into the ocean. Once they were past the churning current, they followed the curving shoreline that jutted into the sea like a leg, its rocky foot curving to the north.

With the sun high, Jastyn shifted in the boat's floor next to Aurelia. Sif sat in front, navigating, while Njal rowed in the center. Rigo and Coran, the latter drifting in and out of consciousness, were packed tightly in the rear.

"May we have some water, please?" Jastyn asked Njal. While her neck still pricked with the ghost of his dagger, she held a kernel of respect for him. He and the other selkies were unlike any fae she'd ever met, yet something about him was familiar. He commanded his troop with a just coldness, but he couldn't hide the soft look in his dark eyes as he glanced back at Coran. "It's so hot," she added, gesturing at the sweltering sun. "Please."

He glanced from the waves to her. "Very well."

Sif turned, tossing Jastyn the flask with hardly a glance.

"Thank you." She took a sip, then handed it to Aurelia. "Drink a little, it'll help." Aurelia, who had appeared excited at stepping into a boat for the first time in her life, was looking rather green now. Jastyn encouraged her as she took a slow drink and gulped hard to keep the water down.

"I feel like I'm going to be ill," she breathed, clutching her stomach.

Jastyn smiled. "I thought the royal family had a strong constitution."

Aurelia shot her a look, though it withered quickly as she hiccupped. "Now is hardly the time for teasing."

Jastyn turned to watch the waves lift their boat before setting it into the gentle swells. She'd gone out to sea a few times with Coran and his family and other times with her mother when they'd been desperate for food. But the western sea held a different sort of enchantment; the sunlight glistened off the blue-green depths like glittering diamonds. She took comfort in the fact that, despite the awful conditions of the trek, they were at least on the coast. The caves were only a few days north, according to Eegit's old calculations. Even though this was another unexpected interruption, she was not too far off track from her goal.

Wherever they were going, Jastyn hoped this council would see reason. The river they had been fishing in was on public fae lands, as far as she knew. Selkies were not ones to wander so far inland. As her head lolled, the bruises on her neck added an ache to her already sore body, and she wondered what had driven the selkies there. Over the last twenty years, all of the fae had grown more territorial, more protective of land after they'd lost more than a third of its vastness to encroaching humans. The three royal kingdoms had taken what was rightfully theirs, in their minds, anyway. As Aurelia had recounted weeks ago around the fire, cohabitation between fae and humans had been attempted in the early days of the royal families, nearly two centuries before. Peace had reigned for a short time.

Then a deadly famine brought to their realm by fae magic swept over the kingdoms of Gultero and Venostes. This triggered an endless tirade by the mighty royals until the responsible fae and anyone suspected of being privy to the awful plague had been eradicated. Lines had been drawn, and the three laws of Venostes had been locked into ink.

The nose of the boat dipped, water splashing up its sides and spraying their sunburned faces. Perhaps, Jastyn thought as she kept her gaze on Njal, the selkies had already fallen prey to the dark force that seemed intent on bringing back the old, hateful beliefs of the first royal families. It would explain their behavior.

Sunlight glinted off the dagger on Sif's hip as she faced the bow, her beady eyes scanning their choppy path. The bright light blinded Jastyn momentarily. It hung from a ring at her right side. The handle was off-white, most likely carved from bone. The silver blade was beautifully sharp, a sign that she took great care to maintain it. Jastyn's hand drifted to the vacant sheath of her right boot. She hated that she'd lost it. Even more, she hated the sense of insecurity she felt without it.

The hot sun mixed with lack of sleep was causing her mind to drift. Her eyelids heavy, she fought to stay awake.

"Watch the starboard side!"

Njal's voice cut through the sleep. Next to her, Aurelia stirred as a deep crunch, followed by an awful scraping sounded from the side of their boat. They'd landed on shore.

Blinking, Jastyn discovered the sun was already sinking toward the horizon, burning yellow giving way to deep pinks and streaks of lavender.

"Where are we?" Coran asked.

Jastyn jerked her head at his first words since the river.

Njal pulled the oars in as Sif jumped out onto wet black rock covering this new stretch of coastline. As Njal joined her, Jastyn scurried to the back of the boat. "Coran, can you hear me?"

His eyes were dilated and his body limp. To her dismay, his eyes fluttered shut.

"Coran?"

"Everyone out." Njal's stocky figure looked even more intimidating framed by the layers of cragged rocks. "I said out."

Jastyn glared as Rigo lifted Coran. She followed them out of the boat, helping Aurelia step carefully onto uneven rocks pocketed by deep crevices waiting to claim unsteady feet.

Sif was already twenty yards ahead, Rigo's bow over her left shoulder as she walked easily along the treacherous boulders.

"How much farther?" Jastyn asked, still holding Aurelia's hand. She looked pale as she placed one of their satchels over her shoulder, her eyes darting frantically as a crab scurried across her boots.

Njal tugged the boat onto a gritty patch of sand between two rocks. "We'll be with the council by dark."

They staggered to the shoreline via a well-worn path cut into the black rock. The narrow path continued toward the towering cliffsides, their plateaus jutting menacingly overhead. Jastyn wondered how their bases—cut five yards farther inland—managed to withstand the weight of their upper halves. On the beach, the sea sent a continuous spray up against their left sides as they turned northwest between the black rock and the cliffs.

They walked single file, Jastyn close behind Aurelia with Rigo and Coran at her back. Sif became a dark shadow up ahead as the sun set to their left. She motioned for their attention. "Through here."

Jastyn tried not to panic at the gaping mouth of a cave. Aurelia's breath caught. "Gods, not another one."

Sif turned, and Jastyn saw the gleam of her smile. "What is it with humans and their irrational fear of the dark?"

Next to her, Aurelia could only squeak.

"At least let us conjure our saols," Jastyn said as she stepped closer.

Behind them, Njal's deep voice echoed. "Don't bother. It's a thoroughfare. We'll be in and out of it before you can even conjure it."

Aurelia reached back, and Jastyn took her hand briefly before saying, "It'll be okay." She wasn't sure why, but she actually believed what she said. An odd sense of calm washed over her as they stepped into darkness. It was the same calm that had kept her from panicking upon their capture. The selkies were a hard fae, but part of her knew they were victims of an obscene regime. This familiarity gave her comfort. She only hoped her sense of security would be justified.

They walked only a few minutes before the passage curved again and a smaller mouth spit them out into fast-fading twilight.

It was Jastyn's turn to stop in her tracks as Aurelia took the words from her mouth. "By the gods."

An expansive, moon-shaped cove opened before them, sand running up against the cliffsides towering over the curved shore. A path bordered by rocks led from where they stood toward the cove's center. But it wasn't the cove itself that took Jastyn's breath away. In the lazily swirling water sat half a dozen ships. Or what used to be ships. Only one retained its complete shape, the massive wooden hull marred by a scattering of gaping holes in its side. The tall mast had splintered and leaned to the left, looming ominously over the deck. The immense structure looked like a giant fairy's nest under the darkening sky; twinkling lights filled every hole within, and figures moved in and out of the ship's bulky body.

"It's like a village," Aurelia said, her voice conveying the same sense of awe Jastyn felt. From the center ship, long planks of wood stretched like arms, connecting to the other shipwrecks resting along the shore or anchored in the shallow water. Those on the shore appeared to have fallen victim to the rocks as the slick black boulders jutted through the boards, splitting open bows and sterns and redistributing their pieces along the cove. More planks weaved in and out of the decrepit parts, creating dozens of walkways. From where they stood, Jastyn imagined she was staring up at the Diarmaid castle, the glimmering lights and layers of the selkie colony gleaming regally from its secret cove. It was, indeed, a sprawling city all on its own.

"Keep moving."

Sif shoved a fist into her lower back. She'd doubled back while Njal stood at the front of their group. As they moved closer to the towering ships, Jastyn heard splashes. Dark outlines of seals poked their curious heads out of the sea. A few swam closer, dove under, then reappeared as their forms stretched and grew until human figures walked onto the land before disappearing into one of the many ships.

"Up here." Sif led them up an inclined plank twenty yards from the water. Jastyn walked carefully as that board led to another resting on top of it that twisted left, followed by three more leading them higher until, ducking low, she and the others entered the extensive hull of the main ship. The area was dimly lit, its floor damp and covered in seaweed. The unmistakable scent of fresh trout laced with salt overwhelmed her as she spotted barrels upon barrels of fish. A storage room? She could practically taste the open ocean as they continued toward the opposite end where another ladder waited, this one climbing straight up into the second deck.

"Coran," Rigo said quietly as Aurelia, trailing Sif, gave Jastyn a wary glance before ascending. "We have to climb now."

Jastyn's heart ached as he stumbled when Rigo set him down and struggled to keep his balance. Njal watched as she helped Rigo push Coran up the ladder, his trembling hands barely gripping the rungs.

When his torso made it up, Jastyn pushed until he could crawl through. She followed, Rigo at her side. In moments, he scooped Coran up, propping him under his shoulder.

Coran's eyes opened and closed slowly. "Jas," he muttered. "Where are we?"

Glancing around as Njal climbed easily through the hatch, she took in a space that was as large as her village. The floorboards seemed stronger than those below, their higher position allowing for less water damage over time. A single, circular window opened into this deck, but the dark night allowed little in the way of a view. Ahead, Sif stepped through a hanging curtain, its woven reeds swaying in her wake. Jastyn caught a glimpse of a vast, well-lit chamber before the reeds closed.

Her heart racing with uncertainty, Jastyn stepped closer to Coran. She squeezed his arm. "I'm not sure. But we're going to be okay."

I hope we're going to be okay.

Rigo looked nervous for the first time, his typically calm veneer swept away with the tumultuous happenings of the last few days. Aurelia's eyes brimmed with frightened tears as Njal stood patiently behind them, one hand on his dagger.

When Sif walked back through, holding the curtain for them, Jastyn's chest tightened.

"The council is ready for you now."

Chapter Eighteen

A urelia was blinded by blazing light. Stunned, she shielded her eyes as she was shoved through the curtain and into the council chamber. Blinking, she thought for a moment she'd lost consciousness as the light gave way to a dark star, its five looming points encircled by a flaming yellow glare. She'd imagined the palace of the gods looking like this, foreboding and awesome in its grandeur.

Slowly, the bright lights shrank and revealed their true nature, the flames of torches encircling the vast chamber. The light danced off wooden beams racing overhead and running down the curved walls of the ship's belly before snaking beneath their feet. The old wood creaked under each step. Stumbling, she reached for Jastyn to steady her and glanced behind to find Rigo still holding Coran. Njal quickly walked past to join Sif, who stood proudly in the center of the room.

"Four prisoners for your consideration." Sif's words sounded boastful, spoken with her hands on her hips. "They were discovered stealing trout from our river to the east, the river that flows directly into *our* sea."

Aurelia's vision cleared as she leaned into Jastyn. The dark shape before them was not a heavenly body at all but the shadowy edges of a pentagon, each point a single, looming chair whereupon a member of the council sat.

"Bring them forward." The feminine voice came from the top of the star, in the chair opposite where Aurelia stood. She forced her tired gaze onto the black-haired selkie, whose brown skin seemed more leathery than smooth. Her dark eyes were large, reminding Aurelia of a giant bat. The seal skin sitting atop her tall forehead was framed in a mask of white. Its brown spots ran past her shoulders along with her hair, landing atop her large bust.

"Is the orange one even alive?" Beside the aged female sat an equally old male with age lines etched into his skin. "He looks ready for the Otherworld," he added with a disgusted sneer on his thin lips. He pushed back his shoulder-length black hair. His seal skin wasn't as white as the female's but still looked worn with time.

"I think he's only unconscious, Colborn." The warmth of the third voice drew Aurelia's attention to the other side of the room. This selkie was younger, his dark eyes softer and filled with curiosity as he tilted his head as if to get a better look. "My, what a great many spots he has." The chair to his right was vacant.

"No doubt from some disease." Turning, Aurelia found the fourth councilmember. She looked to be Aurelia's mother's age, her seal skin gleaming, and her black hair in two beautiful plaits running over her shoulders.

"Yrse, not all humans carry disease," the younger male said defensively.

"You're right, Fortan. Only the ones too stupid to protect themselves."

The older male selkie, Colborn, chuckled. Jastyn tensed beside Aurelia, who swayed with the voices pinging back and forth around a chamber that smelled like salt and something she couldn't place, something of the earth, like the quartz she'd found once with Brennus.

Holding up a vein-riddled hand, the oldest female's voice rose above the others. "That's enough."

The other selkies' eyes fell, and they muttered, "Apologies, Revna."

Revna glared at them a moment more, then refocused on the human group. "Njal, speak."

Aurelia was surprised to see him take a trembling knee before the council. "Revna, what Sif speaks is the truth. The orange one and those women were caught fishing in the western river. They'd taken nearly twenty of our summer supplies for themselves, with no consideration as to where they were."

Yrse snorted, but Fortan said, "Perhaps they did not recognize the terrain."

"Perhaps they knew exactly what they were doing." Colborn sat back in his chair, the white frame bright against the darkness of his tunic and general demeanor.

Revna rolled her eyes before she said, "Please, everyone."

The room fell quiet. Coran whimpered and curled into a tired ball in Rigo's arms.

Revna looked them all over. "Where are they from?"

Njal and Sif exchanged glances. The latter stammered when Njal bowed his head. "We were hasty in their arrest."

"You did not think to ask?"

Sif stammered, "With respect, Revna, they were in our river. What right did they have—"

Revna stood, suddenly as tall as the room itself. Thunder clapped, and the torchlight threw menacing shadows over her formerly serene face. "What right did *you* have to snatch the princess of Venostes up from the Wildlands and bring her into our sacred space?"

Sif was on her knees, her forehead pressed to Revna's feet. Njal stared at the ground, shaking. "Princess?"

Aurelia was as shocked as the others. How did this selkie know who she was? Trembling, she clutched Jastyn's arm. Rigo stepped closer behind them.

"What is a member of the royal family doing so far from home?" Yrse's question was laced with malicious intrigue, and Aurelia shrank as she leered at them hungrily.

"Oh, sit down, Yrse," Fortan said. "You'll frighten the poor thing."

The room slowed its rocking from Revna's tumult. Sif stood, cowering behind Njal. Colborn's baritone echoed. "So we have a half-dead human, an elf, a princess, and…" Aurelia watched him scrutinize Jastyn. "You look familiar."

Jastyn clenched her hands into fists. "I do not know you."

"What is your name?"

Aurelia, sick with worry, glanced between the selkies. She didn't like the way these fae were eyeing them. Selkies were notoriously slippery, silver-tongued cousins of the sirens, able to lure ships toward their haven before devouring the unfortunate souls on board.

Jastyn pulled her tired shoulders back. "My name is Jastyn Cipher."

Revna took her seat slowly, a small smile gracing her lips. "An Odium rounds out the group."

Fortan, crossing his legs and lacing his fingers beneath his chin said, "My, how intriguing."

"Are we to believe the princess of Venostes walks with an Odium and a fae?" Yrse asked, disbelief obvious in her tone.

The malice in her voice gave Aurelia the smallest ounce of fortitude, and she lifted her chin. "The Diarmaid family is not what many believe them to be."

"Is that so?" Colborn asked, an interested eyebrow up.

"Aurelia," Jastyn muttered.

She ignored her, standing taller and stepping toward Revna. "I travel willingly with Jastyn, the Odium, as you call her. She is on a journey for a cure, and we are committed to fulfilling our mission no matter the consequences."

Fortan's mouth was open, amused. Yrse looked on the verge of pouncing. Colborn and Revna exchanged glances. After a moment, all except Revna burst into laughter. Confused, Aurelia muttered, "I do not see the humor in such a situation."

"Forgive my council," Revna said, glaring daggers toward her fellow selkies when each failed to quiet their laughter. "As you know, Your Highness, human and fae do not walk the same path, thanks to the very laws set in place by your family."

Aurelia stepped back. Something in Revna's tone made her skin itch. She was nearly impossible to read.

"Still, humans and fae have mingled in the shadows for centuries. But never in my lifetime has a human given up their home to *help* an Odium."

Aurelia blushed. Glancing at Jastyn, she wondered if the council could sense her feelings.

Revna's tone was even. "You must understand, then, how inconceivable your story is."

Frowning, Aurelia replied, "With respect, what I say is true. Jastyn is on a quest to help her ailing sister. Our paths crossed unexpectedly nearly five moons ago and…" She faltered, turning to Jastyn, whose face was hard, her eyes glued to the selkies before them. When Aurelia grabbed Jastyn's left hand, intertwining their fingers, Jastyn finally met her gaze. "The gods made sure that we met. Much has happened since then." Her gaze swung back to the council. "A great dark force has swept over my kingdom, as well as many of the fae lands to the east."

The selkies fell quiet. Colborn cleared his throat, exchanging glances with Yrse and Revna.

Aurelia, sensing she'd caught their attention, continued, "You are familiar with the darkness I speak of?"

"There have been rumors," Fortan said. He fingered a worn coin at the end of a leather necklace resting over his gray tunic. It was the same as each of the council members wore. "But stories of a Dark Fae have circulated for ages."

"He is more than story." Jastyn said, still holding onto Aurelia's hand. "The Dark Fae has followed me more than half my life."

Aurelia took a breath, adding, "We believe he is the same dark force whose influence has injected itself into our homeland. It robbed my brother of his life and has even penetrated the northern territories." She felt Jastyn's gaze but felt a sharp desire to explain.

Rigo's light voice added, "My queen has fallen prey to his will. I fear she has been misguided and seeks to protect her people through the ways of the Dark Fae. Ways that brings death and destruction to those who don't agree with her vision."

For a time, the only sound was the constant creaking of the ship from the gentle rocking of the sea below.

"Why do you all care about this Dark Fae?" Colborn asked. "If this is the Dark Fae of legend, the Odium is the only one he desires."

Jastyn's jaw stiffened, but Aurelia squeezed her arm. "The Dark Fae's beliefs led to my brother's murder. He poisoned the weak mind of a member of our court. As a result, I am the remaining heir to the Diarmaid throne. It is on my shoulders to right the wrongs of my kingdom's past." Pointedly, she looked at each of the selkies. "If that means helping to defeat this Dark Fae"—she paused—"so be it."

Yrse barked a laugh. "Your family is responsible for the murder of thousands of fae. And everyone knows how the Diarmaids treat women who bear offspring without a mate." She scoffed. "It's archaic."

The sting of her words burned Aurelia like fire, but she fought the shame inside her. "I have come to understand that," she said. "I understand the Dark Fae must be defeated before his teachings can penetrate more of the realm. I trust he has not made his way to you?" she asked, pulling her courage up to meet Revna's gaze.

"The selkies' cove is a secret to all, save for the unfortunate sailors who find themselves adrift."

"Fortunately, they never get a chance to reveal what they found." Colborn's wide smile was unsettling, and Aurelia shivered.

It fell quiet again. Revna watched them, her dark eyes analyzing each piece of their story.

Yrse broke the silence. "Revna, please tell me you do not believe this outlandish tale."

"Humans and fae walked together once before," Fortan mused. "It's not impossible."

"Only highly improbable," Colborn muttered, his dark gaze fixed on Jastyn. Njal and Sif, who had taken a knee next to Revna's chair, appeared stunned.

Finally, Revna spoke. "This has been quite the story." She glanced around. "We mustn't forget the reason you were brought in. The river you were found trespassing in does belong to the selkies. You have been charged with stealing food that is rightfully ours."

"Wait," Aurelia said. "We didn't know." This was not how she'd hoped this would go. Revna wouldn't show pity? Surely she could see Aurelia was telling the truth? "Please, we didn't know it was yours. We were tired and hungry, that's all."

Revna ignored her. "Our council is incomplete. When Tove returns, we will deliberate and reconvene with their sentence."

Aurelia's knees felt like water, and her head spun. "Wh...what does that mean?"

Standing, Sif and Njal moved toward them. Sif sneered gleefully. "It means you belong to us."

Aurelia stepped back, running into Rigo. "Wait. You don't understand."

But her voice was lost over Revna's orders. "Take them away. I want them in separate chambers."

"No." Aurelia held tighter to Jastyn as Sif grabbed her shoulders, pulling her backward. "Jastyn!"

Jastyn struggled, but Njal picked her up easily. Aurelia tried to hold on to her, but they were torn apart. Jastyn kicked, but it was no use. Aurelia turned to Rigo, but a third guard appeared and tied a lasso of seaweed tight around him, and he slumped in defeat with Coran in his arms. The guard shoved him forward. With one more glance back at Aurelia, he disappeared through a doorway.

"Please," Aurelia cried. "Let me explain." Her shouts were in vain. Sif yanked her arms behind her back, and she screamed at the pain in her shoulders.

"Aurelia!" Jastyn's voice was muffled as Njal covered her mouth. Aurelia held her gaze for a moment before she was hauled from the room behind Fortan's chair, disappearing into the shadows.

"Jastyn!"

Sif pulled her arms again, forcing her into submission. "Gods, you humans are loud."

Then a searing pain struck Aurelia in the back of the head, and there was darkness.

Chapter Nineteen

Jastyn drifted in and out of consciousness. The splintered wood floor she slept on stank of rotten fish, the smell waking her sporadically with fits of nausea. Her eyelids lifted heavily each time, meeting the faintly lit room. A pair of candles sat in a metal tray on the floor, flickering sadly. The first time she'd woken, she reached for her braid and heard the soft clink of metal from the shackles around her wrists. The attached chain snaked behind her to a thick, grime-encrusted bolt. Exhausted, she'd fallen asleep once again.

The second time, she stirred from a loud creak and sudden light as the door opened. A quick tread moved close, followed by the dull thud of something placed a foot from her grasp. When the steps left and the door closed, she reached out to find a cup of water. Sniffing it first, she gulped it gratefully.

Later, when she opened her eyes to Aurelia, Jastyn knew she was at the point in starvation where her mind was conjuring images.

"I'm sorry," she muttered tiredly to Aurelia, who lay on her side, stroking Jastyn's face.

"You need to stop blaming yourself for everything." Aurelia's gaze was like a rock, anchoring Jastyn to what was real.

"I haven't been honest with you." Jastyn's eyes watered, her body weak with hunger. "I don't know how to be."

She only wiped her tears away. "I trust you, Jastyn."

"We're so close to the cure."

"I know."

"I'm so tired."

"Hold on, Jastyn."

"What if I can't?"

Aurelia smiled, then leaned in, kissing her. Though she knew it wasn't real, Jastyn relished the feel of Aurelia's lips. She drank in Aurelia's scent, earth and tulips.

Drifting off again, Jastyn tried not to think about the pain in her stomach as it twisted, searching for nourishment she hadn't had in days. She hated the feel of the chains around her wrists. She didn't remember the dungeons of Diarmaid castle. Her mother had never spoken of it. Jastyn wondered if this was what it had felt like, this sickening sense of helplessness.

Lying on her back, she tried to focus her thoughts. If she dwelled too long on the misery, she'd be lost. She had to try to remember the good: she was alive. That was something. She hoped the others were, too. Perhaps they would show mercy to Coran. She smiled, knowing Aurelia was too stubborn to give up. Her vision had been right. If she could hold on, they had a chance. Alanna's time was slipping away, but they were close. Jastyn could feel it. But how to get out of these ships and to the caves?

Again, the door opened. Jastyn met the harsh light that poured in. The boots stepped quickly over the wooden boards. A dagger was strapped to the right one, below a pair of pants that hung loosely. She blinked. For a moment, she thought she saw the sway of a coin at the end of a necklace, catching the faint candlelight. But her gaze shifted to the tray hosting half a loaf of bread and something that made her stomach growl.

The tray was placed where her empty water cup sat. "Good, you drank it." The unfamiliar selkie's voice was matter-of-fact but held an edge of relief, as if he was truly glad she hadn't perished from thirst. "Eat this. It'll help."

Her mouth watered at the sight of a steaming plate of fish next to the bread that glistened with butter and oil, and she tried not to dive forward like the starved animal she was.

The selkie grabbed her cup, muttered something, then placed it back down. Her eyes bulged at the clear water. When she looked up, the selkie's shoulders and face were in shadow.

There was a shout from somewhere above, and they both lifted their gazes to the ceiling. Again, the selkie said, "Eat." He turned and was gone.

Her first instinct was to shove the tray away. She was imprisoned. She shouldn't give in to the wishes of her captors. What if they were only feeding her to hand off to somebody, or something, else? She knew little of selkies, but their legend painted a cruel picture.

Even Eegit had little to say about the shape-shifters, only calling them "wickedly clever" and warning Jastyn that if she ever found herself at sea to be cautious. "Selkies are worse than sirens, they are," Eegit had told her when she was young. "Sirens give you the mercy of thinking you're happy when they kill you. Selkies don't bother with such benevolence."

Sitting up, Jastyn pulled her legs close to her chest, staring at the bread that smelled fresh, like the loaves from the market back home. The fish looked even better, with steam rising lazily from the cooked white meat.

Eventually, her stomach decided for her. After all, what use would she be if she starved to death? She had a mission to finish.

An hour later, she leaned against the wall, satiated. She sipped leisurely from the crisp water. Like her meal, she took the water slow, knowing all too well that a starved stomach would reject a quickly consumed meal. She'd learned that hard fact when she was nine, during one of her and her mother's particularly rough bouts, where meals were twice a week if they were lucky. Back then, she'd gone to stay with Eegit for a few days so her mother could barter at the market. Eegit had prepared a stew that Jastyn had eaten within minutes of it being laid before her. Of course, it had come back up soon after.

Shaking her head at the memory, Jastyn cleared her mind. She could feel her energy returning, and she conjured a small saol to reassure herself that she still could. When the chamber door opened, she quickly vanquished her companion flame.

"I thought you might like the fish."

The same male selkie wandered in, torchlight from the hall flooding in behind him. His frame was much slighter than the others she'd encountered. His brown skin shone, even in the dim candlelight, and his shoulder-length black hair fell in soft waves onto his slim shoulders. When he crouched to pick up the tray, his face caught the candlelight, and Jastyn was met with a genial smile set below a straight nose and kind, dark eyes.

"Were you watching me?" She hadn't expected the selkies to show pity. Fortan had seemed sympathetic at the council meeting, but she imagined his empathy a rarity. This selkie looked almost excited to see her.

He laughed, revealing a missing canine on his lower jaw. Wrinkles etched around his eyes. "Would you judge me if I was?"

Confused, she asked, "Who are you?"

He stared as if counting the freckles running over her nose and forehead. "My name is Tove."

Jastyn sat straighter. "You're the fifth councilmember."

He nodded, a small smile gracing his thin lips. "I was on an excursion with my clan. We had ventured north on a visit to Uterni. Their royal family called upon all fae-folk who had gotten word of the dark force penetrating the realm. They sought our counsel on how to best plan a defense, if needed. I only left the meeting two days ago."

Two days, how long have I been here?

"Uterni?" Jastyn conjured the image of the twins. They must have gotten word to the king and queen about what they'd seen near Vreis's cave. She nodded. "Uterni is much more reasonable when it comes to working with nonhumans in times of unrest."

The selkie raised an eyebrow. "And Venostes is not?"

"How did you—"

"Revna briefed me."

Jastyn was grateful for the darkness as her cheeks grew hot. "Of course." She sat back against the wall, the clink of her shackles the only sound for a moment. "Venostes could learn a lot from the northern kingdom," she said, biting back the desire to spew more hatred toward her homeland. "Wait," she said, glancing up at Tove. "Why is a councilmember tending to a prisoner? Why not Sif or Njal?"

Tove looked thoughtful as he swept one leg beneath him to kneel, placing his bare forearms atop his right knee. His dark brown tunic looked worn, and his boots bore frayed edges. The same necklace worn by the others hung around his neck, the council's coin shining in the candlelight. The light also gave Jastyn a better look at the seal skin atop his head. The face looked peaceful, its shining skin almost glowing.

When he reached out, Jastyn shot back against the wall.

"It's all right," he said, gesturing to the shackles, which she'd yanked closer to her chest. "Are you always this untrusting?"

"Why do you care?"

His gaze turned forlorn. She bit the inside of her cheek. He had brought her food and water. Perhaps he was a friend of Fortan's, a selkie sympathetic to her cause.

Slowly, she reached out. He muttered a spell and waved one hand over the metal bands. A faint *click* signaled her release, and she quickly shed the shackles. Rubbing her wrists, she avoided his gaze, unsure how to interpret this. "Thank you."

"How little kindness you've been shown." Each word was filled with such sadness that her gaze was pulled to his.

"What do you know of my life?" she shot back.

His shoulders rose and fell. "Not nearly enough."

Frustrated, she was ready to conjure her saol as she said, "Speak plainly, selkie. I do not like twisted phrases."

The coolness of his palm shocked her when he gently cupped her cheek. Despite the shock, she found she couldn't pull away. He was looking at her in a way only one other person ever had. "You look so like your mother."

Instantly, Jastyn was seven years old. She fell back, cradled in her mother's arms. Together, they huddled into the hollowed trunk of an oak tree. Biting winter wind blew over them, threatening to freeze them both. A single, frozen flask of water sat between them. Jastyn pushed her small frame back into her mother, who wrapped strong arms around her.

"Which one would you like to hear tonight, love?"

Jastyn began to forget about the hunger pangs racking her young stomach. "The one where Father fights the mongrels during a sea storm."

Her mother chuckled tiredly. "I told you that one two nights ago."

"But it's my favorite."

"Very well." She shivered and clung tighter to Jastyn. "Listen, love, to the story of your father. A man whose sense of adventure and love is so grand, the only way to satisfy his thirst is to sail the wide oceans, exploring untouched lands and new worlds."

Smiling, Jastyn listened eagerly to the tale her mother wove as they fought to survive another winter in the kingdom that had cast them out. A kingdom that had shunned them because of the fae sitting before her now.

Lunging forward, Jastyn ripped the dagger from his boot and pointed the sharp tip against the pulse in his neck.

Rage boiled in her veins. The dagger trembled against his skin, years of lies bubbling to the surface as she faced the fae who'd left her mother alone. The fae who was too much a coward to face the repercussions of the kingdom's laws. The fae who'd left Jastyn without a chance in this world.

Seething, she pushed the tip into his skin. Tove continued to kneel, his dark eyes watery as he tilted his head, giving her the best angle possible to do as she might.

She grew angrier. "Are you such a coward you won't even try to fight?"

Slowly raising his right hand, he placed it over Jastyn's left, which was shaking as it held the dagger. "You have every right to call me a coward."

She sneered in disgust. His apathy only fanned the flames of her hatred. With a flick of her wrist, she rearranged the dagger on the other side of his neck, ready to drag it across the length of his throat. She could feel her mother's pain, her own unanswered questions holding the dagger's hilt, willing it to gain her revenge. Her breathing haggard, she stared into Tove's gaze when he said, "I don't want to fight you."

That was all she needed to pull back the dagger, ready to strike. As she did, Tove trapped her hand between his own. When she tried to yank free, he surprised her with his strength, and she was quickly upended, landing with a hard thud on her back as he held her down.

"Coward," she yelled, summoning all the strength she had to push him away and get up. Swinging, she landed a hard elbow to his cheek. He released her, and she stood, the dagger firmly in her grasp.

Standing slowly, Tove held up his hands, palms toward her. "Jastyn. Please."

In her free hand, she conjured her saol. He looked sadly at the fire. With a flourish of his hand, a wall of water shimmered to life, creating a barrier between them. Jastyn threw her saol, but it simmered and died, consumed.

"I don't want to fight you," he said again, his voice garbled by the water.

"Tough." She lunged through the cascade, which disappeared at her touch. She narrowly missed his torso with the blade. When she dove forward again, he sidestepped, grabbing her right arm and twisting it behind her. She cried out as he held her in place against him.

"I said, I don't want to fight you, but I will if I have to."

She gave in. Her body ached. She was still too weak to do any real damage. The surge of life that had invigorated her moments before withered.

"Let go," he whispered behind her, his hand around hers on the dagger. "It's okay. Let go, Jastyn."

When her grip released, so did her will to keep fighting. She was no longer the stone-faced twenty-two-year-old determined to walk through whatever life threw at her. This was one thing she had not prepared for. No matter how often she had thought about him, no matter what her mother had told her, Jastyn wasn't ready for the tumult of emotions raging in her heart upon meeting her father.

Her knees buckled.

Tove caught her. He helped her against the wall. She tried to slow her breathing as he stepped back carefully, giving her space.

Dropping her head in her palms, she steadied her breathing. Tears welled in her eyes, but she held them back, refusing to show him an ounce of emotion, though she feared he could already see how their reunion had unraveled her. Thoughts of her mother surfaced, images of the years they'd fought together to survive a life of suffering neither of them deserved.

"I don't understand," she said through her teeth. "Why now?"

His boots shuffled as he sheathed his dagger. "The gods work in mysterious ways."

She lifted her head, glaring. "Since when do fae believe in the gods?"

His body radiated calmness as he clasped his hands behind his back. "Since I met your mother."

She raised a warning hand. "Don't—"

"Talk about her? Say her name?" For the first time, his tone took on that of a frustrated parent speaking to their child. "Jastyn, Branna was a part of my life. You are, too. I wish neither you or her any harm."

Snorting, Jastyn said, "You've done enough harm already."

He raised an eyebrow. "Was it I or the Diarmaids who hurt you?"

Swiftly, she stood. "The Diarmaids wrote the laws, but you broke them."

"Because I loved your mother."

"You left us!" She didn't care that her voice cracked, emotion slipping through her words. "I was born in the dungeons because of you."

His jaw clenched. "I never wanted that."

"Then why did you leave?"

"I had no choice."

"Like the Otherworld you didn't."

"Watch your tongue."

Taken aback, Jastyn faltered. She crossed her arms. "Then why?"

Exhaling, Tove lowered his voice. "I will tell you. But first, I must explain why I have come to see you now."

She eyed him warily, keeping her stance defensive.

He stepped closer. "I know why you and your group have traveled so far. I know of the cure you seek."

Her heart began to race.

"And I can get you into the western caves before your time is up."

Chapter Twenty

"For a princess, you sure do puke a lot."

Aurelia retched again, her face pressed against the rim of a bucket whose original purpose she hoped to never know as it now hosted a truly terrible stench. She blinked back tears that accompanied her first experience with, as Sif called it, "starving sickness."

Sif had stayed to witness Aurelia eat in a manner that would have appalled her mother and father. But Aurelia hadn't cared; she was starving. The steaming fish smelled tantalizingly fresh, and the bread had been as good as anything she'd eaten in the castle. It had gone within minutes.

Unfortunately, it was all back, staring up at her from the bottom of the bucket.

Groaning, she leaned back, cradling the bucket between her legs as a sad child held a doll. "By the gods, that was awful." She ignored Sif's laughter and wiped her sweating forehead with her dirty forearm while attempting to slow her breathing. Her cheeks were hot from expending so much energy, as well as from embarrassment at not remembering the first rule of eating after a prolonged fast. Or in her case, forced starvation. All reason had left her when that tray of fish and bread had been laid before her.

"I don't imagine you have a stash of ginger root nearby?" she asked, her eyes closed as she pressed her head back against the wall.

"I'm afraid not, Princess." Sif snorted. "Even if we did, I wouldn't give you any."

Aurelia sighed. "Is it my title or my weak stomach that bothers you so much?"

Sif squinted from where she leaned against the opposite wall. "I don't trust any human. Especially a Diarmaid."

Feeling her stomach lurch again, Aurelia took a deep breath, willing her insides to quell their unrest.

Sif took her silence as a chance to add injury to insult. "As I'm sure you're aware, your family has done more damage to the fae than any other dynasty in history. The selkies used to roam every inch of the sea surrounding the realm. Now we're relegated to this corner of the island, thanks to your laws."

Aurelia opened her eyes, wincing at hearing more awful history.

"One year of bad crops and you blame a fae for the famine that followed." Sif paused, and shadows from the candlelight added a malicious glow to her round face. "You know what I think?" Her words were filled with such disgust, they made Aurelia shiver. "Humans have only ever cared about themselves. The Diarmaids were simply the first to wear that prejudice on their sleeves."

Trembling, Aurelia asked, "Is that all?"

Sif's eyes widened. "You don't disagree?"

"I never said that."

"You simply don't care, then."

Aurelia straightened. "I do care." Sif laughed, but Aurelia was undeterred. "I want to fix what my family has done to this realm. Starting with my kingdom."

"More empty promises from a monarch who can't even keep down her dinner."

Fueled by Sif's impudence, Aurelia set the bucket aside. She placed her shackled hands in her lap, pulling up the little dignity she had left. "Do not presume to know me. My word is good."

Sif scoffed.

"I may be a Diarmaid, but I am not like my family." She looked at the dirty wooden floor. "Admittedly, I was unaware of the terrible things my family has done. I knew the laws, but I did not understand the extent of the pain they caused. I was naive, but I was only privy to what I had been taught."

"The little princess didn't know what the world was like?"

"I did not."

"And now you do?" Sif raised an eyebrow.

"More than I did before. Leaving the castle was the best thing that ever happened to me. Albeit I would have liked to have done it under different circumstances."

A question knit itself between Sif's brows.

"I was kidnapped during my brother's Remembrance ceremony."

The surprise on Sif's face only lasted a moment, but Aurelia caught the shift in her posture.

"It was a blessing from the gods, it turns out. I met Jastyn and have traveled far."

"You think because you've gone on a single journey, you know the realm?" Sif sneered, but her spite wasn't as sharp as before.

"It's not the journey that opened my eyes to what's wrong with the way my family has ruled. It's the people I've met who have taught me the most."

Sif didn't look impressed. "You shake hands with a fae or two, and then you seek to rectify a century of wrongdoings?"

Aurelia faltered, stammering. "It's difficult to explain." She blushed. Meeting Jastyn had triggered a series of events that had exposed the dark underbelly of her family's past. She hadn't known the consequences of the laws; Jastyn was those consequences incarnate. Yet she didn't let those circumstances keep her from fighting for what she deserved. Aurelia loved that about her. She would do whatever she could to help Jastyn live the life she deserved.

Looking satisfied, Sif turned to go.

"Wait," Aurelia called. "Please, how are the others?"

One hand on the door, Sif paused as if considering answering her. "The male human is weak but gaining strength. The elf hasn't said a word."

"And Jastyn?"

Sif's eyes narrowed. "What care you of the Odium?"

Aurelia met her gaze evenly. "How is she?"

Sif's eyes flickered with recognition. She pursed her lips, then said, "She fares the best."

Falling back against the wall, Aurelia exhaled. "Thank you."

Again, Sif turned to go. But she stopped in the doorway. "Feelings for an Odium don't change my perception of you. The council may buy your quest for reform, but they would be fools to do so." Aurelia shrank against the wall, the words hitting her hard. "There's only one type of human worse than the rest, and that's a Diarmaid."

With a harsh thud, the selkie slammed the door shut, leaving Aurelia alone in the darkness.

❖

"Do you mean to say you can get me out of here and to the caves without the council's knowing?"

Tove shook his head. "That would be impossible. The council is cunning. They would know in a moment if I tried to sneak you out."

"Then how?"

"Once this entire misunderstanding about the river fish is cleared up, I will go with you and your friends to the caves."

Jastyn eyed him. She took another sip of water, her other hand on her hip as she stood across from him in the dim room. "Why?"

He gave an exasperated sigh. "Jastyn."

"It's a valid question. I spent twenty-two years without you. What makes you think I need or want your help now?"

Her father's face possessed a flicker of pain, but he smiled nonetheless. "Nearly twenty-three years now. Winter will be here in another six moons."

"You're deflecting."

He leaned against the wall beside the closed chamber door. The candles flickered, their bright light dancing as if entertained by this new showdown between father and daughter.

"I know the quickest way to the cure because I helped make it."

She nearly dropped her cup. "What?"

He gestured to the floor. "Why don't you sit down?"

"I'm fine."

"Very well." He ran a hand through his hair. "You asked earlier why I left you and your mother. I told you I didn't have a choice."

She opened her mouth to protest, but he held up a hand. "Twenty-four years ago, I was only a little older than you are now, a carefree selkie enjoying the best of our world, the open sea and the lands it opens up to. I'd met your mother at a festival in Venostes." He smiled, and his eyes shined with memory. "It's not uncommon for selkies to shed their skin and walk on land. I'm glad I did that day. Branna stole my heart instantly."

Jastyn tried to hold on to her anger. But as he spoke, she was thrown back into a memory of when her mother had told a similar story. The look she had worn was the same one Tove wore now, one of unmistakable adoration and love. Shaking her head, she tried to extinguish her growing sympathy. "Why don't you skip ahead?"

He refocused on her, his face falling. "Very well. Once my clan got word of my union with a human, panic erupted."

"Why? Selkies are known for their relationships with humans."

"That was before the Diarmaids." His gaze turned dark. "The council was furious, claiming I was risking the security of our entire nation by loving a woman in a kingdom built on the hatred of relationships like ours." Again, his face shifted, this time to stoic resolve. "They requested my immediate return, but I couldn't leave Branna. Especially once we learned she was pregnant."

Jastyn felt light-headed, her knees like water, but she refused to sit. She could handle the truth. She'd waited years for it.

After a moment, he continued. "My father was a councilmember. He was a brave selkie but not a kind soul. I knew he didn't approve of my decision to stay in Venostes, but it wasn't until later I learned how against it he truly was." He rubbed his hands together, surprising Jastyn with his first sign of anxiety. "When Branna was six months pregnant, I received word that he had died."

Their chamber was quiet as Jastyn filled in the blank. "You had to take his seat on the council."

He nodded. "It was my birthright and my duty as a selkie to join the council and fill the vacancy." He hung his head. "Upon my return, Revna was the first to speak with me. She told me my father died with boiled blood in his veins. Blood he had used to fashion a curse. A curse that, he hoped, would ruin the life of the woman I loved."

Stunned, Jastyn could only listen.

"I didn't know what form his curse would take at first. So I left your mother with a gift to help protect you." He leaned down, pulling out his dagger. For the first time, Jastyn really looked at it. When it had been in her hands, she had sensed a twinge of familiarity in its hilt, but she hadn't seen it. Not until now.

"My dagger." She stepped closer. He held it out.

"Yours is just like it," he said. "I'd hoped you would find it useful. It was built with serpentine stone, along with a bit of other selkie magic in the hope that the luck inside the blade would always walk with you."

Luck does not walk with you this night.

Jastyn gaped. "My dagger…that's what's protected me from the Dark Fae."

"That was its purpose. To keep you safe."

Blinking, she stared at the blade. "The Dark Fae…he was your father's curse?"

"No. He is another beast entirely. My father only wished to hurt Branna. It wasn't until years later that I realized the manifestation of what he'd done. Nine years later, to be exact."

"Alanna." She stumbled back, finding the wall and sliding to the ground.

"Your sister bore the curse of my father. What better way to hurt Branna than to force her to watch her child suffer?"

Jastyn felt sick, the fish in her stomach trying to swim its way back up. She had spent her entire life hating the Diarmaids for what they had done to her mother. The royal family was to blame for many things. But now a selkie had a hand in her family's suffering, too. Part of her had always held on to the idea that the fae had, somehow, been on her side in life. Eegit had been kind. The kingdom's fae were respectful. She never thought they would be out to hurt her, too.

Was there no safe place in the realm for someone like her?

"As soon as I realized what he'd done, I tried to fix it. I worked with Revna to make a cure that would heal Alanna. It took some time, but eventually, we were successful."

"But why not share that with us?"

"The council deliberated. Obviously, as a member and the subject of investigation, I had no vote. But it didn't matter. All except Revna decided I was guilty of risking the safety of our nation. I was forbidden from ever stepping foot in Venostes again."

"Revna, then, she could have brought it."

"No. She would not compromise the safety of her clans."

"So you left it in the western caves?"

"It was the safest place. The caves belong to a leprechaun clan. We made a deal. They would secure the location for the cure that awaited my Odium daughter. In turn, the leprechauns could add a single stipulation to the acquisition itself."

Jastyn shook her head. "Sounds like the leprechauns." Then she added, "That's how the Red One knew where to send me."

He nodded.

Jastyn sighed, her body growing as tired as her mind. "Why does none of this ever come easy?"

Tove moved across the room and sat beside her. He was a few inches taller than her, but both of their frames were so slight that even together, they were hardly as wide as the door frame standing across from them.

"I know this is all unfair."

The chamber door opened. A selkie Jastyn didn't recognize stood in the light. "The council is ready to meet."

"I'll be there in a minute," Tove replied. The selkie nodded, then left, leaving the door ajar.

Jastyn turned to meet her father's gaze. Her eyes traced over his lean arms, the sheen of his seal skin. Part of her thought this might all be some elaborate dream. She might wake up back in Vreis's cave or on the side of the river where they'd been fishing. She reached out, setting her hand atop Tove's, his skin cool and smooth.

He seemed to read the unspoken words between them. His lips curved in a smile. "We'll get the cure. I promise."

Jastyn watched him stride out of the room. Dazed, she ran a hand down her braid, wondering at the reality of meeting her father. Despite herself, she laughed, relishing the kernel of hope that lit itself inside her mind. For the first time in a while, Jastyn had a good feeling about whatever was coming next.

CHAPTER TWENTY-ONE

Aurelia winced at the glaring sunshine as Njal led her out of the prison ship on their way to the council chamber. Blinking, she asked, "What day is it?"

"The last quarter moon of summer," Njal grunted behind her.

Five days? Had they really been separated that long? Aurelia staggered along the rickety planks connecting one ship to the next. They wound their way under tattered sails and low-hanging ropes that had long ago been resigned to hang listlessly in the dull wind that swirled inside the selkies' cove. Eventually, Njal nudged her onto the deck of the largest, center ship, the same one they'd stumbled onto the night of their capture.

Ushered inside to wait to enter the council's meeting room, she was thrilled and relieved when Coran and Rigo joined her minutes later.

"Coran," Aurelia practically squealed, her shackled hands clanging against his as she gripped his forearms. "How are you?"

He looked like himself again, his wild orange hair detangled and the color back in his freckled cheeks. "I feel much better, m'lady. Though,I was mighty confused when I woke up in the hull of a ship. Never been on such a thing in my life." He turned to Rigo, who also looked livelier, his green tunic dirty but his effervescent skin shining. "Rigo filled me in on what happened." He lowered his voice, throwing a glance to the selkies standing nearby. "Do ya think they'll let us go?"

"They'll see reason." Jastyn entered from a doorway to their right, followed by Sif.

"Jastyn!" Rushing to her, Aurelia threw her shackled arms over

Jastyn's head, pulling her into an embrace. She had missed her terribly, but only now registered how unbearably awful it had been being apart.

Jastyn breathed a laugh, then pressed herself close so Aurelia could pull back her arms. "How are you?"

Aurelia didn't care if the entire room heard the pitter-patter of her heart. "Better," she replied.

"She stopped vomiting, so that was something," Sif called.

Flushing, Aurelia said, "I may have eaten too quickly. But I realized the error of my ways," she said, shooting Sif a look. Sif gave half a smile before turning to speak to Njal.

Coran stepped closer. "Jas." He reached out a hand, and Jastyn took it. "It's good to see ya."

Aurelia saw the emotion flash through Jastyn's eyes as they embraced. "You look like you've had a go with the back end of a horseshoe," Jastyn said, clearing her throat.

Grinning, he said, "Better than you. You're as scrawny as a twig."

Aurelia watched the two dear friends stand awkwardly across from one another, silly smiles exuding relief. Overcome, she rushed forward, embracing them both. "Oh, I missed you two."

Fumbling over one another, they all laughed. Coran leaned back. "Rigo, get in here."

Rigo, whose wrists were still bound in the seaweed shackles, gave an exaggerated sigh before joining their group hug, squirming in between Coran and Jastyn. Aurelia beamed.

A voice cut in behind them. "The council is ready for you now."

They separated, standing in a line before the open curtain. Revna sat stone-faced in her high-backed seat. The joy at being reunited fizzled at the sight, and Aurelia felt a sudden pang of dread as they were escorted into the room.

When Njal and Sif took their places at either end of the chamber, Revna spoke. "The council has had time to deliberate on the matter of your party stealing selkie property from the river."

Swallowing, Aurelia pressed closer to Jastyn, who looked oddly relaxed, considering they were about to be read a potential death sentence. Examining her face, Aurelia wondered at her clear gaze. Normally, she looked to have at least five different things running through her mind. Now she appeared almost excited to hear what the council had to say.

Revna asked the room, "How do you find them?"

Aurelia was pulled from her thoughts as Yrse announced her verdict. "Guilty," she said, a glint of resentment in her icy gaze.

"Not guilty," came the second vote. Fortan.

The selkie that had been missing from their first encounter with the council spoke next. "Not guilty," he said. A small wave of relief washed over Aurelia, but it was replaced by curiosity as she noticed this selkie's gaze linger on Jastyn. Perhaps he'd learned she was an Odium and, like Fortan, was genuinely intrigued by their unorthodox quartet. The look he wore held something different. Aurelia couldn't pinpoint what it was, but when the next verdict rang out, she was brought back to her frightened thoughts.

"Guilty," Colborn said proudly, scowling.

It would be up to Revna to decide their fate. Aurelia trembled as the torchlight danced over her face. For a moment, a flash of something lit in them…sympathy? Understanding? Aurelia wasn't sure, but the pounding of her heart was deafening, and she hardly heard Revna when she said, "Not guilty."

"Gods above," Coran sighed. Rigo nodded, and Aurelia's knees nearly gave out as she turned to Jastyn, who gave her a smug look.

"Told you we'd be fine."

"But how did you know?"

Colborn and Yrse were on their feet. "This is outrageous," Yrse shouted.

Colborn held out an arm to block her from going for Revna. He spoke heatedly. "With respect, Revna, the council is wrong. I demand another recess to deliberate further on the matter."

Revna ignored him. Instead, she watched their group, her dark eyes drifting from Aurelia to Jastyn, then back again.

Fortan waved a hand. "When will you two realize the entire world isn't out to get us?"

"The rules are in place for a reason," Yrse fired across the room. "If we waver on matters like this, who's to say the next time won't see us losing more than just our food supply?"

"Matters like this?" Revna's voice was eerily calm as she stood. Yrse shrank, climbing back into her chair.

Colborn set his jaw, but he slowly sat. "Revna, the council's judgment on this matter has been compromised."

Confused, Aurelia watched as the verbal volleys continued. Meanwhile, Njal and Sif reluctantly undid their shackles.

"On the contrary," the fifth selkie said, "this matter holds more clarity than any other sentencing before it."

"I beg to disagree," Yrse said, her nails digging into the arms of her chair. "Just because she's your daughter doesn't mean they should be held to a different standard."

"Daughter?" Aurelia asked, glancing from Yrse to the fifth selkie.

Coran asked the follow-up question blaring in her mind. "What're they talkin' about?"

Rubbing her free wrists, Jastyn gave a knowing smile.

"Is something funny? I fear I don't understand." Aurelia turned to Revna. "Will the council please explain themselves. I demand to know what's going on."

The fifth selkie chuckled. "My, she is quite commanding, even for a princess."

Aurelia faced him, ready to dish out a verbal lashing. But it hit her then: the familiar teasing she'd heard for the last few months. The words that, to the untrained ear, sounded harsh but in reality held a note of admiration. She scrutinized the selkie, whose face held a raised brow she had come to know well, only in a fair-skinned, female form.

"By the gods." She stepped back.

"Jas?" Coran asked. "Your Highness?"

"Oh, come now, Revna," Fortan said, "let the poor lad in on it."

Revna's formerly stern face shifted to one of serene amusement. "Very well. Business first, though. The council finds your party not guilty. We have deemed your innocence true and your ignorance of where your party sought nourishment accurate. The forgotten daughter of a selkie will always be given the benefit of the doubt," she added with a smile.

Grumbling came from Yrse and Colborn's side of the room. The other half beamed with pride.

The fifth selkie leapt from his chair. "May I?" he asked Revna.

"You may."

Grinning, he walked over to their group, eagerly clapping his hands. "Come," he said. "We have a lot of catching up to do."

Later that evening, Aurelia sat in the warm, brightly lit quarters of a different ship. This one was smaller and had been anchored closest to the edge of the cove where the entrance to the ocean's waters met the thin rock line delineating the selkie's territory. It belonged to Tove, the mysterious fifth selkie, who had spent the last half of the day explaining everything.

Aurelia sat with a cup of water, listening intently to the lengthy tale of Tove's meeting with Branna, Jastyn's mother. It was a beautiful story, and Aurelia could see how deeply the selkie loved Branna, despite how short their time together had been. All throughout the story, she had thrown glances to Jastyn, who listened with her eyes glued to the floorboards. She seemed lost in her father's words. Aurelia had found all of it so surprising that she imagined Jastyn had to be having trouble grasping all he was telling them.

Coran, meanwhile, had transformed from the polite stable boy and loyal best friend into a skeptical and untrusting older brother. With each new layer to Tove's story, he questioned the selkie hotly. Why had he been in Venostes in the first place? Did he have reservations about entering into a relationship with a human woman? Was this common selkie behavior?

Aurelia had to admire his gusto, and the overprotective net he cast over Jastyn was quite a wonderful new side to witness.

"Answer this," Coran said, pointing at Tove from where he sat cross-legged next to Rigo on a blue cushion on the floor. "Why leave? Did you not want to stay and raise your daughter? You had to have known Branna was with child."

Aurelia took another sip. Tove smiled at the question he had to have known each of them was thinking. As she leaned forward, covered by the folds of a rough blanket, she was surprised to feel Jastyn's hand reach over and rest comfortably in her lap. The knowing look on Jastyn's face told Aurelia she had already heard this part of the story.

"While I was in Venostes, my father sat on the council as its fifth member. The others were already there, though Fortan had been a recent, controversial addition." Aurelia chuckled as he threw a grin to each of them. "I was expecting to stay in Venostes much longer, especially once I knew Branna was pregnant. It was a surprise, I will admit, but a welcome one." His gaze fell on Jastyn. "Unfortunately, at that same time, my father fell ill. Had he been younger, he might have been able to overcome it. But the illness took him quickly, faster than the council could have anticipated. As soon as it happened, they sent word to me." A glimmer of regret flashed through his dark eyes. "The council summoned me to fill my father's seat. It is a selkie's duty to respect and uphold the tradition of taking over from the previous generation."

"You had no choice but to return," Rigo said. He and Tove exchanged knowing looks. Aurelia wondered if, as fae, they held some sort of understanding.

"I had no choice," Tove echoed. "It pained me greatly to leave your mother." This he said directly to Jastyn, who had lifted her head. "It hurt me even more to leave knowing I might never know you."

Aurelia's eyes brimmed with tears, and she wrapped Jastyn's hand between her own. "Gods, that's terribly sad," she muttered.

Coran looked moved by Tove's words, too. He cleared his throat. "Why not leave a message or something?"

Aurelia knew what Jastyn would say before the words left her mouth. "He couldn't. If the Diarmaids had known his identity, they would have hunted him down and killed him."

Tove nodded solemnly.

Aurelia took a deep breath. "With you gone, all my parents could do was lock up your mother." She faced Jastyn. "Gods, I hope they didn't torture her to try to find out who you were." Covering her mouth at the thought, she dropped her gaze, ashamed.

The room fell quiet with the horrible idea. Jastyn squeezed Aurelia's hand and whispered that it was okay. Aurelia shook her head, knowing it really wasn't. Why was Jastyn being so forgiving? She feared she didn't deserve it.

Tove broke the silence. "Though I knew I might never be able to see you, I hoped Branna had given you my gift." He drew the dagger outside of his boot, holding it flat. "I had it fashioned to look like mine."

"I knew it looked familiar." Coran reached for it as Jastyn's eyes grew cloudy.

Aurelia frowned. "What's wrong?"

Jastyn took the dagger, holding it in her open palm. "I'm afraid I've lost it."

"The battle with Drest in the Wood," Aurelia said. Jastyn nodded. "I had forgotten about it."

"There was a lot going on." Jastyn sounded as if she was trying to be reassuring, but Aurelia could hear the thick sadness.

"It's completely lost?" Tove's voice, meanwhile, grew concerned. "How long have you been without it?"

Jastyn handed it back and rubbed her hands together thoughtfully. "Several moons now."

Tove's eyes widened. "It's no wonder the Dark Fae has been on your heels."

"What do ya mean?" Coran asked, now admiring the dagger.

"The blade's handle was fashioned from serpentine stone and citrine. Selkies believe those are two of the key elements in fashioning tokens of luck and good fortune." He quickly told of the curse placed on Alanna and of giving Branna the dagger to protect Jastyn, who he had presumed would be the target of his father's curse.

Aurelia wondered at the realm's fascination with trying to capture the essence of luck.

"Luck does not walk with you," Jastyn said.

Aurelia faced her. "What?"

Jastyn shifted her legs, speaking animatedly. "Luck does not walk with you." She cast her excited gaze around the group. "That's what the Dark Fae said to me that night in the Wood. And again when we were in the mountains."

"Your dagger," Tove said, awe evident in his voice. "It really did work."

Aurelia held up a hand. "Wait. Are you saying that your dagger"— she pointed to Tove—"has been a real lucky charm for Jastyn all her life?"

"Yes," he and Jastyn replied together. They stared at each other, expressions equally surprised.

"You heard the stories, then?" Rigo asked. "Of the Dark Fae who collected Odiums?"

"I had, though I'd hoped they weren't true. I fashioned it more as a means to combat my father's curse." He turned to Jastyn. "It really worked?"

Jastyn stared into the middle distance. "I think so. The Dark Fae found me when I was ten summers old. I was alone in the Wood. He could have taken me easily then, but..." She fingered the empty holster in her boot. "I had the dagger. I carried it every day. The closest he ever got to me was in my dreams."

"Until now," Coran added, his face pinched in concern.

"You can fashion another one." Aurelia said to Tove. "Can't you?"

He smiled. "I can. But it will take time."

"Which we don't have a lot of," Aurelia mumbled.

"The cure you seek for Alanna."

Aurelia raised her brows at Tove's knowledge of their journey's purpose.

"She's got two moons left, at best." Jastyn set her jaw. "I have the vial from the Red One, but I need to get to the caves quickly."

"I can help with that," Tove said. "There's a shortcut up the coast. Compared to traveling by foot, it'll save a week's time."

"It's a boat?" Aurelia asked, her stomach turning at the memory of their recent journey to the selkie cove.

Jastyn and Tove exchanged amused looks. "I'm afraid it is," he said. "I know a remedy for seasickness. Perhaps Sif can prepare it before we leave."

Aurelia swallowed, nodding gratefully but certain Sif probably wouldn't volunteer for such a job.

"When do we head out?" Coran asked.

"Coran," Jastyn said, shooting him a look.

"Jas," he said, "you know there's no talking us out of going."

Shocked, Aurelia squared with her. "You weren't truly going to try to convince us to stay behind, were you?"

Jastyn bit her lip, throwing a pleading glance to Tove.

He chuckled. "Your friends are almost as stubborn as you."

She glared, but it was half-hearted. She sighed. "Very well. I suppose we could leave at first light tomorrow."

"Tomorrow?" Tove cut in. "Absolutely not."

The four of them turned in unison. Aurelia, who hadn't heard an authoritative parental tone in months, nearly fell into Jastyn, who said, "We need to move quickly."

"And we will. But there's a very important matter to attend to first. It will take two, three days at most."

Aurelia frowned. She looked to Coran, and he squinted curiously at Tove.

"You really don't have to," Jastyn said, looking uncomfortable.

"Don't have to what?" Aurelia had been in the dark for most of this conversation, and she was beginning to feel as if she was back in the castle, always the last to know things. Her skin itched at having to pull information out of everyone, but she had to laugh at how elusive Tove seemed, not unlike his daughter.

"The selkies would hardly let one of their own return to the cove without the traditional welcome celebration." He grinned, leaning back on his hands.

"Really," Jastyn said, "it's not necessary."

"Nonsense. Besides, I've already made the arrangements. The celebration begins tomorrow night."

Aurelia couldn't help smiling. Perhaps it was her upbringing—which had been littered with festivals and reasons for the royal family and their court to enjoy themselves—but she latched on to this new opportunity to shine a loving light on Jastyn. She had to sit on her hands to keep from clapping.

"Think of it as a much belated birthday party," Tove said, winking as he stood.

Aurelia moved to her knees, calling out as he turned to go. "Wait, Tove. The celebration tomorrow, may I offer my services to help prepare?"

He tilted his head slightly. "Is the princess of Venostes offering to help a fae?"

She lifted her chin, determined to prove she wasn't just in this for the fun. "It would be an honor to be of assistance."

He looked satisfied and threw a glance at Jastyn. "Very well. Meet me on the deck of this ship when the sun is high tomorrow."

"I will see you then," Aurelia replied before he bid them all good night.

Chapter Twenty-Two

Jastyn woke the next morning to the soft, persistent lapping of ocean waves against the nearby cliffs. Stretching, she felt blissfully rested for the first time in several moons. Last night, they'd all had cooked fish for dinner, which they ate together alongside Fortan and a cluster of curious selkie families eager to meet the newcomers. Afterward, Sif—still sour at their release but appearing to lighten up out of sheer curiosity—showed each of them to their rooms. On the same ship as Tove, all four were given small quarters just belowdecks. Jastyn didn't mind the tight quarters, the space reminding her of the small room she and Alanna shared.

The night had lasted longer than she had anticipated once dinner was done. Over a shared platter of sweetened figs, she'd spent nearly an hour convincing Coran that he didn't have to follow Tove around, though she appreciated his newfound interest in keeping a watchful eye on her father. It was rather hard to believe she'd met him, she thought as she lazed on the bed of blankets and stared at the rocking ceiling. Sunlight shone dimly from her western porthole, the frame long ago eaten into jagged edges by time. A tray of candles in the corner sat atop a wooden table. Otherwise, the room was vacant. Turning on her side, she tugged her satchel closer, pulling out the Red One's vial.

She traced the glass, remembering the ghostly banshee blood that had helped alleviate her sister's ailment.

"Soon, Alanna," she said to the empty vial. Lying on her back, she fiddled with it. Her mind drifted to Eegit, wondering if she'd managed to bottle luck back in her meadow. Jastyn smiled at the image of her hopping around gleefully at what would surely be a wild success. It might explain the sudden meeting with Jastyn's father. She refused to believe the gods had a hand in all of this but wouldn't put it past Eegit to conjure up something to throw a wrench in Jastyn's plans. Of course, Aurelia respectfully disagreed, convinced the gods had a mysterious plan. Just last night, she had explained their last three months together in detail, pinpointing things that couldn't be explained away by chance or happenstance.

Jastyn smiled at the sound of footsteps approaching her curtained doorway. The fabric rippled, and Jastyn called, "Come to convince me more of the gods' abilities, Princess?"

"That sounds like a fun conversation."

Jastyn tilted her head back to find Coran. "Oh, good morning."

"Mornin'," he called, waving and stealing one of the blankets from under her before wrapping himself in it and sitting cross-legged to face her. He nodded to the vial. "Thinkin' about Alanna?"

"We're so close, Coran." She sat up, leaning one arm over her bent knee. "With Tove's help, all of this will be done soon."

He opened his hands, and she tossed him the small glass. "You trust him?"

She considered his question, holding back a quick retort. When she didn't answer, he added, "I only ask because, well, since knowin' you, I could count the number of people you trust on two fingers." She snorted. "Your mother and yourself."

Snatching the vial back, she said, "You're forgetting somebody."

"Me?" he asked. The uncertainty in his voice surprised her.

"Coran, you're the only person I'd ever trust to help my family if something happened to me." She stared at the vial. "You're who I'd trust to get the cure to Alanna if something goes wrong in the caves."

"Jas—"

"I mean it." She stared at her hands for a while, and when she looked up, she saw unwavering loyalty in his eyes, his willingness to always help.

Scratching his chin, he asked, "What about Aurelia?"

She avoided his gaze. "I trust her. It's just…different."

He raised his eyebrows. "Well, strike me down and call me a druid. Jastyn Cipher trusts a Diarmaid?"

"Shut up." She threw the vial at him, but he caught it and tossed it back. Grinning, she shoved it into her satchel.

"Speaking of Her Highness." His gaze lifted to the ceiling, where footsteps wandered back and forth. "When are you gonna tell her about, you know…"

She flopped back onto her blanket, hands over her eyes. "I don't know. I can't ever seem to find the right time."

"I'm not sure there is a good time to tell your girlfriend she may need to be sacrificed in order to save your sister."

She lifted her hands, glaring sideways. "Don't make light, Coran."

"Is that not what is going on?"

Clasping her hands behind her head, she closed her eyes. She imagined herself back in Eegit's meadow. The stiff floorboards transformed into soft grass that waved lazily around her. She could smell the boysenberry shrubs and feel the dew that stuck to the grass each morning. Her mind calmed. "Before we leave for the caves, I'll tell her."

His voice was low. "If you need me there…"

He didn't have to finish. "Thanks, Coran." The meadow faded to the edges of her mind as she opened her eyes and was once again in the cool, damp cabin.

Coran fingered the toe of his boot, and Jastyn could feel a question in the air. "What is it?"

"I was just wonderin', what are you gonna tell Branna?"

After hearing Tove's story, Jastyn's frosty feelings toward her mother had begun to thaw. After all, it had been nearly four moons since their fight back in the village. She still couldn't believe her mother had lied to her as much as she had about her father, but, perhaps, like him, she'd had good reason.

"I'll figure that out when we get home."

"Home," he mused, pulling the blanket tighter around him. "That will be nice."

"Miss your mum?" she asked, teasing.

"O'course I do." He kicked her playfully, and she gave his knee a smack.

"She's lucky to have you."

More footsteps scurried overhead. There was a loud thud, followed by a peculiar sound, like a stone rolling across the deck, followed by the faint echoes of Aurelia's shouts.

"What d'ya reckon she's gotten into now?"

Jastyn laughed. "I could only guess. Come on." She stood. "We've got a festival to get ready for."

❖

Aurelia completed the final twist of her braid, squinting into the foggy glass of a broken mirror she'd discovered while helping Tove and the selkies prepare for Jastyn's welcome celebration. The anticipation was palpable throughout the entire colony. Apparently, word had traveled quickly that one of the councilmember's daughters had appeared from the Wildlands on a journey, walking with a member of the royal family. Aurelia had been delighted at the enthusiasm the selkies had shown in preparing to celebrate and welcome their half-fae kin. She'd met dozens of selkies during the day, young and old.

She'd also watched them admire their new clan member. Many had followed Jastyn along the shoreline as she'd gone for a walk with Rigo. In seal form, they'd swum alongside her in the water, leaping up to say hello when she had wandered onto an outcropping of rocks near one of the ships. Curious adolescent selkies had run up to her, then giggled and fled when she turned to find them.

Jastyn seemed to be opening up more with each greeting, even joining a game Aurelia didn't quite understand with a group of selkie children which involved Jastyn being tackled and tickled by the game's end.

Helping to hang green and white sails upon the main ship's mast, Aurelia felt happy Jastyn had found at least one of the answers to the many questions in her life. At the same time, she felt guilty as jealousy took root within her. Aurelia hated to admit it, but she couldn't help wondering if Jastyn, after finding Alanna's cure, would want to stay in the selkies' cove with her father. She seemed at home on the ships, surrounded by fae who shared her blood. What if she sent the cure back to Venostes with Coran but didn't want to return herself? Or what if, after going back to the kingdom, she realized she was no longer happy there and came back to these western shores?

Tying off the end of her braid, Aurelia sighed. She was happy Jastyn had found her father, but she hated the thought that this might mean losing her. She wasn't completely naive. She knew things would be difficult when they returned to the kingdom. But at least there, they would be together. Aurelia had hoped Jastyn might be able to ease the pain of living in a kingdom without her brother.

What if she left Aurelia, too?

"You're looking clean, for a human."

In the mirror, Aurelia found Sif standing in the doorway, the curtain swaying behind her.

"Thank you." She smiled. "You look lovely yourself."

Sif walked stiffly across the chamber, ever the soldier, her hands behind her back. She'd donned a newer-looking tunic, its teal fabric stunning against her dark skin. During the preparations, Aurelia had noticed Sif sporadically lending her a hand in hanging a curtain or lighting a finicky candle. She noted each time Sif kept away those selkies eager to badger Aurelia with questions. Over the course of the day, she saw the cold, calculated exterior that Sif boasted melt away, and she grew fond as Sif acted much like an older sister might, keeping a careful eye on Aurelia in this new and unfamiliar world.

Sif spoke to her reflection. "Tove would like you to know that it's selkie tradition for the guest of honor to share a dance with the one who accompanies them to the celebration." Her face shifted to a sly grin. "I hope they've taught you how to dance in that stuffy castle of yours."

"Of course." Her stomach flipped at the idea of dancing with Jastyn, but she forced her face to remain neutral. "I would be delighted."

Sif's eyes sparkled. She shifted her feet, glancing down.

"Is everything all right?"

Sif's hard features looked softer in the glow of the candles bouncing around the chamber. Even her scar wasn't as prominent, and her dark hair had been pinned elegantly beneath her sealskin. "I, um, thought you might like this."

Aurelia turned as Sif presented her with a hairpin, one end hosting a small golden starfish tied around the copper metal. Eyes wide, she looked up to meet Sif's gaze. "Sif, it's beautiful."

"I misjudged you before," she said, hesitating a moment. "While I still think your kind have a terrible lack of respect for rules, you have shown great poise through this misunderstanding."

"I'm not entirely sure that's true."

She stared at Aurelia's reflection. "You're not the Diarmaid we all expected."

Aurelia looked down at the hairpin. It had the faintest of rust lines on one edge, but was in good condition. The starfish looked as if it had been polished recently; the gold shone. It was a beautiful keepsake, and she wondered what motivated Sif to offer it.

Her fingers lingering over the pin, Aurelia whispered, "I can't take this."

The snark returned to Sif's voice. "Who said I was giving it to you?"

Flushing, Aurelia stammered, "Oh. I assumed…I only thought—"

Sif laughed. "Humans are hilarious. Of course I'm giving it to you. You should wear it tonight."

Blinking, Aurelia asked, "Are you sure?"

"It's been sitting in my chamber for years. It should be worn, and tonight seems like a good time to break it out of hiding." Her lips lifted in a teasing grin. "Besides, how often does a Diarmaid dance with an Odium?"

Aurelia was grateful when Sif motioned for her to turn around, as words became lost in her throat. Sif pulled back several strands of hair, setting the pin to rest above her right ear. The starfish shimmered in the candlelight.

"It's breathtaking," she said, touching the pin lightly. "Thank you."

The faintest smile graced Sif's lips as a discordant chorus of string instruments sounded above deck. "That's our cue, Princess. Let the fun begin."

Chapter Twenty-Three

Jastyn stuffed the fourth sampling of poached fish in her mouth, savoring the oils and spices with each bite. Standing on the center ship's main deck, she watched a dozen selkies begin a rather exuberant dance, one that involved stomping their polished boots and stamping individual staffs onto the deck in tune. Upon each fifth stamp, they all gave a hearty shout, throwing up their hands, their seal skins waving as some spun around, leaping high.

The night sky was clear, the waning quarter moon shining on the elaborate ship-city that was now teeming with torchlight on every available surface for the special occasion. Jastyn had tried to insist that such a celebration wasn't necessary. After all, she'd just met everyone. But Tove had insisted she was a member of their community, half-fae or not. The selkies, he'd told her, enjoyed any excuse to celebrate, but Jastyn was still surprised to see the entire colony present as the dancing continued. Even the council members were there. Fortan was in the middle of the dance, twirling a young selkie before another enthusiastic stomp-and-clap routine. Revna spoke with Tove near the former captain's quarters. Yrse was doing her best to look angry, but Jastyn could see her frustrated exterior beginning to wither.

"So what do you think?"

Standing against the ship's railing, Jastyn turned at the sound of Aurelia's voice. Her breath caught at the shine to Aurelia's hair under the moonlight. She had fashioned it into an elegant braid, with a pin Jastyn didn't recognize holding back a few loose strands just above her ear.

Blinking, Jastyn swallowed and turned to the festivities. "It looks wonderful." Aurelia beamed. Her heart beating wildly, Jastyn cleared her throat. "I didn't see you come on deck."

She laughed. "Did you think I enter each gathering with a musical pronouncement?"

Shrugging, Jastyn said, "Don't you?"

Aurelia nudged her elbow. "How high and mighty do you think I am?"

"I imagine it's a nice soft drumming." She mimicked a quick beat, then cupped her hands around her mouth. "All stand for Princess Aurelia Diarmaid."

Laughing, Aurelia said, "You're impossible." They shared a smile. "And my pronouncement music is actually a melody on a lyre, I'll have you know."

A shout from the center of the deck caught their attention, where the final spin of the selkies' dance called for a *hurrah* from everybody on board. Those who had cups raised them.

"They sure do know how to throw a party," Jastyn said.

Aurelia nodded. "It's quite inspiring. They're an astoundingly resourceful group. They utilize all of the belongings from each ship they, well, repurpose." She gestured to the shoulder-high black iron stands lining the broad deck. Their circular welding hosted prickets where candles sat, wicks flickering in the light breeze. "All of this came from the ships surrounding us. Even the dinnerware." She held up the wooden cup filled with a savory mead Jastyn had tasted earlier in the evening.

"Impressive."

Aurelia nodded to the musicians, whose notes were also plucked on instruments formerly owned by the unfortunate sailors whose ships had found their way into the cove. The musicians changed to a lighter tune.

When Aurelia looked at Jastyn expectantly, Jastyn frowned, but her stomach fluttered. "What?"

"They didn't tell you?"

"Tell me what?"

Coran rushed to her side, himself into his third cup of mead and looking entirely too happy at whatever was about to happen. "You're up, Jas."

"What are you talking about?"

The selkies cleared out of the middle of the deck, forming a haphazard circle. Eyeing the jubilant crowd as the music continued, Jastyn was still frowning when Tove joined them. "The guest of honor is required to have one dance with a companion." He looked between Jastyn and Aurelia, giving a wink and taking her cup. Then he leaned in, whispering, "That's you and your princess."

Jastyn blanched. "You couldn't have told me about this?"

He grinned, and Coran pushed her forward. Jastyn skidded through the selkies, all of them shouting and barking in encouragement as she weaved through them, Coran helping her along. Faster than she would have liked, Jastyn found herself in the middle of the circle with dozens of excited eyes watching expectantly. Feeling light-headed, she was determined to have a conversation with her father about this afterward. But when a lone pair of sky-blue eyes met hers, Jastyn forgot all about her father and stood locked to the planks beneath her feet. Aurelia stood ten paces across from her on the opposite side of the circle, a soft smile on her face.

Jastyn gulped. She'd never learned to dance, not properly, anyway. She had only gone to a handful of the equinox festivals in Venostes. And she'd typically kept to the edges of the crowds.

The music lifted, and Jastyn found the source of the sound. A band of selkies played lutes, a lyre, and another stringed instrument she didn't recognize. When she looked back at the circle, Aurelia was only two paces away.

"What do we do?" Jastyn asked, her voice a whisper.

Aurelia bowed, and Jastyn did the same. "We dance."

She held up a hand, and Jastyn pressed her palm to Aurelia's. They walked a small circle as the music continued, the strings plucking merrily. Jastyn stared at her feet when they switched palms, repeating the steps in the opposite direction.

"Relax," Aurelia muttered.

"I don't know what I'm doing."

"Follow me."

Jastyn let her gaze linger on Aurelia's. She focused on the pools of blue staring back at her and forgot to worry about what her feet were doing. When their third circle was completed and their palms parted, Jastyn frowned, and panic set in.

As if sensing her worry, Aurelia said, "Do as I do." She took two steps back, then pulled back her shoulders and raised her hands in a clap. Jastyn mimicked her on the second clap. By the third, the selkie colony had joined in. Aurelia stepped closer, pressing her palm to Jastyn's.

When they once again fell into the circling from before, Jastyn exhaled. "This isn't so bad."

Aurelia's eyes twinkled as other selkies cheered and broke from the circle, pairing up and striking their own poses on the deck. A couple of feet away, Revna and Tove bowed elegantly to one another before joining the dance. When the entire deck was packed, Jastyn looked back at Aurelia and lost herself in the dance. She tried to relax, but each time their palms pressed together, she felt a fire ignite inside her that grew stronger with each touch. The music spun around them, the selkies and the grand ship disappearing until it was only her and Aurelia dancing in the cool summer night. Jastyn's throat went dry as Aurelia's gaze shimmered with the same look she'd had back in Vreis's cave, the look before they'd shared their first kiss.

Heat ran through her body, and she stumbled as the musicians played their final notes.

"I've got you." Aurelia stepped forward, laying her hands on Jastyn's hips, bracing her. Now Aurelia was all she could see. Jastyn was struck—as she always was—by Aurelia's beauty. But this time was different. This time, Jastyn wasn't just looking at a beautiful princess. Now she was gazing upon a woman who had shared in her struggles the last few months. A woman who had willingly given up the comfortable life she'd known to join Jastyn on this journey. A woman who had stood alongside her in the face of danger.

Jastyn was staring at a woman who made her want to be better, who made her want to share everything, every truth, no matter how dark. "Aurelia…"

Aurelia smiled as applause scattered through the ship.

"Well done, Jastyn." Tove clapped her on the back, beaming with pride.

"You were great, Jas." Coran shouted. "Here I thought you had two left feet."

Jastyn muttered her thanks, then was caught up in a flurry of handshakes and shoulder pats, so many that she lost count. A chorus of congratulations rang out, and Jastyn raised her hands in gratitude.

The noise and congestion didn't let up, and she quickly felt stifled by the attention. The adulation constricted her like a snake over its prey. The words of adoration and affection became scathing knifes, pricking at her skin. The feeling that she didn't deserve all of this crept into the back of her mind.

Next to her, Tove's face lit with recognition as she wriggled free from a selkie hug. "Excuse us, everyone," he announced, his voice booming over the noise and a new song. "I would like a moment with my daughter." A few jeers rang out. "Don't worry, I will return her. Until then, carry on with the celebration." Just like that, the boos returned to jovial cries, and the selkies began another dance.

Jastyn glanced back. "Go on," Aurelia said, "I'll see you later."

Her heart hurt at parting from Aurelia, but Jastyn was grateful when her father led her through the throngs of festivalgoers and up a set of steps, past where Rigo looked to be in a very serious conversation with Njal and onto the quarter deck above the former captain's cabin. Clear of the crowds, Jastyn breathed deeply, holding on to the wooden rail gratefully.

"Thank you," she said.

Tove stood beside her, looking out at the dark waters below. "We don't have guests often. I forget that we can be an overwhelming group."

She smiled and watched the pale crests of waves crashing against the distant shoreline. "I'm not used to parties, that's all."

He fingered the coin at the end of his necklace and said nothing.

Feeling the need to explain, she said, "The festivals thrown by the Diarmaids never appealed to me."

"I can imagine why."

"Coran would drag me to some, but most of the time, I'd stay away."

"So it's safe to say this is the biggest celebration you've been a part of?"

She snorted. "Definitely." Memories rushed back. "When it was just me and Mother, we only celebrated my birthday. She would take me to the beach." She looked at the night sky, breathing in the salt air. "We would walk to the southern shoreline of Venostes. I would run along the sand, kicking up the water each time it pulled onto the shore." Warmth settled over her shoulders, and she held her arms across her chest. "My mother always took me there, despite the danger of being seen by the guards. We'd go every year and touch the edges of a sea that had come from lands far away." She paused, glancing at Tove. "Lands I thought you might have come from. Places I dreamt you might be."

His voice was filled with sadness as he said, "But then you stopped going to the shoreline."

Confused, she turned. "Yes. When she married Elisedd. He thought it was too dangerous."

"He was probably right."

"How did you know?"

He stared at the coin between his fingers. He let it fall against his chest and met her gaze. "Branna sent me a message the day you were born. I was ecstatic, knowing you were finally a part of this world. She even told me your name. But I knew nothing else of you." He scanned her face as if straining to etch it into his mind. "The week of your first birthday, I pleaded for leave from Revna. She let me go, and I swam to your southern shores, waiting in the water, hoping to see you at least once."

Hardly able to comprehend what she was hearing, Jastyn stood quietly.

"When Branna and I were together, we spent most of our days at the beach. It was a far-flung hope that she might take you there, too. Lucky for me, she did." His eyes filled with tears, and he reached out, taking her hand. The sounds of the party faded with his words.

"You…you were there?"

"Each year until you were ten."

"The year my mother married."

"Not only did I get to see you once, but I got to witness you grow into a strong young girl. I wouldn't give that up for all of the shipwrecks in the world."

Turning her face to the sea, Jastyn bit the inside of her cheek. Thinking back to her mother, she conjured that old resentment. "Why didn't she say anything?"

"Your mother never knew. I never made contact with her after the message of your birth. If the royal family had known the fae who fathered you was near, they would have stopped at nothing to find me and would have thrown your mother back in the dungeons, even after she married."

Knowing he was right, she shook her head. "It's all so unfair." Her mind drifted to the Wood. She pictured herself alone with her mother as they fought to survive. She felt the ever-impending presence of the Dark Fae, constantly at her back for being an Odium. She once again felt the eyes of disdain and scrutiny from the villagers who knew her only as the bastard orphan of a woman who'd broken the laws. The lonely life wrapped itself around her mind, threatening to burst in a fit of rage.

"Jastyn," Tove said, turning her to face him. She hadn't even realized tears were running down her face until he gently wiped them away. "You weren't alone. You were never alone."

He pulled her into a hug. At first, she braced herself against the cool slickness of his seal skin, the hardness of his body. "You're not alone, Jastyn," he said again, and slowly, she wrapped her arms around him, letting him console her the way she'd always imagined a father might. They stood like that a moment, and she stored it in that place in her mind where pleasant memories resided, like the day after Alanna drank the banshee blood. The day she and her sister laughed and laughed alongside her mother and Elisedd. Now her father could be a part of that sacred place, too.

When she stepped back, they looked at one another, slowly breaking into awkward laughter. "Well," he said, wiping his own face. "I've always heard reunions were tearful, but I hadn't truly understood until now."

"I'm sorry to interrupt." Rigo's voice cut between them. He looked truly concerned at having intruded.

"It's all right, Rigo," said Jastyn. "What is it?"

He gestured toward the steps near the captain's cabin that led to the main deck. Aurelia was there, leaning against the wall in conversation with a rather striking selkie.

Rigo glanced worriedly at Jastyn. "Your mate is being approached by another."

Heat flew to Jastyn's cheeks, and she dipped her chin, turning her shoulder to block Tove's view of her face. "Rigo, Aurelia is not my mate."

His brows knit together. "Your human rituals continue to perplex me."

She could only laugh. "Aurelia may speak with whomever she

likes, Rigo." All three of them watched as Aurelia and the selkie continued to talk. When she laughed at something he said, the selkie reached out a strong-looking hand to touch the starfish pin in her hair. Jastyn took a step forward.

At the same time, a pair of young selkies ran up the stairs, parting Aurelia and the man, who looked unhappy at the distance. As the pair ran past and found a spot near the other end of the railing, Aurelia caught Jastyn's gaze. She said something to the selkie, then bowed and excused herself.

"I see Her Royal Highness can handle herself just fine," Tove said, amused.

Jastyn clenched and unclenched one of her fists as the male selkie's eyes trailed Aurelia. When his gaze met Jastyn's, she glared. He stumbled back, giving a slight bow before sprinting down the staircase.

"Good evening, everyone." Aurelia beamed at their group. "What were we all discussing?"

The three of them exchanged looks.

"Why, the woman of the hour, of course." Tove shoved Jastyn's arm, and she couldn't help but enjoy the fatherly gesture.

Rigo looked between them, muttered, "Humans," then walked back to the center of the ship.

Aurelia frowned after him, then turned back to Jastyn. "So were you ever going to tell me about how you could dance, or was I going to be left in the dark for years to come?"

Jastyn's stomach fluttered at her talk of a future. She swallowed, avoiding Tove's knowing gaze. "I wasn't sure I could."

Humming, Aurelia said, "If you say so."

Over Aurelia's shoulder, Njal appeared at the top of the stairs and called, "Tove, it's time."

"Time? Whatever for?" Aurelia asked.

Jastyn groaned. "Not another dance, I hope."

Laughing, Tove said, "You'll see. Stay here. These will be the best seats on the ship."

"Best seats for what?" Jastyn shouted after him as he hurried after Njal before disappearing belowdecks.

"Your father is as enigmatic as you."

Jastyn turned to Aurelia, surprised. Aurelia also seemed taken aback, perhaps surprised she'd said that out loud. "You look alike, too."

"Do we?"

She nodded and leaned her forearms onto the railing, looking out over the smaller ships and gentle waves. Jastyn let her eyes rove over Aurelia's figure. Her tunic was fitted, hugging her curves. Her legs, quite muscular compared to when their journey began, were shown off inside her snug pants. Jastyn's mouth grew dry as her gaze lingered at Aurelia's waist.

"I never thanked you for the dance," Aurelia said, still looking at the night sky.

Jastyn pulled her gaze away, mirroring her position and lacing her fingers while resting on the railing's edge. "I'm not sure there was much to be thankful for."

Aurelia chuckled. "You were better than you think."

"I suppose we can't all be trained by the kingdom's finest."

"That's true."

Jastyn shot her a look, catching the mischievous light in her eyes. "Has it been a good night?"

Considering the question, Jastyn grew quiet. Her mind flooded with images from years past. There had been bad nights, ones spent next to a scant fire in the Wood, huddling for warmth with her mother. There had been good nights, when she and Alanna had stayed up listening to stories by the hearth, enjoying a rare sweetbread and cup of milk. But never had there been a night like this.

Before Jastyn could respond, a bright orange light lit up the night in the middle of the vast cove. They both shielded their eyes at the unfamiliar glow. Below, a flurry of splashes met the water, and Jastyn caught sight of two dozen selkies taking to the sea, their seal skins wrapping around them in fast transformations.

"What's going on?" Aurelia asked.

Jastyn smiled. "I think this is what my father was talking about."

The selkies swam into a formation, dark shadows beneath the water. The orange glow sat over the sea like a giant saol bobbing several yards above the current. The selkies leapt from the sea, their paths crisscrossing. Trails of water crested and broke in beautiful patterns, each one lit by the orange light. The selkies swam down, then leapt in a new pattern, the water erupting from the surface in intricate arches, their movements so precise, Jastyn wondered how long they had spent practicing such a feat.

"It's breathtaking," Aurelia said.

Jastyn could only nod. The sight was like nothing she'd ever seen. Looking behind her, she searched for the source of the orange glow. She spotted Coran atop the captain's quarters, his hands out as he controlled the dancing flame, giving light to the elegant movements of the selkies.

"Happy homecoming, Jas," he cried.

Overcome, she shook her head, looking back at the spectacle below. More selkies had taken to the shoreline, embracing their seal skins to join in the revelry.

Aurelia intertwined her fingers with Jastyn's over the rail of the ship. When she met her gaze, Jastyn's heart raced, and she squeezed Aurelia's hand. Desire pricked her skin and enveloped them both, pulling Jastyn's attention from the show below.

When the light burst into a red-orange glow, illuminating the finale of the selkies' dance, Jastyn straightened. Aurelia did the same. The fire that had ignited between them during their dance returned, burning hotter than Jastyn had ever felt. Instinctively, she tried to pull away, but Aurelia's grip tightened.

Jastyn opened her mouth to explain that they shouldn't do this. The same tired mantra ran through her mind. *You're the princess. I'm an Odium. We could never be together.* But she knew Aurelia had heard all of that before. Back in Vreis's cave, when she had said those very words, none of it had mattered. Jastyn had felt Aurelia's longing then, the same way she did now.

Closing her eyes, she tried to see things the way Aurelia did. She tried to embrace the feeling of allowing herself to want something she couldn't have. Somebody she shouldn't have.

She felt Aurelia step closer. Taking a deep breath, Jastyn opened her eyes. As Aurelia's gaze fell to her lips, Jastyn decided.

After all, it *was* her party.

CHAPTER TWENTY-FOUR

Aurelia could no longer hear the music from the deck, the waves against the ship, or the selkies barking in the water below. All she could hear was the pounding of her own heart as she leaned in and kissed Jastyn the way she so desperately longed to.

The softness of Jastyn's lips was better than anything she'd ever experienced. Granted, she had little to compare it to. She had kissed one other woman before, when she was eighteen. Her first kiss had been a wine-fueled adventure with a daughter of one of the ladies of the court. She and Gilda had snuck into the eastern tower one rebellious evening after dinner, giggling and clasping each other's hands as the guards searched for them at the requests of their mothers. Feeling invigorated by the whole thing, Aurelia had leaned in and kissed her, something she had considered doing for a while. Alas, it had happened only once, and afterward, Aurelia had been left alone with her own imagination and dreams.

Until Jastyn.

Now here she was, kissing the woman she was certain she'd been destined to meet. The woman whose strength and bravery stoked endless embers of admiration and longing. A woman who cared for others more than herself. A woman who Aurelia wanted more than anyone she'd ever known.

Kissing her deeper, Aurelia moaned in protest when Jastyn pulled back. Their shoulders rose and fell as their breath came quickly. Aurelia ran her hand up Jastyn's arm, then cupped her cheek. Tracing Jastyn's bottom lip, she smiled at its swollen feeling.

Aurelia's entire being felt light when Jastyn let her head rest in her hand, eyes closed in brief contentment. When they opened, Aurelia saw the familiar glint of regret beginning to swirl. Before Jastyn could say anything, Aurelia grabbed her hand.

"Come with me."

For the first time, Jastyn didn't protest and let Aurelia lead her across the quarter deck. Aurelia led them into the captain's quarters. The room was bigger than their chambers on the other ship. Aurelia had stumbled upon it during the preparations for tonight. Many decorative sails were stored there, piles of material strewn on the floor and over an old desk cluttered with sailing instruments while others spread across chairs with missing legs.

Still holding Jastyn's hand, she turned and walked carefully backward toward a pile of sails below one of the portholes that looked out on the night sky. It wasn't the bed Aurelia longed to lie Jastyn down upon, but it would do.

But the sudden, stark quiet stoked Aurelia's uncertainty. The tension between them felt palpable, as if their saols were lit and competing for space, creating a white-hot heat Aurelia felt in her bones.

She faced Jastyn, their hands clasped. Slowly, she knelt. Looking up, she hoped Jastyn could feel the yearning that filled her heart, raced down her arms, and pulsed through her fingertips. After what felt like an eternity, Jastyn joined her, and Aurelia knew this night would hold more magic than any before it.

This time, it was Jastyn who reached out, pulling Aurelia into another kiss. When her lips parted, Aurelia breathed her in, wanting nothing more than to lose herself in the feeling of Jastyn's strong body pressed against hers. When Jastyn's tongue met hers, its slick wet heat lit a fire deep inside Aurelia, and she leaned forward, craving more as she lay Jastyn down with herself on top, the sails beneath them. Aurelia didn't break their kiss as she straddled Jastyn, relishing the feel of her fingers tracing up her legs, then gripping her thighs hungrily. Aurelia cried out at the sensation, breathing into another kiss.

When Jastyn leaned back again, Aurelia tried to steady her breathing. Her body hummed, taut like an arrow yearning for release, and she ached to run her hands under Jastyn's tunic. "What is it?" she finally asked, unable to stand the space between them.

Aurelia was surprised when Jastyn swiftly rolled them over. Now

Jastyn lay alongside her, one leg between Aurelia's as their bodies pressed together.

Aurelia bit her lip as Jastyn delicately pulled the starfish pin from her hair. "I don't want to ruin such a beautiful gift," she said, her voice a whisper.

When she placed it on the other side of them, Aurelia raised her eyebrows. "And how do you imagine that might that happen?"

The grin on Jastyn's face told Aurelia everything she wanted to know.

Sunlight streamed through the porthole. Jastyn stirred, stretching beneath a green sail that she'd wrapped around herself in the night. Wondering at her tired limbs, she felt another body stirring and found Aurelia draped over her, one arm and one leg holding on tight.

Jastyn watched her chest rise and fall. She ran her fingertips along Aurelia's forearm, tracing lines into her skin. She still wasn't sure that everything that had happened between them had been real, every touch, every kiss they had shared as the ship rocked gently with them through the night. But while holding Aurelia in her arms, Jastyn knew she wasn't dreaming. She had discovered Aurelia's desires as the stars shone overhead and matched their brightness with her own.

She ran her fingers toward Aurelia's face and brushed the brown locks, tucking them behind Aurelia's ear. When Jastyn returned to her arm, Aurelia muttered sleepily, "That feels wonderful."

Jastyn grinned. "You said something similar last night."

One side of Aurelia's lips turned up in a smile. "You're feeling clever this morning."

Pulling her close, Jastyn held her tight. She'd let her guard down last night, but for the first time since meeting Aurelia, she didn't regret what they had done or how she was feeling. She'd known she was falling in love. But things were different now. She understood more. The veil of uncertainty that had hovered over her life had begun to lift in the last two weeks. Questions she'd had for years had finally been answered. And with the help of her father, she'd have her sister's cure in time. For once, things might actually work out.

When Aurelia lifted her chin, clear brightness shone in her eyes, and Jastyn leaned down, pressing their lips together. She smiled into the kiss.

A sudden clamor broke the blissful spell, and they turned at the sound of voices coming from overhead.

"We need to put things away, Coran. The festivities are over."

"Can't it wait?"

"Why wait when it can be done now? Truly, you humans are so prone to procrastination, it's a wonder anything ever gets done."

A rush of footsteps was followed by their cabin door banging open. Njal fell into the room, a pile of food trays resting on a sail hanging over his wide arms. Jastyn and Aurelia sat up, holding their material up to their chins.

Njal dropped his sail. Coran halted behind him. Njal's gaze went from Jastyn to Aurelia's discarded tunic lying on a nearby chair, then back to Jastyn.

"Sorry, Jas. Many pardons, m'lady," Coran said, his own eyes fixed on the ceiling. "I tried to tell him."

Aurelia giggled, and Jastyn nodded to Njal. "If you'll give us a few minutes, we can be out of here so you can take care of things."

The selkie, still wearing a look of shock, only stared. Finally, he said, "Very well." He hurriedly placed the rest of his things on the old desk then ran from the room. Coran, hands behind his back and still staring at the ceiling, said, "See you two upstairs." Jastyn didn't miss the grin on his face before he left, closing the door behind him.

❖

"You've got a lightness to your step today," Coran said from across the table where they sat munching on lunch inside his chamber.

The celebration had ended, but the effects of the evening lingered. Many selkies lounged lazily on rocks scattered throughout the cove, their seal forms happy to do nothing but sunbathe until the next day. Colborn had finally emerged, scowling at the remnants of food and used candles strewn about the main ship. But even his bitter demeanor couldn't dampen Jastyn's mood.

"I have no idea what you're talking about," she said.

"Uh huh." He bit into his bread, tearing off a bite.

She threw a cherry at him, which he chucked back before she

popped it in her mouth. Its sweetness reminded her of Aurelia, and she lost herself in the memories of their night together.

"I'm guessing you didn't spend the night telling her about the noble sacrifice."

Her face fell. "Must you do that?" she asked, glowering. "I can't even have half a day to enjoy myself?"

"I'm sorry," he said, holding up his hands. "Tove wants to leave in two days for the caves." He shrugged. "You're running out of time."

She stabbed at her fish with a fork, frustrated at being brought back to the reality of her situation. The gray cloud of what she still had to do crashed down around her. Sighing, she held on even tighter to the memories from the night before. Last night, she had never felt the way she had with anyone before. No woman had ever evoked such pleasure, such happiness inside her. Being with Aurelia had made sense in ways so many things never had in her life. When they had been together, when Jastyn had felt Aurelia in ways she'd only dreamt of, a new hope had blossomed. A hope that Aurelia would understand why she'd kept the sacrifice secret for so long. Jastyn only ever wanted to protect her, only ever wanted to make her happy. She hoped after last night, Aurelia could feel that, too.

"I'll talk to Aurelia soon," she said.

"Talk to me about what?"

Aurelia strolled into the chamber, plopping down next to Jastyn and plucking a strawberry from her plate. She bit into it eagerly, chewing through a smile as she glanced between them.

Coran pursed his lips, busying himself with his bread. Jastyn grimaced but turned to Aurelia, grabbing another strawberry and taking a bite. "I was telling Coran that I wanted to talk to you about…" She searched for words that were as close to the truth as she could get. "Well, about us."

Aurelia's swallow was audible. "Oh." A bashful smile lifted between her rosy cheeks. "I see."

"That's what we were talking about before you came in." Jastyn fixed Coran with a look, and he nodded.

"Yep, that's it," he said overeagerly.

"Anyway," Jastyn said, "what are you doing today?"

Aurelia looped her arm through Jastyn's. "I thought we might go explore the cove a bit." When Jastyn and Coran stared, she added,

"Rigo has already scouted a few spots for us. Sif said she and Fortan would join, as well. Maybe Tove would like to go."

Jastyn finished the last of her fish, giving her a sideways glance.

"It's only an idea," Aurelia added, one hand waving casually.

"Sounds fun," Jastyn replied as Coran gave her an expectant look. "And," she added, "it's a good place to have our talk."

Aurelia leaned forward, planting a kiss on Jastyn's cheek. "Wonderful. I'll gather everyone, and then we will head out."

She hopped up and scampered from the room, her excitement trailing after her and bringing Jastyn's gaze along with it.

A low whistle pulled her attention back to Coran. "You've got it bad," he said, shaking his head.

She chucked another cherry at him. "Hush."

CHAPTER TWENTY-FIVE

This was one of the most wonderful days Aurelia had ever had. Since sunrise, a warm contentedness had settled within her. It was the first time she'd felt anything like it since her brother's passing. Waking up in Jastyn's arms had been like a dream, one she never wanted to end. The night had been magical, surreal, full of such love like she'd never known. Now, walking hand in hand with Jastyn along the shoreline of the selkies' cove, Aurelia was certain this must be what the gods felt when walking among the clouds.

"So you two *aren't* together?"

Sif's teasing voice passed her as she walked by to join Tove and Rigo, their steps imprinted in the sand before being washed away by the retreating waves. Aurelia laughed and held tight to Jastyn, who flinched in her grasp.

"It's all right, she's only poking fun," Aurelia whispered, leaning in as they walked behind the others. The late afternoon sun began its descent overhead.

Jastyn grimaced, but she relaxed as Aurelia placed a kiss on her cheek, brushing back some hair as the wind swept it out of her braid.

Aurelia relished being so near a shoreline, and it took everything in her not to spend every moment on the sand or running her hands along the cliffsides, feeling the smooth beneath her fingertips. The openness of it all was so unlike the dark, tight quarters of the castle.

"That looks like a good spot," Coran called from behind, his satchel bouncing at his side. He pointed across Fortan, who he'd been having a lively conversation with.

"I completely agree," Fortan said, his step light as they all veered toward a shallow cave pocked with smooth boulders, a perfect spot for a picnic.

Once they were all settled, Aurelia and Coran opened their satchels while Tove and Fortan transformed into seals, diving into the water to fetch fish. Rigo started a fire with Coran's help, and Aurelia shifted driftwood around to form a half-circle for seats.

"Can't resist, can you?" Jastyn asked, tossing her a grin as she pulled more berries and apples from the satchel before placing her own bag outside the cave.

Aurelia smiled back. "I only want us all to be comfortable."

Coran continued to stoke the fire as Rigo arranged wooden cups and poured sweet wine into each. Once the driftwood was arranged, Aurelia straightened, placing her hands on her hips and meeting Jastyn's gaze, which seemed cloudy.

"Is everything all right?" Aurelia asked. Gods, she hoped Jastyn didn't regret what had happened between them.

Jastyn nodded but avoided her gaze. She tossed Aurelia an apple. "I need to talk to Coran about something."

"All right," Aurelia said as Jastyn motioned for Coran, who left the fire to Rigo.

"We'll be back," Jastyn called as they started off in the opposite direction.

Aurelia waved. "Hurry back." Her hand falling to her side, she watched Jastyn walk away.

"Is she always like that?"

Turning, Aurelia found Sif standing nearby, her hands on her hips and her seal skin resting atop her dark hair.

"She's got a lot on her mind," Aurelia said, hoping that one of those things wasn't wishing last night had never happened. She watched Jastyn and Coran a moment more, then reluctantly turned to face Sif. "Her sister isn't well."

"That's why you've journeyed west?"

Aurelia nodded. "It's the reason for all of this. We're so close to her cure now."

Sif looked at her thoughtfully.

"What?"

Sif shook her head. "You are not the Diarmaid I expected."

"Well, if I'm being honest, you're not exactly the selkie I expected."

Sif raised her eyebrows, her scar lifting with it. "Oh?"

"The texts I read paint your kind as a vicious, vindictive group." Aurelia motioned to the shipwrecks cluttered in the cove's waters. "Sailors faint at the sight of you on the ocean, knowing what fate lies ahead of them."

Sif lifted her chin. "We sound rather impressive."

"People fear you above sirens."

"Is that so?" She chuckled. "Stories are a powerful thing."

Aurelia nodded.

"They can also create a persona that was never deserved." Sif started for the wet sand, and Aurelia followed as they moved closer to the water. Sif's voice was calm as she spoke over the waves. "Our feelings toward the royal family are built on decades of stories. None of us has ever actually met a member until now. The Diarmaids are a construct in our minds based on hearsay." She lowered her gaze. "I realize that now."

"Fae have good reason to dislike my family." With guilt creeping up the back of her neck, Aurelia crossed her arms. "We have not been kind to those who are different from us."

"But you are not like the others in those tales," Sif said, motioning to their group. "Look around, Princess. You rejoice with selkies and have befriended an elf. You walk with an Odium and, if I may, have fallen deeply in love with her."

Aurelia's mouth opened at Sif's candidness, a blush filling her cheeks. Glancing sideways, she met Sif's kind gaze.

"You are not the Diarmaid I expected."

Standing quietly on the shoreline, Aurelia breathed deep, relishing the scent of salt water and the cool breeze sweeping over them. "This realm is full of wonderful beings," she mused. "It holds so much magic in it, more than I could have ever imagined. I know one day, my kingdom can be like this." She pointed to their group. "It may take years, decades even, but when I'm queen, the bigotry will end. Prejudice will be vanquished." She looked longingly at Jastyn down the shoreline. "Venostes will live in peace when the laws of hate no longer exist."

Sif's dark eyes shimmered. "I look forward to that day, Princess."

A series of splashes drew their attention. Fortan and Tove emerged from the water and shifted back into their human forms. Each held a bundle of fish as they walked toward the cave.

"Only ten?" Sif asked.

Fortan scoffed. "I didn't see you out there."

"Quit your squabbling, you two," Tove said. "We've got a feast to prepare."

Sif laughed. "We'll be over in a minute to help."

When the two selkies joined Rigo near the entrance of the cave, they began to skin the fish and skewer them above the fire. Sif looked pointedly at Aurelia.

Feeling scrutinized, Aurelia asked, "What is it?"

"You're worried about something."

Aurelia sighed. Her gaze slid toward Jastyn, who was still in conversation with Coran. "Jastyn told me she wants to talk about 'us.' I'm afraid she's going to tell me she doesn't think we should do…this." Aurelia faltered, emotions making her words difficult to find. Her heart raced, and fear mingled with the newfound hope rising in her chest. "She's been elusive since I met her. I understand why, but I also know she feels for me the way I do for her. It's difficult, though. She's not one to let others in."

"That is obvious."

Aurelia spoke softly, afraid at her own words. "What if she says we can't be together?"

Sif frowned, looking out at the colony of ships in the middle of the cove. "She loves you, Aurelia. Even if she can't say it. The road to love is never straightforward. Things will work out."

"How can you know that?"

Sif smiled. "Call it a selkie's intuition."

"I hope you're right."

"Come on, Princess." Sif wrapped her arm around Aurelia's shoulders. "Let's get the food ready before your Odium returns."

The sky's edges gained tints of pink as they finished the last of their meal. Aurelia leaned back, content and swimming in the bliss of a cup of wine and Jastyn sitting beside her. She listened as Tove explained the process of making another dagger.

"It can be ready within a few days," he explained. "Our blacksmiths are efficient, but getting hold of the materials is what takes time."

"Too bad Eegit's not here," Coran said. "She's got everything you'd need."

Jastyn smiled. "I'll just be happy to have my dagger again."

A comfortable silence fell over their group. It had been hours since Jastyn had gone off with Coran, and Aurelia, despite the joy of an afternoon at the beach, had grown more nervous with each passing minute. Jastyn had mentioned she wanted to talk, but they had yet to do so. Finishing the last bites of her fruit, Aurelia stood.

"If you'll excuse us for a few moments, Jastyn and I are going for a quick stroll."

Tove raised his brows knowingly, and Coran asked, "Now?"

"Of course." She reached out to Jastyn, who set her cup down. Aurelia didn't miss the look she shot Coran, which confirmed her decision that whatever this talk was going to be about, she might as well get it over with now. Clearly, something was weighing heavily on Jastyn's mind.

When they were down the beach, out of earshot of the others, Aurelia pulled Jastyn down beside her on the sand, just out of reach of the water's edge. The sky's edges began to darken as sunset drew nearer.

They sat quietly, nothing but the sound of the water and the distant barks of selkies aboard the ships in the distance. It was complete reverie, save for the tense feeling of Jastyn beside her. She hated that Jastyn could never feel at ease for long, and she feared the worst of what could be on her mind. When Jastyn swallowed, pinching the bridge of her nose, Aurelia rested a hand on her knee.

"Talk to me."

Pursing her lips, Jastyn bored a hole into the sand with her index finger. "There's something I need to tell you about the caves."

Not expecting this, Aurelia said, "You mentioned already it will be dangerous."

Jastyn closed her eyes. "It's not just that." She fidgeted, shaking the sand free from her hand. "Do you remember how I went to trade your bracelet with the Red One?"

Aurelia nodded. She recalled the cool metal on her wrist, the dazzling rubies that had been set within the band. Now her fingers ran over the thin scars left by the ropes upon her kidnapping. Jastyn had followed her gaze but quickly averted her eyes as if unable to look at the remnants of what Aurelia had gone through.

"The Red One gave me banshee blood for the bracelet," Jastyn continued, "along with information on where to find Alanna's cure."

Aurelia tried not to squirm. She knew all of this already.

Jastyn's swallow was audible over the lapping of the waves. "That night, the Red One told me something else." Jastyn began to tremble beneath her touch.

Gods, what could be waiting for them in the caves? What could make someone as brave and strong as Jastyn shake the way she did now? Bracing herself, Aurelia's confusion turned to fear when Jastyn's gaze met hers.

"The Red One told me that upon reaching the caves, a noble sacrifice would be required to obtain the cure."

At first, the words washed over her like the swiftness with which the waves claimed the sand. Perhaps she'd misheard. "I don't…I don't understand," she finally said.

But Jastyn's gaze didn't waver, and Aurelia felt a pang of dread at the hardness in her eyes. "It's the only way to get the cure," Jastyn said.

Slowly, events began to align. Aurelia stared, stunned, at the water. She remembered the Wood and how it was Jastyn who'd found her at the leprechaun lodging. She recalled Jastyn's aloof nature, constantly analyzing their route. She saw her own stubbornness at the rash decision to join a journey that held the promise of danger at every turn.

"Is that why you agreed that I could join you?" Aurelia fought to keep her voice even. She remembered the look on Jastyn's face when Aurelia's parents had found her in the Wood. Aurelia had misread it as fear, when it had actually been disappointment at the prospect of losing the key piece to her sister's cure. "You wanted me to come but not because you cared for me. You needed me to come because you needed *me*." More images flew past her vision. She saw Jastyn making sure that, at each step of the way, Aurelia went unharmed. For what? Aurelia had thought it had been because Jastyn cared and loved her. But now…

Jastyn was shaking. "It's not like that."

Her chest tight, Aurelia let out a hollow laugh. "That's why you worked so hard to make sure I made it through this journey. You needed me in one piece for…what…a sacrifice to save your sister?"

"Please," Jastyn said, holding up her hands. "Let me explain."

Aurelia, seething, couldn't find her words.

"At first, yes, I thought maybe, somehow, I would need to be the one to find you when you were kidnapped. If I did, I could convince you to come to the caves." Her gaze fell. "I never wanted to hurt you, and I have been trying to think of ways to avoid this. Every night, I thought of other possibilities. But Aurelia"—she looked up, her eyes shining—"it's my sister's life."

"Are you saying her life is more valuable than mine?"

"Of course not." Jastyn leaned forward, reaching for her hands. "You know that's not true."

Astonished, Aurelia stood. "Do I?" She began to pace. Her mind felt like it was swept up in that awful whirlwind Drest had cast upon her that night in the Wood. Fuming, she squared up to Jastyn, who slowly stood. "Why didn't you say anything? You have had every opportunity." She waved, gesturing at the cove. "We've been traveling for months."

Jastyn's voice was low, her gaze drifting to the water. "I spent weeks trying to convince myself that the Red One had to be wrong. She's full of riddles, and I tried to unravel her words, convinced she had to mean something else. It still could be anything—"

"How could it be?" Aurelia shot back, gesturing to herself. "You've had a noble in your hands this entire time." Anger boiled in her throat and burst forth with her next words, "She's a fae, Jastyn, they're always after something. Especially when it comes to my family."

At this, darkness fell over Jastyn's face. "You don't mean that."

Turning away, Aurelia wiped at the tears falling down her face. She knew she didn't mean those words, but how could she not think that after hearing all of this? What if her parents had been right to protect her and Brennus from the awful things of the world? What if they knew nothing good could come from trying to change the way things had always been? Aurelia let her thoughts dwell in misery, so much so that she hardly felt Jastyn grab her hand.

"Aurelia, please understand. I was trying to protect you." She winced as if the words hurt her as much as they dug like a sword into Aurelia's heart.

"You lied for months to *protect me*?"

Jastyn stammered. "I didn't lie. I only wanted to wait until…until I could figure out a way to get around the Red One's words."

Aurelia's mind fell into a twisted haze. She felt dizzy and sick. How could this be happening? Looking at Jastyn's hand over hers, a terrible thought came to her. "Last night…was that to ensure I would go with you?"

"No, Aurelia—"

"You touched me in ways no one has. I thought it was because…because…"

Hesitating, Jastyn shifted her weight. Tears filled her gaze.

"Or was it only to fulfill your plan? Sweep me up and make me blind to your scheme? Walk me like a lovestruck fool into the caves and watch me give myself up for you."

Her jaw clenched, Jastyn said, "That's not it at all. Aurelia, my feelings for you are not something I planned. But they're real."

"Then why, Jastyn?" Aurelia was surprised at the hard edge in her voice as she shouted.

"I never wanted to hurt you. I didn't tell you because…" She looked at her boots. "Because I was afraid."

For a moment, Aurelia was caught in the anguish filling Jastyn's face. She had to stop herself from reaching out, stop herself from comforting her. But like the nights she'd sat beside her brother's body, a cold emptiness filled her chest, and she couldn't bear to listen to Jastyn a moment longer.

"Wait," Jastyn said as she turned, holding on to her hand. Aurelia yanked it away. "Aurelia, please."

"Don't follow me," was all Aurelia could manage to say, sobs choking any other words. She couldn't stand to be near Jastyn. She didn't understand how, not half a day before, she had been utterly happy, madly in love with the woman who hadn't given a second thought to breaking her heart.

She could hear Jastyn crying, and the wind carried her desperate pleas, but Aurelia refused to turn back. She couldn't. All she wanted was to put as much distance between herself and Jastyn as she could, something she'd never imagined could be possible.

Chapter Twenty-Six

Shattered. That was all Jastyn felt. She felt as if her very soul was shattered and left in irreparable pieces on the ground.

Collapsed on the sand, she watched her nightmare come to life: Aurelia walked away from her, as far from Jastyn as she could, all because Jastyn had been too afraid. Too afraid to let her in. Too afraid to trust her with the truth. Too afraid to surrender to her feelings.

And now Aurelia was gone.

Sand kicked up around her. Coran was at her side. "What happened?"

Jastyn coughed, her throat aching from crying. She shook her head.

"Jas, did you tell her?"

Looking up, she found his worried face through bleary eyes. "What do you think?" she asked, pointing disdainfully at Aurelia's distant figure.

"It's gonna be okay, Jas."

"Nothing is ever okay." She dropped her head in her hands. "All my life, nothing good ever lasts."

"Hey." He crouched in front of her and pulled her hands apart, making her look at him. "I'm still here. I could've drowned in that river. But you dove in after me. And gods know the number of times we barely escaped the guards in the market." He gave her half a smile. "We'll get through this."

"I love her, Coran."

"I know." He looked past her. "I'll talk to her."

"She's so angry."

He squeezed her shoulder. "Go back to the others. I'll talk to her and bring her back."

She couldn't respond as he took off after Aurelia. More tears threatened, and she rubbed her palms into her eyes, forcing them away. She didn't deserve to cry. She didn't deserve to feel better. And she didn't deserve somebody like Aurelia. She never had, and she never would. The last few months had been nothing but a wishful fantasy. And like all fantasies, it had come to an end.

Taking a shuddering breath, she watched Coran run after Aurelia, but she wasn't slowing down. They were nearly around a curve in the cove, toward the entrance to the inlet leading out to sea. Turning, Jastyn caught a glimpse of their campsite. The selkies were laughing as Rigo told an animated story. Her gaze fell on Tove. Part of her wanted to run to him. She wanted to ask him what to do. But as she watched, his boisterous laughter echoed over the rocks, and she knew she couldn't. He might be her father, but that didn't make him the person she could run to when things were hard. She'd been raised without him and knew deep down that she could never have him as a part of her life beyond this cove. Even if she wanted it, it wasn't something an Odium like her deserved.

A faint *pop* sounded off to her right, and Jastyn imagined she was back in the Wood. When a familiar voice shouted at her, Jastyn nearly fell backward. "Child! I leave you for the summer, and you crumple up like a leaf in autumn. Stand and wipe the water from your face."

Jastyn had to be imagining things. She couldn't be looking at the waifish, swaying frame of Eegit. Stunned, she reached out, but Eegit slapped her hand away.

"Get up, child."

"Eegit?"

"I can see the journey took your backbone, but did it take your brain, too?" She guffawed, motioning for Jastyn to stand.

"I don't understand."

"Clearly." She shook her head, the wind whipping her mane of frazzled gray hair every which way. "Come, I have urgent news."

Aurelia and Coran had disappeared around the edge of the cove. "What do you mean?" Jastyn asked, looking back at Eegit. "Come where?"

"I've somethin' to show you, and it'll only last a few moments more."

Before Jastyn could ask, Eegit gripped her forearm tightly, and the solid pack of sand beneath their feet dropped out from under them. They fell into darkness, and Jastyn would have screamed at the sensation of falling if not for the solid grip Eegit had on her arm.

Seconds later, they landed hard on a familiar dirt floor.

"Where did you—"

Eegit held up a finger in front of her thin, chapped lips. Her eyes were wide, and she pushed Jastyn against the wall. They were back in the kingdom, back in the village.

Back in her home.

"Eegit," Jastyn whispered, "what are we doing here?"

She clucked as if annoyed at Jastyn's confusion. "We're not really here."

"I don't understand."

Reaching up, Eegit slapped her forehead.

"Ow."

"Pay attention, child," was all she said before pressing them both against the wall as the unoccupied room filled with the figures of Branna, Alanna, and Elisedd. Her mother was seated by the fire, reading a book with Alanna while Elisedd sat in the corner, bent over a horseshoe.

"Alanna," Jastyn said, stepping forward. When she did, it was as if an invisible wall kept her from moving any closer. Pressing against the air, Jastyn turned to Eegit.

"It's a complicated spell. We've only a few minutes." She pointed again to the room. "Wait."

Jastyn, weary with wonder at being back home, stood reluctantly against the wall. She felt dazed as she looked once again at her family. She hadn't realized how much she'd missed them. Looking harder at Alanna, her happiness shrank at her sister's ashy complexion and the stained rag bundled in her hands to quiet her coughs.

Suddenly, the door burst open.

A group of royal guardsmen flew into the room.

Elisedd stood. "What is this?"

"You all are under arrest by order of the royal family."

Branna put Alanna behind her. Elisedd rushed over, standing in front of them. "On what grounds? We're guilty of nothing."

"You have been charged with harboring the fugitive responsible for kidnapping the princess Aurelia Diarmaid."

Elisedd glanced back at Branna. Alanna looked petrified.

"Jastyn," Branna muttered.

"She's not here," Elisedd told the guards, his goatee trembling with his chin. "She hasn't been here for months."

"We have our orders." One of the guards motioned, and the others stepped forward.

"Mother," Alanna cried as Elisedd was pulled away, one of the men yanking his arms behind his back.

"It's okay, sweetheart," Branna said, but Jastyn heard the wavering conviction in her voice as another guard separated her from Alanna. When one of them grabbed her sister, Jastyn pounded against the invisible wall.

"Please," Elisedd cried as they bent Alanna's arms behind her. "Leave our daughter out of this. She's done nothing wrong."

"We are to take every member of the household in for questioning. You can take up your concerns with the royal magistrate."

"Alanna!" Jastyn pounded harder on the wall, her fists sending pulses across the barrier. But her sister didn't hear her. None of them did. She watched tearfully as her family was torn from their home at the hands of the royal guards.

"No, wait," she yelled. "I'm here. Don't take them away." Jastyn screamed, but it was no use. When the door slammed shut, she was left with nothing but the dull crackle of her family's hearth.

"We have to go after them," she shouted, rounding on Eegit. "They can't do this."

Eegit's eyes were sad, and she gently took Jastyn's arm. With a snap of her fingers, the ground once again fell out from under them. Jastyn felt sick in the twisting darkness until they landed once again on the beach. Bending over, she retched into the sand.

"Take me back," she cried, shaking and clutching her stomach. "Eegit, please, take me back."

"I can't, child. That moment has come and gone. I was lucky to have enough strength to get us back here." She walked gingerly around Jastyn, one hand on her waist. Her raspy breathing came in wheezing bursts, and her wrinkled skin was pale. Jastyn couldn't recall the last time Eegit had looked so tired. She had known the hedgewitch possessed the ability to pull herself from one place to another, but she'd never thought to ask at what cost such magic came.

"If they hurt them…" Jastyn said, falling to her knees, but the rest of her words were lost as Eegit spoke tiredly, exhausted from her spell.

"It's a sordid pile of spoiled scraps. The whole kingdom has gone topsy-turvy." She closed her eyes, steadying herself. "The prince is gone, the king is a whisper of the ruler he once was, and the queen has disappeared."

"What?" Jastyn forced her mind to focus on Eegit's words. "What do you mean the queen has disappeared?"

"She left months ago to find Her Royal Highness."

A chord of fear struck Jastyn's chest. "Aurelia. She's not safe."

"None of us are." Eegit crouched, pulling Jastyn's chin so she looked her in the eye. "You've got to hurry, child. Your sister doesn't have time. Nor does your princess. You've got to get to the caves before—"

"Before what?" Jastyn asked as Eegit's gaze grew unfocused. She tilted her head, staring past Jastyn.

"I'm of no use in this state," she whispered. "Be brave, Jastyn."

Another *pop* and Eegit was gone.

"Eegit! Eegit, come back." Standing, Jastyn turned, searching. Twenty yards behind her, the Dark Fae sat atop his horse.

"Odium Child." His voice echoed around her like the horrible clanging of a bell.

"No," she muttered, "not now."

The sky darkened as the Dark Fae and his horse stood unmoving on the beach. Behind them, the selkies and Rigo continued to laugh and joke, unfazed by the fae's appearance.

Meanwhile, his voice sounded again. "Odium Child."

"You're not real," Jastyn said. She shook her head, shouting, "You're not real."

Memories invaded her mind. What had he said to her all those months ago in the Wood? This journey would be her undoing? Had he come now to taunt her, declare his victory; he'd been right all along. Jastyn struggled to stand as she felt herself unraveling with each passing second since Aurelia had walked away.

She slammed her eyes shut, digging her palms into them until the dark burst with lights. "You're not really here. You're not."

Opening her eyes, Jastyn glanced down the beach. The Dark Fae was gone.

Slowly, she started forward. Then she remembered Aurelia and Coran and ran for the others.

"Jastyn. Welcome back," Fortan said, his arms wide in greeting. "Tell your father he's ridiculous to think he could take me in a blade fight. Look at me." He stood, tilting a little, his wine sloshing in his cup. "I'm twice his size."

Tove sat up. "Jastyn, what is it?"

"He's here."

"Who's here?"

"The Dark Fae, he found me." She pointed toward where she had been standing, but there was only the darkening beach.

Fortan and Sif exchanged glances. "Jastyn," the former said, laughing, "our cove is blanketed in numerous spells. It's impossible to get in. Well, unless you're one of those unlucky souls," he added, gesturing to the ships and taking another drink. Sif laughed along, but Rigo stood.

"You saw him?" he asked, stepping closer, his grip firm on his bow.

Panic rose in Jastyn's voice. "He was just there."

"Are you certain?" Tove asked. When she nodded, his jaw clenched, the muscle below his ear pulsating. "Fortan." He turned back to the others. "We need to get back."

"Come now, Tove. You know the water plays tricks with the light. Surely it was a passing vision or a shadow from the clouds above." When they all looked up, the sky stretched empty, darkening. Fortan's face fell. "Oh."

"Something's not right," Jastyn said. "Aurelia and Coran aren't here. They need to be warned."

Sif stood. "Where did they go?"

Pointing toward the cove's entrance, Jastyn said, "Coran followed her out of the cove, around that bend." Frightened, still feeling the presence of the Dark Fae, Jastyn turned fearfully to Tove. "It's not safe out there."

He nodded. "We'll gather our things." Then he gripped Jastyn's shaking hands. "We will get them back. Whatever is following you, we will face it together."

Her throat dry, all Jastyn could do was nod. Tove bent to help Fortan stand. As he did, a faint rumbling started in the earth beneath their feet.

"What is that?" Fortan asked, falling back against the boulder he'd been sitting on. All of them glanced around. Jastyn held on to Tove as the shaking intensified.

Rigo leapt ahead to stand on the sand where the quaking water lapped against his legs. He peered across the cove, past the ships where selkies had emerged from their cabins, scrambling across the torchlit deck to investigate the disturbance. Jastyn followed his gaze to the opposite cliffside.

As Fortan fell again, Sif hurrying to help him stand, Rigo spun around. "Your colony is in danger," he said, his voice the most worried Jastyn had ever heard it.

"What do you mean?" Tove asked, the legs of his seal skin waving across his chest as the earth continued to shake. The rumbling grew louder, and Jastyn's heart sank at the familiar sound of thousands of feet storming toward them.

"My queen," Rigo said, "has sent her army to the west."

As if on cue, hundreds of tall, lean bodies poured over the far cliffside, spilling over like water from a basin. They moved swiftly, a horde of ants swarming down the edge of the cliffs and onto the beach in seconds. A boom sounded from the ships, and an old cannonball shot into the air in warning as chaos broke out over the selkies' shipyard. Some of the selkies took to their seal forms, diving into the choppy waters, barking for their children and young selkies to follow. Others remained on two feet, shouting across the planks, gathering weapons and taking up posts along the decks.

"Fortan," Tove said, "can you get back?"

He struggled to keep his feet as the ground shook, but his amused face was now serious as stone. "Yes, of course."

"Go help the council. Keep our families safe. Tell Njal to lead the children out to sea. He knows where to take them."

"I'll go with you," Rigo said, seemingly vibrating with anger. She had never seen him convey such emotion. His serene face was contorted, as if in great pain at once again seeing his own kind. "I do not stand with my brothers and sisters," he said. "I will fight to defend your colony."

Fortan looked ill but started for the water while Rigo draped his bow over his chest. He looked back at Jastyn. "Be safe. I will see you after."

A sense of dread grabbed Jastyn's chest, but she managed to hold out her arm. Rigo shook it, then swiftly leapt onto the boulders jutting up from the water. Within a few bounds, he was back on the ships.

"I'll get Aurelia and your friend back." Sif stood, turning to Jastyn, who could hardly focus. Fear consumed her mind at the presence of the Dark Fae. She was so close to the cure; this couldn't happen now. He wasn't supposed to find her here. This was a safe haven. What if she was too late? Or worse, what if he had gotten to Aurelia?

Sif braced her shoulders, forcing Jastyn to meet her gaze. "I will find her. She'll be all right."

"Please," Jastyn finally managed to say. "If anything happens to her…" She couldn't bear to finish the thought. Tears stung her eyes, and she barely registered Sif promise Aurelia's safety before she took off down the beach.

Still in a haze, Jastyn was pulled back into the shallow cave.

"I thought we had more time." Tove was with her, one hand on her arm as he tugged them inside. He scooped up her satchel. "We've got to move."

"The ships," Jastyn muttered, trying to shake her head of the horrible vision of the Dark Fae and the fear at Aurelia being left to the elements. She wanted to break free from Tove's grip and run with Sif, but her father's determined step drew them farther into the cave.

"The council is strong. Revna predicted something like this might happen while your group was here. The curse," he said, glancing at her, "that damn curse follows you every moment of every moon. She knew he was coming. The colony is strong. It will be all right."

"Where are we going?" The cave they'd spent the day in front of had appeared shallow, but Tove, after muttering a quick spell, revealed impossible depths traced by a narrow path of sand deeper into the cliffs.

"We've got to get you to the caves."

"But the others—"

"Jastyn." He paused, spinning around. "There's no time. The cure waits for you."

Then she remembered. "The noble sacrifice…" She'd unveiled the terrible bargaining point to her father days before the festival. He knew Aurelia might be needed to obtain the cure, and like Jastyn, he'd hoped the leprechaun's words didn't mean what they feared it did.

"Sif will bring her."

Hating everything about this, Jastyn felt sick. "This isn't how it was supposed to go."

"Things rarely work out the way we think they will. I'm sorry, Jastyn. I wish your dagger was ready."

"I never meant to bring this to your world," she said, regret and disappointment seeping into her gut. "Nothing good ever happens where I go."

Tove pulled her chin up. His dark eyes swam with pride, and the look in them shook Jastyn, planting the smallest seed of hope inside her chest. "You are good, Jastyn. Believe that."

The tumult from the selkies' shipyard grew louder. She heard the cries of the elves, the selkies' barks, and the clash of daggers against elven shields.

"There's another way to the caves through here. Only the council knows of it." He glanced fearfully over his shoulder, at his colony taking a stand against the dark force. A dark force Jastyn never wanted to burden anybody else with but which seemed to follow her, destroying the lives of everybody she met. It had ruined her family. It had hurt Vreis. And now, it had its sights set on her father's home.

"Come," Tove said, pulling her from her thoughts. "We have to go. Now."

CHAPTER TWENTY-SEVEN

Y our Highness, wait!"
Here comes Jastyn's little lap wolf to make amends on her behalf.

Aurelia stomped away, kicking up sand and determined not to look back at Coran. To fuel her steps, she let her mind dwell in this newfound negative space.

Not this time. She tripped slightly over a broken seashell as she stormed farther from the selkies' cove. *He can't fix her mess this time.*

The bruised feeling beneath her boot distracted her for a moment, but the pain disappeared too quickly, leaving only the intense ache in her heart, in her soul, from her conversation with Jastyn. It pounded drums in her chest. She had to keep walking. If she stopped, she had time to relive the betrayal. She had time to remember the horrible plan Jastyn had had for her all along. She shook with the irony of it all. She'd wanted to be useful on this journey. Little had she known how useful Jastyn had hoped she'd be.

"M'lady, please."

"I won't hear it, Coran."

"But, Your Highness, if you'll only let me explain—"

"There's nothing to explain," she shouted over her shoulder, catching a glimpse of him trailing behind her. "She has been using me this entire time. You can't reason that away."

Sand stung the back of her legs, and Coran's tired breaths drew near. Boiling with anger, she refused to slow, marching away from Jastyn and toward...toward...

She paused. Aurelia wasn't entirely certain where she was. When she had been angry back in the kingdom, she'd known every nook and cranny of the castle, making it easy to disappear into a forgotten corner or an abandoned room where nobody could find her. There, she had space to sulk and stew in her dark thoughts. Out here, her pain was exposed, open to the biting wind from the wild sea. Looking around, the cove was far behind.

Where *was* she?

As she squinted at the cliffs, at the sliver of sun resting above the wide, dark stretch of ocean, Coran caught up and took a divisive stance before her. When she continued to avoid his gaze, he exclaimed, "Aurelia, please."

The use of her first name startled her. Despite her efforts, he'd insisted on continuing to use her title. Eventually, she had found it endearing. But now she stared, surprised at his sudden decision to throw all of that away. "Coran, I—"

"Jastyn doesn't want to hurt you."

Aurelia laughed. "That's amusing. I suppose she didn't fill you in on our conversation, then?"

"I know exactly what she told you."

Her skin prickled with the sand blowing past, and the throbbing in Aurelia's chest intensified. "Oh?"

His gaze shifted to his feet. "I know because she told me about the sacrifice."

The prickling turned blazing hot, and rage dripped from her lungs, running to her hands as they balled into fists. "You, too, Coran?"

"It's not like that," he explained as Aurelia tried to step away. He grabbed her arm. "Please, listen."

Huffing, she tugged away from his grasp. "You have my attention. But it's waning quickly."

He straightened. "The Red One told Jastyn she would need a noble sacrifice in order to obtain the cure. Initially, yes, she thought you might be that missing piece the Red One spoke of."

Aurelia raised her brows. "This does not make me feel better."

"But Jastyn never wanted to do that. She thought if you came along, she could work somethin' out. This entire time, she's been tryin' to think of another way around this."

"And did she?"

"No, but—"

Aurelia turned, furious.

He ran forward, putting himself in front of her. "She loves you, m'lady. Jastyn wouldn't let anythin' hurt you. Whatever is in the caves, she was goin' to face it. She won't let whatever waits in there do you harm."

"How am I supposed to believe that?" she cried, hurt twisting her words and making them come out in choked gasps. "How, Coran? I left my world behind for her. I journeyed across the realm to be with her. I…" She faltered, flashes of her night with Jastyn bursting in her mind. The joy she'd felt, the love that had blossomed between them came rushing back. "I gave her everything," she said, her voice barely audible over the wind. "And she betrayed me."

"No," he said, shaking his head. "She loves you. She just…she didn't know what to say."

Aurelia's head was heavy, thick with hurt. It spilled out onto her cheeks in tears. "Why didn't she tell me?" She sniffled, wiping her nose. Waving her arms, exasperated, she added, "She could have mentioned it so many times. I could have helped her come up with a plan. Why didn't she trust me?" she asked again, pleading with Coran, who looked at her with sad eyes.

His next words hit her like a crashing wave. "She doesn't know how, m'lady."

Instantly, Aurelia was back in the Wood, sitting around a gentle fire. Coran slept nearby, next to Jastyn, who Aurelia watched from her seat next to the dancing flames. She was talking to Eegit, who spoke in riddles as she studied her runes.

"She does not trust easily," Eegit had said. "She doesn't understand it." In the memory, Eegit's wide eyes held Aurelia's. "Be ready to forgive her."

Clasping her hand over her mouth, Aurelia fell onto the sand.

"M'lady!" Coran rushed forward, landing beside her.

"She knew," Aurelia muttered behind her hand, more tears falling. "Eegit knew this would happen."

Confusion knit between his brows. "Eegit?"

"She told me to be ready to forgive her."

Coran studied her, realization forming in his eyes. "It's scary, what she knows."

But Aurelia hardly heard him. If Eegit knew, then she knew Jastyn wouldn't be ready. Honestly, Aurelia wasn't sure if Jastyn would ever be ready to open herself up to someone. She'd hoped one day, she would. Aurelia had hoped for months that Jastyn would let her in, would trust her. In some ways, she had. Aurelia had felt it, seen fleeting moments of it. She'd felt it during late night conversations by the fire in the Wood. She'd felt in Vreis's cave. And she'd felt it, without a single doubt, that night on the ship. Eegit was right. Jastyn didn't know how.

But she was learning.

If Aurelia didn't forgive her now, all chances of Jastyn ever trusting her or anyone in this world would vanish.

"Gods," she said, pulling herself up to stand. "I've got to get back. I've got to help her."

"M'lady?"

"I understand, Coran." Her mind cleared. She saw all of it now. She saw everything lining up. She knew her fate was tied to Jastyn, but it wasn't her own nobility that needed to be sacrificed inside the caves. It didn't have anything to do with her. "Come on," she said, clasping Coran's hands. "Jastyn needs us."

Before they could move a step, the earth began to shake. For a brief moment, Aurelia was again in the Wood. She saw Jastyn lying on the ground, an arrow lodged in her shoulder. She saw Drest unconscious at her feet. She saw her family's soldiers gallop out from the line of trees. But there were no trees now. Only an endless stretch of sea and the feeling of dismay settling like piles of sand atop her shoulders.

"What's happening?" she asked.

Coran fell, unable to keep himself steady. She hurried to help him. "I don't know," he said, wide-eyed. "Sounds like it's coming from the cove."

Terror exploded like spell-fire in Aurelia's stomach. Gods, the cove. The selkies.

Jastyn.

"Coran," she said, "we have to run. We have to get back."

As they started back toward the entrance of the cove, a thin sliver of sand that snaked around the cliff next to the water, Sif sprinted around the corner. She ran at full speed, unfazed by the quaking ground.

"Aurelia," she cried, her face awash in relief at the sight of them.

"What's going on?"

"An invasion."

Aurelia's heart sank. "Elves?"

When Sif nodded, Aurelia pushed past her. "They will not take another person whom I love away from me."

But Sif grabbed her hand, spinning her around. "Aurelia, you can't go back. It's not safe."

"You don't understand. Jastyn thinks I've left her. She has to know I still stand beside her."

Coran echoed her sentiment. "I agree with m'lady. We can help the others. We should return to the cove."

"No." Sif's clear dark eyes met Aurelia's. "Your Highness, stay with me until it's done. It's too dangerous. I'll keep you—"

A swift *thwump* cut her words at the knees. She grabbed her chest.

"Sif!" Aurelia struggled to catch Sif as she fell forward. A long, slender arrow protruded from her back, bright red blood seeping around the shaft.

"Gods, Sif, no."

Coran's voice cracked as he said, "M'lady, the cliffs."

Aurelia tracked his finger to find a lean figure atop the cliffside, fifty yards behind where Sif had stood. The elf had already nocked another arrow, aimed right at them.

"Get down," Coran cried, pushing Aurelia and Sif to the ground. Sif groaned at the weight of their bodies as the elf's arrow zoomed past, landing right next to Coran's feet.

Aurelia turned Sif over. The arrow had penetrated through her back to her chest, the small arrowhead exposed below her collarbone. Her breathing was ragged, a sickly crackle emitting with each shallow breath.

"You have to move," Sif said. "Get back to the cave."

"The cave?" Coran asked, putting up an orange saol just in time to block the elf's next arrow.

"Tove, he's with Jastyn."

"You're hurt," was all Aurelia could say as Sif coughed. Blood sputtered from her mouth, shining unnaturally on her bright skin. "Let me help you, please." She could hardly conjure the steps for a healing spell before horrible memories overtook her. Her brother's stiff body lay before her, dragged in from the Wood, his veins riddled with poison. Shuddering, the image shifted, and she saw Jastyn in the Wood, taking an arrow to protect her, lying in her arms not unlike the way Sif was now. How many were going to die? How many were going to put their lives on the line to protect her?

She wouldn't let it happen anymore.

As Sif shook with coughs, Aurelia gingerly set her upon the sand, which was now dark brown beneath the wound. She faced the elf, who leapt easily down the cliff. He nocked another arrow.

"M'lady," Coran said warily, "what're you doin'?"

Aurelia took all of her hurt, all of her pain, all of her feelings and pushed them into her hands at her side. She balled her fists and conjured her saol, relishing the hot heat of the flames as they licked against her knuckles. As her anger grew, so did the flames. She hardly heard Coran's cries as she broke into a run.

The elf paused a moment, then let his arrow fly. It rushed past her left thigh. She kept going. Another arrow zipped past her right shoulder, but it didn't break her stride. She conjured more flames. Rearing her right arm, she fired.

Her saol hit at the elf's feet, exploding red light up into his face. He shouted, rolling quickly to the side as she fired a second saol. The elf knelt, shaking away the lingering flames holding to his tunic. As he did, Aurelia forced herself to see her brother's face, made herself feel the pain he'd felt that night. She forced herself to watch again as Brennus writhed and spasmed in agony.

She raised the blazing saol high above her head. "Not anymore," she said, staring down at the elf.

He said something in elven, and she was thrown onto her back, her saol vanishing in a puff of smoke. "Oh," she gasped, the breath gone from her lungs. As the elf got to his feet, moving to stand over her, Aurelia tried again to conjure her saol, but she needed more time, just a few more seconds to regain her strength. Then she'd have him. Then she'd stop this.

A gust of wind blew a wall of sand over them both. The elf's nostrils flared, and a familiar scent struck her. Chamomile and sage.

The fae's small gray eyes widened as something caught his eye. A second later, she shielded her face as a massive glare of blinding magenta light raged over them both. Aurelia prepared for the end of an arrow. But a twisted cry came from the elf, followed by a thud upon the sand. When the light dimmed, Aurelia opened her eyes.

The elf lay in a motionless heap, the thin sharp blade of a sword buried in his chest. Aurelia gaped at her mother, who held the elf down with one boot while she yanked the sword from his corpse.

Chapter Twenty-Eight

Jastyn felt as if she was back in the Mountains of Ionad. The cold, damp walls Tove pulled her through seemed endless, like the claustrophobic tunnels leading to Vreis's cave. She conjured her saol, but it did little to light the way, barely penetrating the darkness.

Tove seemed unfazed as he sped them through the winding, cramped walkways leading to the western caves. "We're almost there," he called over his shoulder, his frame hunched to keep his seal skin from scraping the low ceiling.

Jastyn's entire body was numb, her mind in shock as she struggled to comprehend the last few hours. She couldn't believe another invasion had followed her. She tried not to think about the danger she had put the selkies in. Worst of all, she tried to shake the horrible images of Aurelia caught in the crossfire.

"Aurelia," she muttered, wiping tears from her eyes.

"She'll be okay," Tove said. "She's strong. Sif will keep her safe and bring her to the caves."

Jastyn hoped he was right. Now wasn't the time to divulge their argument and Jastyn's betrayal. All she could do now was hope. She had to. The dangerous alternative was too much to consider.

Eventually, the pitch black of the tunnel faded, giving way to a moonlit path. Jastyn blinked at the night sky, the dark water. How long had they been walking? "Through here."

Tove released her hand, and Jastyn reclaimed her saol as they stepped out onto a new shore. Before them, what Jastyn had spent the last three months searching for came into view. Two ship lengths away stood the looming, gaping mouths of the western caves.

"We're here."

Tove slowed, and she did the same, both of them leaving heavy tracks in the sand. Shells crunched beneath them. On this side of the cliffs, the wind was harsh and the waves crashed like thunder against the rock face connected to the left wall of the first cave. All three cave mouths stood taller than two village homes and were as wide as three meadows.

Staring into each, Jastyn saw only shadow. "How do I know which one to go through?"

Her father scanned the jagged edges of each. "I placed the cure in the last one," he said, pointing to the cave closest to the raging sea. "It should still be there."

"It should?"

"The leprechauns promised not to move it, but you and I know they're shifty. Manipulating is one of their favorite things."

Biting her lip, Jastyn studied the cave. It seemed unassuming enough. She tried not to lean too much into the small seed of relief at finally being here. The cure was near. After everything, after traveling so far, she was finally here. The first step to healing her sister lay before her at last.

Tove's voice interrupted her thoughts. "Sif should be here soon."

Jastyn swallowed. Aurelia would be with her. She shuddered. "I'm not sure what to say." When her father only looked at her, she added, "To Aurelia." Her gaze fell. "I betrayed her. I was too afraid to tell her about the sacrifice."

Her father searched her eyes. He held up a hand, holding her cheek in his palm. "Jastyn, Aurelia loves you. She will understand."

"How?" She shook her head, rubbing her tearstained cheek against her sleeve.

He looked past her, toward the caves. "You'll find out."

Frowning, Jastyn was about to reply when a high, piercing screech broke across the sky. Tove pulled her to the ground as the pooka careened toward them at full speed.

"He's with the Dark Fae," Jastyn shouted over the bellowing screech as the pooka dove, its claws narrowly missing Tove's shoulders. Huddled low on the sand, they watched as the creature flapped its wings, carrying its body into the sky for another try.

"We better hurry then."

"But Sif—"

Eyes on the pooka, he shook his head. "When they get here, I'll send them in, but you have to go."

Knowing he was right, Jastyn started for the caves but not before shooting a blue saol at the pooka. It howled, delightedly dodging her spell-fire. Tove ran behind her as cover, his dagger ready should the pooka dive again. Running, Jastyn didn't look back. She felt a rush of air as the pooka flew toward them. She heard Tove's shout, followed by a piercing yell as the pooka once again retreated. Meanwhile, the sky darkened.

Jastyn shouted, "He's coming."

"Keep going," Tove yelled after her. "I'll handle it."

They were almost to the cave. Whistling wind swirled around the entrances of the first two. Jastyn swore she heard the beckoning call of a siren as she passed the first. A low, guttural growl echoed in the second. As she reached the third, she slowed. Turning, she found Tove standing ready, his dagger out as the pooka followed close behind. Black clouds twisted into a funnel over the creature.

"The others should be here," Jastyn said, anxious at the sight of the impending arrival of the Dark Fae.

"They'll get here. Jastyn, you have to go in, now." Tove swiped at the pooka bobbing menacingly overhead.

"But the Dark Fae—"

"I can handle him."

"He's stronger," Jastyn argued. "You shouldn't face him alone."

"Jastyn, I'll be fine." He gripped her shoulders, turning her until her back was to the cave opening. He met her gaze resolutely. "Your sister needs you. Go, now!"

She glanced into the darkness. It was there. She knew it was. Her sister's cure was only steps away. Looking back at Tove, she felt stuck. Her feet couldn't move. She was here, and she was frozen, petrified at finally having what she needed.

He handed her the satchel he'd snatched from the sand before. Only now did she realize it was hers. "You'll need this. The vial's inside."

She opened it to find the empty glass staring up at her. "Father, I—"

He smiled, his face serene despite the bedlam breaking loose above. "You are loved, Jastyn. Don't forget that." Then he pushed her, and she stumbled backward into the cave.

Her father's gaze held hers, and she cried out, angry at his pushing her away. But after regaining her steps, the dark clouds, the pooka, and her father disappeared.

"Tove?" She walked back to the entrance, where the dark sand of the shore met the light, untouched sand of the cave floor. As she hit the borderline, an invisible force halted her tracks. It was just like the barrier she'd run into when Eegit had taken her home. She pressed her hands against what felt like a wall. Gazing past it, out onto the beach, there was no sign of her father or the pooka. The sky had returned to dark blue, the edges laced with purple as the moon shone bright.

Footsteps hurried behind her.

"Who's there?" Jastyn spun, peering into the cave's depths. When she took another step, the walls of the cave burst with light. Blinking, Jastyn watched as lines of torches lit themselves, casting an eerie orange glow over a path leading to the belly of the cave.

Despite having the light to guide her, Jastyn conjured her saol. It stayed close as she walked.

Adjusting the satchel draped over her chest, she took a deep breath, trying to slow her heart. She tried to imagine what could be waiting. What beast, what nightmarish ghoul was standing guard over Alanna's cure, waiting to confront her with unimaginable horrors?

The path curved as she followed it deeper. Eventually, the cave ceiling shot up, and she found herself in a vast open chamber. Stalagmites littered the rim of the room, shooting up from the sand in all sizes. Torches lined the walls here, too, and Jastyn followed the light into a circle around the room's center, where a large, flat boulder sat vacant atop a rounded dome of sand. The rock resembled a bed, curved up slightly at its head, ready to welcome a tired guest. Scrutinizing the chamber, Jastyn searched for something resembling the cure. She walked a wide circle around the cave, her saol bobbing in step with each careful placement of her foot. Knowing the leprechauns, unforeseen traps could be anywhere, and she was careful where she placed her feet.

Footsteps ran past, so close Jastyn could hear the light tread of whoever hurried by. She spun around but found no one.

"My name is Jastyn Cipher," she said. The torchlight danced as if intrigued. "I've traveled far at the Red One's request." She reached into her satchel, pulling out the empty vial that once held the banshee blood. Holding it up, she said, "I've come for the rest of my sister's cure."

Feeling wind at her shoulder, Jastyn turned again. A dim figure sprinted past, then disappeared into the shadows.

"Alanna?"

Carefully, Jastyn stepped sideways, her eyes roving the shadow-filled walls, scanning the darkness that fell between rock formations.

Her sister's voice came from the dark. "Jastyn!"

"Alanna!" She ran between the stalagmites, pushing against the rocks as she searched behind each one, trying to find her sister. "Alanna, where are you?"

Again, her sister's voice called out, this time from the other side of the cave. Jastyn paused, listening, then ran for the opposite wall. "Alanna, I'm here."

The lights flickered, leaving Jastyn for a moment in darkness. Her steps faltered as the lights returned, beckoning her gaze toward the broad rock in the cave's center. Alanna sat atop it.

"Jastyn," she said again, one thin arm reaching out. Hurrying forward, Jastyn reached her in seconds. Setting aside the vial, she took her sister's delicate wrist.

"Alanna."

She smiled weakly. "You made it."

"I did." Jastyn held her sister's hands, which seemed smaller than she remembered. Sitting, Alanna was nearly her standing height. Her skin was pale, her shoulders narrow. Jastyn winced at how frail she seemed.

"I knew you would make it." Alanna's eyes sparkled.

Jastyn couldn't help but smile back. She knew this Alanna wasn't real. She knew it was a conjuring of the cave's magic. But she didn't care. She didn't let that stop her from pulling her sister into an embrace.

"Were you careful?" Alanna's small voice asked over her shoulder.

Leaning back, Jastyn studied her face.

"I told you to be careful." Her sister's expression turned serious.

"I was," Jastyn stammered. "I tried to be."

"Vreis."

Jastyn's face fell. "His injuries were an accident. He didn't deserve to get caught in this fight."

Tilting her head, Alanna's mouth scrunched, the expression she wore when trying to recall something. "And Coran."

"Coran is fine," she said. "He wasn't, but he's okay now."

"You can't say the same for Sif."

Worry wrapped its claws around Jastyn's chest. "What do you mean?"

"Sif," Alanna said matter-of-factly. "Don't you know?"

"What happened to her?"

"So you weren't careful, then."

Jastyn dropped her hands, which had turned as cold as the look on Alanna's face. "What happened to Sif?" Jastyn asked again. If something had happened to her, that meant something might have happened to Aurelia.

"You left a trail of misery behind you." Alanna's voice wasn't her own now.

Jastyn stepped back, her saol at her side. "That was not my intention."

"Will you follow it back?" Alanna asked, standing. "Will you retrace the wreckage left in your wake?"

Her muddled words did little to quell Jastyn's worry. Then she remembered the leprechauns behind all of this, and fear erupted into anger. "Enough of your riddles. Reveal yourself. I come for the cure. Nothing else."

"How many, Jastyn?" The Alanna-thing walked closer, forcing her backward. "How many are going to be hurt on this journey? How many are going to die so your sister can live?"

Her form shifted, growing taller, broad shoulders now covered in a seal skin. Sif stood before her. Jastyn gaped at the arrow sticking out of her chest.

"Sif," she said, examining the wound. "What happened?"

"I was trying to protect your precious princess." She sneered. "And look what I got for it." Sif reached up and snapped the arrowhead from its shaft. She gestured to the blood dripping from the pointed tip. "You're nothing but a filthy Odium."

"No, please."

When Jastyn reached out, Sif began to change. She grew taller, thinner. A fine beard lined a strong jaw. Now Vreis walked forward. His typically kind eyes were hard when he spoke. "I'll never be the same after what the pooka did to me." His smooth voice had a searing edge, slicing into Jastyn's mind, opening it up to dread and uncertainty.

"Vreis, I'm sorry. You were kind to us. You didn't deserve that."

"You should have known this is what happens to Odiums like us." He held his thin arms out. "We are destined to be alone forever. Destined to fall prey to the Dark Fae and his forces."

Her jaw clenched. "This is the Red One talking." She clamped her hands over her ears. "I won't hear it."

Again, the figure before her shrank and shifted. For a moment, the barmaid from the leprechaun lodge stood before her. The woman's bright green eyes were empty, her freckled chest and arms stiff. Guilt clanged inside Jastyn's heart.

"I'm sorry," Jastyn muttered. She couldn't stand to look at the woman who had been alive until they'd met.

Crouching, her saol shrank to fist-size, cowering with her on the cave floor. When the figure changed again, Jastyn slammed her eyes shut, unwilling to look. When a strange new silence hovered over her, she peered through her nearly closed eyes to find a familiar pair of boots. But the legs inside the leather pants were thicker, the torso wider. The face was nearly the same as Aurelia's, but it wasn't her.

There was no mistaking the prince.

He didn't speak. He only stood, stock still, one hand on the hilt of the sword resting at his waist.

Jastyn managed to stand, her legs quaking. In the torchlight, she studied his face, his brown hair, his proud posture. He was so like Aurelia. Only his eyes were different, a light hazel. But they were vacant of any emotion. His pallid complexion held no sign of life.

When she reached out, her fingers inches from his arm, he screamed. The sound was high and unnatural, like the pooka outside. Wincing, Jastyn shot back into a crouch, covering her ears. Her saol disappeared as fear overwhelmed her. She rocked on her heels, trying to block out the horrible sound. As it threatened to rip her open and tear her mind to shreds, she realized this was exactly what the leprechauns wanted. They wanted to drive her mad, wanted to make her quiver with fear until she had no choice but to flee, emptyhanded.

"No," she said, staring hard at the ground as the wailing continued. "You won't make me go." Raising her voice, she said, "I don't care how many ghosts you send me. You won't scare me off. Do you hear me?" she screamed, her voice hoarse over the high-pitched howl. "You don't scare me!"

The screaming stopped. The only sound was the pounding of blood in her ears. The lack of noise was so sudden it hit her hard, and she fell back onto the sand. The prince was gone. She'd retreated nearly to the entrance of the chamber. The torchlight continued to flicker lazily. In the center of the cave, a new figure sat upon the broad stone.

"Mother?"

Her legs dangled casually over the side of the high rock seat, her toes dancing above the floor. She wore the tunic Jastyn had always seen her in, the kingdom's colors tied around her waist in a belt that matched Jastyn's own. Her hair was twisted into a loose braid, one end of it resting over her right shoulder.

All of the fear that accompanied the Red One's earlier forms disappeared. As Jastyn slowly stood, the only thing she felt while staring at her mother was guilt.

"Jastyn."

Her mother's voice was the same. The sound of it was like home, compelling Jastyn's senses into a place on the other side of the realm. A place where the river trickled happily nearby. A place where fresh stew brewed on the open hearth, where the warm fire kept the cold nights at bay. Her mother's voice was like that worn, ragged blanket Jastyn shared with Alanna, and for a second, Jastyn longed to wrap herself in her mother's arms, to feel that comfort of home again.

But then she remembered the last conversation they'd had. She remembered her mother telling her the first pieces of truth about who her father was. She recalled the feeling of betrayal as her mother revealed the secret, one she had believed was better kept from Jastyn, the truth of her mother's unlawful actions.

Renewed frustration steeled her, and Jastyn straightened. "Why are you here?" she asked.

Her mother looked genuinely thoughtful. "I'm not sure."

Not buying into this, Jastyn stepped closer. "Tell me why you're here."

"Jastyn—"

"Don't play ignorant with me. I've come too far for this."

Her mother's face changed from curiosity to a look Jastyn knew well: concern. "You've come too far?"

This glamour was good; her tone made Jastyn falter. "I have traveled half the realm to get here. To get Alanna's cure." She mustered as much disdain as she could. "I don't understand why you're here. It has nothing to do with you."

"Doesn't it?" She pulled her legs up, crossing them where she sat. "I broke the laws of the kingdom. I dealt you your fate before you were even born."

Jastyn bit the inside of her cheek. Over the last three months, she had dreamt about hearing such words from her mother. Words she believed were justified for the life Jastyn had to live. The life her mother built.

"It's my fault," her mother said, frowning. "Everything is my fault."

Before she could stop herself, Jastyn was standing before her mother, no more than a step between them. Her mother's confessions pulled her in like a siren's song. Blinking, Jastyn forced herself to concentrate. Things couldn't be this easy.

"The Diarmaids," Jastyn said, sifting through her mother's words. "The Diarmaids wrote the laws. They created this world."

"But it's not them you harbor hatred for."

Jastyn blazed, inhaling sharply.

Her mother's gaze, which had fallen to the ground, lifted. "Jastyn, I never wanted to make this so difficult. I wanted to protect you. Keep you safe."

The back of her throat itched, and Jastyn shifted uncomfortably. The look her mother wore was one of such heartbreak, Jastyn couldn't bear it. Glancing around, she fell back into memories of that last night outside her home. "You lied to me."

"I didn't tell you because I was trying to protect you, sweetheart."

Jastyn shook her head. "No. You made me believe my father was somebody else. Somebody human."

"Every truth has its time, Jastyn. I didn't tell you when you were young because there was no point. It wasn't right."

"You made me hate him. You made me hate my father for leaving you." She shook with anger, spewing her words. "You made me hate you." The words flew from her like a sword plunging into its unsuspecting target.

"I only wanted to protect you."

Trembling, Jastyn stared into her mother's eyes. The colors were bright as tears spilled onto her cheeks. When her mother reached out, placing her hands on either side of Jastyn's face, she didn't move. She hated what her mother had made her feel, she hated what her life had been, and she hated—more than anything—how she ached to feel her mother's touch again.

When her cool palms cupped Jastyn's cheeks, both of them froze.

Gasping, Jastyn felt a surge run from her mother's hands. It was like a shock, like the prick of a blade or the singing of a flame. The sensation hurt at first, every fiber of Jastyn's body wanting to pull back, to step away from her grasp. But just as Jastyn felt she couldn't stand the pain another second, it subsided. In its place, Jastyn was projected back in time as a series of moments played out before her eyes.

Her mother and Tove danced together along the market streets of Venostes. They were alone after the festival had ended. Tove's seal skin bounced atop his shoulders, his dark complexion shining under the moonlight. Her mother laughed as they held one another, turning to a tune only the two of them could hear. Jastyn watched her parents dance down the dirt road, spinning blissfully around a corner. When they did, the market vanished, and Jastyn knew where this next memory took her: the dungeons of the Diarmaid castle. Her mother sat against a grimy, cobweb-covered wall. She was crying and laughing all at once, holding a tiny bundle in her arms.

Another memory. Jastyn saw herself, four years old and waist deep in a hole she'd dug in the sand. The half-moon hung overhead, glinting off the ocean. Behind her younger self, her mother stood a few yards back. She waved, staring out into the water. Jastyn looked out at the waves, catching a glimpse of a seal diving under.

The next vision was one Jastyn remembered: the day her mother presented her dagger to her. It had been a winter solstice gift. Looking at it now, Jastyn felt the same elation her younger self was feeling as she jumped around, brandishing it as only a young hunter could. Despite herself, Jastyn smiled, her mother's hands still holding her face as they stood together in the cave.

A brief plunge into darkness, and Jastyn was in the Wood. Her mother was bundled beneath a cloak, the forest ground covered in snow and more of it falling in heaps all around. It took Jastyn a moment to recognize the meadow her mother had wandered into. Eegit's hut was different, a mere tent of pitched sticks. Skulls and rocks littered the area, but the familiar purple fire burned nearby.

She couldn't hear the conversation her mother was having with Eegit, whose hunched back was less severe. After a time, her mother held out a hand. Eegit shook it, and she nodded gratefully before retreating into the trees. Time rushed forward, and Jastyn saw herself on the day she'd met Eegit. The day she'd gone hunting, starved and desperate for food. The day she thought she'd stumbled accidentally upon Eegit and her meadow.

The air was kicked from her lungs, and Jastyn was thrown from her mother's memories. Gasping for breath, she opened her eyes, surprised at the tears in them. Her mother looked almost embarrassed as she lowered her hands.

"It was you."

Her mother kept her gaze on the ground.

"You're the reason I met Eegit. All of the magic she taught me, the hunting skills I learned," Her voice was hoarse with this newfound knowledge, her legs weak. "You orchestrated our meeting. You brought her into my life."

"I only wanted to help you."

Stunned, Jastyn didn't know what to say.

"I may have molded you into the woman you are today, Jastyn. But it was never to help myself. I only ever wanted to see you thrive." Her mother brushed her cheek, her fingers wiping Jastyn's tears. "This world was against you from the beginning, but I did everything I could to give you a chance. To give you the life you deserve."

Jastyn's composure snapped. She had tried to be strong. She had tried to be brave. She had tried to hold on to her anger. Resentment had made her hard, but just like that, the truth had shattered her resolve like a rock thrown against glass. Now Jastyn knew the truth. It racked her body with sobs, and she fell forward into her mother's arms.

"I'm sorry," she cried, clinging tight as her mother wrapped her arms around her, pulling her into a hug. "I'm so sorry for what I said to you that night. I didn't know."

Her mother's voice was soft, "How could you?"

"I could have let you explain," Jastyn said between sobs. "I could have stayed that night and listened to you."

"You had a right to be angry."

"I'm so sorry," Jastyn said again, weeping openly against her mother's neck. "I don't hate you."

Her mother cradled her head and ran her fingers down Jastyn's braid. The feeling was so intimately her mother that Jastyn leaned back. In her mother's eyes was a look Jastyn had longed to see. "I'm so proud of you, my darling."

Hardly able to breathe, Jastyn smiled. "I love you."

Smiling, her mother said, "Do you know what the noblest quality is that one can possess?" Jastyn sniffled, her body weak. "The ability to forgive."

She pulled her into another embrace. Her mother's voice tickled her ear. "Hurry home, Jastyn."

Stumbling forward, Jastyn fell onto the smooth face of the boulder. It sat alone in the chamber, her mother gone.

Spinning around, Jastyn searched for any sign of where she could have gone when something caught her gaze.

Upon the open seat was a small wooden box. Stepping closer, Jastyn reached out. A thin line ran across its front edge. When she lifted it, she found three vials resting upon plush velvet lining. The first held a swirling liquid, gold and shimmering. The second contained some sort of herb. The third Jastyn lifted carefully, squinting to better see the contents.

A tiny rolled scroll sat against the glass. A recipe for the cure? She could only hope. Closing the box, Jastyn tucked it into her satchel. Glancing around one more time, she hoped all of this hadn't been a dream. She waited for another figure, another obstacle to overcome. Instead, a newfound lightness settled upon her shoulders. There was no denying it.

Finally, she had the cure.

CHAPTER TWENTY-NINE

A urelia stared up, dumbfounded, as her mother wiped the elf's blood on her cloak, then sheathed her sword as if she'd done so a million times.

"Mother?"

"Aurelia, sweetheart." Her voice exuded relief as she knelt, embracing her. "Oh, my sweet girl, I found you."

Pressed tight against her, Aurelia blinked, rocked with disbelief and unable to find the words at seeing her mother again. She opened her mouth to speak, but nothing came out. All she could think about was the soft material of her mother's fine cloak, the unfamiliar scent of dirt that clung to her unkempt braid, and the tight grip of her arms as she leaned back. "I thought I might be too late." Her mother's sky-blue eyes searched her own. A groan from Sif pulled Aurelia from her frazzled thoughts. Coran leaned fearfully over her.

"My friend," Aurelia said, motioning to Sif. "She's hurt."

Her mother turned, quickly analyzing the wound. With a look back at Aurelia, she brushed Coran aside, broke the shaft, and cast the same spell over the wound Aurelia had seen her perform on Jastyn moons ago. One thing Aurelia couldn't deny about her mother, no matter the situation, was that her instinct to heal was too great.

When she gripped the shaft to extract it, Sif's hand shot up, halting the queen. "Don't," she muttered. "It's a waste of time."

Aurelia hurried to Sif's side. "Please, let her help." But Sif wore the same look Aurelia had seen on Jastyn's face when her mother had lent her healing hand. Swallowing the reality of her friend's fate, she wiped tears away, nodding.

"I'm sorry," her mother said, shifting her attention back to Aurelia. "Darling, we have to go." Coran stood, moving to speak when her mother looked at him as if only now realizing he was there. Then she muttered a spell, her saol leaping to Coran. He couldn't even utter a protest before his eyes rolled back and he collapsed onto the sand.

Aurelia recognized the sleeping spell she'd been shown years ago by Brennus but could never master. "What are you doing?" she shouted, rounding on her mother. "He's my friend."

"It's safer for him this way."

"What are you talking about?"

Her mother's eyes were frantic as she spoke. "There's a horse waiting for you on the other side of the cove." She pointed to the opposite end of the cliffs, where Aurelia and the others had been brought in for questioning over a week ago.

"A horse," Aurelia said, still stunned, "what do you mean? Mother, what are you doing here?" She stepped back, scanning her mother's worried face, her forehead creased with lines and crow's feet at the corner of her bright eyes. Her frame was slighter, as if she hadn't eaten properly in some time. What had her mother been doing? Why wasn't she in Venostes, back in the castle? None of this made any sense.

"I searched for you, Aurelia. I've been searching for nearly three moons."

"Why?" Then Aurelia remembered the saol snares. "Were your snares not enough? You really couldn't stand for me to be away, could you?" Her voice rose with her frustration. "All I wanted was the smallest taste of a life away from the castle, the tiniest morsel of freedom, but you couldn't even give me that, could you?" Her mother started to speak, but Aurelia cut her off. "I told you Jastyn had unfinished business." She glanced to the cove's entrance, not caring at the indignant tone her voice was taking, like that of a frustrated teenager. "She needs my help, Mother. I won't return until we are done."

When she paused to catch her breath, her mother looked exasperated. "Aurelia, please listen to me."

"Why, Mother? Are you going to tell me you searched far and wide only to drag me back to the castle so you and father can groom me to take over as another tyrannical Diarmaid? Well, I've seen the world, Mother, and I understand now how wrong we've been. I understand now how beautiful the world can be if everybody would set aside their hate. The hate our family upholds," she cried, ignoring her mother's pleading look.

"Aurelia, enough."

Her mother's voice sent a chill down her spine. Gulping, Aurelia tried to keep her voice steady. "Mother, I'm not going back with you."

"Your father has been taken."

"Taken?" Aurelia's heart sank. "What do you mean?"

"I had to come and find you before they got to you, too."

"Where has Father been taken? By whom?" Aurelia licked her lips, regretting her earlier tirade. "Mother, who are you running from?"

Before her mother could answer, a funnel of wind ripped between them, blowing Aurelia yards away until she landed hard against a boulder jutting up from the sand. Her back throbbed with the impact, and she cried out at the sudden pain. Air left her lungs. Colors swirled past her vision as the searing ache in her back radiated through her limbs. Slowly, she managed to push herself up.

When she did, she couldn't believe what she saw.

Baroness Enya stalked toward her mother. She hardly looked like herself. The expensive jewelry and fine clothing were gone. Only her dragonfly pin remained the same as the baroness strode forward in her riding pants and long tunic. The kingdom's colors were woven beautifully into a cloak draped over her thin shoulders. Her eyes held such hatred, they turned Aurelia's very blood to ice.

Her mother seemed undeterred by the baroness's presence as she hurried to her feet, sweeping her cloak behind her and readying her saol. Magenta flames blazed bright above her palm. Aurelia tried to make sense of things. Had the baroness followed her mother all this way? And what had become of her father? Questions swirled through her mind like a wind-filled torrent.

"You won't get away with this, Enya." Her mother's voice was carried by the blustering wind whipping her braid behind her back.

The baroness tilted her head, a satisfied grin on her face. "Oh, Dechtire. We already have."

Her mother fired a saol. Aurelia watched, astonished. What was happening? Her mother had fired on a member of her own court? Then a thought hit her. Did the baroness have a hand in the invasion? Or worse, Aurelia thought, her stomach twisting, did she help orchestrate her brother's death? That would explain her mother's behavior. Enraged at the idea, she stood, lumbering forward, still aching with the collision against the boulder. She winced at the pain in her shoulders but moved quickly to help her mother, who launched another saol.

Baroness Enya was fast as she conjured a golden shield of light to stave off her mother's spell-fire. Moments later, she retaliated with shots of light. Her mother blocked them with speed Aurelia hadn't known she possessed. The baroness remained relentless, and she fired saol after saol at her mother, forcing her back, her boots digging into the sand to keep herself upright. Finally, Aurelia crossed the stretch of sand to her side.

Her own red saol joined her mother's as they fired on the baroness.

"She's cast a spell over your father," her mother shouted over the explosions. "He's been compromised. They're after the throne."

"Baron Louarn, too?"

More golden light shot from the baroness's hands, pushing Aurelia and her mother back on their heels. She hadn't remembered the baroness ever using magic. Everybody in the kingdom was capable, but after years of never seeing her cast so much as a conjuring spell, Aurelia had simply come to believe the baroness didn't know much magic. Not even a simple saol of hers ever flitted about the castle. Clearly, as another series of light bombarded the saol shields Aurelia and her mother held, she'd been holding back.

Her mother responded, breathless, between hisses of smoke. "The baron is dead." She shifted her feet, facing Aurelia, her mouth a tight line of concentration as they struggled to keep their saols lit against the overwhelming magic.

"What?" Aurelia stumbled. As she did, their saol shield cracked, pulling apart and leaving them exposed. A blast of gold split the air. Aurelia cried out, diving to the sand just in time to miss the spell-fire.

Her mother dove, too, then crawled to her through the sand.

"Who is helping her, then?" Aurelia asked as she helped her mother stand. "She couldn't possibly do this alone. Is it the elf queen?"

Another funnel of wind plunged to the earth, snatching Aurelia and her mother up in its grasp. Peering through her shielded eyes, Aurelia saw the baroness's gleeful face, a maniacal smile on it that matched one Aurelia now only saw in her nightmares.

The baroness closed in. Aurelia crouched on the wet sand. Her mother stood, her arms outstretched, shielding Aurelia. "You won't get away with this, Enya. Do you hear me?" Her voice roared with loathing, but Aurelia shivered at the desperate grip of her mother's arms.

"Mother," she whimpered, angry at her own cowardice. "What's happening?"

Her mother turned, locking her gaze on Aurelia's. "Be strong, my darling. We will get through this."

"What do you mean?"

"Sometimes, sweetheart, you have to give up the battle to win the war."

"I don't understand," Aurelia said, glancing past her mother as the baroness conjured another golden saol, aiming at her mother's back.

Her mother's gaze turned sad, tears spilling onto her cheeks. "I love you."

Aurelia stared as her mother muttered an incantation similar to the one she'd cast over Coran, only a few of the words varying. Seconds later, her mother's face contorted in pain, and she grabbed her chest, a shaking hand over her own heart.

"Mother!"

Her knees buckled, and she collapsed. Aurelia knelt, trying to lay her down. Her mother groaned, agonized, as she clutched her ribs. Seeing this, the baroness slowed, lowering her saol, one thin, curious brow raised.

Reaching up, her mother kept her eyes closed as she shook with pain. "Get me back to the castle," she said as Aurelia grabbed her hand. "We will fight this together." Then her eyes flew open as her body seized for a moment, then stiffened. With one final look at Aurelia, her mother's eyes glazed over. Her body went still, and for the second time, Aurelia stared down at the body of a loved one.

"I knew Dechtire was too weak." Enya's voice pulled Aurelia back to the shoreline. Pulled her back to the place where her mother's body lay unmoving upon the sand. "I did think she'd perish on the journey to find you, so I must give her credit making it this long. Still, she doesn't have the stamina of a Gulteran." Her bony hands resting proudly on her narrow hips, the baroness shook her head. "Venostes women are so weak."

Swiping tears away, Aurelia stood. "What do you want, Enya?"

"It's Baroness Enya, to you, young lady."

Aurelia glared, willing her gaze to pierce this horrible new layer the baroness had revealed.

"I want what any woman wants, the freedom to make my own choices."

"You have freedom," Aurelia countered. "You have more freedom than half of the kingdom. You're a baroness, for gods' sake. Is that not enough for you?"

Enya's eyes flickered with something, then narrowed. "My grandfather will rise again. And with him, this realm will return to its once great state."

Aurelia cringed at the same awful sentiment she'd heard back in the Wood. "You're the granddaughter of King Taranis?"

The baroness didn't answer at first, looking through Aurelia, lost in a vision only she could see. "He will return to this world and claim the last of the Odiums. With them gone and the Diarmaids under our command, we will cleanse the land of its fae filth." Her proclamation warped into a cackle, and Aurelia knelt over her mother as the baroness leaned back, relishing the relentless wind. It took Aurelia a moment to notice the dark clouds forming overhead, the funnel of wind spinning its way to earth.

Aurelia tugged her mother's limp figure close, shielding her from the sand that stung her face. The Dark Fae and his horse appeared in the sky, galloping down, each hoof clapping thunderously against the air.

Her mind racing, Aurelia tried to come up with a plan. She tried to figure a way out of this. But looking around, all she saw was hopelessness. Coran's unconscious form lay beside Sif. Aurelia thought she saw Sif's chest move, but it was probably her own desperation conjuring false hope. And in her own arms, her mother lay helpless.

Aurelia was alone.

With a clap of thunder, the Dark Fae landed below the dark sky, next to the ocean's raging waves crashing on the shore. The water broke hard in curious currents, now battling for a spot to see the spectacle about to unfold.

The Dark Fae's horse cantered over to the baroness, who looked up at the figure like a young pup begging for approval. "Dechtire is gone. Her cowardly heart gave out before I could take her myself." She gave a disdainful look back at Aurelia and her mother. "Now all that's left is her."

"Well done," the Dark Fae said, nodding.

"Can I finish her here?" Enya asked, her eyes wide and wild as she rubbed her hands together, eyeing Aurelia like a slice of fresh meat.

"Not here." The Dark Fae adjusted the reins of his horse, shifting the beast to better see. "The kingdom awaits her return. We will bring them back to Venostes." He tilted his head, the dark space beneath his hood seeming to scrutinize Aurelia as she tried not to shake with fear. "This one may be able to help us."

Enya's face fell. "But, Grandfather—"

"Take them back. That is my final word."

The baroness's shoulders hunched, but she nodded reluctantly. "Come on, then," she said, gesturing for someone to follow her. Aurelia looked on, confused. She couldn't have been speaking to the Dark Fae that way. But if not him…

A figure she hadn't noticed dismounted behind the billowing, black cloak of the fae. Powerful legs, a barrel-shaped chest, and a mane of blond hair took form upon the sand.

"No." Aurelia felt as if she had been plunged into an icy river. "No," she said again, the old scars on her wrist burning. "It's not possible."

Alongside the baroness, Drest stared down at her, his eyes clear as glass. "Oh, Aurelia," he said. "Anything is possible."

CHAPTER THIRTY

Tove!" Jastyn sprinted for her father, who lay on the sand, clutching his side, struggling to hold himself up against a tall rock. The satchel holding her sister's cure bounced against her thigh as she ran. Within moments, she was at his side, her eyes tracing his pained face, the torn fabric of his tunic, the slashes to his sealskin, and the wound beneath his bloodstained hand.

"I'm all right," he said. "That damn pooka doesn't know when to quit."

Glancing around the empty inlet, blinking at the dark blue sky, Jastyn asked, "The Dark Fae, where did he go?"

"Oh, he didn't stick around for long." Groaning, Tove hunched over.

"You're hurt," Jastyn said, "we need to get back to the ships."

"I'll be fine." Carefully, he lifted his hand. The wound was wide beneath his palm, but the blood flow was slowing. Frowning, Jastyn started to protest, but her father spoke first.

"The Dark Fae, he went that way." Tove nodded toward the beach they'd spent the day at. "I think he found something better than an Odium."

The elation at having the cure left her, and Jastyn was left with a ringing dread. "Aurelia."

"Come on." He managed to stand, and Jastyn helped steady him as they stumbled back through the passageway's tunnel. Her saol led them through the dark pathways, flickering with trepidation as Jastyn's anxiety filled her mind with horrible images.

After what felt like an eternity, they made it out onto the familiar sand of the cove's beach. Jastyn's saol vanished.

"Gods." Tove's breath caught along with Jastyn's at the sight of the selkie ships. Or rather, what was left of them. Half the smaller vessels had been upturned, their bellies punched through and floating like dead fish in the stagnant water. The main ship resembled a carcass, the wooden planks like the bones of a vessel that had once sat proudly among the others, but now was no more than a corpse, fed upon and left to rot. The masts had collapsed, their sails ripped and floating like lilies in the water. The ship's broad, sturdy deck had been splintered, split nearly in two.

"It's all right," Tove said, and Jastyn knew he was speaking more to himself. "The council had a plan. Everybody evacuated to the ocean." He nodded, reassuring himself. "It's all right."

"Tove," Jastyn said, taking in the ghastly destruction left behind by the elves, "if you need to go, I'll understand."

His eyes glistening, he pulled himself up. Jastyn helped him balance as he gazed upon the cove. After a moment, he faced her. "Did you find the cure?" His eyes held a distant look, and Jastyn wondered what memory he had fallen into.

"I did. I have it." She patted the satchel at her side.

"Good. And no need for Aurelia." It wasn't a question despite the lilt in his tone. Jastyn, still incredulous at the happenings within the cave and the true meaning of the sacrifice, could only shake her head.

Tove looked once more to the ships sitting listlessly, empty of all the life they'd held not two nights before. "Come on, we need to get to the beach. I don't know what, but something drew the Dark Fae there."

Together, they followed the narrow stretch of sand snaking around the cliffs, shrinking to only a few feet of land before the cove's entrance opened and curved around the cliff's edge. On the wider, windswept beaches that met the ocean's waters, Jastyn's steps faltered.

"Coran!" He lay a ship length's away, flat on his back and unmoving.

"Go," Tove said. Not hesitating, Jastyn ran, willing her feet to carry her faster, hating that each step seemed to sink deeper in the sand trying to slow her down.

"Coran." Breathless, she fell to her knees beside him. The knot in her stomach unclenched a little when she heard him moan, his chest rising in a deep breath. "Coran?" she helped him sit up.

"Jas," he mumbled, "what're doin'?"

"I could ask you the same thing," she said before noticing Sif a few yards away, an arrow protruding from her chest.

Coran followed her gaze. "The elves," he started to say, but the rest of his words were cut off as Tove, having caught up, stood over Sif.

Jastyn feared the worst as she watched Sif's body lie still. Slowly, Tove reached both hands out over her, running them inches above her chest, not unlike the way Jastyn had seen Rigo do.

Swallowing, she asked, "Is she…" But she couldn't finish the thought. She couldn't stand to add another tally to the death toll that followed wherever she went.

"She's weak," he replied, his shoulders trembling with relief. "If I can get her to the others, she may have just enough strength to pull through."

Nodding, Jastyn looked around the beach. It was only Coran and Sif there, but examining the sand, Jastyn saw more pairs of footprints. Boots like Aurelia's. And were those hoofprints?

"What happened here?"

Coran took a shuddering breath. "The queen was here."

"The queen?" Jastyn and Tove spoke in unison. Exchanging glances, Jastyn asked, "Coran, are you sure?"

He nodded weakly. "She did somethin' to me. Knocked me out."

Confused, Jastyn looked around again. Near the hoofprints were two larger sets of imprints.

"Jas," he said, reaching up.

"What is it?" She was trying to understand what could have happened. But all questions halted when she saw what Coran held.

Aurelia's starfish pin. Staring at it, Jastyn tried not to cry. She tried not to scream. She tried to be calm as she reached out, taking the pin delicately between her fingers.

"They took her, Jas." Coughing, Coran fell back down, exhausted. "She's gone."

Jastyn stared at the starfish, its golden arms glistening against the moonlight. She adjusted the satchel. Inside, she felt the small weight of the box shift. It reminded her that she had what she came for. She had her sister's cure. This was what she'd wanted, what she had journeyed across the realm for.

But of course, the journey wasn't done. Her sister was in the hands of the guards. Her family was in trouble. And now Aurelia had been taken by the same dark force that had haunted Jastyn for years.

Her gaze drifted out to the water. Churning waves reached up onto the sand only to be pulled back out by the unrelenting current. She sighed, her chin falling to her chest. She should be tired. She should be weary and worn from months of travel. She should be exhausted from lack of food, makeshift shelters, and narrowly escaping trap after trap. She should have wanted to lie down, give up, and succumb to the wretched life the royal family and the Dark Fae had spent years trying to convince her it was all she was worth. She also had no idea if Aurelia would, could, forgive her. As much as that prospect hurt, Jastyn knew she had to at least find out.

Pocketing Aurelia's pin, Jastyn stood. She felt anything but tired. Instead, she was invigorated with a new sense of purpose. She wasn't going to give up, not now.

"Jas?" Coran asked.

"Come on," she said, helping him stand. "We're going to stop all of this once and for all. But first, we've got a princess to save."

About the Author

Originally from Dallas-Ft. Worth, Sam Ledel now lives in Southern California with her girlfriend and their Jack Russell terrier. Her debut novel, *Rocks and Stars*, was a 2019 Goldie finalist. She is currently working on her next book.

Books Available From Bold Strokes Books

Bet Against Me by Fiona Riley. In the high-stakes luxury real estate market, everything has a price, and as rival Realtors Trina Lee and Kendall Yates find out, that means their hearts and souls, too. (978-1-63555-729-9)

Broken Reign by Sam Ledel. Together on an epic journey in search of a mysterious cure, a princess and a village outcast must overcome life-threatening challenges and their own prejudice if they want to survive. (978-1-63555-739-8)

Just One Taste by CJ Birch. For Lauren, it only took one taste to start trusting in love again. (978-1-63555-772-5)

Lady of Stone by Barbara Ann Wright. Sparks fly as a magical emergency forces a noble embarrassed by her ability to submit to a low-born teacher who resents everything about her. (978-1-63555-607-0)

Last Resort by Angie Williams. Katie and Rhys are about to find out what happens when you meet the girl of your dreams but you aren't looking for a happily ever after. (978-1-63555-774-9)

Longing for You by Jenny Frame. When Debrek housekeeper Katie Brekman is attacked amid a burgeoning vampire-witch war, Alexis Villiers must go against everything her clan believes in to save her. (978-1-63555-658-2)

Money Creek by Anne Laughlin. Clare Lehane is a troubled lawyer from Chicago who tries to make her way in a rural town full of secrets and deceptions. (978-1-63555-795-4)

Passion's Sweet Surrender by Ronica Black. Cam and Blake are unable to deny their passion for each other, but surrendering to love is a whole different matter. (978-1-63555-703-9)

The Holiday Detour by Jane Kolven. It will take everything going wrong to make Dana and Charlie see how right they are for each other. (978-1-63555-720-6)

Too Hot to Ride by Andrews & Austin. World-famous cutting horse champion and industry legend Jane Barrow is knockdown sexy in the way she moves, talks, and rides, and Rae Starr is determined not to get involved with this womanizing gambler. (978-1-63555-776-3)

A Love that Leads to Home by Ronica Black. For Carla Sims and Janice Carpenter, home isn't about location, it's where your heart is. (978-1-63555-675-9)

Blades of Bluegrass by D. Jackson Leigh. A US Army occupational therapist must rehab a bitter veteran who is a ticking political time bomb the military is desperate to disarm. (978-1-63555-637-7)

Hopeless Romantic by Georgia Beers. Can a jaded wedding planner and an optimistic divorce attorney possibly find a future together? (978-1-63555-650-6)

Hopes and Dreams by PJ Trebelhorn. Movie theater manager Riley Warren is forced to face her high school crush and tormentor, wealthy socialite Victoria Thayer, at their twentieth reunion. (978-1-63555-670-4)

In the Cards by Kimberly Cooper Griffin. Daria and Phaedra are about to discover that love finds a way, especially when powers outside their control are at play. (978-1-63555-717-6)

Moon Fever by Ileandra Young. SPEAR agent Danika Karson must clear her werewolf friend of multiple false charges while teaching her vampire girlfriend to resist the blood mania brought on by a full moon. (978-1-63555-603-2)

Serenity by Jesse J. Thoma. For Kit Marsden, there are many things in life she cannot change. Serenity is in the acceptance. (978-1-63555-713-8)

Sylver and Gold by Michelle Larkin. Working feverishly to find a killer before he strikes again, Boston homicide detective Reid Sylver and rookie cop London Gold are blindsided by their chemistry and developing attraction. (978-1-63555-611-7)

www.ingramcontent.com/pod-product-compliance
Lightning Source LLC
Chambersburg PA
CBHW032210030726
47494CB00020B/935